DANGEROUS WATERS

SUSAN HUNTER

SEVERN RIVER PUBLISHING

DANGEROUS WATERS

Severn River Publishing
www.SevernRiverBooks.com

ISBN: 978-1-64875-130-1 (Paperback)
ISBN: 979-8-53863-167-4 (Hardback)

ALSO BY SUSAN HUNTER

Leah Nash Mysteries

Dangerous Habits

Dangerous Mistakes

Dangerous Places

Dangerous Secrets

Dangerous Flaws

Dangerous Ground

Dangerous Pursuits

Dangerous Waters

Dangerous Deception

Dangerous Choices

To find out more about Susan Hunter and her books, visit

severnriverbooks.com/authors/susan-hunter

For Mary Starnes

*"There is nothing on this earth more to be prized
than true friendship."*
~ Thomas Aquinas

PROLOGUE

Bryan Crawford steps from his warm house into the cold air of a March night. He is heading to his outdoor sauna, as he does every Friday evening of the year. The light rain that hits his face makes him shiver. He's glad his sister Rhonda isn't here. She'd be nagging him to wear a coat and put on shoes instead of flip-flops. It's not even 40 yards to the sauna. He's 54 years old, and she still treats him like he's a little boy. She's always been like that, but her constant hovering can be hard to take.

She's not the only woman in his life who's starting to get to him. His wife Rachelle was all sexy, and pretty, and whatever-you-want-Bryan before they got married. But she's different now. She wants him to do this, she doesn't want him to do that. She's even talking about him selling his hunting cabin. That's never gonna happen. Maybe all wives get like that after a few years. That's how it was with Jackie. He's going to have to lay down the law with her. He doesn't need a nag for a wife. Rhonda can handle that. That's another thing that bugs him. The two of them, Rhonda and Rachelle, are always picking at each other, fighting over him like he's a winning lottery ticket.

He laughs a little then. In a way, he kind of is. He's good-looking, owns a business that makes plenty of money, and he's not stingy about letting them spend it. He has a brief thought that it's Rhonda who puts in the effort at Crawford Plumbing and Electrical, not him, but he tamps that down. He's the owner. He's the one his dad left the business to, not Rhonda. She's lucky, when you come to think of it, that he gives her as much freedom as she has to run things. Where would she be without him?

At the sauna door, he reaches down under the Badgers welcome mat for the key. As he stands up, he's startled by a noise coming from the woods behind him. He turns and peers through the darkness. He can't see anything. A week or so ago, he set up a trail cam to catch footage of a black bear he saw out in the yard one night. So far, no luck. Not tonight either, he decides after hearing nothing else.

He unlocks the padlock and slides the security bar back, then bends down to put the key back under the mat. Whoa! He gets a head rush as he stands back up. He puts his hand on the door to steady himself, then goes inside. He's been feeling off all afternoon. He would've checked his blood sugar, but he didn't have any test strips with him. Rhonda always has them—she never lets him forget he's diabetic. All that checking is a pain in the ass. He's strong, he's healthy, he takes his insulin, he eats right. Most of the time he doesn't even think about his diabetes. Nothing says you're a candy-ass like poking your finger a hundred times a day.

He did a test when he got home, though. His sugar was high, but he jacked up his insulin, so he should start coming around soon. He always has before when he's had an issue.

The sauna is warm when he steps in. He told Rachelle to set the heater to preheat before she left for the weekend. She remembered, so score one for her on the keeper side. She has her faults, yeah, but as long as she keeps her looks, doesn't get fat, and backs off on nagging him, he'll probably stick with her.

He sets the timer for 15 minutes and sits down on the bench. He's thirsty even though he polished off a bottle of water just before he came out. He shrugs. He's got one in the pocket of his robe. He takes the cap off and brings it to his lips, draining half the bottle in one swig. He loosens the belt on his robe and leans back on the bench, closing his eyes.

They fly open as he hears the sound of the safety bar on the door sliding into place. He jumps up, but he has to pause a second as a wave of nausea hits him. He hears the snap of the padlock clicking shut. By the time he reaches the small window in the door, all he can see is the back of a hooded figure running away.

Damn it! He put the lock on to keep whoever got in and trashed the place out. Are they playing a stupid joke to pay him back? He pounds on the door and shouts, but of course they don't turn around. If they can even hear him. He reaches reflexively for his phone, then remembers that he doesn't have it. It's on the counter in the kitchen where he always leaves it when he uses the sauna.

He sinks back down on the bench. There's nothing he can do but wait for them to come back. He's thirsty again. He reaches for the bottle and drinks the rest of the water. He sits back once more, but after a minute he feels a sharp pain in his gut. He's still nauseous. This isn't good. His blood sugar must still be out of whack. If he doesn't get it straight, he's in real trouble. But he can't get out, until whoever locked him in lets him out. But when will that be? When will they come back? He needs to get his insulin. He feels the first, faint stirrings of fear. He tries to push it back with anger.

He's going straight to the cops as soon as he gets out. Hell, he's gonna offer a reward to anyone who finds them. A big one. That wasn't a bear he heard in the woods, it was someone waiting for him to show up, so they could lock him in for a not-funny joke. He gets up again, looks out the window again, sees nothing again.

God, he's starting to feel awful. He's beginning to sweat, and he's dizzy, and he has to pee. He has to get out of here, now, not later! He pounds on the door. He shouts. Then he stops, as the stark reality of his situation hits home.

They're never coming back. Why would they, and chance getting caught? They don't know that there's no one at the house to come looking for him when he doesn't return after twenty minutes.

Rachelle is at a retreat. Her son Adam is in Chicago. His daughter Stephanie is at college. Even Rhonda isn't around. He told everyone that he was going to his hunting cabin in the morning. No one will check on him. No one will even miss him. Not until Monday. By then it will be way, way too late.

He feels a rush of despair as sickening as the nausea that rises with it and he sinks to the floor. He doesn't deserve this. How can this be happening to him? He has to think. But he can't think. His thoughts won't hold still, his mind is jumbled and confused, and his body is in pain.

He doesn't know how long he sits there, his mind a tangle of half-formed thoughts. He can't concentrate. He's sweating profusely now. His heart is racing. His mouth and throat are dry but there's no water. His abdominal muscles spasm painfully and he cries out. But no one hears him. He tries to stand, but he stumbles. His head hits the corner of the bench as he falls. He loses consciousness, and it's a blessing.

Throughout the night he moves in and out of wakefulness. His cries for help grow fainter until they're no louder than a whisper. It doesn't matter. Only the night visitors—the deer, the raccoons, the bear—are there to hear. Sometime the next day, the light coming through the window stirs him awake. He's confused and frightened, like he was that time when he was a little boy and got lost. Rhonda found him, and she hugged him, and she told him not to cry. She said she'd always find him. For a second, he feels her arms around him. He feels safe. He tries to hug her back, but she's gone. Where is she? Where is he?

He feels so bad. He's been sick. He has a foul taste in his mouth. His stomach muscles keep cramping, and it's hard to breathe. He just wants to go home so Rhonda can fix it. He's so very tired. His voice is a bare murmur as he calls her name. Rhonda, who has always been there for him, though he rarely has been for her, doesn't answer. Even with his mind so muddled, he knows. She isn't coming. No one is. He's going to die alone.

Late Sunday afternoon the door opens. A face peers around the corner. The killer stares intently for a moment, looking for signs of life. There are none. Bryan Crawford is dead.

1

I've never killed anyone before. I hope I never do again. Sometimes at night I still wake up in a tangle of sheets and sweat, my heart racing, my hand gripping a gun that isn't there. I can feel the rage coursing through my body just as it did that day. I can hear the shots ringing in my ears, once, then twice, then three times. My voice is a ragged whisper and my breathing is harsh as I repeat out loud, over and over again, *I had to do it. I had no choice.*

But there's always a choice, isn't there? Was killing another human being truly what I had to do, or was it what I wanted to do? I'm still not sure. But then, I'm not as sure as I used to be about a lot of things.

My name is Leah Nash. I write true crime books. I also co-own a weekly newspaper in the small town of Himmel, Wisconsin. I bought the local paper with a business partner a year or so ago when it was about to go under. Yes, I know. Buying a newspaper these days seems about as sound a business decision as investing in a training school for switchboard operators. But I'm a big believer in community journalism, and I can't resist an underdog—whether it's a person or a business.

We run the *Himmel Times* on a shoe-string—an editor, two reporters, and a few stringers. It's not ideal, but it's what we can afford. I'm saying "we run" the paper, but Miller Caldwell, my business partner, and I usually leave the day-to-day operations to our very capable editor. Miller is definitely hands-off and never interferes with editorial decisions. I have a harder time staying out of the newsroom. In fact, I'm pretty much proof positive that you can take the reporter out of the newsroom, but you can't take the newsroom out of the reporter.

But on the late February afternoon when this story begins, the newspaper wasn't on my mind at all. Instead, I was mulling over a proposal that had taken me by surprise. No, not that kind of proposal. This one came via a phone call from my agent.

"Leah, if you're standing up, sit down. If you're sitting down, lie down. It's for your own safety, because what I'm going to say will knock you into next week!"

Clinton Barnes, my agent, rarely bothers with hello—or goodbye. He's always on the move. I don't mind. His frenetic energy and persistence sold my first true crime book, and when my original publisher dropped me, he found me another one, which is not an easy thing to do in a tough market. But he's a relentless taskmaster when it comes to pushing me to meet deadlines.

"Hi, Clinton. I already made the corrections to the manuscript and sent the pages back to my editor. On time, in case you didn't notice. You don't have to hound me anymore."

"If I weren't so excited, I'd be offended. When I call you, it's support and concern. Support and concern, Leah. Not 'hounding.' Now, listen, I had a brainstorm. I talked with your editor and she is totally on board. It's going to be great!"

"What's going to be great?"

"You haven't settled on the subject for your next true crime book, right?"

"Hey, I just finished the one that's coming out this summer. I thought this wasn't a hounding call. Don't I get even a little break? You're making my left eyelid start twitching again."

"Yes, yes, of course you do. But listen. I think—we think— you should try your hand at fiction."

"Fiction? I'm a journalist, Clinton, not a novelist. I don't know anything about writing fiction. No. Not interested," I said firmly.

"Mark Twain was a journalist, Maya Angelou, Nora Ephron, Michael

Connelly. They all made the move to fiction. It worked out pretty well for them, wouldn't you say?"

"Well, yes, but ..."

"Stand-alone nonfiction sells, yes. And you know I love yours. But it's an uphill climb every time. The only sure-fire non-fiction hit is a celebrity tell-all, something by Malcolm Gladwell, or a heart-tugging story about a feisty little rescue dog who changed his owner's life. Do you have a dog frolicking lovably around your house? Is he your sidekick in crime-solving adventures? Does he snuggle next to you intuitively offering comfort as you silently weep over a bad book review?"

I glanced down at Barnacle, the small dog of indefinite heritage who belonged to Gabe Hoffman, my partner in romance and sometimes crime. Barnacle was staying with me while Gabe was out of town. Far from meeting Clinton's criteria for a dog companion, Barnacle could easily be mistaken for a rug, except for his not-so-gentle snoring as he slept in front of the fire.

"Uhhh, no, not exactly. Not at all, as a matter of fact. I have a dog here, but he belongs to my beau. And you know I don't 'silently weep' when I get a bad review. I just show it to my mother, and she hunts the villain down and makes him sorry he ever learned how to type."

The odd word choice I'd used to describe Gabe distracted Clinton for a minute.

"Your beau?"

"Yes. You know Gabe. You met him when I was in New York last month, remember? I feel like it sounds too high school to call him my boyfriend. And too awkward to call him my significant other. Partner doesn't quite fit either. The word of the week is beau. How do you feel about paramour?"

"Not good. Why don't you just get engaged and call him your fiancé?"

"You've been talking to my mother, haven't you?"

"Stop distracting me. Seriously, just listen for a minute. You need to write a mystery series. A fiction series would give you a reliable income stream, not the highs and lows of stand-alone books. You get readers hooked and they keep coming back. Plus, you won't have to spend days researching, weeks interviewing, and months writing. You can just think of an idea, and bing, bang, boom, you write the book. Plus, and I know this will appeal to you, you can get revenge on real-life people you don't like."

"Clinton, you've been reading my diary. How would that revenge thing work?"

"Easy, just turn them into characters in your books and do what you want with them. Expose them to humiliation, leave them penniless, have their lovers dump them, give them a fatal disease, whatever strikes your fancy. Then just stick to your disclaimer. You know, 'any resemblance to actual persons, living or dead, or actual events, is purely coincidental.' Besides, who's going to take you to court to insist that the corrupt politician character in your book is really them? With fiction, you can do whatever you like. You'll be in complete control, Leah."

He said the last part enticingly, like the devil tempting Jesus in the desert. And I have a much lower temptation threshold than Jesus.

"I don't know," I said. Despite the misgivings I had about my ability to create a fictional world out of nothing, the dual prospect of control and steady income was appealing. Clinton sensed my resistance fading and moved in for the kill.

"Yes, you do. You know you'll be great at it. I've got another call coming in. I know you're going to do it. It's perfect for you. Talk soon."

2

After talking to Clinton, I poured a Jameson over ice and sat down in my favorite thinking spot—the window seat in my apartment. From there I can overlook the downtown—such as it is—of my down-at-its-heels hometown. Years of factories closing and stores shuttering have taken a toll on the population of this once busy little city. The 15,000 or so souls who still soldier on are either too settled in their ways to move, too young to have a choice, or too delusional to realize that Himmel isn't coming back.

At least that's what I thought when a self-inflicted career injury forced me to move back home a couple of years ago. I took a temporary job at the *Himmel Times*, the place where I'd started my reporting career 10 years earlier. I never intended to stay. It was just a stopgap gig while I regrouped. But it didn't turn out that way.

I don't believe in many things, but the few that I do—the need for community, the obligation to keep your word, and the importance of seeking the truth—I try to honor. That's why, after my first book made some decent money, I used the profits to resurrect the *Times*.

The newspaper was the main reason that I seriously mulled over Clinton's suggestion as I sipped my Jameson. Meeting payroll and overhead was a constant struggle. Everyone worked for less than they were worth because we all shared the same goal. But I didn't feel good about barely breaking even. Although we'd started with a doable three-year business plan to self-sufficiency, the appearance on the scene of *GO News* has created an unexpected challenge. It's a digital-only publication with an approach to news that is more sensational and less fact-based than ours. And it's managed to siphon off a significant number of our subscribers and advertisers—who weren't that plentiful to begin with.

I'm happy that my business partner Miller Caldwell is both wealthy and generous, but he's had to provide more financial support than we planned. It isn't fair to rely on him to rescue the paper while we battle it out with *GO News*. If writing fiction could produce a steadier stream of income for me as Clinton predicted, maybe it was worth a try.

But could I even do it? I'd been all about the facts all my writing life. And even if I did manage to create readable fiction, would I enjoy doing it? Writing true crime books has all the elements of journalism I like—research, chasing down leads, interviewing, putting the pieces of the story together—and none of the things I don't like—meetings, timid corporate attorneys, editorial-to-advertising ratios, and bad headline writers. Fiction would be very different.

I probably agonize over change more than most people do. Intellectually, I understand that nothing stays the same. Without change butterflies wouldn't exist, trees wouldn't burst into glorious fall colors, whalebone corsets would still be a thing. But something in me always fights against it.

It started when I was a kid, after my sister Annie died and my dad left. I tried to feel safe by taking control, keeping things steady, making sure there was always firm ground under my feet. I think that's why I like reporting so much. After you ask all the questions, chase down all the answers, then you can finally hit on what's real. And that's when you know you're on solid footing. You can rest easy, then. Sort of. My version of "trust but verify" is "relax but be wary."

How would things change if I moved away from true crime to pretend crime?

Well, if I was a miserable failure, then I'd lose my publishing contract, the *Himmel Times* would be on even more tenuous financial ground, and I'd be letting down everyone at the paper from Miller Caldwell to Courtnee the receptionist. Worst of all Spencer Karr, the publisher of *GO News*, would be able to gloat. I realize that it doesn't say much for my character that the last item on my list would probably bother me the most, but there it is. I would hate more than anything to fail in front of Spencer.

That would be the downside of making the switch. The upside could be that I became a successful mystery fiction writer with a series that developed a solid fan base and turned out a respectable and steady stream of revenue. Something my standalone non-fiction had not done.

I had no illusions about being Sue Grafton-level successful. However, it would be very nice to have a reliable source of income that was enough to help keep my little paper alive, my lovely apartment roof over my head, and my requisite bottle of Jameson in the cupboard. Still, it would be a big change.

I was just about to consult my Magic 8-Ball for an answer when the buzzer at the back entrance of my place went off.

3

"Hey, you," Gabe said as he stepped inside my apartment. "I missed you." He offered a long hug and a lingering kiss to prove it.

"I missed you, too. So did Barnacle. Look how ecstatic he is."

We both glanced in the direction of the living room, where Barnacle had deigned to open one eye and give a slight wag of his tail by way of acknowledgement that his master had arrived.

Gabe laughed.

"He only brings out the big guns when Dominic is on the scene. Maybe if I ran over, shouting 'Barnacle! Barnacle! It's me, I'm back!' then dropped down, snuggled his neck, and kissed him, he'd respond with more excitement."

"Well, if you're going to display that much enthusiasm I'd prefer to see it directed at me."

Dom is Gabe's five-year-old son, who he didn't know existed until a few months ago. His son's surprise appearance complicated things a bit for me and Gabe, but we were working our way through it. Dom is a funny, smart, affectionate kid and I enjoy him. Gabe is totally into being a father, which is a good thing when you actually *are* someone's dad. But I've never seen myself as a parent. It's a huge, lifetime, scary commitment. I haven't made my mind up yet, but the need for a decision will come one day. Meanwhile

I've chosen the Scarlett O'Hara problem-solving method. I'll think about that tomorrow.

"I've got some good news," Gabe said with a smile that was reflected in his dark eyes.

"Yeah? Well, I've got some interesting news that could be good—or not. I'm having a Jameson. Let me fix you one and we can share."

We each claimed a corner of the sofa and faced each other at an angle. At Gabe's insistence I filled him in on my news first.

"Tell me, what do you think?"

"I think yes. You're a good writer, Leah. Stretch your wings a little. See where fiction takes you. I can tell you're seriously considering it."

"Yeah, I am. It's just a little scary."

"Scary doesn't usually keep you from doing things."

"Some things, no. But what if my fiction is terrible? What if I don't have the imagination for it? What if it's so bad Spencer Karr puts the worst parts on the home page of the *GO News* website, along with a video of him dancing on top of piles of unsold copies of my book?"

"See, that's imagination right there. Just put it to work on your series instead of on disaster scenarios and you'll do fine."

He set his glass down then and leaned over to put a hand on mine. His eyes, my favorite thing about him, were intense under his thick, straight eyebrows. A piece of his dark hair flopped down on his forehead.

"I'm serious. You can do this, Leah. It's always hard to start something new. I felt the same way moving from New York to join Miller's law firm. But that decision turned out to be one of the best I've ever made. I met you, didn't I?"

"You know, you keep talking like that and I might have to move you from boyfriend to swain status. I'm searching for the perfect term for you. What do you think?"

"Swain isn't a good fit for me, sorry. But I can think of another word that I'd rather have you call me."

Okay, I had walked into that minefield. Time to beat a retreat. I smiled and changed the subject.

"Tell me, what's your good news?"

"Dominic's coming to stay for a while. Lucy is putting him on a plane this coming Friday."

"That's great. But I thought he was going to be in New York with her until spring break. Did she get another acting job?"

Lucy Paine is Dominic's mother. I've never met her, but Gabe's told me a lot about her. When she and her not-so-nice ex-husband divorced, she was shocked to discover via a paternity test that her ex wasn't Dominic's father. Gabe was. Their relationship had ended just before Lucy had met and hastily married the man she *thought* was Dominic's father. Gabe was even more surprised at the news, but happily so. In addition to regularly scheduled time with Dom, he's always glad to step up when Lucy needs him.

"Not this time. Lucy's grandmother—the one who raised her—is in hospice care in Florida. Lucy wants to be with her for the time she has left. It could be a few weeks, but it might be as long as a few months. Either way, it's no place for a rambunctious five-year-old."

"That makes sense. And Barnacle will be in heaven. Can you stay tonight? You haven't told me anything about your conference. Also, I bought eggs, onions, green peppers, and mushrooms, in case you want to make your famous omelets in the morning. And I have a new nighttime ensemble. *Star Wars* pajamas. I know how you feel about Princess Leia."

"I was hoping you'd ask."

4

Shortly after Gabe and Barnacle left in the morning, I got a text from Miguel Santos. He's the senior reporter at the *Times*, but since there are only two on staff, it's not much of a job title. He also happens to be one of my favorite people in the world.

Just finished story on Kiwanis Pancake Breakfast. Can I come up?

When I opened the door, I marveled yet again at how very good-looking he is. Tall, slender, skin a light caramel color, long, long eyelashes, and dark, dark eyes. His hair is always perfect, and his fashion sense is strong. Plus, he's funny, thoughtful, and kind. I would marry him in a nanosecond if he weren't gay and 10 years younger than me. Maybe I would anyway, if he asked.

"Come in. What can I get you? Coffee? Diet Coke? Water? Half of a great omelet Gabe made?"

"I'll take the Coke, *gracias*," he said, pulling up a bar stool and sitting at the kitchen island.

"Anything exciting in your life?"

"No, but the day is young, and I have hope. What about you?"

"Maybe. I'm not sure yet," I said.

I told him about Clinton's idea and my ambivalence.

"Oh, but you have to do it, *chica*. You would be so good. It will be just like *Murder She Wrote*."

"Great. That's what I aspire to be, the Jessica Fletcher of Himmel. And how do you even know what *Murder She Wrote* is? You weren't even born when it was on, were you?"

"I was just a tiny baby. But very precocious," he said with a grin. "When I was in elementary school, I used to watch reruns with my grandma. I love Jessica."

"My sister Annie and I used to watch it on Sunday nights with my mom and dad. It was the last show before bedtime. We loved it," I said.

Annie had died in a fire when she was eight and I was ten. It was years before I could think of her without crying. Sometimes I still do, but mostly I smile at her memory. As I did then at the mental image of Annie and me with a bowl of popcorn each, snuggled between our parents on the living room couch, watching Jessica Fletcher solve crimes.

"But still, I'd like to think I have more of a Veronica Mars, hot-young-chick thing going than a bike-riding-older-lady thing."

"Don't even say that. Jessica is ageless. And she is smart like you. And she lives in a small town like you. And she solves crimes like you. But, and I'm sorry to say it, *chica*, she is styled better than you. Eighties fashion was not so good, but Jessica, she is always on point."

My sense of style has always pained Miguel, who at various times has accused me of dressing like an Amish lawyer—that's when I pull out my black blazer, black trousers, and white shirt; like an airline counter person —that's when I'm wearing my break-out red blazer, white shirt, and black trousers; and a sad gamer—that's when I'm dressed as I was at the moment in my Badgers hoodie and jeans.

Miguel, on the other hand, is always pulled together, even for a casual Sunday morning. He was wearing a sort of tweedy-gray, shawl-collared sweater over a button-down gray shirt and black jeans. His feet were clad in black boots.

"We can't all be fashion icons like you and Jessica," I said.

"Very true. But I will get you there, one day, I swear on my collection of vintage *GQ* magazine covers. But I want to talk more about your new mystery series. They must have romance with the mystery."

"No."

"Yes. People like a little romance with their murders. My grandma, she watched because she wanted Jessica and Seth to get together. Me, too."

"You think everyone should get together. Actually, I liked the sheriff better than Seth."

Oops. That was an unfortunate reference point. As soon as I said it, I wished I hadn't.

"I don't think everybody should get together. But you and Sheriff Coop, yes. Gabe, I like him, but he's not the one. Tell me, what's happening now with Coop and you, *chica*."

A couple of months earlier, right after my best friend Coop had won the election for sheriff, something odd had happened between us. I'd made the mistake of telling Miguel about it, immediately regretted it, and then made him pledge never to mention it again unless I alluded to it. I very carefully hadn't, and he'd kept his promise. But I had just given him the tiniest of openings, and he was leaping right into it.

"Nothing is happening now. Nothing happened in the past. And nothing will happen in the future. Except that Coop and I will always be good friends. No, make that great friends. Without a scintilla of romance in the relationship. Now, get that out of your head," I said, a note of crossness creeping into my voice.

"Ah, but how can I? Romance is in my blood. Also, did you forget, I am Miguel Santos, D.L." He said the last with a flourish.

"I know I shouldn't ask, but what does D.L. stand for?"

"I've told you before, they call me the Doctor of Love," he said, in a low, seductive voice that made me laugh in spite of myself.

"And I told you before, no one calls you the Doctor of Love. And you are going to leave what I told you in a moment of weakness alone."

"Oh, I would like to, but you brought it up. And once the doctor has been alerted, he is ethically obliged to take action. Now, let's go over things again, so I can prescribe for you properly."

"There's nothing more to say."

"No. I cannot accept that. On the very night of the election, after you have saved Coop's campaign, after you share the unexpected kiss—"

"I told you, that was an accident. I was just going to kiss him on the cheek to annoy Sherry and then he turned his head and we bumped lips. That's it."

"Ah, but Dr. Freud and Dr. Love—that's me—we say there are no accidents. Why would you kiss him at all? No, you were manifesting your *unconscious* desire. Then, you tell him, 'I'm sorry.' Then he says, 'I'm—' but he's interrupted. He doesn't finish. The crowd, they want his victory speech, and you are already walking out the door. It is too late. The moment is lost."

He had jumped to his feet to act out the scene, and he finished his historically inaccurate reenactment with an impression of what I guessed was supposed to be me. He pressed the back of his hand to his mouth like a silent movie heroine, an anguished expression on his face as he looked over his shoulder and walked away.

"That's not exactly what happened. Especially not the unconscious desire part. I was there, remember? I'm the one who told you about it."

"Yes, but you are blocking now. I remember everything. You pull into the driveway at Gabe's. Your cell phone pings. Coop has sent you the text, 'I'm not.' He's not sorry about the kiss! That's what happened, yes?"

"You put a lot of embellishment in there, Miguel."

"It did happen though, yes?"

"Yes, but—"

"No, no. You cannot 'yes, but.' You cannot ignore it. Coop was reaching out. He was pulling together all his courage to take the chance, to tell you that he wants to be more than your friend. And you? What do you do? You ignore it."

"I didn't ignore it."

"No?" He leaned forward, his expression eager. "You've talked to him about it? I knew it! Tell me everything. What did you say? What did he say?"

"I didn't say anything. He didn't say anything. Because we didn't talk about it."

"But you just said—"

"I said I didn't ignore it. Coop's the one who did. Which proves my point that it was nothing. He started a text, got distracted, hit send, and didn't realize it. In the excitement that night, he forgot all about it. If it had been anything major, he would have said something later. He didn't, so I didn't."

"I disagree."

"I know you do. But listen, Coop and I, we love each other, yes. Only it's not in the fairy tale way you think it should be. Coop has a girlfriend he's happy with and I have Gabe."

Miguel heaved a sigh so heavy that it fluttered the napkins I'd set out.

"What?" I asked, a little exasperated.

"What if Mr. Darcy never told Elizabeth Bennett how he felt? Where is *Pride and Prejudice* then?"

"Which one am I supposed to be, Mr. Darcy or Elizabeth?"

"Coop is Mr. Darcy, he tried to tell you. You are Elizabeth, but a very bad one. She told him no, but she let him try again. You're just ignoring him. You're getting good advice here from Dr. Love, and you don't even have to call my podcast."

He looked so disappointed, I couldn't help laughing.

"I'm sorry, Dr. Love. Dr. Reality, here, and I prescribe less Jane Austen and fewer Hallmark movies. Now, we're done with that, okay? Let's move on. Are you bringing Anthony to Mom's surprise birthday party?"

"No."

"No? I thought you guys were a thing."

"We were, but you know me. I'm just a boy who wants to have fun. Anthony, he's too serious."

"You're a heartbreaker is what you are. I hope you're still friends. I like him."

Miguel changes boyfriends fairly often, which I think is a good thing at his age. He's too young to settle down. Still, I felt a little sad about Anthony. He's just starting a practice as a family physician in Omico, the next town over from Himmel. I think Miguel was good for him. But then I think Miguel is good for everybody.

"Well, if things change, or you want to bring someone else, feel free. Mom likes meeting new people almost as much as you do."

5

"So, I've reached the point where I'm seriously leaning toward doing it, Mom."

I sat in my mother's kitchen on Sunday afternoon, having explained Clinton's idea as she finished up the molasses spice cookies she was making. She pulled out the last batch and set the pan on the counter before answering.

"Good. You should," she said, turning her full attention to me now that her baking duties were done. I wasn't surprised that she responded decisively on the question. My mother rarely hesitates.

"But I'm still kind of nervous about whether or not I can actually write fiction."

"What? Of course you can. Why would you even say that? The stories you invented to keep yourself out of trouble growing up were some of the finest pieces of fiction I've ever encountered," she said, pushing an errant strand of hair off her forehead as she spoke.

"Ah, but you never believed me—or hardly ever. What if I write fiction, but it isn't good enough to make people feel like, for the moment, it's real? What if they just go 'meh,' and toss my book aside after one chapter?"

"Oh, stop. Are you fishing for compliments? You're a good writer. You'll use the same skills to write an imaginary mystery that you use to write about real-life mysteries—drat!"

She broke off her pep talk to jab at another piece of hair.

"I don't know what I was thinking when I told Lydia I'd like to try letting my hair grow out a little. Now it's too short to pull back out of the way, and too long to stay spiked up." She raked her fingers through her silver-threaded black hair to make her point.

"You're looking kind of Rod Stewart there, Mom."

"Well, we can't all have nice, thick, straight hair like yours. Wait a second. Did you get highlights?"

"Nope. It must be the lighting in here. Same old reddish-brown. Miguel's always pushing the highlights, though."

"He's right. It wouldn't hurt you to get out of your comfort zone once in a while. You've got such pretty, shiny hair, Leah. You should make the most of it. Do something with it that plays up your hazel eyes. You know, I think—"

I was saved from a makeover conversation by Coop knocking on the door just then.

"Coop, hi! You're just in time for cookies," my mother said. "Sit down, I'll get a plate for all of us. Milk, too. Nothing goes better with warm cookies than cold milk."

"Can I help?" he asked.

"No, you sit. This kitchen is too small for both of us to maneuver in."

It's true. Coop is tall, six feet, and while not bulky in a professional wrestler way, he has a big presence. He took off his jacket and draped it over the back of the chair opposite me. I was a little surprised at the cardinal red of his long-sleeved Henley T-shirt. It looked good with his dark hair and gray eyes, but he usually sticks to darker colors.

"You're looking festive," I said. "Are you trying to ward off the gloom of this endless rain with your red shirt?"

"It's Kristin. She says I'm too basic, so she picked this up for me the other day. I'm going over to her place for dinner later, so I thought I should wear it. Not exactly my style, though." He smiled and shrugged.

"Nonsense," my mother said, pausing for a moment from her snack gathering. "You look very handsome in red."

Coop's phone rang then. "I have to take this, excuse me," he said, and stepped into the living room.

When he returned, I asked him around a mouthful of molasses cookie, "Anything serious on the phone?"

"Not at the moment, but it could be trouble down the road."

My ears pricked up immediately.

"What's going on?"

"That was the county emergency manager, Barb Dunaway. I asked her for some projections on flooding over the next week. The heavy rain's supposed to let up, but the Apple River is pretty high right now. I'm worried about the dam north of Towson Road, too."

My mother shuddered.

"We're sure paying for a mild winter with all this rain we've had. If the dam goes, I don't even want to think about the damage," my mother said. "I don't understand how private owners can be allowed to let a dam deteriorate like that. Where's the enforcement?"

"Tangled up in court cases, red tape, and competing agency jurisdictions," Coop said.

I got up from the table.

"Where are you going mid-cookie?" my mother asked.

"I'm just going to text Maggie and let her know to get in touch with the emergency manager. She should assign Troy or Miguel to do a story on the dam."

As I reached for my phone, which was charging on the counter, I caught a glance between my mother and Coop.

"I know what you're thinking. But I'm not micromanaging. I'm just helping, in case Maggie doesn't think about the dam. I'm allowed to help, right? That doesn't make me a control freak."

My mother shook her head.

"Do you seriously think that it won't occur to an editor with Maggie's experience to check in with the emergency manager? That's another reason you should say yes to Clinton's idea. You need something to keep you busy other than thinking about what everyone at the paper should be doing."

"What idea?" Coop asked.

"A career change. I'm thinking about switching up my writing life."

I laid out Clinton's proposal and waited. Unlike my mother, Coop is a very deliberate thinker, and almost never says things off the top of his head. He seemed to be taking a little longer than usual to weigh in, though.

"So?" I prodded him when I couldn't wait any longer. "What do you think? Can you see me as a fiction writer?"

"Well, I'd say you've got the imagination for it."

"That's what I told her," my mother said.

"And if she's busy making up crimes, she won't get in the way while I'm solving real ones. I think this fiction writing thing could be in the best interests of everyone."

"It's settled then," my mother said.

"You guys are very funny," I said. "But I'm trying to make a big career decision here, quit teasing me."

"Who says we're teasing? You imagining murder mysteries instead of mixing it up in the real world is bound to make my life easier. And just think how happy Charlie will be," Coop said.

Charlie Ross is a detective in the sheriff's office. We clash sometimes, but basically, we respect each other. I think.

"Really? I believe Ross was pretty grateful that I mixed it up with Gretchen Fraser. And what about last summer? When—"

I was winding up for a full-scale rebuttal itemizing a number of times when I'd actually gotten to the answer before—or at least at the same time —they did. Then I saw the glint of laughter in Coop's eyes.

"You just love to get me going, don't you?"

"It is pretty entertaining."

I rolled my eyes, but not too hard, because I had a favor to ask.

6

"Coop, if you're serious that you think writing a mystery series is something I should try, would you be willing to help me out?"

"I'm sure you're not asking me to co-write with you. But you know I'll support you any way I can. What is it?"

"Well, I've been looking at the idea from all angles—not just whether or not I should do it, but how I'd do it. What the setting would be, and who I'd use as a lead character."

"What about a reporter, like you?" my mother asked. "You already know what it's like."

"See, that's the thing, Mom. I don't want to write a character who's like me at all. I want my real self to stay totally separate from the characters I create. My lead will definitely be female. It's going to be hard enough to write fiction without trying to figure out how a man would suss things out. But I'm thinking she'll be a cop. That's where your help comes in, Coop."

"You mean you want to interview me about being in law enforcement? Sure, that's not a very big ask."

"Well, that would be helpful, yes, and I'll take you up on it, but I had something more hands-on in mind."

"Oh?"

The wary look on his face told me he'd leaped ahead and suspected where I was heading. He may be a deliberate thinker, but that doesn't mean he's a slow one.

"I'd like to job shadow a detective in the sheriff's office. And I don't mean just a one-night ride-along. I mean hanging out on regular shifts with him for a couple of weeks. It would have to be him because you don't have any female officers except Marla and she's not a detective." I couldn't resist bringing up a point I'd been hammering him with for weeks—the lack of females in his office.

"Art Lamey filled the only detective spot we're likely to have open for a while before he left when he hired Owen Fike. I'm working with the county on the budget, but it's a tough sell. Let's not get derailed here, though. Can you be more specific about this job shadowing?"

I hesitated because I knew if I didn't make the right pitch, that would be the end of it. On the other hand, I had Coop's full attention, we were on my home turf, and there were cookies. I wouldn't get another setup as good as this. I went all in.

"Okay, well, I want to job shadow because I need to know the ins and outs of the work—not the detecting part, but the everyday things—what's frustrating, what's fun, what the obstacles are, the kind of paperwork a detective has to do, the pressures from above, the interaction with citizens, with the other cops, how it feels to respond to a call. How does the day start? How does it end? In short, I want to understand what the job is all about. I don't mean the heart-in-your-throat exciting stuff, I can make that up. I want to understand what real, everyday stuff is like."

The phone rang then—that would be the one on the wall. My mom has a cell phone, but she still likes her landline.

"That's Paul," she said. Paul Karr is our family dentist, my mother's long-time suitor, and the father of my mortal enemy Spencer Karr. "I'll take it in my room, so I don't disturb what looks like some delicate negotiations. Have another cookie, Coop," she said, patting his shoulder as she left. "You're going to need the strength."

"Coop, I know it's a big ask. But it would help me make the story world seem real. I know the big picture, it's the details I need. Come on. How often do I ask you to help me?"

"Do you want that reported out on a monthly, annual, or lifetime basis?"

I bit back a smartass response and took a different tack.

"All right, why don't you just tell me why you think this will be a problem? Because I can tell by the way you're looking at me that you do."

"Okay."

He then held up his hand and used it as he began enumerating his concerns, folding down each finger in turn as he listed them.

"One, you'll be a distraction. Two, there are privacy concerns. Three, GO News could make an issue of me granting unfair access to the Times. Four, morale—some of the guys aren't very fond of the press. I'm trying to build trust. Injecting a journalist into the mix could be a problem. Five, it could be dangerous."

"All right, those are reasonable concerns to raise. Now, let me tell you why you don't have to worry about any of those things."

I followed his lead and held up my own hand to rebut each of his points.

"One, I won't be a distraction. I'll be there to shadow, not to shine. Like a fly on the wall or a mouse in the corner. I'll absorb the atmosphere, observe the rhythms, and pay attention to the ordinary things that are part of a detective's day. I won't be recording, writing, or asking bunches of questions —at least not until after the shift ends.

"Two, as far as privacy concerns, I promise that nothing I see during my job shadowing will turn up in the Times, unless it gets there by good reporting from Troy and Miguel. I promise. You know that you can trust me to keep a promise, right? Please tell me you do know that?"

"Yes, I know that."

"All right then, three. As for GO News raising a ruckus because Spencer Karr or Andrea Novak thinks you're playing favorites, it's a non-issue. You can shut them down with this: Do either of them have a contract to write a mystery series? No, they do not. This isn't about daily reporting, it's about gathering background for my new series.

"Number four, morale. I understand the tension between journalists and public officials—not just cops. We both want to serve the public, but we don't always agree on the way it should be done, or when transparency beats the need for confidentiality, and vice versa.

"But, and this is for real, I'm not going to be taking down names of cops who take too many breaks at Bob's Donut Shop. I won't be getting all up in anyone's business, and I won't be talking about what I observe or hear to anyone, not even you. You have my word."

I still had one more objection to counter, but Coop obviously had something to say.

"Okay, I yield the floor—but I'm not done yet."

"I'm sure you're not. Leah, you made some good points, and I think I could probably sell the job shadowing to everyone, more or less, except—"

I was pretty sure I knew what he was going to say but forced myself to be quiet and hear him out.

"You could get into a very bad situation. If you're shadowing a detective for two weeks, it'll probably be pretty routine, even boring. But there's still a chance that you'd be out on a routine call and suddenly a witness interview becomes a hostage situation, or the surveillance turns into a car chase. It's not an everyday occurrence, but dangerous situations happen. I can't have a civilian at risk out there, especially not you."

Secretly I thought I would be extremely lucky if a routine surveillance morphed into a 90-mile-an-hour car chase, but I sensed that wasn't something I should share with Coop at the moment. He had a very earnest—and a very mind-made-up—expression on his face. He gave me no choice. I had to bring out the big guns.

"Look, I know being a cop can be dangerous. But so can being a journalist. We've had this conversation before, and I know we don't, and probably won't ever, agree on it. So, I'm skipping over rational arguments and going for my big finish. You owe me one."

He raised an eyebrow indicating he was curious to hear why.

"You're the one who said you wouldn't be sheriff if it wasn't for me. I'm not bragging, but I did stop Spencer from writing all that *GO News* garbage about you and your dad, remember? And exposing Art Lamey's lies cleared the way for you to get elected. Now, I'm just asking you to clear the way for me. It's only for two weeks. You can set any parameters you want, I won't object. Please?"

He hesitated a second, then nodded.

"All right, all right. You can job shadow for two weeks on one condition."

"Sure, what's that?"

"It has to be with Charlie Ross, and he has final say on whether or not he agrees to do it. If he says no, that's it and you don't keep badgering me—or him—about it."

"Fine. And for the record, I don't 'badger.' I persistently persuade."

7

Ross answered my knock at his front door with a surprised expression on his face. I don't usually do home visits to him. In fact, I've only ever been to his house to drop his daughter Allie off when she needs a ride home from her part-time job at the paper.

"Nash! What are you doin' here?"

"Hi, Ross. I'm sorry to bother you at home, but I need to ask you something. It'll only take a minute, I promise."

"Yeah? Well, come in then. You're lettin' in all the cold air standin' there. I was just watchin' the game. It's half time. We can talk in the den."

He ushered me down a short hall and into a small, knotty-pine-paneled room. A plaid rocker-recliner with a sagging seat cushion sat directly in front of a big-screen TV. The walls were hung with photos, most of them sports oriented, though I noticed several of Allie at different stages in her life. Ross gestured for me to take a seat on the brown corduroy couch that sat at a right angle to his chair.

He grabbed a beer from the six-pack on a tray table next to his chair, popped it open, and took a swallow. "Want one?"

"No, thanks. I won't stay long, so you can get back to your game."

"Nah. It's all right. It's not that exciting."

He clicked off the television and looked at me expectantly. Ross is gruff and quick-tempered, distrusts anyone not in law enforcement, and despite us working together pretty well a few times, still regards my abilities with a certain amount of doubt.

"Okay, what is it?" he prompted.

I laid everything out for him as I had for Coop, but Ross was a tougher audience.

"No. Not gonna happen."

I took another run at it to no avail. He remained extremely skeptical about my repeated promises to stay in the background while job shadowing, and adamant that he wanted no part of having me with him every shift for two weeks.

Until, that is, Allie entered the room. Her father's face softened at the sight of his teenage daughter, and I was reminded again of how well he'd made the transition from weekend dad to full-time father after his ex-wife, Allie's mother, took off with a boyfriend.

"Hi, Leah," she said, and smiled at me before turning to her father.

"Dad, what are you guys talking so loud for? I could hear you with my headphones on and Billie Eilish turned all the way up."

She joined me on the sofa, and I explained the situation.

"Leah, a mystery series—that's fire! I love mysteries. Dad, how can you even *think* of saying no to Leah?"

"Bein' a detective isn't a game, Allie. I don't need an amateur gettin' in my way." He stopped and took another drink from his beer, which he kept in his hand and waved in my direction as he continued.

"Plus, I don't need Nash here writin' down everything I say and do, and then usin' it to make me into some dumb cop character in her book. Everybody will know she means me 'cause she was learnin' all about the job from me. Also, I don't wanna be responsible for her dumb mistakes in her book either."

His small, rather close-set eyes glared in my direction. I realized then that I'd been answering the wrong objections as I tried to persuade Ross. He wasn't seriously concerned that I'd be underfoot, or that I might not follow his lead. He was more or less used to that. No, he was worried that he was going to show up as a character in my book and I'd make fun of him or make him look bad. I regrouped and reframed my case.

"Ross, seriously, I am *not* putting you in my mystery series, not even heavily disguised. That is unless you think people might suspect that you're the model for my female cop. But you know, I don't feel you're enough in touch with your feminine side for that to be a problem."

I smiled at him, but he didn't smile back.

"The job shadowing thing is just for background. I swear that I won't be profiling you. I won't even mention you in the acknowledgements if you don't want me to. I need to really understand what the day-to-day is like because that's what will help make the story ring true."

The stubborn look remained on his face and I faltered. He wasn't going to budge. Allie seemed to sense the same thing, because I felt her body tense by my side, and I glanced over at her.

She was returning his glare with a steely-eyed stare from eyes that are very like his, except hers are a brilliant blue framed by thick, dark lashes. In fact, Allie looks quite a lot like Ross, but somehow features that are harsh and unyielding on him—thick eyebrows, a determined set to his mouth, and a straight, strong nose—are transformed into a striking and attractive combination on her. One thing she didn't get from him is her tumbling mass of dark curly hair. Ross is mostly bald with just a fringe of hair around his head and a small, receding patch on top.

I watched as Allie tucked her unruly locks behind her ears, put her hands on her knees, and leaned toward her father, ready for battle.

"Dad, you're always complaining how the writers on cop shows and movies get it all wrong. Now's your chance to make sure Leah gets it right."

When Ross started to shake his head, Allie ignored him and continued before he had a chance to speak.

"I don't know how you can even think of saying no to such a small favor. She gave me a job at the paper, which I happen to love. And she let me stay even after I messed up so bad. All she wants to do is ride with you for a couple of weeks, and you won't let her? Not cool, Dad, not cool."

Then she went in for the kill. She thrust her verbal knife into the weak spot in every parent's armor—guilt.

"Are you forgetting that she risked her life for me? This is one tiny thing you can do to repay her. Or isn't my life worth a couple of weeks of inconveniencing yourself?"

That was a bold move. I'm not above using guilt when necessary. I'd used much the same tactic with Coop, but I hadn't considered trying it with Ross. Allie's brush with death had been so devastating for him that I wouldn't have been able to bring myself to use it as a bargaining chip.

But Allie, with the blissful obliviousness of adolescence, felt no such compunction. It's hard for teenagers to recognize parents as creatures with feelings that can be as deep and painful as their own. I held my breath, then he sighed.

"All right. Fine. Two weeks. I got day shift, but it don't always end after eight hours, so I don't wanna hear any complainin'. In fact, I don't wanna hear much from you, Nash. You get in my way just once, this little favor is done, got it?"

"Got it," I said happily.

Allie leaped up from the couch and gave her dad a quick hug. I wished not for the first time that I'd had a dad who'd been there for me the way Ross was for Allie when I was her age.

"Thanks, Ross. This will be fun. You'll see."

"I'm not lookin' for fun," he said. "I'll have you glued to my side for two weeks. I'm just lookin' for you to be quiet and for this shadow thing to be over."

"Okay, Clinton, I'll do it. I'll try, anyway."

I'd called him as soon as I got back from talking to Ross. I knew if I didn't, I was in for a late-night phone call. Or an early morning one the next day. Clinton operates on his own swing shift schedule, sometimes working late into the night, other times on the phone to me about the time the sun rises. Maybe, though, he just works round the clock. He has the energy for it.

"I knew you would. How soon can you have a plot line for the first book? I'd like to see an arc for the series, too. At least the first three books."

"Hey, I only just decided to try it. I'm not JK Rowling. I don't have a six-book story arc at the ready. I have a bit of an idea, I'm doing some research, and that's as far as I am."

"How soon?"

"Give me a few weeks to come up with something. And don't send me any snarky reminder texts, either, please."

"How can you say that? I'm happy to let the creative process unfold."

"Uh-huh."

"Talk to you next week. Are you as excited as I am?"

He was gone before I had a chance to answer.

8

"Here, Ross, I brought you a coffee. That's what partners do on all the cop shows," I said as I handed it to him on Monday morning, and then slid into my side of his unmarked cop car.

"We're not partners."

"Sure we are. Do you want to be Rizzoli or Isles? Or, we could go deep cut and you be Cagney and I'll be Lacey. No?"

His ongoing silence as he put the car in drive and we left the sheriff's office parking lot told me he didn't find my cheerful morning banter as amusing as I did. But I was not deterred.

"Ohhh. I get it. Can't see yourself as a female detective, right? Okay, I'll be Olivia Benson and you can be Elliot Stabler. Or you can be Lennie Briscoe and I'll be Ed Green. I don't have any gender hang-ups. Yes, I think that's the right combo. You're the crusty old-school detective and I'm the smart, cool one."

He was shaking his head as if in disgust, but I thought I saw a smile tugging on the corner of his mouth.

"Come on, that's funny, right? Why is it always so hard for you to give it up for me, Ross? Admit it, this is your dream come true."

"Are you finished?"

"Well, I can be, but I do have more partner repartee. Seems a shame to waste it."

"Tell ya what. You waste away while I drink my coffee. I'll let you know when it's time to talk."

Given that I'd had to use pleading, promising, and the intervention of an outside force in the form of Allie to get myself into the seat, I knew it was probably best not to push it any further.

"All right. Fair enough," I said, then subsided into silence.

———

Our first stop of the day wasn't very exciting. Ross had to follow up with the victim of a break-in in the western part of the county. We drove twenty miles on rutted gravel roads for a twenty-minute interview, at the start of which Ross had introduced me as his personal assistant.

"That wasn't funny, Ross," I said as we got back in the car.

"I thought it was."

"I'm doing everything you asked me to do: staying quiet, cooperating, not causing problems. You don't have to act like such a jackass."

"How do ya want me to explain you? Say I'm your therapy human and ya have to come with me?"

He laughed at his own joke so enthusiastically that he snorted.

In response, I rolled my eyes so far that they almost stuck in the back of my head. But I knew if he was making what he thought was a funny joke, he wasn't as irritated by the situation as he'd been pretending.

"This will all be over before you know it. And then you'll miss having me around. Come on, Ross, let's let this be the beginning of a beautiful friendship," I said.

"Me and Allie watched that movie after you told her about it last week. It's not bad."

I was somewhat amazed that he got the reference to the last line in *Casablanca,* but I tried not to show it. I find Ross to be full of small surprises.

"I'm glad you liked it. My offer still stands. I'll take you to the Classic Film Festival at Alcott College next month. You can watch some more not-that-bad movies. We can bond over Humphrey Bogart. They're going to show a bunch of his gangster flicks. You'll like those. The cops always win."

"No thanks. Take Allie instead. Two weeks in a car with you is my bonding limit. But I agreed to do it, so let's just make the best of it. Who knows, maybe you'll learn a thing or two from me."

"That's what I'm here for, Ross. I mean that. I want to learn from you. I know there are some things you can teach me."

I waited in vain for him to respond in kind.

"You know, you *could* say that maybe you'll learn a little something from me, too." Into the silence that followed, I added, "Or not."

I noticed then that we were heading away from, not back to, the sheriff's office.

"Hey, why are we on Linwood Road? Don't you want Brandle?"

"Like I haven't been drivin' these roads since practically before you were born. No, I don't want Brandle. I wanna swing by and take a look at Ponder Dam, the one north of Towson Road. See how high the water is."

"Why? Coop said yesterday that if the rain lets up, it's okay for now. Do you know something different?"

"A buddy of mine has a place downstream from it. He's outta town and kinda worried. Thought I'd just run by as long as we're out this way, see what things look like."

"Do you think it might not hold?"

"A dam like that, it could go fast. A cousin of mine lives in Michigan. Same situation as here, old earth embankment dam, private owner, maintenance not taken care of. The state flagged it, but nothin' got done. That one went and it took out a whole town. We'll just take a look see."

"Sounds like the *Times* should be digging into that."

"Yeah well—"

Whatever he was going to say was cut off by an incoming phone call and he motioned for me to be quiet.

9

As soon as Ross finished talking, we changed course and headed south. He spent the drive repeating that the call was routine, that I should stay out of the way, and that I'd better remember I wasn't there to do a write-up for the paper.

"I'm just checking in at a death scene. Deputies and EMTs are there. Don't be gettin' all excited like it's a crime scene."

"I know, Ross. You said that about a hundred times already. I'll just stay in the background like I promised. This isn't the first police call I've ever been on, you know."

In a way it was, though. I'd gone out on calls we picked up over the scanner lots of times, but this was my first time seeing things from a detective's perspective. It was exactly the kind of background insight that I was looking for. I was determined not to give Ross any reason to send me to time out.

We pulled into the long curved driveway of a large two-story house set so far back from the road that you could easily miss it. Two SUVs, one blue, one gold, and a red Mustang were in the drive, along with two cop cars. The responding ambulance had parked near a small wooden building about thirty yards from the house on the edge of a woods.

Ross and I tromped our way across the muddy yard toward the small group of people standing behind yellow tape marking off the area around the building. A deputy was talking to them.

"We need to get those people outta there. Family just gets in the way," Ross said.

"Do you think that building is a sauna? It looks too small for a workshop and too nice for a storage shed."

"Yeah. That's where the guy was found. Lotta people have outdoor saunas around here. Crazy if you ask me. Goin' out in the cold, gettin' all sweaty, then back into the cold? Not for me."

When we were halfway to the taped-off area, a woman spotted us and detached herself from the group. She was tall, with swept-back gray hair. She looked a bit like the actor Bea Arthur.

"Are you the detective in charge? I'm Rhonda Crawford. Those policemen won't let me in. They say Bryan's dead. But they won't let me see him. Bryan is my brother. I want to see him!"

Her tone was demanding, arrogant even, but from the way her voice cracked at the end and the redness of her eyes, I thought that she was having a hard time holding herself together.

"Yes, ma'am, I'm Detective Ross with the Grantland County Sheriff's Office. I'm sorry for your loss. But I need you and the others over there to vacate the scene so I can do my job."

"I don't understand. Why won't you let me see him?"

"I'm sorry, ma'am. We're waiting on the medical examiner, and I need to take a look around the scene. I can't do that with you there."

"But why? Bryan had diabetes. He must have had a reaction. Why are the police here? Why does the medical examiner have to come? Why do you have to look at the scene? Do you—"

Ross cut her off as her voice grew louder.

"It's routine procedure, that's all. Nothing to get upset about. Lawlor!"

He turned and shouted to the deputy who had been speaking with the family. He came over at a trot, splashing mud and water up his khaki pant legs as his feet hit the rain-soaked ground.

"Lawlor, you take Ms. Crawford here and the others up to the house and have them wait there. Who are the others, anyway?"

"It's the family, sir—the deceased's wife, Rachelle Crawford, his daughter Stephanie Crawford, and his stepson, Adam Harrison. The wife's the one who found him."

Drew Lawlor was hired at the sheriff's office just before Coop won the election. I'd heard Ross refer to him as a suck-up.

"Okay. Well, get 'em outta here. Tell 'em I'll be up to talk to them in a little bit."

"Will do, sir," Lawlor said.

He moved in Rhonda Crawford's direction to escort her to where the rest of the family was waiting, but she waved him away. Tears streamed down her face as she looked at Ross. She didn't sound arrogant when she spoke this time. She sounded utterly broken.

"Please, Detective, I just need to see him. Bryan is my brother, my little brother. I've taken care of him his whole life. I've always been there for him. I can't just walk away. I have to see him!" She began to cry.

Ross answered her in a surprisingly gentle voice.

"Ma'am, I'm very sorry, but you can't. Nobody can until after the medical examiner gets here and looks things over. You go with Deputy Lawlor here, up to the house. I'll get with your whole family in a few minutes, answer any questions."

She drew a shaky breath as she worked to pull herself together, looking embarrassed that she had broken down.

"I'm sorry. I'm not usually so emotional." She reached into the pocket of her jacket for a tissue, then dabbed at her eyes and nose before going on.

"Bryan's had diabetes for years, but it's been a very long time since he had a serious incident. I'm just having a hard time accepting this. It doesn't feel real." She began weeping again.

"Lawlor!"

Ross spoke sharply to the deputy, as much to cover his own discomfort with the inconsolable level of Rhonda's grief as to get Lawlor moving.

"Take Ms. Crawford and the rest of them away from the scene. Now."

This time Rhonda went without balking. I watched as the deputy and she reached the others, and Lawlor shepherded them toward the house. A petite woman I pegged as the wife leaned on the arm of a grim-faced high-school-age boy, who I assumed must be her son. On his other side was an extremely pretty young woman with glossy, light-brown hair that shimmered in the pale spring sun. She must be the daughter. The three of them moved slowly together toward the house.

Rhonda Crawford walked behind them at a distance, as if she were all alone in the world. Maybe now, she was.

10

Once they were gone, Ross called to the other deputy who was talking to a female EMT.

"Hey! Northam! Quit makin' goo-goo eyes at Rita there, and get over here. I need some details."

Unlike Deputy Lawlor, Steve Northam wasn't worried about impressing Ross. He's a pretty laid-back guy in his early forties, with sleepy brown eyes. As far as I can tell, he's got no ambition beyond being a good road patrol officer—which is no small thing. He said something to the EMT that made her laugh and then walked over to us, pulling his notebook out of his jacket pocket as he did.

"Hey, Charlie. Leah. I heard it was 'take your reporter to work' day."

"Hi, Steve. Just pretend I'm not here. It upsets Ross to be reminded."

"Yeah, I'm tryin' to forget, but she's like a mosquito buzzin' around my ear."

"I prefer to think of myself as an angel on your shoulder."

Steve laughed and then got down to business as he referred to his notes.

"Here's what we got, Charlie. The deceased is Bryan Crawford. He's 54, Type 1 diabetic. The wife, Rachelle Crawford, found him about ten this morning when she got home from a weekend retreat. She expected her husband to be at work—he owns Crawford Plumbing and Electrical. She was about ten minutes away from home when she got a call from his office looking for him. He didn't come in this morning, and they couldn't reach him on his cell phone. His sister Rhonda had a doctor's appointment, so she wasn't in either—she's the general manager at Crawford's company.

"The wife says her husband was planning to go to his hunting cabin on Saturday and stay for the weekend. When she got a call from his office asking where he was, she wasn't too worried. She figured he'd decided to stay over on Sunday and drive home this morning. He does that sometimes. The cell phone coverage is spotty up north. She thought he must've been out of range when his office called and that's why he didn't answer."

"Crawford and his wife didn't talk to each other over the weekend? No texting? He didn't tell her he was staying over?"

"She wasn't reachable by phone. This retreat she was at, it was some kind of spiritual thing, she says. 'To get centered in silence,' " he added, reading from his notes. "No talking, and they had to turn in their phones when they checked in and pick them up when they checked out this morning. She couldn't call him. She didn't have access."

" 'Centered in silence,' huh? You ever consider goin' on one of those retreat things, Nash? Might do you a lot of good. It would sure be good for the people around you," Ross said.

I didn't rise to the bait.

"Anyway," Steve said, "they weren't in contact, and that was okay, both the husband and wife expected that. But then she got to thinking. It wasn't like Bryan not to notify the office if he'd be in late. And with him being diabetic that kind of worried her. As soon as she got here, she ran in the house. She saw dishes from his Friday night supper still on the kitchen table, and that wasn't like him either. Then she noticed his cell phone was on the counter and the battery was dead. The only time it's there is when he's in the sauna. He takes a sauna every Friday around six. Right after he eats his dinner. So, she ran out here, opened the door, and there he was, on the floor."

"Okay, wait a second." Ross pointed in the direction of the sauna. "There's a security bar for the door and a padlock. The bar was slid back, and the door unlocked when she got here?"

Steve looked chagrined. "Sorry, she said she pulled the door open, and I just assumed it was unlocked. I didn't ask. I'll go check with—"

"Nah, that's all right. I'll ask her when I go up to the house. What about the body, did she touch it, try to revive him, move him?"

"She says no. She could see he wasn't breathing, and he wasn't moving. We didn't go in, but I did open the door to check. He didn't look too bad. Lucky the temps were in the mid-30s all weekend. But his skin's startin' to get that waxy look. I can see why the wife didn't want to touch him. She called 911, pretty hysterical. The dispatcher sent an ambulance. Both me and Lawlor were in the area, so we responded to the call. Got here just a couple minutes after the ambulance. I talked to the EMTs, got the basics. Lawlor called dispatch to get hold of the M.E. and we set up the yellow tape to keep everyone back.

"The wife called her son, he goes to the local high school, and her step-daughter. The stepdaughter goes to Robley College, but she was on her way to the house to pick up some clothes she left last time she was here. She swung by the high school and picked the boy up. The deceased's sister came separate. They all got here maybe 15 minutes before you did."

"Anything from the EMTs on cause of death?"

"EMTs can't make that kind of call, you know that, Charlie."

"No unofficial guess even?"

"Not from them. But the guy had Type 1 diabetes. I got a cousin with that. Diabetes is a real balancing act. If Crawford wasn't monitoring his blood sugar regular-like, and didn't adjust his insulin right, he could've had a bad reaction. We didn't do anything but look quick, but I didn't see anything suspicious."

"Well, no use speculatin'. We'll let the medical examiner tell us. That's why she gets paid the big bucks. How much longer before she gets here?"

"I'd say about 60 seconds," Steve said, pointing to the black van that had just pulled into the driveway.

A short, sturdy woman with glasses and close-cropped auburn hair got out of the vehicle, then reached back in for a small black bag. Connie Crowley is an old friend of my mother's. Since her retirement from her medical practice a few years ago, she's been the part-time county medical examiner. She moved toward us with short, quick steps, and arrived in front of Ross slightly out of breath.

"Sorry you had to wait. I was at a drowning on Barnett Creek. Bridge is washed out after all the rain. Two kids either didn't see the warning sign or blew right past it. Eighteen years old, both of them. Senseless," she said, shaking her head. Then she noticed me.

"Leah? What are you doing here?"

"I'm job shadowing Ross."

"Try again. I don't believe you're thinking of joining the sheriff's office."

"No," I said, laughing. "That's not why I'm shadowing him. I'm going to try my hand at fiction. A mystery series. I'm with Ross for a couple of weeks observing how he does his job, for background."

"Better you than me," she said to Ross. "I don't like an audience when I work. Speaking of which, what's the situation here?"

Ross explained.

"All right, let me take a look and then you can have the scene."

<hr>

Connie finished as quickly as she'd promised and reported that she'd found nothing suspicious in her initial examination.

"Any idea on cause of death?" Ross asked.

"Some, but you know I can't tell until—"

"Yeah, I know, until you open him up. But what about this diabetes thing? Could that be a cause? Or a heart attack? Or something else?"

"There's a small bruise on his forehead and slight bruising on the hand, but that could be from falling after fainting. No evidence of a struggle. If he has Type I diabetes, there's always a chance of diabetic ketoacidosis."

"Say again?"

"Diabetic ketoacidosis. DKA for short. It can happen when blood sugar levels get dangerously high. Without treatment, it's fatal."

"How long's he been dead?"

"Well, rigor's come and gone and that takes about 36 hours give or take. The smell isn't bad. We can probably thank the cold weather for that. I doubt he's been dead more than a couple days. I can tell you more after the autopsy."

"How soon will that be? I'm goin' to talk to the family, and I know they'll ask."

"Depends on what else the day brings. Could be tomorrow, late. But I'd say Wednesday for sure. The scene's all yours, Charlie. Good luck with your new series, Leah."

"Thanks, catch you later," Ross said.

"Bye, Connie," I added.

She had already started toward her van as we answered, and she acknowledged our goodbyes with a backwards wave of her hand overhead as she hurried away.

"All right, let's go, Ross. Do you have gloves and a pair of booties for me?"

I knew he had no intention of letting me follow him into the actual death scene, but I gave it a try anyway.

"Don't push it. You'll be standin' behind the yellow tape, not over my shoulder."

"But I want to see you in action up close, Ross. That's part of the shadowing thing."

"Then you're gonna hafta get your binoculars out, because you're not comin' with me."

11

A flagstone path led from the house to the sauna. We followed it to the point where the crime scene tape blocked our access. Ross slipped his gloves and booties on and stepped over the tape with unexpected nimble-ness. I scurried around to a vantage point that gave me a view of the sauna from the front, so I could watch him from a distance.

The sauna was wooden, about eight by ten feet. The door had a small window, a pull handle, and brackets for a security bar that was not in place at the moment. A Wisconsin Badgers welcome mat sat in front of it. When Ross pulled open the door, I could see a body in a white terrycloth robe, lying on the floor. He was on his side, his head resting on one arm stretched out above his head, the other curled in front of his face. From my line of vision, he looked like he was asleep. Ross stepped carefully inside, bent down, checked the pockets on the robe, then stood up and looked around. When he moved a little farther inside, I couldn't see as well. After a few minutes, he came out. I noticed him lift up the mat in front of the door and then put it down as though it were crooked, and he was straightening it. He must have a touch of OCD I didn't know about.

"That was awfully quick. I didn't see you picking up a piece of fiber with tweezers and dropping it into an evidence envelope or getting out your magnifying glass to examine the body for unusual marks. Are you sure you did a good job?"

"That's for TV, Nash, and for medical examiners. I didn't see anything surprising. Before you ask, nothin' in his pockets. The sauna has two benches to sit on. The shelf had a pair of flip-flops on it and a towel. There was an empty water bottle on the floor. That was it."

On the way back to the house, Ross stopped to talk to the EMTs.

"Hey, Rita. Cal. Can you do me a favor?"

"Maybe," Rita said with a smile. "Depends on who you're asking—and what."

Was she flirting with Ross? Well, why not? Just because I didn't see Ross as a romantic possibility didn't mean no one else would. Rita looked close to his age, had a nice smile, and her eyes were a very pretty shade of blue. Ross could do worse.

His face had turned slightly pink at her teasing. He quickly said, "I'm askin' both of you."

"What is it?" the guy named Cal asked.

"Nothin' that big. I'm done, but could you get the body loaded up quick and out of here? The sister is kinda hysterical, insists she wants to see the body, but I can tell she won't be happy to just look. Nobody needs a scene with deputies holdin' her back and everybody wailin'. I'd appreciate it if you just double-time it out of here before the family knows you're leavin'."

"Sure. Moving fast is kind of in our job description, Charlie. The sister looks to me like the kind who would hold things together. But you never know how a death'll hit somebody," Rita said.

"Yep, that's for sure. Thanks, guys, I appreciate it," Ross said.

"Anything, anytime, for you, Charlie," Rita said with a smile and, I could swear, a wink.

"Aren't we going to take our shoes off?" I asked Ross, pointing at our muddy footwear as we stood on the side patio of the Crawford house.

"Nash, ya don't wanna talk to the family in your socks. It's not a good look. Just scrape the bottoms on the mat and keep your feet off the furniture. If God wanted us to go around in our stockin' feet, he wouldna made shoes."

I did the best I could with my muddy boots and followed Ross through the glass door and into somebody's Pinterest page of dream kitchens. The massive range, glass front stainless steel refrigerator, farmhouse sink, and miles of quartz countertop looked like they belonged on the set of a cooking show.

Beyond the open concept kitchen, Bryan Crawford's family waited, clumped together on a dark gray sectional in front of the fireplace. No one was talking. Everyone turned in unison to look as Ross and I clomped our way across the wood floor.

"Detective Ross? Does this mean I can see Bryan?"

Rhonda Crawford rose to her feet without waiting for an answer as Ross moved to stand in front of the fireplace to face the family.

"Please, Ms. Crawford. I got a couple things to tell you all. First off, my condolences to all of you," Ross said. "I already met Ms. Crawford, but not the rest of you. I'm Detective Ross with the Grantland County Sheriff's Office."

Ross didn't introduce me, and nobody asked who I was, which was just as well, because I had no official standing and they'd be perfectly justified asking me to leave.

"A detective? Why do we need a detective? Bryan's dead. He had diabetes and he died, right?"

The teenage boy had asked the question. Up close he was a good-looking kid with a thin, oval face and slightly pointy nose. His eyes were deep-set and a soft brown. He had the kind of decisive eyebrows I like—thick but not bushy. His voice was a pleasant tenor, but at the moment it was a little intense.

"You're Adam Harrison, the stepson, is that right?" Ross asked.

"Yes. I don't understand why you're here. Bryan had diabetes. That must be how he died," he repeated.

"Easy does it, kid. Don't get upset. It's just routine. Deputy Lawlor here, and the other officer who responded, Deputy Northam, they took care of things just fine. But it's my job to make sure everything gets buttoned up."

"I'm Stephanie Crawford," said the pretty girl with the light brown hair. "Bryan was my father. What does that mean, 'buttoned up?' What needs buttoning? My father had diabetes for years. Isn't it obvious that's what killed him?"

Stephanie had a delicately featured face with a flawless rosy complexion, pale blue eyes that showed no sign of tears, and a voice that, while softer, carried an echo of her Aunt Rhonda's arrogance.

"Like I told your brother—"

"Stepbrother," Adam quickly corrected Ross. No love lost there, I guessed.

"Stepbrother, okay. It's just routine. Now, Mrs. Crawford," he said, turning his attention to Rachelle Crawford, "was anyone with you when you found your husband in the sauna?"

She shook her head. Her eyes were large and wide-set, and they had a disoriented look—like they would, I guess, if you had just discovered your dead husband in a sauna. She kept twisting the wedding ring on her finger.

"I was alone. I called the rest of the family after I found Bryan. I told your deputy that."

"Yeah, I know. I just like to double-check things. I'd appreciate it if you could just go over with me how you found him."

She repeated the story Steve Northam had told us and to my ears it sounded the same.

"Okay, now when you got to the sauna and opened the door, did you touch your husband or try to move the body?"

"No!" She looked horrified at the thought. "As soon as I pulled the door open, and I saw Bryan, I knew he was dead. His skin was so pale, and he was so still. It was terrible," she said, dropping her face in her hands and letting out a small sob.

"Okay, okay, now. Take it easy. I noticed there was a security bar for the door. Was the door unlocked when you got home?"

"Yes, of course it was. Bryan would have had to unlock it to get in."

"It's a little odd, lockin' up a sauna, isn't it? It was pretty much empty as far as I could see, what's anybody gonna steal?"

"Not steal. Vandalize. Someone got in when we were gone a year or so ago. There were empty beer cans inside, and they left burn marks from cigarettes on one of the benches. Bryan had to replace it. He was very particular about things like that. He installed the security bar so he could keep it locked."

"Makes sense," Ross said. "Where do you keep the key?"

She looked surprised. "Under the mat. Why? Isn't it there?"

"Detective, why are you asking questions about a key, and how Rachelle found Bryan? Is there something you're not telling us?" Rhonda asked.

"I'm sorry for the questions, it's just procedure. We have to tick all the boxes in an unexplained death. But we'll have all the answers for you after the medical examiner does the autopsy."

"Autopsy?" Rachelle asked, her voice rising and trembling slightly as she looked up at Ross. "No! Please, Bryan wouldn't want that!"

"Your husband—" Ross started, but she cut him off.

"Don't I have to sign something, give permission? Please. Bryan didn't even like the idea of embalming. He always told me if he died before I did, he wanted to be cremated. He would hate that his body was autopsied. I can't let you do that. Please," she added, her eyes filling with tears and her voice nearing hysteria levels.

Rhonda moved from where she'd been standing near Ross to a spot directly in front of her sister-in-law. She towered over the seated Rachelle as she unleashed a venomous tirade.

"You don't have the right to object. He wouldn't be dead if you'd been home. Instead, you were wasting his money again, pampering yourself at some luxury spa. Bryan gave you everything. A beautiful home, a housekeeper so you didn't have to lift a finger, clothes, spending money. He took in your son when his own father didn't want him. But Adam never showed one ounce of respect or gratitude to Bryan. And you didn't either. You might not care, but I want to know what killed my brother. It's not up to you if there's an autopsy or not. I—"

Rachelle sprang up like a jack-in-the-box, all trace of cowering gone. With her fists clenched at her sides, she looked ready to throw a punch right at her much taller sister-in-law's head.

"Well, it sure isn't up to you, Rhonda! You weren't the most important person in Bryan's life, no matter how much you wanted to be. He only put up with you out of a sense of family obligation. I'm Bryan's wife! I'm the one who had to reach out my hand to open that sauna door, knowing what had to be on the other side, but praying that by some miracle it wasn't. But it was, Rhonda, it was. My husband, my Bryan, lying there on the floor! This has been traumatic enough. You—"

"You've been jealous of how close Bryan and I are since the day you met me, Rachelle. You tried to cut me out of his life, but it didn't work, did it? And I'm going to—"

"Don't be ridiculous. You're the one who's jealous. You—"

"He was my father. Don't I have a say in this?" Stephanie's voice broke in. "I'm his daughter. I'm the one who—"

"Don't even start that. He spoiled you rotten with the clothes, the car, the college. And you always wanted more. Well, finally your daddy's-little-girl act stopped working, didn't it? And believe me, Bryan was not going to let you twist him around your little finger again!" Rhonda's voice had moved from her distinctive alto almost to a screech on the last.

"It's none of your business how my father wanted—"

The only one who wasn't participating in the family melee was Adam. I had noticed his shoulders slump when Rhonda shot out the barb about his father not wanting him, and now he seemed to have totally checked out of the proceedings, his eyes staring straight ahead.

"All right. Enough," Ross said. "This isn't helpin'. You're all upset. But none of you makes the call on the autopsy, so quit fightin' about it. It's not optional. It's required in a situation like this. The death was unexpected. He wasn't bein' treated for a terminal illness. He was alone when he died, and we got no visible cause. The autopsy is happening. We'll have the results by Wednesday, maybe before. The body will be released then. I'll leave my card here," he said, taking one out of his wallet and placing it on an end table.

"You call me if you need to, otherwise, I'll be in touch as soon as the medical examiner gives me her report."

"Well, those were some interesting family dynamics," I said as Ross and I headed back to the sheriff's office.

"Yeah, well, you get that sometimes. Nothin' brings a family together or splits it wide open like an unexpected death. Lotta feelin's come up, not just grief."

"What happens now?"

"Lawlor and Northam write up their reports, I review 'em, write my own. Connie does the autopsy, we get her report. I give the news to the family, the body is released, and we're done."

"You're coming through for me in a big way, Ross—a death scene first thing Monday morning. What have you got lined up for the rest of the week? A bank heist? A major drug bust?"

"Not hardly. I gotta give a talk at the high school to a bunch of smartass kids who only signed up to get outta English class. Got some interviews, a ton of paperwork. And oh, yeah, if a workshop on 'Emotional Wellness for Law Enforcement' floats your boat, then you got a treat comin' on Thursday."

"Sorry, you're not going to discourage me. I'm okay with dull. I told you I want to get the whole picture, not just the exciting parts. And being your partner at an Emotional Wellness seminar is basically the stuff dreams are made of. I can't wait to help you get in touch with your inner child. You know, that EMT, Rita, she'd probably find emotional vulnerability very attractive," I said with a sly grin.

"Rita's just a friend."

"Oh? Is that why she practically gave herself a concussion batting her eyelashes at you?"

That wasn't fair to Rita, she hadn't been that obvious, but maybe Ross had been out of the game so long he needed a little help seeing what was in front of his face.

"You read it wrong. Rita's just friendly with everybody. She's a nice person. That's all."

"Hey, I'm a nice person too, but I don't vamp you when you talk to me."

"That's somethin' I never wanna see. And this conversation is somethin' I don't wanna have. Let's drop it."

"All right, all right, you don't have to get so crabby about it."

I settled into silence for the rest of the ride, but I couldn't help trying to figure out if Ross didn't recognize flirting when he saw it, or if he didn't want to let himself think it was real. Maybe he was afraid. I'd never heard him talk about anyone he was seeing, even casually. I realized it wasn't any of my business, but that didn't mean it wasn't interesting to speculate. I tucked it away for possible future exploration.

12

"Why do you have a dress on, Leah?" Dom asked when I arrived at Gabe's on Saturday evening. I was dropping Allie off for babysitting and picking Gabe up for party-going.

"Because it's my mom's birthday and we're having a surprise party for her at a nice restaurant tonight."

"I like birthday parties. And I like Mrs. Carol. Can I go, too?"

"She likes you, too, Dominic. But it's not the kind of party you'd enjoy. No games, no prizes, not even a real birthday cake."

"No cake?" The shocked look on his face made me laugh.

"Well, there is a sort of cake, but it's called tiramisu and I'm pretty sure you wouldn't like it."

"Dom, we're going to have our own party here," Allie said, dropping down on the floor next to him. "A much better one. At theirs, the grown-ups have to sit up straight, and not use their fingers to pick up their peas, and they're not allowed to burp. Me and you? We're gonna eat pizza with our hands, make slurping noises with our straws, and see who can burp the loudest. And we don't even have to say, 'excuse me.' Our party, our rules."

Dominic giggled as Gabe entered the room.

"Wait a minute, that sounds like a lot of fun, Dom. Can I stay here with you guys?"

"No, Dad. It's not for grown-ups. It's just for me, and Allie, and Barnacle. You have to go now."

"Oh, I see. You've got a better offer, so now you want me out of here, eh?"

He leaned down and began to tickle his son, who responded—or tried to—in kind. Allie stood and walked over to me.

"Leah, do you think my dad is dating somebody?"

I was surprised by the question, but my mind flashed to Rita, the flirty EMT from earlier in the week.

"I don't know, Allie. He hasn't said anything, though he probably wouldn't to me. Why do you ask?"

"He's just acting kind of weird. Like wearing aftershave and saying he wants to lose a few pounds. And one day this week, he had music on in the car. He never listens to music."

"How would you feel about it if he is?"

She shrugged. "Good, I guess, depending on who it is. I'll be going to college in a few years. I don't want him to be alone. He doesn't do so well when he's alone."

"Well, he didn't mention bringing anyone to the party tonight, but I told him he could."

"Okay, well, don't tell him I said anything. I was just wondering."

"No problem."

"I think my work here is done," Gabe said as he stood, leaving a giggling, gasping Dominic lying on the floor. "You two have fun. Let me know who wins the burping contest."

Ariana's is an Italian restaurant in a converted Victorian farmhouse on the other side of Omico, a little more than half an hour from Himmel. The addition that expanded the kitchen and dining room capacity had been carefully constructed to fit with the architecture of the house. The restaurant is situated on a hill that overlooks the Apple River. From April through October, if you snag a table by the window or choose the outdoor seating, you can watch kayaks, canoes, and fishing boats going by. In the summer, sometimes people come to the restaurant by water and pull up at the dock that juts out into the river. It's a great setting, but the reason people come to Ariana's is the fantastic Italian food.

All was in readiness when we walked into the private dining room I'd reserved for the party. Coop and his girlfriend Kristin Norcross, an attorney in the DA's office, were chatting with Miguel in one corner. In the opposite corner, I was surprised to see Courtnee Fensterman, since I had deliberately left her off the guest list. She is, if not the worst receptionist in the world, certainly among the top 10. My mother and Miguel have quite a bit of patience with her. I do not. She was chatting at, rather than to, Father Lindstrom, who's a family friend and the priest at my mother's church.

"I don't know what Courtnee's doing here, Gabe, but I'm going in. Father Lindstrom has that look people get when she starts telling them about her uncle who was abducted by aliens. I'll cut her off and you grab Father Lindstrom and get him to safety."

Gabe followed as I moved swiftly in their direction.

"Hi, Father. I'm glad you could come," I said to the little priest. With his fluffy white hair and gentle smile, he reminds me of Clarence the angel in *It's a Wonderful Life.* "I hate to interrupt but I need to talk to Courtnee for a minute."

"Of course," he said, a little quickly, but I don't think Courtnee noticed. As he and Gabe moved away, she said, "It's all right. You don't have to apologize for not inviting me. Miguel already did for you. He said you forgot because you had all that typing to do or something."

I had told Miguel to bring someone in place of his ex, Anthony, if he wanted. It hadn't occurred to me that the someone would be Courtnee.

"Courtnee, I'm not up in my office doing random typing jobs. I just finished my third book. And I'll be starting a new series, fiction, soon."

"Uh-huh."

Courtnee is uninterested in my literary pursuits. Her large, slightly vacant blue eyes had begun scanning the room past my shoulder. I knew she'd spotted someone, because she patted her shoulder-length blonde hair and made sure that on one side it was tucked fetchingly behind her ear and on the other that it draped artfully over her shoulder.

I turned. Miller Caldwell, my business partner, was just walking in.

"Courtnee, you do know Miller is gay, right? And old enough to be your father?"

"Duh, yes, everybody knows. I don't want to hook up with him. I'm going to ask him for a raise. I already asked your mom and she said no. So, *my* mom said I should go to the top."

"No, you are not going to ask Miller for a raise. It's my mother's birthday party. It's totally inappropriate. Besides that, Miller doesn't get involved in personnel decisions. I'm the court of last resort there, and I can tell you right now, the answer is no. We don't have the money in the budget."

Her lower lip began to protrude in a pout. I caught Miguel's eye from across the room and signaled for him to come over. He had brought Courtnee, he could manage her.

"*Chica*, you are looking good," he said. "That burgundy dress—and your hair! You used a flat iron like I showed you, didn't you?"

"I did, thank you. Tell Courtnee what you said to me yesterday."

"What I said?" he asked.

"Yes, when you told me you were bringing her," I said with a bright smile.

"Ohhh."

"Yes, oh."

Miguel is quick on the uptake and he knew that having brought her, I expected him to take care of her. He began talking to her about a jacket he'd seen at Nordstrom Rack that would be perfect for her.

Any talk that centered on fashion and herself immediately held Courtnee in thrall.

I slid away without notice, waved a quick hello to Miller, and walked over to say hi to Coop and Kristin.

"Hey, how are you and Charlie doing?" Coop asked.

"He hasn't said?"

"I've been afraid to ask."

"Pretty good, all things considered."

"Coop mentioned you were job shadowing," Kristin said. She's very attractive, with shoulder-length auburn hair and green eyes. She seems to make Coop happy, and she's not bothered by our friendship, so I've given her the Leah Nash seal of approval.

"Yeah, you know, funny you should mention that, Kristin. I've been wondering if I could tag along with you for a while, too. Not for two weeks like I'm doing with Ross. Maybe just a day or two, to get a feel for life in the district attorney's office."

"Sure," she said. "I'll have to check with Cliff, but I doubt he'll mind. Call me Monday to remind me?"

Cliff Timmins, the district attorney, is Kristin's boss.

"I will, thanks."

I looked at my watch. We had about ten minutes before my mom and Paul were due to arrive.

"I wonder where Jennifer and John are. If they don't get here soon, they might run into Mom and Paul coming in and that will kind of mess up the surprise."

Jennifer Pilarski and I have been friends since kindergarten. She works in the sheriff's office now. Jennifer is warm and easygoing with deep-set brown eyes in a round face, and a small plump mouth that always seems on the verge of a smile.

"Jennifer's here," Ross said, coming behind me. "I saw her going to the ladies' when I walked in. She said John can't come, though, he had some work thing come up."

"Oh, that's too bad. Hey, Ross, you clean up pretty good," I said, noting his navy sport coat and light blue shirt. "I don't think that I've ever seen you in a sport coat before. Are you trying to impress someone? You're not meeting Rita after the party, are you?"

"I told ya, Rita's just a friend. Don't start that again," he said. A slight blush had crept up his cheeks, and I suddenly felt bad about the teasing.

"Okay, okay. Sorry. You do look nice, though. I'm going to the restroom to hustle Jennifer along. Mom and Paul should be here in a few minutes."

13

"Jen, what's wrong?"

I had expected to find Jennifer adjusting a strap or combing her hair. Instead, she was leaning toward the mirror, trying to repair mascara that kept smudging because tears were running down her face.

She turned with a start and began dabbing at her eyes to hide the evidence.

"Leah, hi. My eye won't stop watering. I must have an eyelash or something."

She tried to smile, but an involuntary snuffle came out instead. I stepped toward her and put both hands on her shoulders.

"Jen, what's going on?"

"I'm sorry. I'm being ridiculous, I know. It's just that John called this afternoon. He was supposed to get back from Menominee in time for the party. He's been there most of the week. But the CEO of the company he's consulting with wanted him to go to dinner. John said he couldn't say no, so he isn't coming."

John Pilarksi works for a firm that specializes in operations analysis. I'm not exactly sure what he does, though he's explained it several times. It's something to do with data mining and analytics and supply chains.

"Is that why you're crying?"

I was surprised that what seemed like a minor disappointment would affect her so deeply. Jennifer is not an easy cryer.

She nodded. "I know, it's stupid. It's just that I've been looking forward to a night out with John so much. He's been gone so much for work lately. I'm just feeling a little sorry for myself, I guess. Forget it, I'm fine."

She turned back to the mirror and removed the smudgy mascara from under her eyes, then patted her face with a damp towel.

"You know, maybe tomorrow I could pick your boys up for a play date with Dominic, give you and John some time together."

"Thanks, I know they'd love it. But John's parents are coming for dinner tomorrow. Don't look so worried. I'm fine. Come on, we'd better get going or your mom and Paul will be there before we are."

I could tell something still wasn't right, and I felt like a bad friend for not probing more deeply, but she was right. We had to get to the party.

"Now that was a wonderful meal," Paul said as he used a piece of bread to sop up the last bit of sauce on his plate.

"I agree," my mother said. "Leah, thank you for planning this. What a nice way to enter a new decade, here at my favorite restaurant, with some of my favorite friends."

"To you, Carol!" Paul said, lifting his glass in salute and beaming at her. We all followed suit. Lifting our glasses, that is; none of the rest of us discernibly beamed. However, Paul usually does when he's around my mother. He's not super handsome, but looking at her the way he does goes a long way to making him seem so in my eyes.

"Well, it looks like you're all enjoying yourselves. How was the food?"

The exuberant voice preceded the entrance of a short, curvy woman in a white chef's outfit. She wore red-framed glasses and her long, glossy brown hair was pulled back in a single braid that hung down her back. As she smiled, she revealed a dimple in the left cheek of her heart-shaped face.

"Liz! Everything was just perfect. When did you add the clam risotto to the menu? And what did you do to make it taste so wonderful?"

"Last week, Carol," Liz answered. "But the taste secret is classified. I'm glad you enjoyed it."

"Liz, will you cater our wedding?" Paul asked.

"You're getting married? When?"

"Whenever Carol finally says yes. I thought throwing you in to cater the reception might be enough to get me across the finish line. What do you say?" he asked, turning to my mother.

Paul asking her to marry him, and my mother saying no, is a running joke between them—though Paul isn't joking. He would in a heartbeat. Mom loves him, too, but she likes her life the way it is. I co-sign that sentiment.

"It's tempting, but only if Liz comes on board as our personal, permanent chef."

"I tried being a personal chef once. The pay was great, but I need more than a two-person audience for my food," Liz said with a laugh. "What about the rest of you? Did your meal meet your expectations?"

"Leah told me to set the bar high. I did, and you managed to exceed it," Gabe said. "The best Italian food I've had outside of New York. I'm Gabe Hoffman, by the way."

"Good to meet you, Gabe. I'm Liz Moretti. Leah, thanks for the advance PR."

"No problem. I knew you'd live up to it. My scallops were delicious, by the way."

"How about you, handsome?"

I thought she was talking to Miller, who reminds me of Robert Redford in his *Sneakers* era, absolutely fits the word handsome. Instead, as I glanced down the table, I saw that she was talking to Ross, who had a startled expression on his face.

"Don't tell me, let me guess, you're the spaghetti Bolognese, aren't you? How was it?"

"Good. How did ya know that was me?"

"You look like a man who enjoys a meal with substance. I'll bet Pabst is your favorite beer, isn't it?"

Ross looked very uncomfortable.

"Don't worry, hon, I'm not psychic. You've got a touch of sauce on your shirt. And it was just a good guess on the beer. Next time you come, I'll treat you to a Campari. You'll never look back," she said. Ross looked embarrassed and had begun dabbing at his shirt with a corner of his napkin dipped in his water glass.

Liz spared him and moved on to Miller. Or tried to.

"Miller, when are you—"

Courtnee interrupted before she finished.

"Liz, I'm Courtnee. Um, well, I don't want to hurt your feelings or anything but ..."

Uh-oh. I exchanged a quick glance with Miguel intended to convey that he should kick her under the table and/or put his hand over her mouth because what was coming couldn't be good.

"My Chicken Alfredo was fine. No, really, it was. Only the mushrooms were kind of big. And sort of brownish? When my mom makes it, she uses Campbell's mushroom soup. Their mushrooms are more grayish, like real mushrooms, and they're cut into these little squares? And the sauce isn't so thick. Maybe you'd like to try that? I think people would like it a lot."

Liz stared at her, nonplussed for a second, but recovered quickly.

"Thank you, Courtnee. I'll think about that. For a long time."

"You're welcome," she said with polite obliviousness. "My mom's Chicken Alfredo is always the first to go at the American Legion potluck dinners."

"High praise indeed," Miller said, stepping into the awkward silence that followed her last comment. He has the least experience with her, but the best manners.

"Everything about your restaurant is lovely, Liz," he said. "But I've never asked. Why the name Arianna's?"

"Arianna is the owner's wife. He named it after her. I'm the executive chef, but I'd love to own this place someday."

"With your skill in the kitchen, I won't be at all surprised when you do, Liz," Father Lindstrom said.

When she smiled, she reminded me of Jennifer. She had the same kind of engaging grin that makes people feel happy for no particular reason. That prompted a look down the table at Jennifer, who had been uncharacteristically quiet. She was staring down into her wine glass without even seeming to realize a party was going on around her.

Something more than John missing a party was going on with her. I made a mental note to follow up as soon as I could.

14

On Monday morning I arrived at the sheriff's office early, hoping to get a chance to talk a little more with Jennifer before I hit the road with Ross. I'd called on Sunday to see if she was okay after her mini meltdown in the ladies' room, but she didn't pick up and she didn't return my call.

She was sitting at her desk in the open area outside of Coop's office. I noticed right away that her eyes were puffy behind her glasses. She usually wears contacts. When I pulled a chair up beside her desk, I could see the whites were crisscrossed with the tiny red veins that come from a serious crying jag.

Nevertheless, she pasted a bright smile on her face as I plopped down next to her.

"Leah, hi! Sorry I didn't get back to you. The kids were wild yesterday, and John's parents stayed and stayed. The boys forgot to tell me that they had to bring eggshells to school for some project. Then while I'm in the kitchen, cracking open and cleaning out a dozen eggs, the boys are playing hospital with the poor dog. They put Band-Aids all over him! John was so mad, and ..."

I expected that kind of frenetic chatter from Courtnee, but not from Jennifer.

"Hey, I can tell you've been crying. What's going on? Did you and John have a fight?"

"No." As she shook her head, her lip trembled slightly.

"Jen, you didn't tell me everything on Saturday night. And now you can barely hold it together. Come on, what's up?"

"John and I aren't fighting, Leah. How could we? We barely see each other and when we do, it's like we're polite strangers. He's not even engaging with the kids like he used to do. The other day, Ethan asked me why his dad was mad at them."

"Have you talked to John about it?"

"That's just it, we don't talk. We just exchange information. I hate it!" Her tone was both bitter and frustrated.

"Jen, I—"

My thought was cut off as Coop's office door burst open. A woman stood in the doorway, her back to us as she raised her voice.

"He's dead, and she killed him! I've given you the proof, and you're telling me you won't do anything with it? Unbelievable!"

"Ma'am, that's not what I said." Coop's voice was controlled, but his frustration was evident.

I cocked an eyebrow at Jen, and she shook her head to indicate she didn't know what was going on either.

I had recognized the voice. It was Rhonda Crawford.

Bryan Crawford's sister was shedding no tears today about her brother. Instead, she was shouting at Coop, and beginning to draw a crowd. Out of the corner of my eye I saw Ross and Drew Lawlor, the young deputy who'd been at the Crawfords', emerge from the breakroom door and come toward the front. Coop, who had stepped out of his office and joined Rhonda, gave them a subtle shake of his head. Ross signaled to Lawlor and they fell back.

She stood only a few feet from Jen's desk, but in her fury, Rhonda didn't seem to notice us.

"What does it take to get you to do your job? His wife killed my brother.

I did your work for you. I gave you the evidence! You have Bryan's laptop. What are you going to do about it? Nothing?"

She had drawn herself up to her full height and was jabbing a finger in the air in Coop's direction as she listed her demands. "You need to reopen this case. Get Rachelle down here for questioning. Find out where she truly was the night Bryan died. Because I can guarantee you that she wasn't at any retreat. She was right in Omico, murdering my brother in cold blood!"

"Ms. Crawford," Coop said, when she took a breath that allowed him to speak. "Please, come back into my office and let's finish this conversation."

His quiet but firm voice seemed to persuade her to lower her own by a decibel or two, but she didn't change her stance.

"I think you've said it all, Sheriff. You're not going to do anything. I am absolutely sure that my sister-in-law Rachelle killed my brother. She's got the motive, for God's sake. She's going to inherit over a million dollars! I don't give a damn what the medical examiner's report said. It was wrong. Rachelle should be under arrest right now. I've got a copy of the video. I'm taking it to *GO News*. They'll do something about it."

"Ms. Crawford, I said that we'll look into it, and I meant it. All I tried to point out was that it's a difficult situation. The medical examiner ruled on cause of death, and your brother's body was cremated. I'll talk to the district attorney today about the case. I will keep you informed. Trust me, going to *GO News* is not going to help anybody."

"That's where you're wrong. It's going to help me get justice for Bryan. Because *GO News* will make sure you don't get away with not doing your job. And I'll be speaking to the district attorney about you, too. I've always been a strong supporter of Cliff Timmins. I'm sure he'll remember that."

With that she swept away down the hall and out the front door.

———

Coop motioned for both Ross and me to come into his office.

"What the hell was that? Is she crazy, or what?" Ross asked as he and I took the visitor chairs on one side of Coop's well-ordered desk, while he sat across from us, shaking his head. I saw that there was an additional laptop on his desk—the one Rhonda Crawford had brought to him, no doubt.

"Actually, she's not. She's convinced her brother was murdered, and after what she showed me and what she told me, she could be right."

"What did she bring in?" Ross asked.

"One piece is solid evidence—the other, well, it's suggestive, I guess you could say, but it's part of the picture."

"No. No way," Ross said emphatically. "The guy had diabetes. He had a diabetic reaction and he died. I was at that death scene. The M.E. was there, too. There was nothing suspicious. If something was hinky, I woulda seen."

"I agree, Charlie. If there was something at the scene, I'm sure you would have found it. The reason you didn't is that it wasn't there by the time you arrived."

"You mean like the sister found it and took it?" Ross asked.

"Not exactly. Take a look at this," Coop said.

He turned the second laptop around to face us and hit play. The screen showed the sauna in the Crawfords' backyard, flanked by the woods. The line of sight was at an angle to the front door of the sauna. It looked like the video had been shot by a trail cam mounted on a tree. Two deer emerged from the trees and ran across the yard. The date/time stamp was 10:15 p.m. on the Friday night Bryan Crawford had died.

As we watched, there was a slight flicker before the next scene, which featured a raccoon couple heading toward the house. The raccoons were followed by a black bear that crossed in front of the sauna. That time stamp was 4:45 a.m. Coop then fast-forwarded through additional footage on Saturday and Sunday that showed more deer, a repeat of the raccoons, and a skunk. He stopped it at a coyote caught on camera at 9 p.m. on Sunday of the weekend Bryan died.

"Did you notice anything?" Coop asked.

"Yeah. They got a damn nature preserve in their backyard. But what's that got to do with Bryan Crawford dyin'?"

"Leah? How about you?" Coop asked, without answering Ross.

I had absolutely noticed the bear. Bears have been the stuff of nightmares for me since I was 8 and saw a bear-centered episode of *When Animals Attack* the babysitter let me watch. However, I knew that wasn't what Coop meant. I shook my head. "No. What are we supposed to be looking for?"

"Let me run it one more time."

He hit play again as Ross and I stared at the screen. This time when he stopped the video, I realized what it was that he had wanted us to see.

"It's the door," I said. "The sauna door."

I looked at Ross. He nodded in agreement.

15

"That's why Rhonda Crawford brought Bryan's laptop in," Coop said. "The footage is from a trail cam Bryan set up the week before he died, according to Rhonda. You can see there's a security bar and a padlock on the sauna door at 10:15 p.m. on Friday night. It's there all through the video on Saturday night, too. But then when the coyote shows up at 9 o'clock Sunday night, the security bar on the door is off."

"Which means somebody locked Bryan Crawford in, so he wouldn't have access to his insulin. If he went long enough without it, there was a good chance he'd die and it would look like a natural death from diabetes complications," I said.

"Exactly. That way, no suspicion, no investigation, and the killer walks away free."

"But what if he didn't die? You couldn't be positive that would happen. What if he was still alive when the killer came back to unlock the door?"

"I don't think it mattered to whoever killed him. Even if Bryan wasn't dead when the killer unlocked the door, he'd most likely be unconscious, or at least out of it. He wouldn't even realize anyone had been there. And he might still have died before the family got home to help him. The killer could just walk away and wait. If it didn't work, he could try something else later. Bryan's diabetes and his sauna habit made it a low-risk plan. The odds were good that his death would be attributed to his diabetes. And that's what we all thought, including the medical examiner. We would've kept on thinking it, if it weren't for the video."

Ross had been mostly quiet, but he'd started shaking his head in self-disgust as Coop finished.

"I knew there was somethin' off, but I didn't follow up. It wasn't anything big, but ya know I don't like loose ends. The key to the padlock was missing. I asked the wife about it. She seemed real surprised it wasn't there. But I got off track when the family started snipin' at each other. And I didn't get back to it. Then Connie Crowley did the autopsy and said it was that diabetic whatsit thing—DKA. I shoulda stayed with my gut on the key. Two things ya gotta pay attention to at a murder scene—what's there that shouldn't be, and what isn't that should."

"Don't beat yourself up, Charlie. Why would you think a missing key mattered, when everything, including the autopsy, pointed to a natural death? Even now that it looks like murder, I'm not sure that the key means anything," Coop said.

"Here's another thing. Everything else that went past the sauna got captured. How did the killer avoid the camera?" I asked.

"You can program a motion sensor camera to go on and off at a specific time. There's nothing recorded before 9 p.m. or after 6 a.m., so it must have been set to go on at nine at night, and off at six in the morning. As long as the killer avoided that time frame, he'd be safe," Coop said.

"Okay, but even if he did his dirty work before the camera was programmed to go on, or after it went off, the video still shows the door locked when it should be unlocked. Why didn't the killer disable it, or even take it down altogether? Because he didn't, we've got evidence now that Bryan's death was engineered, not natural. It seems pretty sloppy."

"I'd say more unlucky than sloppy," Coop said. "According to Rhonda, Bryan just set the camera up recently. He was trying to get footage of a black bear he thought was coming into his yard from the woods. He mentioned it to Rhonda but told her not to tell Rachelle. He didn't want her freaking out about the bear when he wasn't even sure he was right about it. Which, I guess he was. But only Bryan and Rhonda knew about the camera."

"Why didn't Rhonda say anything about it before now?"

"She said she forgot all about it with everything else. She didn't connect it with Bryan's death because why would she? Last night, she checked Bryan's laptop for work-related files before she wiped the hard drive clean. She found a folder marked trail cam. She looked at it, thinking it might have some video of Bryan on it. She was waiting for me in the parking lot when I got in at seven this morning to show me what she found instead."

"Ya know, we keep sayin' 'he.' " But this seems more like a woman's game than a man's to me. It doesn't take any strength, there's no blood, you don't even have to be there when he dies. It's like a poisoning without the poison. And I can tell you who my number one candidate is," Ross said.

"The wife, right? You're always *cherchez la femme*, Ross, but I don't disagree if you throw in 'follow the money.' When you talked to the family, Rhonda said Rachelle stands to inherit a million or more. That's a pretty good motive. She'd know all about Bryan's sauna routine, about his diabetes, and what lack of insulin would do to him. And that he wouldn't have his phone with him to call for help," I said.

I turned to Coop. "You told us that Rhonda had something solid—the video—and something else that was 'suggestive.' What is it? Tell us so we have the whole picture before we go out to talk to Rachelle—or whoever Ross thinks we should see first," I amended quickly, so it wouldn't appear like I was trying to run the show.

"Leah, no," Coop said.

"No? What do you mean?"

I knew, but I wasn't going to make it easy for him.

"He means there's no 'us' in investigation, Nash. No more job shadowing. This is the real deal, an open murder case. Time for you to step out."

"But you both agreed to two weeks. It's only been one. I just want to ride with Ross for another five days. I don't expect to stick with it for the whole thing. I'll go quietly when my two weeks are up. Although, if you want me to, I'm available to stay longer and help."

I paused to insert a winning smile. "Come on. It's what we all agreed to."

"I'm sorry you didn't get your full two weeks, but you can't be part of this, Leah. I can't have a civilian involved in an investigation like this."

"Tough luck, Nash," Ross said. But I didn't detect much sympathy in his words.

Jen wasn't at her desk when I left Coop's office, but Drew Lawlor was standing in the hall, so close to Coop's door that I bumped into him and caused him to drop his phone.

"Oh, sorry!" I said as I bent down and scooped it up to return to him.

"No, my fault. I was checking a text, not paying attention. I'm Drew Lawlor, by the way. Detective Ross didn't introduce us, but I know who you are. I saw you with him at the Crawford place. Wow. Rhonda Crawford, she's something else, isn't she? Sounds like she's got the DA where she wants him, though, doesn't it?"

He was pleasant and quite friendly. Ironically, that's what raised my suspicions. I know a lot of cops who are pleasant enough and whose company I enjoy—like Coop and Ross. But I don't know any good cops, and I mean that both in terms of competence and ethics, who casually chat about police business with someone they don't know. Especially if that someone is connected to a newspaper. I wondered how long Lawlor had been hovering in the hallway outside Coop's door. With Jennifer not at her desk, he could have done so with ease, and picked up much of what Coop, Ross, and I had said.

"Yes, I remember you, Drew. Again, sorry for just about knocking you over, but I was in a hurry. Still am, so I've got to run. Good meeting you," I said as I moved past him and headed for the door.

Drew Lawlor had reversed the natural order of things—he was a cop pumping a journalist for information instead of the other way around. That seemed very odd to me.

After being unceremoniously dumped from shadowing Ross, I drove home. I was disappointed, but it wasn't unexpected. At least I'd gotten a week out of the deal. If I was honest, it was probably for the best. I needed to start committing to the idea I had for the series by putting something down on paper instead of just thinking about it. Clinton hadn't called to check in yet, but it was inevitable. As though just thinking had conjured him up, my phone rang.

"Yes, Clinton, I have a general idea worked out. It's not ready for prime time, but I'll give you the gist. The lead character is female. I think she's a detective in a county sheriff's office in the UP—the Upper Peninsula—in Michigan. But I might make her a disgraced detective who's a private eye now, I'm still working on that."

"Why the UP?"

"It's kind of like Wisconsin, so I won't have to do a ton of research. I visited my Aunt Nancy there every summer and every Christmas vacation for years when I was growing up. The UP has a great landscape, a shoreline on three of the Great Lakes, waterfalls, mountains, bears even. Plus a few decent-sized towns and plenty of small ones. It's home to strong women, brave men, and plenty of quirky characters. There's a lot of room for action."

"What's her name?"

"Not sure yet. I'm thinking a unisex nickname, like Jo for Josephine or Eddie for Edith, or maybe Rory for Aurora. Last name short, sharp, maybe Clark, West, Burke, something like that."

"I like Rory West."

"Okay, I'll take it under advisement."

"What's the plot for the first book?"

"I'm not quite there yet, I'm still turning some things over in my mind. Hey, I thought you'd be happy."

"I am. Keep going. Can you have a plot and characters for the first book fleshed out in a couple of weeks?"

"Yes. Absolutely."

At the time, I thought I could.

16

"Jen, this is nice. I can't remember the last time you and I met for drinks on a Saturday night. I don't suppose you invited me so you can feed me secret information on how the Bryan Crawford investigation is going?"

Jennifer and I were sitting in a booth at McClain's, my favorite bar in Wisconsin. Maybe in the world. I love the 1940s noir feel with its creaky wooden floors, dark booths, and a bartender who considers gin and tonic a fancy drink.

"Leah—"

"You don't have to say it. I know. You can't talk about open investigations. And far be it from me to call in my marker for taking the blame when your mother found that six-pack of Miller High Life in your room."

"You've called in that marker about 600 times already."

"Well, but who's counting, right? We can make it six hundred and one. It can be my birthday present."

"Your birthday isn't for months."

"Avoid the rush. Give me my present now. Come on, I was so close to being in at the start of an investigation. In fact, I was in the room where it happened, so to speak. It's killing me not to know what's going on, who they're talking to, what other information Rhonda gave Coop besides the video. It's not for the paper. I just want to know for myself."

"Not happening," she said before taking a long drink of her second beer. I briefly, but not seriously, considered plying her with drinks to see if she'd loosen up. I opted instead for another try with emotional blackmail.

"Jennifer, you do recall that I got grounded for a month when your mother told mine that I had gotten hold of the beer and stashed it in your room. And if I had ratted you out, you would've been the one grounded. Instead, you got to keep your date to the Homecoming Dance with John.

"And you guys fell in love, and you went together all through high school, and you got married, and now you have beautiful twin boys. When you think about it, I sacrificed my freedom to protect your future and guarantee you a lifetime of happiness. With that in mind, are you sure you won't even answer one little question about the investigation—or two?"

I tried my winning smile. It had an even worse result with Jennifer than it had when I'd given it to Coop earlier in the week. He had just ignored it, but it made Jennifer cry.

"Jen! What is it?" I reached across the table and put my hand on hers.

"Nothing. Everything. The same thing," she said with a shaky sigh as she struggled not to break into full-on sobs in the middle of the bar.

I remembered the conversation at her desk on Monday that had been interrupted by Rhonda Crawford's outburst.

"Did something else happen with John? Is that why you invited me for drinks? Jen, I'm so sorry I didn't get back with you earlier. I meant to. I got caught up in my own stuff—you know, coming up with a plot, working on an outline for the book. But still, that's no excuse. I apologize for my stupid babbling just now. Please, tell me, what's going on?"

"Don't apologize, Leah. I know you've got a lot on your mind with your book and everything, but I just don't have anyone else to talk to. My mother would just tell me to ignore it, and my dad would probably challenge John to a duel." She gave a small laugh that ended in a sob. "I don't even know how to start."

"Just start wherever you want, I'll keep up."

"Like I said before, we're not fighting. We're just not connecting—at all. At first, I thought it was his new job—he got a promotion at work—I told you that, right?"

"Yes. You said you're not talking anymore, that he doesn't seem very engaged with you or the kids. Have you said anything to John about how you feel?"

"I've tried, but it doesn't go anywhere. He says he has to put in the work because he wants his boss to know he made the right decision promoting him. And then he turns it around to me and says that it seems like all my attention is on finishing my bachelor's degree and there's not much left over for anything else. And then I get mad because that's not true."

I could feel myself getting irate on Jen's behalf. She'd put aside her own college studies to go to work and help John get through school. But when he finished, instead of her going back as they'd planned, he'd said she should work a couple more years so they could buy a house. She did. But then after they had enough for a down payment on a nice place, she unexpectedly got pregnant. And then she had twins. There was no thought of taking classes again until the boys hit kindergarten, which they just had. And now, it sounded like instead of supporting her, John was trying to make her feel guilty for finally pursuing her own dreams.

"I know it's not true, Jen. You're a great mom, you do a great job for Coop, and you've always been super supportive of John's dreams. Deep down he knows that, but it's inconvenient for him to be honest with himself. He knows he should be in your corner the same way you've always been in his, and he feels guilty about it. So, he's trying to make it about you."

"John's not like that," she said.

"Well, it kind of sounds like he is, only maybe it's been going on long enough that you don't recognize it. Look, I've always liked John, but we can all get a little tunnel vision when it comes to our own wants and needs. I'm not saying he's a bad guy. I'm sure that he loves you and the twins. But he needs a wake-up call. He's taking you for granted. You need to lay it out for him."

Is there anyone more confident in giving marital guidance than a single, divorced friend? Not if that friend is me. But what Jen said next made me realize how surface and facile my advice had been.

"No. It's not just that we aren't communicating, or we're too busy and not taking time for each other. John doesn't *want* to spend time with me. This is so hard to say. It's the first time I've said it out loud. I'm afraid he doesn't love me anymore. I think John is having an affair."

The pain in her voice cut through to a still tender place in my own heart. My ex-husband and I had divorced years earlier for the same reason. The wound, though healed, is still there. Sometimes it throbs a little in sympathy and makes me wince. This was one of those moments.

"Are you sure? Why do you think that?"

"Yes. I'm sure. About a month ago I ran into Marty Angstrom at the grocery store. He asked me how I liked the B&B weekend John had won with the Sports Boosters raffle ticket Marty sold him. When I said I didn't know he'd won, Marty got kind of flustered. He said, 'Oh-oh, it must be a surprise, there. Don't let on I spoiled it for you, Jennifer.'"

Jen said the last part in a very credible imitation of Marty's northern Wisconsin accent.

"But that should make you feel good, not bad. John knows you're unhappy, and he wants to take you away for a romantic weekend as a surprise."

"That's what I thought—what I hoped anyway. I was so excited, and I waited for John to mention it. Only three weeks went by and he never did. Finally, I asked him about it outright."

"And?"

"And he told me that he forgot about winning it. He said he gave it to his secretary for her birthday, because he's too busy to take a weekend trip right now. He thought it would be a nice treat for Mindy and her husband, because they don't have much money."

"And you didn't believe John's story?"

"I tried to. But last night I saw Mindy when I ran into Bonucci's to pick up a pizza. I asked her what she thought of the Beale House Inn—that's the B&B the ticket was for. She looked at me funny, like why was I asking her a random question like that. I kind of stammered and said, 'Oh, I thought John said that you and your husband had been there recently. Must have been someone else.' And she said it must have been, because she and Derek hadn't been anywhere since the baby was born in January."

Oh, boy. That didn't sound great.

"Okay, well, John lied to you, and that's not good. But could there be another reason besides him having an affair?"

"I've been racking my brain trying to think of one and I can't. Can you?"

I shook my head. "Not right offhand, no. I take it you haven't said anything to John yet?"

"He's not coming home until Thursday, and I don't want to talk to him about it over the phone. Besides, I don't know what to say. What if he lies again? Or worse, what if he doesn't, and he says yes and he wants a divorce? Or what if there's some weird explanation for everything, and he realizes that I don't trust him?"

"But would any of those scenarios be worse than the limbo you're living in now?"

"Yes, they would! If John says he doesn't love me anymore, if he wants to leave me, I don't know what I'll do, Leah. I just don't."

"Jen, I get how it feels when you're afraid someone you love doesn't love you back. But you can't go on like this much longer."

"I know that. But there's one last thing I'd like to try before I confront John."

"What?"

"I want *you* to find out for me if John is having an affair. I don't know how to do it, but you could. Please? I just want to know for sure what I'm facing before I face him."

"Jen, I'm not a P.I. I'm all in with you, however things turn out, but I don't want to get caught in the middle here. You should hire a professional."

"I can't. I don't have the money. Even if I did, I don't know where to find one, or who I could trust. I trust you, Leah. I don't want to know, but I have to know. I can't eat, I can't sleep, I can't do anything until I know for sure. Please, you have to help me."

In the end I agreed. But I didn't feel good about it.

17

"John is having an affair? No!" Miguel's voice carried a mixture of emotions: interest in the latest gossip, sympathy for Jennifer, and censure for John.

"Shhh!" I said. "Keep your voice down. I don't want everyone in here to know what we're talking about."

"There's no one else here."

It was true. Miguel and I were at the EAT restaurant—though not to eat. Only those bargain hunters with the sturdiest stomachs choose the EAT for a meal, especially on a late Sunday afternoon. That's why I had picked it when he wanted to meet for coffee. It's reliably good there, and I knew we wouldn't run into a million people he had to say hello to.

"Okay, okay, you're right. I just don't want this to get spread around."

"By me? *Chica*, why do you say that?"

"Because nobody likes being in the know—and sharing what they know—more than you."

"That is true," he conceded with a self-aware smile. "But something so sad for Jennifer? No, that is not the kind of tea I would ever spill. But are you going to find out for her?"

"I said I'd try. I'm not allowed to know anything about the Bryan Crawford murder, according to Coop and Ross, except what I read in the *Times*— or *GO News*. I guess I might as well try being a private eye for a friend."

"Can I help?"

"Maybe. I'm going to look into the B&B weekend John won. It might involve a road trip. Want to come?"

"Of course I do! Do you want me to do some checking at Making Waves? I'm getting a haircut tomorrow. You know it's Tea Central there."

"Well, that might help. But just be sure you're sipping the tea, not spilling it."

"I will be discretion itself."

"Hey, on another romance-related subject, you haven't heard anything about Ross having a girlfriend, have you? That would be something to check out delicately."

"Charlie is seeing someone?"

I'm the only one who consistently calls Ross by his last name, as he does me. It started when we first met and didn't exactly hit it off. Now, it's our thing, I guess. The only time we use first names is when a situation is very serious—or scary.

"I don't know for sure. But Allie asked me last week. And when I was job shadowing with him, this EMT named Rita seemed to be coming on pretty strong. I asked him about it, but he said no. I can't help being just a little curious."

"But why would he say he wasn't, if he is?"

I shrugged. "Maybe he doesn't know if it's going to work out. Maybe he's falling crazy in love and he doesn't want us to watch that disturbing spectacle. Maybe he doesn't want to be teased—as if I would."

The look Miguel gave me said quite clearly that yes, that is something I would do.

"All right, I might tease him a little. But I wouldn't if it was something that meant a lot to him. I'm not heartless, you know. I think it would be very nice if Ross had someone in his life. It might even make him less crabby. It's not a big thing."

So much for my fortune telling skills. Within a few weeks, it turned out to be a very big thing indeed.

When I pulled into the parking lot behind the *Times* building, I was surprised to see Allie standing near the back door. And she wasn't alone.

"Allie? What are you doing here on a Sunday night?"

As I got closer, I recognized who she was with. Adam Harrison, Bryan Crawford's stepson.

"Leah, could we talk to you for a few minutes? This is my friend, Adam," she added.

"Yeah, of course. Let's get in out of the rain. Hi, Adam. We haven't actually met, but I was with Allie's dad when he talked to your family the day your stepfather was found."

"Yeah, I know," he said.

"Okay, well, come on upstairs and you guys can tell me what's going on."

Once we got to my place, I offered the two of them seats at the kitchen island.

"Do you want anything to drink? Water? Soda? That's about all I run to at the moment," I said after checking what I had in the refrigerator.

"Not for me," Allie said, squirming a little on her stool, as though now that she had gained access, she wasn't sure what to do with it. She began twisting one of her curls, a habit she has when nervous.

"Adam?"

"What?"

I lifted the can of Coke I held in my hand. "Did you want a soda or water?"

"No. Thanks," he added, as though he realized he'd been a little abrupt.

I considered a Jameson but decided I should model better behavior for the younger generation and settled on the Coke I'd offered Adam. They both watched me as I popped open the can, but neither spoke. They remained silent as I sat down next to Allie and across from Adam.

"I'll bet you're wondering why I called this meeting," I said.

"Oh, right," Allie said with a nervous laugh. "I guess we should get to the point."

"I think that would be good."

"Well, you know I'm doing props for *The Music Man* at the community theater, right?"

I nodded.

"Okay, so, Adam is assistant directing. That's how we know each other."

She stopped and glanced at Adam. He was looking down at his hands.

"And?" I prompted, still in the dark.

"And, well, we got talking and I was telling Adam about you and how you're like kind of a famous journalist. And he was telling me some things, you know, about his stepdad and all. And I could see he was pretty worried and upset. And I thought, well, no, I guess actually I said that I knew that, um, that..."

"Allie, please, the suspense is killing me. What is it you're trying to say?"

But it was Adam who answered.

"The police think my mother killed Bryan. They're going to arrest her. But she didn't do it. She couldn't kill anyone. Not even Bryan." His eyes had darkened with emotion and his voice shook a little.

"Adam, wait a minute. Why do you think the police are going to arrest her? They don't usually announce it in advance."

"They've been to the house three times this week. Allie's dad and another detective. At first, they acted nice, like they just wanted to clear up some things. But they keep asking Mom the same questions about Bryan's insulin, and about the key to the sauna door, and stuff about her prenuptial agreement with Bryan, over and over again. It's like they're trying to trick her into saying the wrong thing."

"I know the sauna key is missing. What are they asking her about it?"

"It's not missing anymore. I found it when I was cleaning up in front of the sauna. I moved the mat to sweep, and it was right there, where Mom told Detective Ross it was supposed to be. It was kind of off to the side, like maybe somebody tripped on the mat and it got shifted or something, but it was there."

"When did you find it?"

"Last week. Tuesday. Allie's dad must have missed it when he looked."

"Did your mom tell the police the key had been found?"

"Yeah, of course she did, right away. I think they just keep asking to mix her up, trying to get her to say something wrong. I can tell by the way they ask the questions that they think it's her. I told Mom, but it's like she's in denial or something."

"What did she say?"

"Not to worry, that she didn't do anything, she has a good alibi, so it'll be all right. But today they asked her to come into the sheriff's office. She was there for hours!"

Okay, now that sounded bad.

"Does she have an attorney?"

"She didn't, but when they said they wanted her to come to the office today she called a lawyer and he met her there."

"That's good. A lawyer will make sure that your mom's rights are protected. They let her go home, so that's a good thing, too."

"For now. But I'm scared for her. It's like they're not even looking at anybody else."

"I'm not trying to minimize how awful this must be for you, Adam. But it's typical for the first focus in a murder investigation to be the spouse. It's not the greatest commentary on marriage, but it's true. I'm sure your mother isn't the only person the police are talking to. They'll be looking at anyone your stepfather had ties to—his daughter, his sister, his business associates, your neighbors, friends. They must have talked to you, too, right?"

He nodded. "Yeah, the first time they came to the house on Monday. But I couldn't tell them anything because I spent the weekend in Chicago with my friend Cam and his family. Bryan was supposed to be going to his hunting cabin and Mom didn't want me to spend the weekend alone. She still thinks I'm 12. Plus, Bryan and I don't—didn't—get along that well."

"Why's that?"

"Because he was a dick."

"And you say that because . . ."

"Because he was. He treated my mom like she was his servant. He screwed around on her, too. I caught him once by accident. I had a half-day at school. Mom was in Milwaukee, shopping with a friend. Bryan was at work—I thought. We have this creek that runs through our woods. I was walking down to sit in the gazebo there and do some writing. When I passed the sauna, I heard something. I stopped for a minute to listen. It was Bryan and some woman. It was gross. I got out of there fast."

"When was that?"

"A couple of years ago. But I'll bet it wasn't the only time either."

"Do you know who the woman in the sauna was? Did you say anything to your mother about her?"

"No. It was too weird, and she was still all into Bryan and this 'great' life he was giving us. I figured it was their thing, not mine. But it just proved I was right about Bryan from the start. I didn't like him, and he didn't like me. He thought I was a loser because I don't play sports, and I don't like freezing my ass off ice-fishing. He was an asshat. And I'm not sorry he's dead." He crossed his arms on his chest by way of emphasis.

"Did you tell the police about Bryan having a girlfriend?"

"They didn't ask me. And I didn't volunteer it. I'm not stupid, you know. I realize that could make it seem like my mother had a motive to kill Bryan."

"Adam, the killer had to be someone who knew Bryan pretty well. Do you have any ideas about who that could be?"

"I told you. He was a dick. It could've been anybody. Maybe a business guy he cheated, or a friend whose wife he was having a thing with. Maybe it was even his sister."

"Rhonda? She's the one who pushed the police to investigate. Why would she do that if she was the killer?"

"Yeah, but who are the police investigating? My mother. And even though Rhonda slobbered all over Bryan, he wasn't very nice to her. He made fun of her behind her back. Sometimes to her face. She just took it, too. Only maybe she didn't. Maybe she got fed up and she killed him. Now she wants to get rid of my mother, too, so she's talking crap about her. She hates her."

Adam's case for Rhonda as the killer wasn't very persuasive, but it was interesting. The dynamics in that family were decidedly odd.

"From the little I've seen of Rhonda and Rachelle together, it's pretty obvious they dislike each other. Why is that?"

"Rhonda started it. She didn't even give my mother a chance. She was always throwing shade at her, making little comments, you know. Stephanie told me that Rhonda hated *her* mother, too. She thinks that Rhonda was the one who told Bryan about her mother having an affair, so that Bryan would divorce her. Then Rhonda could have him to herself again. But then he turned around and married my mother, so she was on the outside again."

"How did Stephanie get along with her dad?"

"All right, I guess. Why? You don't think Stephanie could kill her own dad, do you? That's crazy."

"You'd be amazed what unhappy offspring can do."

"She's not unhappy. Why would she be? Bryan bought her everything she wanted. She's got a cool car, she went to Europe last summer, she has her own apartment. She's hot, she's smart. She's going to New York to be an actor. It's not Stephanie."

I was kind of surprised at his spirited defense of his stepsister. The way he'd quickly corrected me when I'd referred to her as his sister had given me the impression he didn't like her much.

"Adam, I think you need to have a serious talk with your mom, and then the two of you should talk to her lawyer and get his advice. I don't see any role for me in this. You have to trust that the police will do their job if you give them something they can work with."

"I *have* talked to my mother. She won't listen to me. She just tells me to stay out of it. And the cops won't either, because they'll just think I'm trying to protect her. I don't have any real evidence to give them, and they don't want to look for it."

He turned to Allie then and said, "I told you this would be useless. Let's go."

"No, Adam, wait. Leah—" She leaned forward across the island toward me, her expression determined.

"You told me once that you're a journalist because you can't just accept what *seems* to be true, that you have to keep digging for what really *is* true. That's all we're asking you to do now. If you could just dig a little and find something, even just one thing, that would help Adam's mother, I know my dad would listen. He's stubborn, but he's fair. And he respects you. Please. I know you can do it if you want to."

She was laying it on pretty thick. But she was also zeroing in on two gaps in my wall of "No." My curiosity, and my affinity for the underdog.

They both stared at me. Allie's blue eyes were bright with a light that willed me to say yes. In contrast, Adam's brown eyes were anxious and sad.

I'd seen eyes like his once before, a long time ago. I hadn't been able to help then. But I've never forgotten the mix of defeat and sorrow in them when I was forced to say there was nothing I could do.

I knew I shouldn't do it. It would cause all kinds of complications. Ross would be mad as hell. Coop wouldn't be very happy either. And there was the very real possibility that Rachelle had killed her husband, in which case I'd be giving Adam exactly what he didn't want. And yet, those eyes. For the second time I agreed to something I feared was unwise, and that later proved to be so much worse than that.

"All right. I'll see what I can do."

18

Even though it was only 8:30 on a Monday morning, several customers were already wandering among the touchless faucets, the low-flush toilets, and the fans and heaters on display in the showroom of Crawford Plumbing and Electrical. I headed toward a service counter that stood in front of an open doorway.

I could hear doors closing, phones ringing, and muted conversation coming from the office area beyond. When I detected Rhonda Crawford's distinctive voice, I followed the sound to an office with a half-open door. I could see her sitting at a desk, her reading glasses perched halfway down her nose as she looked at some paperwork. In the crisp white blouse and black blazer she wore, she looked like a presiding judge about to issue an order from the bench.

A trim blonde stood in front of her, blocking Rhonda's view of me hovering in the doorway. She leaned slightly forward as she pointed out something in the document Rhonda was reviewing. Rhonda nodded, then took off her reading glasses and looked up at the woman.

"Yes, I see what you're saying. You're right. Make sure Clark has the changes to me by three. That's all, Leah. Thank you."

The sound of my name startled me, until I realized that Rhonda wasn't speaking to me, but to the woman in front of her.

"I'll have him get right on it," she answered. As she turned to leave, my name-twin uttered a surprised "Oh!" as she saw me.

"Hi, I'm Leah Nash. I gather you're a Leah, too," I said with a smile, moving a half-step into the room and holding out my hand.

"I'm Leah Madsen," she said as she gave me a firm handshake. "I'm the accounting manager here. I recognize your name. You own the *Himmel Times*, don't you? I've been enjoying the advice column Miguel Santos writes."

She was somewhere in her fifties, I guessed, with a nice smile that reached green eyes the same shade as the sweater she wore.

"Yes, I do. Co-own it, actually. I'll tell Miguel that I met a fan."

"Please do. I—"

"Leah!"

Both of us jumped in response to "our" name being called, but only one of us turned to Rhonda, apologized, and hurried out. Taking a stand for Leahs everywhere, but especially in the Crawford Plumbing and Electrical building, I met Rhonda stare for stare for a few seconds before saying, "I'm sorry to barge in, Ms. Crawford. I—"

"Then why did you?"

She didn't look pleased, but she did look curious, so that might be enough to keep her from throwing me out.

"I'd like to talk to you about your brother's death. If this isn't a good time, I can come back later, or schedule an appointment with you."

"I've already talked to *GO News*. At least they were willing to listen to me, which is more than the sheriff did."

"I've read the story. And I was in the sheriff's office when you brought the video to him on Monday."

"Yes, I remember seeing you there. And you were with Detective Ross at Bryan's that terrible day. You're not a policewoman. Why are you involved?"

"I was job shadowing him. Research for a book I'm writing."

"Obviously, you're not job shadowing him now. Why are you here?"

"Adam is worried about his mom. He thinks the police are going to arrest her. He asked me to try to find something that might help her."

I had decided straight-up honesty was the best approach with the hostile Rhonda.

"Rachelle killed my brother. You won't find anything to change that. I don't have anything else to tell you."

"I hoped you could tell me more about Bryan. It's obvious you two were very close."

The hard lines around her mouth softened, as did her eyes. I knew I'd hit the right note. She wanted to talk about her brother.

"Yes, we were. Bryan was very special."

"What was it that made him special?"

"From the time he was a little boy, everyone loved him—the teachers, the other kids. The boys wanted to be like him, and the girls? Well, all he had to do was crook his little finger and the girls all came running. He was always so handsome, with beautiful, thick dark hair and the bluest eyes. Mother died when Bryan was just 10. I left business school to raise him."

"That must have been a hard decision, to give up your career hopes for your brother."

"I didn't give up my career. I helped my father in the business, too. But his heart wasn't in it after Mother passed. He died when Bryan was 19. He left the business to him, but Bryan was much too young for all that responsibility. I worked with him to build it from a two-man plumbing shop to what we are today."

Her pride in the company was obvious as her voice grew more animated.

"Now we have 20 employees, a 2000-square-foot building—that we own, not rent—and our cash flow is very good. We own the commercial property, too. And we work all across the state, not just in the county, doing residential and commercial work. We—"

She stopped abruptly and I knew that she'd just remembered there was no longer a "we" in the business.

"As the remaining partner in the business, will you keep it going, or sell it?"

"As I said, my father left the business to Bryan. I worked side-by-side with Bryan, but I've never been a formal partner. Still, that's just a technicality. Bryan trusted me with everything, including his estate. I'm the personal representative. But I'm not distributing any assets until his killer is in prison. She's not getting one penny above what it takes to keep the house running."

"You mean Rachelle?"

"Of course I do. She married him for his money, and she murdered him to get it. Only she won't. Not if I have anything to say about it."

"Rhonda—may I call you Rhonda?"

She gave a brief nod.

"I understand that the sauna was kept locked because vandals had gotten into it while the family was away. Couldn't they have returned and locked Bryan in as a practical joke that went wrong?"

As a theory it was decidedly weak, both in terms of motive and opportunity. But the memory of Adam's sad eyes prompted me to put it forward. Rhonda dismissed the suggestion with a withering look and a scathing tongue.

"Don't be ridiculous. That happened more than a year ago. And it was either kids or some homeless person. How could they possibly know when Bryan would use the sauna? Even that poor excuse for a detective dismissed that idea. He's taking his sweet time, but he's after the right person. Rachelle."

I didn't mind her scorn, because it gave me a bit of information. If Ross didn't have random kids on his suspect list, I saw no need to place them on mine, either.

"I don't disagree that Rachelle has a strong motive, but what about your niece, Stephanie? She's going to benefit financially from her father's death, isn't she? Or maybe the motive was revenge—an employee he fired, or a business deal that went sour, or a feud with a neighbor?"

"Don't be ridiculous. I don't have any illusions about my niece Stephanie, but she had no reason to kill her own father. She never wanted for anything. In my opinion Bryan was far too lenient with her, but she was his to raise, not mine, thank heavens. And no one had a grudge against Bryan. Everyone loved working with him—employees, clients, suppliers, everyone."

"You make Bryan sound like a wonderful man. If that's true, why are you so sure Rachelle didn't marry for love?"

"Her kind never do. She had no money, she was newly divorced with a

12-year-old son, and she had a dead-end job as a medical assistant. She used what she had to get what she wanted. She's good looking enough, I'll give her that. Bryan had just divorced Jackie when he met Rachelle. He was vulnerable. I tried to warn him, but he wouldn't listen. At least he took my advice on the prenuptial agreement. I saved him a lot with Jackie by insisting he get a prenup, even though he thought that was true love, too."

"Jackie is his first wife, Stephanie's mother?"

"She's Stephanie's mother, yes, but she's not Bryan's first wife."

That was a bit of breaking news.

"Bryan was married three times?"

"He got trapped into marrying a waitress who got herself pregnant. She was 18, just out of high school. He was barely 23. Neither of them had any business marrying."

"Bryan has another child, then?"

"No. She lost the baby—if there ever was one. I had my doubts. They stayed married for a couple of years, but I knew it wasn't going to work. Tiffany, that was her ridiculous name, she refused to understand that Bryan had priorities. The business had to come first. He worked hard, and he needed time to enjoy himself with the things he liked—hunting, fishing, playing cards with his friends. She was very self-centered, always whining he wasn't there, always expecting him to give up everything when she crooked her little finger. They finally divorced, and good riddance."

"When was that?"

"Almost thirty years ago. I haven't thought about her in years. I haven't needed to because we were able to keep the business out of her hands. She wasn't smart enough to insist on an interest in Crawford Plumbing. She settled for keeping the house, her car, and a few other small things. If she'd pushed for part of the business, she'd be sitting pretty now. Maybe she is anyway, I wouldn't know. She left town and we never heard from her again. But I am thankful to her for teaching me an important lesson."

"What was that?"

"Always get a prenup. Bryan was the kind of man who couldn't be happy without a pretty woman in his life. I made sure he didn't put the business in jeopardy again. Before he married Jackie, I convinced him to draw up a prenuptial agreement that would hold up against the Wisconsin community property laws. When he divorced her for having an affair, she got a car, a lump sum payment, and that was it. It was only right, after she cheated on Bryan. The agreement Rachelle signed was even tighter."

"Does she inherit everything now, as his wife?"

"No. Bryan left me a half interest in the business. Everything else is split equally between Rachelle and Stephanie. I'm sure Rachelle doesn't like that. She hates Stephanie. In my opinion, neither of them deserve anything. Rachelle is a gold digger if I ever saw one, and Stephanie is an entitled, manipulative brat. Bryan was just a money machine to both of them. He just could never see how the women in his life took advantage of him."

She fell silent then and I noticed that her eyes had begun to fill.

"Rhonda, I'm sorry that talking about Bryan upset you."

She shook her head and reached in a desk drawer for a tissue and wiped her eyes. She waited a few seconds before she spoke.

"I thought I was protecting Bryan by making sure there was a prenup with Rachelle. But I made it impossible for her to get the money she obviously wanted unless he died. Now, if the police don't prove she killed him, she'll walk away with more than a million dollars. And I can't help feeling it's partly my fault. It's why I have to make sure that she pays for what she did."

"If Rachelle does turn out to be the killer, where—"

"She will, because she is the killer," Rhonda interrupted.

"All right. What happens when Rachelle goes to prison for killing Bryan? Where does the money go?"

"Her share will be split between me and Stephanie."

That meant both Rhonda and Stephanie could have a money motive, not just Rachelle. But the hard-edged Rhonda could barely talk about her brother without breaking down. If Rhonda had killed him, it wouldn't be for the money. And at the moment, I couldn't see any reason why she would. But I was intrigued by Stephanie as an alternate suspect. She wouldn't be the first spoiled darling who had killed a parent for money.

19

"Rhonda, how well did Bryan manage his diabetes?"

I had suddenly recalled Adam's remark that the police kept asking his mother about Bryan's insulin. My abrupt shift in topic didn't seem to faze her.

"He was good about it. He always had back-up insulin on hand at home and in the office—in fact, the insulin is how I know for sure that it was Rachelle who killed him."

"How is that?"

"On Tuesday at the office, Bryan mentioned that he'd knocked the bottle of insulin he was using off the counter the night before. It wasn't a big thing, because he had a back-up vial in the fridge, but it was his last one. I told him I was going to the pharmacy at lunch, and I'd pick up his prescription. I did, and I gave him the three-pack that day."

"Okay, so how does that fit in with Rachelle killing him?"

"On Tuesday we were waiting for the autopsy to be done. We couldn't make any arrangements until after that. I stopped by Bryan's house, thinking I'd get his phone and laptop and check them for any business-related files or emails. I had Bryan's passwords in case of emergency. Rachelle was in the kitchen. It was obvious that she'd been clearing out every trace of Bryan in the house. It had barely been 24 hours since he was found! There were boxes on the floor piled with his clothes and his shoes. One of them had all of the trophies he'd won in high school.

"Rachelle was standing at the drawer where he kept his diabetic supplies. She was just tossing everything into a trash bag. It was so uncaring, so disrespectful. I got quite angry at her and I told her to stop."

"How did she take that?"

"The way she's taken everything I've ever said for the past six years. She accused me of interfering and told me to mind my own business. As if Bryan wasn't my business! She said Bryan was dead now and that meant good riddance to me."

"That was harsh. What did you say to her?"

"I told her to stop being such a selfish little witch. That there were less fortunate people who could use Bryan's test strips and syringes and the unopened insulin in the refrigerator. I said even if she couldn't wait to wipe every trace of him from the house, she could at least think of doing something good for someone else, for once in her life."

"So, what happened then?"

"She actually *threw* the box of syringes she had in her hand at me! She said if I was so concerned about it then I could clear things out of the drawer myself. I said fine, I will. And I took that trash bag from her and dumped everything in the drawer into it. Then I went to the refrigerator and took the unopened insulin and put that in, too. Then, I went to Bryan's office, picked up his laptop and phone, and I left. I won't be going back until she's been arrested."

"I'm sure that was an upsetting scene for you, but I don't see how it convinced you that Rachelle had killed Bryan."

"It didn't, not right away. It was later. I didn't do anything with what I'd brought home from Bryan's. It was just too upsetting. I needed to give myself some time. Finally, on the Sunday after the funeral, I knew I had to pull myself together.

"I began going through Bryan's laptop for anything related to the business to forward to myself before I cleaned off his hard drive. That's when I found the video. I realized that someone had locked my brother in the sauna and left him to die. And I had a good idea who it was. Then the insulin popped into my mind. I remembered that there had only been two bottles in the fridge. I double-checked the trash bag I'd tossed them in, and I was right. There were only two bottles."

Though she was looking at me expectantly, like a teacher silently urging a slow student to grasp a challenging concept, I didn't get where she was heading for a minute. But gradually, it came to me.

"You said you picked up three bottles of insulin for Bryan on Tuesday. He was already using a new bottle, the one he'd had in the refrigerator as a spare. There should have been three new vials in the fridge, not two. Where was the other bottle?"

"Exactly!" she said. "One bottle was missing. And why? Because Rachelle put something in the one on the counter that he was using. She threw it away afterward, so no one would know, and replaced it with one from the refrigerator. That's why there were only two, when there should have been three vials left."

"What kind of something did she put in the vial on the counter?"

"Poison, of course. Something that could mimic DKA symptoms. I don't know what kind."

"But is it that easy to buy poison?"

"She wouldn't have to buy it. She could make it from a poisonous plant you could find in any garden—lily of the valley, foxglove, monkshood, oleander—there are plenty of them. And there are instructions for how to do it right online. I looked it up."

The memory of a long-ago murder in Himmel in which aconite, the poison derived from the pretty purple monkshood plant, had been the weapon flashed into my mind. Rhonda's idea was improbable, but to be fair, not impossible.

"Okay, so I have a couple of questions here. First, why poison your brother? It seems like overkill." I immediately regretted the unintentional pun, but Rhonda was too fired up to notice.

"No. You're wrong. Rachelle had to be *sure* that he would die. And there was a chance that he wouldn't. Bryan was strong, he took good care of himself. Rachelle could've come home Monday morning and found him unconscious but still alive. But if she put poison in his insulin, that combined with locking him in the sauna without water or insulin would kill him for sure."

"But wouldn't poison come up in the screenings done as part of the autopsy?"

"I talked to Connie Crowley," she said, referencing the medical examiner. "She said that she screened for the usual: alcohol, narcotics, sedatives, marijuana, cocaine, amphetamines, and aspirin. But nothing else. If Rachelle gave Bryan an *unusual* poison, it wouldn't be found using the usual tests, would it?"

Clearly, Rhonda had been thinking about this a lot.

I was sure by then that Rhonda's idea about the insulin bottles was the additional information that she'd given Coop the day she brought the video to his attention. Her next words confirmed it.

"I've told the sheriff about it, but I don't believe he's taking it seriously. However, I've also spoken to the district attorney. He's ordered Connie to have more testing done. He agreed that she wasn't thorough enough the first time."

In our county, after an autopsy, the medical examiner's office retains blood and tissue samples for six months, even in the case of a natural death. Bryan had been cremated, but additional tests could still be run.

"Aren't you forgetting something?"

"Such as what?" she asked.

"The poison would have to be colorless and the same consistency as insulin, wouldn't it? Or else your brother would see something wrong with his bottle immediately. It seems like the range of poisons that are easily obtainable, could cause symptoms of DKA, are colorless, and are the same consistency as insulin would be very small."

She sat up straighter, if that were possible.

"Because something isn't likely doesn't mean it can't happen."

The irritation in her voice told me my time with her was growing short.

"Rhonda, I'm surprised, as close as the two of you were, that you didn't have dinner with Bryan that Friday night. It seems that with Rachelle gone, it would have been a pleasant evening for you both."

"Is that your clever way of asking me for an alibi? Not that it's any of your business, but I was providing respite care for a friend with a terminally ill husband. I've already provided the details to the police. I'm not giving them to you."

"I'm sorry if I offended you. It was just an observation, not an accusation," I said as I moved toward the door. "Thanks for seeing me."

"Wait."

I turned back to look at her.

"I remember now. Your paper endorsed David Cooper for sheriff. You're here to protect the sheriff's reputation, aren't you? Spencer Karr advised me against talking to your newspaper. He said you were biased and he's right. I don't want to see anything I said in your newspaper. And don't contact me again."

I was in the parking lot buckling my seatbelt when someone tapped on my window.

Leah Madsen, the accounting manager, stood shivering in the cool, damp air. I pushed the button to lower the window, and she leaned in slightly.

"I couldn't help overhearing you talking to Rhonda. Her office is right next to mine. I don't know if this even matters to you but . . ." She hesitated.

"At this point, anything would help. I'm pretty much wandering in the desert right now. Hop in a minute, no sense freezing out there."

"So, what's on your mind?" I asked as she settled into the passenger seat and held her hands in front of the vent pouring out warm air.

"What she said about Bryan, about him never having a problem with an employee. That wasn't totally true. I wasn't going to say anything, but then I thought maybe I should. It's probably nothing, but . . ."

"Bryan had problems with some of the employees?"

"Not some of them, just one. He was a pretty good boss. But there was Mitch. Of course he wasn't an employee, he was Bryan's partner."

"I had no idea Bryan had a partner."

"When I started as a bookkeeper 15 years ago, the business was called C&T Plumbing and Electrical. Bryan Crawford and Mitch Toomey. About

10 years ago, the partnership broke up and things didn't end very well. I don't blame Bryan for that, but Mitch did."

"Why?"

"Mitch was a nice man. But it wasn't a secret that he had a drinking problem and it kept getting worse. He was skipping client meetings, coming into work hungover—or sometimes not quite sober. A couple of his crew quit, because he was so hard to work for."

"I can't imagine Rhonda was okay with that."

"She wasn't. She wanted Bryan to get rid of Mitch, but I guess they were old friends, and Bryan didn't want to. But then Mitch made a big mistake on an estimate that cost the business a lot of money. Bryan finally dissolved the partnership."

"And Mitch didn't take that well?"

"He was furious. He came in one day after it happened, and it was obvious he'd been drinking. Bryan was in the back, talking to some of the guys about a job. Mitch found him and started screaming at him, saying he forced him out, that he cheated him, that he stole his crew, things like that. Only he said it with a lot of swearing."

"How did Bryan react?"

"He yelled back, and he told Mitch he had to leave. Mitch tried to punch Bryan. But he was so drunk, he lost his balance and fell on the floor. Some of the guys laughed. Mitch was humiliated. Bryan told him to get out and not come back, or he'd call the police. Mitch left, but on the way out he kept yelling that Bryan would be sorry some day, that he was starting a new business that would crush Bryan. It was sad. Mitch was a nice man when I first met him. He had a nice family, too."

"Do you know what happened to him?"

"He tried to start up on his own, but within a couple of years his business went under and his wife and kids left him. I haven't seen him in years, but I know he's still around. A couple of contractors we work with see him sometimes. I guess he hasn't gotten over it even after all this time. He still tells people that Bryan cheated him and ruined his life."

"Do you know where Mitch is living now?"

"I heard Hailwell, but I don't know that for sure. Leah, I don't want you to think that I'm saying Mitch had anything to do with Bryan's death. It was all a long time ago. I just thought it might help you."

"Don't worry, I'm not to the thinking part yet. I'm just collecting pieces of information. I have a lot of questions still, and a lot of people to see."

As she reached to open the door handle, she said, "Okay, well, unless you have to, I'd rather you didn't tell him—or Rhonda if it comes to that—you heard this from me."

"No worries."

20

"You're lucky to catch me. Normally I'm not in the office on Mondays," Connie Crowley said as she offered me a chair in her cramped office. "Office" is a grandiose term for the space in the basement of the local hospital that had been allocated to Grantland County's part-time medical examiner. It's the size of a repurposed closet. If Connie were any taller or less compact, she might not fit behind her desk.

The area where she actually does the autopsies isn't all that much larger. It's furnished austerely at best, with old and in some cases outdated equipment, poor lighting, and limited electrical outlets. However, the county Board of Supervisors, struggling to adequately fund the needs of the living, have long resisted increasing the budget for the dead.

"Do you think you'll ever get a better location, or at least one that's outfitted better?" I asked as I took the seat she offered.

"Doubtful. It's a hard sell when the roads are full of potholes and the courthouse needs a new roof. I've been to the Board of Supervisors every year since I started three years ago, asking for a bigger budget. 'More Money for Dead People' isn't the persuasive slogan you might think it is. But you didn't come to talk about funding woes, did you? What's on your mind, Leah?"

"Bryan Crawford."

"Ah. His sister has kicked up quite a little storm, hasn't she? She called me last week, demanding that I send blood and tissue samples to the state crime lab."

"I know. She told me that she went over your head to Cliff Timmins."

"She had to. I told her that I don't send samples to the lab at the request of family members with a score to settle."

"That's what you think Rhonda is?"

She shrugged. "She's one furious sister, that's for sure."

"How soon will you hear back?"

"You're not asking on the record, for the paper, are you? I guess I should have clarified that up front. We're under strict orders that all comments on the case go through Coop or the DA's office. And I'm sure Cliff would prefer if he was the spokesman. He can't get his name in the news often enough now that he plans to run for judge."

"No, this isn't on the record. I wouldn't do that to you without telling you. I'm just poking around a little. Maggie's got Troy on the story. I haven't talked to Coop yet, but I will."

"Well, off the record, let's just say that some pressure has been applied. Seems Rhonda was a reliable and generous contributor to the party of Cliff's persuasion. She made it clear that she expects Cliff Timmins to keep that in mind, if he wants support for his run for judge. In response, our esteemed DA has called in some favors of his own for a quick return on the test results. I'd say we should hear back by the end of next week."

"You did standard drug screening as part of the autopsy, right? That's what Rhonda said."

"Yes. I explained that to her. But she's hellbent on her own idea."

She pursed her lips and blew upward, causing her fringe of bangs to float up and then back down on her broad forehead.

"Everything came back negative on the routine screen. I told Rhonda that her brother's body presented with all the hallmarks of diabetic ketoacidosis. I'm very confident in my report."

"What *are* the hallmarks of DKA?"

"Very high glucose levels, elevated acetone, elevated ketones, I found an Armanni-Ebstein lesion when I examined the kidneys. All indicative of DKA."

"Does DKA kill quickly?"

"Quick is a relative term. In Bryan's case, given the stomach contents, the absence of rigor, and the beginning stage of decomposition, my estimate is that he died around 10 p.m. Saturday night. Given what Coop tells me about him being locked in the sauna around six o'clock Friday night, Bryan was dying for more than 24 hours. DKA isn't an easy death. He would have experienced excessive thirst, vomiting, weakness, confusion, abdominal pain, and probably shortness of breath. Why are you so interested?"

"I'm looking into things for Adam Harrison, Bryan Crawford's stepson. He's worried that the police have made his mother their favorite suspect."

"And have they?"

"I don't know. I haven't confirmed that with Coop yet, or Ross, either. I assume Rhonda told you that she thinks Rachelle poisoned Bryan's insulin to make sure that he died, in case being locked in the sauna without insulin didn't do the trick. Do you think that's even remotely possible?"

"What I think is that Rhonda's been reading too much Agatha Christie. It's obvious someone used Bryan Crawford's insulin dependency to kill him —and that was a very clean and tidy plan. Lock him in the sauna where he can't get his insulin, and he dies. No need to gum it up by adding in poison. Rhonda is off base."

"I suggested that to her and she accused me of protecting Coop at the expense of justice. She's determined to have Rachelle arrested for murder."

"Rhonda's always been intense. And she's always had a blind spot where her little brother is concerned. She and I were in school together back in the day. Omico Central High, Class of 1972. Rhonda was going places, we all thought. She had a lot of ambition, though Lord knows where that came from. Her mother, Helen, was a nice lady, but she made Donna Reed look like a radical feminist. And her dad, Lee, he was a good old boy. He made ends meet with his little two-man plumbing business and that gave him time for hunting and bowling, his two biggest passions. Rhonda, she was different."

"She said she came back home to raise Bryan after their mother died. But she never married or had her own family?"

"She had a fiancé, but he broke off the engagement because she kept putting off getting married, is what I heard. By then we weren't in touch. I think she channeled everything she had, all her ambition and her smarts, into raising Bryan. Then later, she got her satisfaction helping him build up the business."

"That's pretty much what she told me. But she also said that her dad left the business to Bryan. Why not to both of them? I wouldn't be very happy if I worked my butt off to take care of my brother and my father, and then my brother gets the business and I get nothing."

"I'm with you. I've known a few women like Rhonda. They settle for that power-behind-the-throne baloney. I say don't diminish yourself or your abilities for anyone, ever. It never leads to happiness."

"Do you think it could lead to murder?"

I was thinking of Adam and his suggestion that Rhonda could have killed her brother.

"Are you asking do I think Rhonda killed her brother?"

Her expression was so startled that I backed off the idea a little.

"No, not seriously, I guess. Though you just gave her a possible motive besides financial gain. Maybe she got fed up being 'the power behind the throne' for a brother who didn't appreciate her."

"No," she said firmly. "That's not Rhonda. She doesn't see her life that way. She can't allow herself to. Bryan was her creation. She did what a lot of women do. She took a perfectly ordinary man and projected qualities on him that he didn't have: business smarts, commitment, strength of character, and then proceeded to devote herself to keeping up the fiction."

"Why would she do that? Why wouldn't she just strike out on her own? She's obviously intelligent. She certainly projects self-confidence."

"We're getting out of my bailiwick here. I'm no psychiatrist. Maybe her father never loved her. Maybe she was potty trained too soon. Maybe she saw something nasty in the woodshed. I have no idea. But Bryan—her idealized version of him—is what made her feel worthwhile. He's the one thing she gave up everything else for. Killing that dream would be like killing herself. And leaving woo-woo psychological explanations aside, she's the one who pushed for the investigation, right? That would be plain stupid, if she was the killer."

"Yeah, that's my thought, too. I'm just picking at threads, seeing if any pull loose."

"Well, I don't think the poison thread is going to be one that unravels who killed Bryan Crawford. There's not going to be anything there. And you can take that to the bank."

I considered my conversations with both Leah Madsen and Connie Crowley on the drive to Rachelle Crawford's house.

According to Connie, death from DKA would be quite painful, and not very quick—possibly the kind of death a bitter, revenge-seeking former partner might dream of. But Mitch and Bryan had been estranged for years. Would he still feel the level of rage that would fuel murder? And how would he have access to the information that Bryan used his sauna every Friday night, or that he'd be alone all weekend with no one to rescue him?

I returned to Connie's musings about Rhonda's psychology, and her belief that Rhonda could never kill Bryan, because it would be like killing her dream. But what if Rhonda had finally awakened to the fact that she'd wasted her life in service to a brother who had used her, but never loved her? Bryan's death wouldn't have been easy, according to Connie. Rhonda did have a certain fierce, take-no-prisoners quality about her.

But I came back to the same roadblock to that theory. Bryan's murder was a success. It was written off as a natural death due to diabetic complications. Why would Rhonda sabotage her own achievement and possibly put herself in peril by bringing the video to the police and insisting the investigation had to be reopened? Adam had suggested that she hated his mother so much, it would have been worth the risk. But that was a lot of hate.

I was so lost in thought that I almost missed the turn to the Crawford house. I hadn't called ahead, because I didn't expect that Rachelle would welcome the visit. I was right.

21

"I don't understand. You said you've been talking to Adam? What on earth about?"

Rachelle Crawford was standing with the door half open, so that only part of her small frame was visible. She had barely given me time to introduce myself. Now, one of her hands rested on the doorknob, the other on the door itself, poised to shut it in my face.

"Please, if I could just come in for a few minutes, I'll explain. At the very least, I think you should know what your son told me."

That did the trick. She pulled the door open and stepped aside to let me in. I noticed again how pretty she was. Her golden-brown hair was piled in a loose topknot, and she wore a pale shade of lipstick that matched the pink glow of her cheeks. She had on pink slippers with her black leggings and a fluffy, pink sweater. I ignored the advice Ross had given me against going sock-footed into an interview. I slipped my shoes off and padded after her toward the kitchen.

A woman in jeans and a long-sleeved navy T-shirt, her hair covered with a navy and white bandana, stood at the sink, her back to us as we walked in. She, too, was shoeless.

"You can do the upstairs first today, Sheila," Rachelle said. "I'm going to need the kitchen for a while."

She didn't bother to introduce us.

"Excuse me, Rachelle?" the woman said hesitantly as she turned toward us.

Her appearance was fairly nondescript. She was average height, thin, mid-40s. She had worry lines on her forehead and light brown eyes that looked out from beneath overplucked brows. The hair poking out under the bandana she wore was brown and straight.

Rachelle didn't bother to hide the irritation that crossed her face.

"Yes, Sheila, what is it?"

The woman glanced at me, her expression showing her discomfort, as she said, "I wonder if I could have a quick word?"

Before Rachelle could answer, I said, "Rachelle, while you're talking, could I use your bathroom, please?"

"Yes, of course. It's down the hall and to the right."

I stayed there for what I judged to be long enough for Sheila's "quick word." As I walked back down the hall, I could hear that the conversation was ending.

"Thank you so much, Rachelle. I appreciate the advance on my pay. It helps a lot." The words were infused with a mix of gratitude and embarrassment.

"I'm sure you do, Sheila, but you need to understand that I can't keep giving you advances."

Rachelle's voice wasn't exactly unkind, but there wasn't much empathy in it either.

"Oh, right, I understand," Sheila said. "I'm sorry I had to ask again. It's just, we've had so many unexpected expenses. And now the muffler is going on my car and I'm worried about getting a ticket if I don't get it fixed. And the job my boyfriend was counting on fell through, and I—"

"Yes, yes, it's fine. I told you, I'll add the extra to your check. I won't be here when you leave, I have errands to run. Please don't forget to set the alarm when you go."

"No, I won't. And thank you," Sheila said, all but tugging her forelock in deference. Her head was down, and she nearly knocked me over as she scurried out of the kitchen.

"Sheila's a good cleaner," Rachelle said to me, as though she felt she needed to explain. "But she can't seem to manage her finances. Do you want some coffee? I was just going to have a cup."

"Sure, coffee would be nice, thank you."

It's my practice to accept almost any beverage when offered at an interview. The hosting instinct is strong in most people, and a cup of coffee can make an interview seem more like a conversation than an interrogation.

I declined cream and sugar and waited to start while she prepped her own coffee with both. When she sat down across from me, the expression in her eyes—a shade of turquoise so intense it didn't look quite natural—was guarded.

"All right, please tell me what Adam said to you. He's very shy. I can't imagine why he'd even talk to you, a complete stranger."

"Well, not as complete as all that. He remembered me from being here with Detective Ross the day your husband's body was discovered."

"Do you work with Detective Ross? He didn't introduce you that day. Or maybe he did, and I don't remember. Everything about that morning is a little blurry to me."

"No, I don't work with him, at least not regularly. I'm a writer. I was job shadowing him that day, doing some background research for a book. Full disclosure, I also own the *Himmel Times*."

The look in her eyes changed from curious to wary.

"I recognize your name now. Are you trying to interview me for a story for your paper? Or for a book? Is that it? Did you interview my son for a book about Bryan's death? I won't allow that. He's just a boy. He's still in high school. Don't you have to get my permission for that?"

"No to all your questions. I don't want to interview you for a news story, I'm not writing a book about your husband's murder, and I didn't interview Adam about his stepfather's death. He came to me. And as far as allowing me to talk to him, Adam is 18. Even if he weren't, it's not illegal to interview minors. Which I didn't do. We just talked and he asked me for some help. I agreed to try."

Her mood shifted again, this time from aggressive to nervous. She began fiddling with her wedding ring, sliding it up and down her finger.

"What kind of help?"

I recounted Adam's concerns about the police drawing their net tighter and tighter around his mother.

"Adam said he's tried to talk to you about it, but you don't take him seriously. He's afraid they're building a case against you, and they aren't looking at anyone else. He asked me to see if I could turn up anything that the police might have overlooked that would help you."

"Such as?"

"I don't know until I do some looking. I have to be honest with you. I didn't give him much hope for a couple of reasons. First, because I think Detective Ross is good at his job. I only said I'd look into things because your son is so upset, and because sometimes, even the best cop can get on the wrong scent. Second, the money you inherit and the brutal prenup you signed are probably going to weigh heavier against you with the cops than any small facts or discrepancies I might turn up."

"Adam was wrong when he told you that I don't take my situation seriously. He's a very intense boy, with very strong emotions and a very vivid imagination. That's why I don't talk with him about the investigation. It just makes him overanxious and upset. I'm trying to keep him from worrying. "

"Adam is convinced that the police are on the verge of arresting you, so, with respect, it doesn't look like your approach is working that well."

"I know that police always suspect the spouse, but I was hours away from here for the whole weekend when Bryan died. And I have proof. I'm not worried." She said it calmly enough. Though I noticed that she was playing with her ring again.

"You were at a retreat, right?"

"Yes, at the Grace and Blessings Retreat Center. It's near Stratford. I can document it. I have the registration receipt, the payment on my credit card, and I can even produce the weekend program agenda. And I was there with 20 other people."

She rattled off the details of her alibi glibly.

"What was the setup like?"

"We all arrived at 2 p.m. Friday. Vans from the center picked us up at the parking lot down the road where we left our cars and drove us to the center."

She had stopped the ring twisting.

"We all signed in when we got there and turned in all our electronic devices. Then we were basically cut off from the world until we all left together on Monday morning. It was like being on an island with no bridge and no boat. It was my first silent retreat, and it was perfect."

"Silent, huh? That would be hard for me."

"It isn't at all. We had some wonderful talks by some very inspiring spiritual leaders."

"The teachers could talk, but you couldn't?"

"We were allowed to have conversations and ask questions during registration. There was a communal dinner at 5:30 for anyone who chose to attend. And we met as a group at 8 p.m. for Kirtan. It's a kind of call-and-response practice. It's very powerful. After that, we entered our silence. That weekend opened my heart."

Rachelle had the appearance and the trappings of a Peloton-spinning, latte-drinking soccer mom, not those of a spiritual seeker. I reminded myself the two were not mutually exclusive as I tried to stifle my judgy inclinations.

"Open hearts are good, I hear. So, why do you think the police keep questioning you?"

"My lawyer said it's a sign they're not getting anywhere with the case. They're just trying to shake something, anything, loose. But there's nothing to shake. I'm sure they'll move on at some point. I mean, I told the truth, and the truth should set me free, right? Isn't that how the saying goes?"

She had started strong, but ended with a slight, nervous laugh, and the ring twisting had returned.

"Okay, so you didn't kill your husband. Do you have thoughts on who else might have?"

"No, I don't."

"What about Rhonda?"

"Rhonda?" Her voice rose in surprise.

"You don't think that's possible?"

"Only if Bryan died by smothering. There's no love lost between

Rhonda and me, but I can't see her ever doing anything to hurt Bryan. Rhonda just isn't normal about him. She never has been. She wanted to be his everything—mother, sister, best friend, wife. She practically worshipped him."

"I'm kind of surprised that you're defending her. I'm sure you know that she's made it pretty clear that she thinks you're the main suspect in your husband's death."

"I'm not defending her. I just don't think she could bring herself to kill Bryan. To kill me? Then yes, that's absolutely possible. Rhonda can be a horrible witch. She's never been nice to Adam, and she truly hated me from the start. I worked hard to make my marriage a success, but she didn't make it any easier."

"Do you consider your marriage successful?"

"Yes," she said without hesitation. "My first husband, Adam's father, is a dreamer. If he used half the energy he spent on chasing get-rich-quick schemes on his actual job, we'd have been fine. Instead, we went bankrupt and lost everything. I was a divorced mother with a 12-year-old son, struggling to make ends meet when I met Bryan. He was attractive, had his own business, and he offered security for me and Adam. I married him because I loved him. But I appreciated the financial stability he gave me, too. And I won't apologize for that."

"But didn't a prenuptial agreement like the one you signed put that financial stability in jeopardy? You gave up your rights to basically everything, and he gave up nothing."

"I don't see it that way. I didn't bring any money to the marriage. In fact, I brought quite a few debts that Bryan took care of. I understood that Bryan needed to protect his business and his assets. And I knew that as long as I was the wife he wanted, I wouldn't have to worry about the money. I made sure that I was, and I didn't."

She shifted slightly on her seat then, and I knew she was getting ready to wind things down, but I still had questions. I tried to think of a way to keep her there. The ringing of her mobile phone gave me the break I needed.

"Excuse me," she said as she looked at the caller ID. She picked up her phone as she stood and walked to the hallway to carry on her conversation.

As soon as her back was to me, I jumped up, poured myself another cup of coffee, and was seated back at the bar when she returned.

"I hope you don't mind. I don't get coffee this good very often. I couldn't resist pouring myself just a little more."

I could see she wasn't happy, but her good manners overrode her irritation.

"No, of course not. But I do have some errands to run, and I should—"

"Oh, no problem. I'll drink up and get out of your way in just a minute."

22

She didn't tap her fingers on the bar as she sat across from me, waiting for me to finish my coffee, but she might as well have. Her body language conveyed the message clearly: hurry up and get out.

"Rachelle, is there anyone outside of the family—you, Adam, Stephanie, and Rhonda, I mean—who knew about Bryan's Friday night sauna habit?"

"I don't know. There could be. He's done it for years, long before he and I were married. He could've mentioned it to anybody, I guess."

"What about the key to the sauna? Who had access to it?"

When Coop, Ross, and I had talked in Coop's office, Ross had said the missing key was a sticking point for him. Since Ross was still asking about it, according to Adam, it obviously still was. He must have a lead or a theory he was working on that connected to it.

"Again, anyone, I suppose. Bryan hid it under the mat in front of the sauna door. It wouldn't be hard to find. Rhonda told him to put it somewhere less obvious, but he never did."

"I understand Adam found the key that Detective Ross thought was missing. How did he happen to do that?"

I was curious to see if her story matched Adam's.

"I asked him to clean up around the sauna—not inside, I had cleaners do that—but the walkway in front of it and the area around the door were dirty with mud and leaves. Adam moved the mat to sweep, and the key was there. Right under the mat where it was supposed to be. Detective Ross must not have looked hard enough. I called him as soon as it was found. Gave it to him, even."

"Was there only one key?"

"We used to have two, but the other one went missing months ago. I don't know what happened to it. It didn't matter to me, because I never use the sauna. Bryan never bothered to replace it. We keep all the keys there." She pointed to a small wooden key organizer that hung on the wall. Two rows of keys hung in sets of two, each set with a different color head. One hook was empty.

"That's a lot of keys. Why are the tops all different colors?"

"Adam color coded them. He likes things organized. The front door keys are blue, the shed keys are green, the sauna keys are orange, and so on."

"If you gave the key to Detective Ross, then how are you able to get into the sauna?"

"I'm not. I never used it. Neither did Adam. That was Bryan's domain. If I had my way, I'd just tear the damn thing down."

"What's stopping you?"

"Rhonda. She's the executor—the personal representative, that is—for the estate. She says I can't do anything until the estate is settled. And she'll drag that out, I'm sure. I'd like to sell the house, but I'm stuck for now."

"You're moving?"

"I want to. Adam graduates this year, and with Bryan gone, this place is much too big for me. I may move to Florida. I hate the cold weather here, but Bryan never wanted to leave. Not even for a long vacation. I can't do anything without Queen Rhonda's permission. Now that she's decided Bryan was murdered, who knows how long it will take before I can sell?"

"To be fair, she didn't 'decide' he was murdered. The video she found with the locked sauna door was pretty definitive. Did you know about Bryan's trail cam setup?"

"No. I wasn't home when he did it and Rhonda never mentioned it."

"Were you surprised that he didn't mention it to you, but he told Rhonda?"

"No. Bryan has—had—things that interested him but not me, like anything to do with hunting or fishing. Just like I had things that didn't interest him, like yoga and spin class. We tried not to bore each other. But Rhonda always had time to listen to Bryan, even if he just wanted to tell her how he broke his shoelaces and bought a new pair at the Dollar Store."

I was not detecting much love in her comments about Bryan, though maybe it was because Rhonda irritated her so much. Time to check on her feelings for her stepdaughter.

"You said Rhonda wasn't very nice to Adam. How does she get along with Stephanie?"

"Not much better than she does with Adam and me. Though Stephanie is a spoiled brat, so I can't fault Rhonda for that."

"Spoiled? How do you mean?"

"Spoiled as in she got everything she wanted from Bryan. Expensive clothes, school, car. If he ever said no, she guilt-tripped him because he divorced her mother. She lived with her mother, not with us, thank God, but whenever she visited, she was nasty to me and to Adam, too. I think she was jealous. He was here in a beautiful home, while she and her mother lived in some duplex in Appleton. I wasn't sad at all when she got her first no, ever, from Bryan."

A small smile played across Rachelle's lips at the memory.

"What happened?"

"Bryan liked to have family dinners sometimes with the three of us— me, Bryan, and Adam—as well as Stephanie and Rhonda. It wasn't easy because none of us liked each other, but Bryan wanted us all together, so we did it. He wasn't a very complicated man. As long as we acted happy, it didn't matter if we were. I tried, but Rhonda and Stephanie made it hard. They don't like each other much, but they always managed to put that aside to gang up on me. They were always making digs about the money I spent, or the yoga classes I teach, or what I was wearing. Nothing I did was right in their eyes. But Stephanie finally got hers at the last dinner we had in January. She announced that she had decided to move to New York to go to some acting school there, and she'd need $70,000 for tuition and living expenses."

"Wow, that's a big ask."

"Not for Stephanie. She expects to get everything she wants, when she wants it. But Bryan was already a little upset that she was taking so long to graduate from Robley, because she changed her major so often. I told him that he wasn't doing her any favors by giving her everything anytime she asked. We both agreed that she needed to learn how to rely on herself, for her own good. So, her timing in asking for that much money was bad."

Rachelle could barely contain her glee at Stephanie's failure to talk her dad out of an additional $70,000. I suspected she'd done some serious prep work with Bryan that had more to do with payback to Stephanie than with the desire to instill self-reliance in her.

"How did Bryan's refusal go over?"

"I think she was shocked at first. Then she tried her 'daddy's little girl' trick. When that didn't work, she threw a tantrum. She said he owed it to her for abandoning her and her mother. That he had plenty of money, he didn't need to be so selfish. That's exactly the wrong way to get to Bryan. He told her that it was his money and she didn't have any say in how he spent it until after he was dead, and maybe not then if she didn't change her attitude. I've never seen him so angry." Rachelle was almost gloating as she recalled the scene.

"That must have been a pretty uncomfortable dinner for everyone else."

"Adam didn't like it, but I was glad Bryan finally drew the line with her. Rhonda looked like she was going to stand up and cheer. Especially when Bryan told Stephanie that if she didn't stop acting like a spoiled brat, she might not have any money at all. Then he left the table, Stephanie ran off crying, and Adam went after her. Rhonda and I finished eating and it was probably the nicest few minutes we ever spent in each other's company."

"Did Bryan and Stephanie work it out?"

"No. Stephanie tried to persuade him, but when Bryan made up his mind, there was no changing it. Though now she doesn't have to worry about it. She'll have all the money she needs to do whatever she wants."

I thought it unwise to add, "And so will you." Instead, I switched topics.

"Do you know Bryan's old partner, Mitch Toomey?"

Her eyebrows rose in surprise at the question.

"Mitch Toomey? No. Bryan mentioned him a few times. I know they were partners once, but that was long before I met Bryan."

"So, they didn't stay in touch?"

"Hardly. He was an alcoholic who cost the business a lot of money. Bryan tried to help him, but Mitch was a lost cause, he said. Then after Bryan bought him out, he claimed that Bryan had cheated him. To my knowledge he hadn't seen him in years. Why do you ask?"

"I just heard that he'd been Bryan's partner and wondered what the deal was."

I had dragged out my cup of coffee and was down to the last swallow. Rachelle was quick to notice.

"Well, I see that you're done with your coffee, and I do need to go," Rachelle said.

"Oh, sure. Thank you."

I stood and reached for my jacket. I fussed around with it, giving it a shake, slowly putting my arms in the sleeves to give me time for another question.

"I forgot to ask, did your husband manage his own medications—I mean did he fill his prescriptions himself, prepare his injections, that kind of thing, or did you do that for him?"

"Why?"

"Something Rhonda said piqued my curiosity, that's all."

"What, that I was a lazy wife who didn't wait on Bryan hand and foot and manage all his medications? Bryan didn't trust anyone but himself—and Rhonda, of course—with his insulin. Did she tell you she lost her mind when she came over and saw me packing up Bryan's things? She went storming out with all his insulin and supplies."

"She thinks there might be a bottle of the insulin missing. Do you know anything about that?"

"You mean she thinks I poisoned Bryan, right?"

"She does have a theory leaning in that direction."

"I didn't. And I didn't lock him in the sauna. I didn't do anything except be the best wife that I could for the last six years. And with Rhonda constantly trying to be a third party in our marriage, that wasn't easy. Now, if you'll excuse me," she said, signaling her hosting duties were over by reaching for my cup and taking it to the sink.

"Right. Thank you for the coffee and the conversation. I can see myself out."

I was at the door, balancing on one leg while getting my second shoe on, when she called, "Wait!"

I finished tugging it on as she walked up to me.

"I understand why Adam came to you. I can see now that not talking to him about the investigation made him more anxious, not less. But we don't need you in the middle of this family matter anymore. I don't want you to contact him again. Or me, either."

"I'm sorry, Rachelle. I made my promise to Adam. You work it out however you need to with your son, but I'm not done yet. When I am, I'll let him know, and he can decide what to do."

23

It was 11:30 a.m. when I pulled back into Himmel. My growling stomach reminded me that though I'd had plenty of coffee at Rachelle's, she had not offered anything more substantial. Instead of going straight home, where I knew the cupboard was bare, I swung through McDonald's and picked up a favorite meal: Diet Coke with extra ice, a quarter pounder, and a small order of fries. The "small" was my attempt at making healthier food choices. Baby steps, right?

Then I drove to Riverview Park to think.

It's an odd quirk, I know, but I like eating in the car by myself, especially when it's raining, as it was then. I like watching the drops hit and then run down the windows, sometimes in a slow patter, sometimes with rat-a-tat speed. I enjoy being snug inside a dry and cozy space that no one can enter unless I invite them. The park gives me the bonus of indulging in another favorite thing, people watching. When I was a kid, my father used to take me and my younger sister Annie to McDonald's for lunch sometimes, while our mom tended to our baby sister Lacey. We often went to Riverview Park to eat it.

He was the one who started us playing a game he called *Imagine That*. If it was nice, we'd sit at a picnic table. While we stuffed ourselves with Happy Meals—probably the root of my lifelong fealty to fast food—he would point out someone at another table, or on the swings, or walking by. Then he'd say, "Imagine that he's a superhero in disguise . . . "

That, or a similar prompt, would be the beginning of a story that the three of us constructed about the person's fictitious life—what their name was, if they were happy, or sad, or mad, where they were going, what would happen to them that day. Sometimes our stories hewed close to reality and other times they were wild fantasies.

Imagine That isn't only a happy memory for me. I still play it if I'm stuck at a stoplight, or waiting at an airport, or sitting in a doctor's office. I'll sometimes make up stories about the people around me, giving them personal histories and future adventures, imagining the secret hopes and dark sorrows they carry.

As I thought about our family game, my eyes unexpectedly filled with tears. I felt a sharp pang of longing—for my long-gone sisters and father, for what our family was then. I used to push that feeling down when it threatened to break through the protective layer of smartassery I wear to keep it at bay. But over the past couple of years, I've begun to see that it's good, sometimes, to let the hurt out. I credit, or blame, Father Lindstrom for that.

I had learned to sit with the pain, even when it felt as fresh as when the loss first happened. When I didn't fight it, it left me quicker than when I did. Eventually, it would recede, leaving behind the bearable dull ache that is a part of the heart of everyone who has lost someone they love.

This time, though, the bittersweet memories had left something else in their wake. Remembering *Imagine That* had reminded me that I've been creating fiction ever since my dad taught us the game. Writing a mystery series was just the next level of play. Instead of taking real people and giving them imaginary stories, I'd be taking imaginary people and giving them real stories—or at least stories that I hoped seemed real to readers. I felt a sudden certainty that despite my fears, I could do it.

My angst sorted out, I turned my attention to my fries. But I had ignored the cardinal rule of fast-food meals: strike while the French fries are hot. Few things are less appealing than the mouthfeel and taste of cold fries. The burger was cold, too, leaving a light coating of congealing grease on the roof of my mouth when I took a bite. I sighed, because I really was hungry, but I crumpled up the cardboard container and French fries it held, balled up the hamburger in its paper wrap, and shoved them both back in the bag. Then I unrolled the window and tossed the whole thing into a nearby trash barrel, where it landed with a loud thud. Somewhere, a dietary angel just got her wings.

At least I still had my bubbly, fizzy, ice-cold Diet Coke to sip as I made notes on my morning interviews.

Rhonda was hellbent on teeing up Rachelle as Bryan Crawford's killer. To be fair, I could see why. She was far and away the best suspect from a motive perspective. But after spending some time with Rhonda in full avenging-sister mode, I had to wonder if she was pushing so hard only because she hated Rachelle so much. I made a note to get in touch with Bryan's wife one and wife two. I'd like their perspective on Bryan and on Rhonda as well.

Rachelle had been interesting. She'd recited the details of her weekend clearly and convincingly. But on and off throughout our talk she'd displayed the nervous tic of playing with her wedding ring. Her alibi seemed very solid to me, but there must be something wrong with it for Ross to keep going back to her.

Both Rachelle and Rhonda had given me the same piece of interesting information about Stephanie. She had been very angry at her father for thwarting her plans. With Bryan dead she was free to pursue anything she wanted, with plenty of money to support her. I needed to talk to her.

I also couldn't forget the wild card that Leah Madsen had dealt me as I was leaving—Mitch, Bryan's bitter ex-business partner. I wondered if Ross had any information on him.

I was deep in thought when my phone rang. I picked it up reflexively, without checking the caller ID.

"This is Leah."

"*Chica*, where are you? I have some tea for you about John."

I was so focused on the Crawfords that I didn't register what Miguel was talking about at first.

"John?"

"Yes, John! Pilarski? Jennifer's husband?"

"Oh, right. Sorry, my mind was elsewhere. What did you find out?"

"Well . . . " he said, pausing dramatically, as he likes to do when telling a story, "Angela Darmody saw John with a woman last month. Late at night. And it wasn't Jennifer."

"Did Angela recognize the woman?"

"No. She and Dale were coming back from a wedding in Baraboo. It was midnight when they started home. They were stopped to let a car go by so they could make a left turn. The SUV behind them didn't wait and passed on the right. Angela, she looked to give the driver the evil eye and it was John, but he didn't look over at her. She saw the woman, too, but she didn't recognize her. And she was sitting *very* close to John."

"Hmm. That does sound a little suspect."

"That's what Angela and I think. And don't worry," he said, anticipating my next comment. "I told Angela to keep it on the down-low. She will. She likes Jennifer even more than she likes gossip."

"You did good, Miguel. Now I think we need to take a road trip. Can you do Thursday?"

"Yes! Where are we going?"

"I'm not sure yet. I have to do some more checking. Are you at the paper now?"

"No, I'm on my way to shoot some photos in Hailwell at the high school. But I'll be in later."

"Okay. Text me when you're finished, and we can get together for some catching up."

24

On my way back home, I got a call from Coop, but I didn't pick up. I had a pretty good idea what it would be about. Instead, I drove to the Elite Café and snagged a table in the back. It was just past one o'clock, so the lunch rush was mostly over. I called him back.

"Hey, I saw you called. I'm at the Elite. I'll buy you a coffee, or lunch if you haven't eaten yet. I haven't. The special today is roast beef with horse-radish cream on a Kaiser roll," I said, as an added incentive. He ignored my invitation.

"Leah, I talked to Rhonda Crawford this morning. She told me—"

"I'll bet I know what she told you. Don't you want to hear what I have to say?"

"That's why I called. I told you, there's no room for you in our Bryan Crawford investigation."

"I'm not 'in' your investigation. I just—come on, it'll be easier to explain in person. I'll order a sandwich for you. I'm at the table in the back."

I hung up before he could argue.

As I waited in line at the deli counter behind a man engaged in a lengthy discussion with his wife on the merits of ciabatta bread versus a bagel as a sandwich foundation, my phone pinged with a text from Gabe.

Got time for a quick coffee? I've got a half hour before court.

Sorry. I'm having a late lunch with Coop.

Chinese tonight with me and Dominic?

I almost said no, because I wanted to do some more thinking, I had more calls to make, and I wanted to catch up with Miguel. On the other hand, Gabe had been busy prepping for a trial, and we hadn't seen each other for a few days. I hadn't seen Dominic in longer than that.

Six all right?

See you then.

By the time I'd finished texting, the couple ahead had completed their purchase. I gave my order and took our drinks back to the table to wait for Coop. The Elite features rickety tables, uncomfortable small chairs, slanting wooden floors, and by way of decor, a random scattering of sad-looking artificial ferns in metal pots. Still, it's a favorite eating spot in the area. That's because the owner, Clara Schimelman, is a master in the kitchen. Her sandwiches and soups are delicious, and her pastries so good that they're usually sold out by mid-morning. She's a full-bodied woman in her sixties who serves up a steady stream of local gossip and free advice along with her food. She still hasn't lost her German accent despite coming up on 40 years in Himmel, but she loves tossing slang, often outdated, into her conversation.

"I bring this to you myself, because I don't see you for a while. Where is Gabe?" she added as she put the sandwiches down on the table.

Mrs. Schimelman and Gabe have a not-very-secret romance fueled by his love of her pumpkin walnut cookies, and her delight in his enjoyment.

"He's in court today. I'm meeting Coop for lunch."

"Oh, yah. I should know by the sandwich. He was here with Kristin yesterday. Hey, do you know when it is happening with them? It should be soon, I think."

"What should be soon?"

"You know, the ring."

"You think they're getting engaged?"

"I am shipping them so hard. They are good together, would make nice babies. You don't think so?"

"Well, it's just—aren't you kind of getting ahead of things? I mean they haven't even been seeing each other for a year yet."

She shook her head.

"Not everybody likes to go so slow as you and Gabe. You know how the song says. Love comes, you get married."

She laughed, then noticed my expression. "What's the matter, you don't like her?"

"No, no, I like Kristin. She's a much better match for Coop than Rebecca was. I just hate to see him rushing into anything again."

"He's not rushing. You, you're dragging the feet. What do you wait for? Don't you want a nice family? Gabe, he's a good man, and Dominic? Such a little *knuddelmaus*, I think—"

"Mrs. Schimelman, I feel bad. I thought I was your cute little mouse," Coop said.

Mrs. Schimelman turned, laughing, and flapped the white towel she always carries over her shoulder at him.

"You! You been no little anything since you was in middle school," she said. "But, still cute. Kristin thinks so, yah?"

"You'd have to ask her," he said with a smile and sat down. "That roast beef sandwich looks great."

"Is great," she said with justified complacence. Mrs. Schimelman owns her culinary excellence with no false modesty. "Even better, I make kringle today. It's totally lit! I got to get back. I'm training a new one in the kitchen. Good to see you both! I send Wayne over with your kringle, Coop."

She patted him on the arm. Then to me she said, "You think about it. You wait too long, someone else gonna get him."

25

"What's that about?" Coop asked.

"Nothing. Didn't you want to talk about the Crawford case?"

I wasn't eager to have Coop read me out for accepting Adam's request. But I was even less inclined to discuss Mrs. Schimelman's advice on romance with him.

"I do. Rhonda Crawford was pretty unhappy when she called me after you left her."

"Oh? What did she say I said?" I asked, stalling while I decided how much to tell him.

"She said that you're trying to muddy the waters. That if I think I can cover up my incompetence as a sheriff by hiding behind your newspaper's biased coverage, I'm mistaken."

"Hmm." I took a large bite of my Reuben and used the chewing time to settle on my answer.

"Leah, I know you feel some kind of ownership because you were with Charlie when Bryan Crawford was found, but I thought I was clear. You can't be part of this investigation. It's way outside the parameters of the job shadowing you pitched to me."

"I know that, and I'm not trying to be part of your investigation. I'm doing my own."

"Oh, and that makes it so much better?"

He shook his head and ran his hand through his dark hair in a familiar gesture of frustration. He then continued in the controlled, reasonable voice he uses when he's trying not to lose his temper.

"Look, it doesn't matter if you're doing it on your own or not. I still spent my morning taking calls from Rhonda Crawford and the district attorney. Yes, she called him, too. You stirred something up. What are you doing? And why are you doing it?"

"What I'm doing is just asking a few questions to help out a friend. Adam Harrison, specifically. He's worried that his mother is going to be arrested for Bryan Crawford's murder. Is she?"

"I'm not going to discuss this case with you. I'm serious."

"Fair enough. But don't expect me to discuss my case with you, either."

"You don't have a case. You have a kid who's worried about his mom, and maybe he should be. But you've got no standing to be involved in asking anybody anything."

He frowned at me and his voice was stern, as though he were admonishing a troublesome rookie.

"I don't need standing and I'm not claiming any. I can ask anyone anything I like, just like any other citizen. No one has to answer. I get that you're the sheriff—the top dog, the big boss, if you will. But as long as I'm not doing anything illegal, you're not *my* boss. Eat some of your sandwich. I think you're hangry. And stop yelling at me."

"I'm not yelling at you."

It was true, he hadn't yelled in the traditional sense of raising your voice and shouting. Coop's version of yelling, however, is an emphatic way of speaking that conveys the emotion behind yelling even better than the real thing does.

I didn't say anything, just took another bite of my Reuben and stared at him. He took a bite of his roast beef and returned my steady gaze. We continued eating and locking eyes for a while without speaking, like gunfighters waiting to draw. Finally Coop put his roast beef down and spoke in a conciliatory tone.

"I'm sorry. I'm not trying to be your boss. I pity the person who does. We've kind of hit a wall with the investigation. Getting an earful from

Rhonda Crawford and Cliff this morning didn't improve my temper any, I guess. Now, would you please tell me how exactly you're trying to help Adam Harrison, and help me understand why you don't trust my office to get to the truth?"

"I give you eight points for that apology. I have to take two points off for your passive-aggressive assertion that me asking questions means I don't trust your office. Now, my turn. I'm sorry that my visit to Rhonda this morning got her and Cliff so riled up. For the record, I do trust you and your office to investigate the murder. But I'm going to flip that around. Don't you trust me? Don't you know that if I find anything, I'll share it?"

I ignored his raised eyebrow.

"I'm not doing this because I think Ross can't. I'm doing it because Adam asked me to, and because I know, and you know too, even if you don't want to admit it, that sometimes people will say things to me they won't say to a cop. And if something I hear gives me an idea, or I think of a different angle on something, you don't want me to ignore it, do you?"

"No, of course not. But—"

"I know what you're going to say. You're a cop, and I'm not. It's your job, not mine, to investigate crime. But sometimes it *is* my job to ask questions. Bottom line, we're both trying to get to the truth."

"Leah, things are a little different from when I was just one guy in a police department. I'm the sheriff now. I'm responsible for the whole office and for its reputation. I told you before, morale isn't great. I'm trying to build a good team." He stopped talking while he took another bite. When he started again, he was very serious.

"There are some holdovers in the office who were pretty happy with Art Lamey in charge. They're pretty unhappy now that I am. They like to stir things up. I want to see if I can turn them around. To do that, I need to keep everyone in line and keep all of us moving forward. What I don't need is Rhonda Crawford running to *GO News* with stories about me leaking to the *Times*, or giving anyone the inside track, or ignoring facts because a friend is pushing a different theory. I'm doing the best I can to steer things in the right direction. It would be easier if I didn't have to steer around you, too."

"Coop, I hear you. I'm sorry some asshats are giving you grief. I don't want to get in your way. If you let me know which direction you're going, it would be easier to stay out of your lane. Can you at least tell me if you think Rhonda's insulin theory has any legs?"

"She told you about that?"

"I hate to break it to you, but I think she's probably telling everyone. Connie confirmed, off the record, that Timmins told her to send samples in for additional testing. Do you expect anything to turn up?"

"No, I don't. Rachelle—or anyone—putting poison in Bryan's insulin is pretty out there as a crime theory. But at the same time the missing bottle is a loose end that bothers me as much as it does Charlie. We checked out Rhonda's story. The pharmacy records show that she picked up a three-pack of insulin for her brother on Tuesday of the week he died, like she said. The pharmacist even remembered her mentioning that Bryan had broken a bottle and that he was on his last one, with no backup. That means there should have been four bottles of insulin in the house—one open on the counter, and three new in the fridge—when Bryan died. But there was just the open bottle on the counter, and the two in the refrigerator. So, where's the other bottle? I don't think the missing bottle is a case maker or breaker, but like I said, it's a loose end. And it's not the only one related to Rachelle."

"Oh? What else? She's got a solid alibi. She was hours away all weekend."

"Was she?"

"Wait, you don't think she was? Why?"

"Nope. That's all I'm giving you, and it's more than I should have. I told you, we hit a wall. If you find a crack in it, let me know."

26

When I got back home after lunch, I stopped in the office to say hi to my mother. I found her in the conference room, deep in discussion with two of her friends, Donna Record and Ann Lynn Bailey. Donna's house was just up the street from ours in my growing-up years. I don't know Ann Lynn as well.

"Hey, ladies, what's going on? It looks like you're plotting something," I said, gesturing to the paper-strewn table. "Mom, you're not planning a coup to overthrow Richard, are you? You know how the last one went."

Richard Whitlock is the autocratic president of the Himmel Community Players board. His claim to knowledge about all things theater is the year he spent as a production assistant on *The Dukes of Hazzard*. Some members defer to his judgment based on that. My mother does not.

"Only a minor one. We're planning the annual awards dinner without his input," she said.

"We want to have it all organized so that we don't have three hours of debate over what the starter should be," Donna said.

"Where are you having it?"

"At Ariana's," Ann Lynn said, looking up from the needlepoint she was working on—a colorful likeness of a male and female cardinal on a snow-laden evergreen branch.

"That's stunning," I said as I leaned over the table to see it better.

"Thank you!" Her blue-green eyes flashed with pleasure at the compli-ment. "It's coming together nicely, I think."

"Oh, Ann Lynn," Donna said, "all of your needlepoint is just lovely. I wish I had your talent. Leah, I hope we'll see you and Gabe at the dinner."

"You can count on it. But party planning isn't my strong point, so I'll leave you to it. It was nice to see you both. Mom, I'll catch you later."

"Oh, stay just a minute, can't you? I haven't seen you in so long, and Carol told us that you're going to be writing fiction now. I'd love to hear about it. You can finish these off for us," Donna said as she pushed a plate holding two chocolate chip cookies toward me.

She smiled with a warmth that reached her soft brown eyes and I couldn't refuse. Besides, she had cookies. I sat down and updated them on the turn my writing career was taking.

"Oh, I think you'll be very good at that, Leah," Donna said. It's nice to have a few unconditional cheerleaders in your life.

"I agree with Donna," Ann Lynn said, "but won't you miss the investiga-tive part of your work?"

"Good question. I don't know. However, I think I might like being in charge of a murder—figuratively speaking. That way I can choose the villain I want, and make things come out the way I think they should, instead of trailing along behind a killer whose motives I can't figure out and whose next moves I don't know."

"Speaking of murder, the paper hasn't had very much about Bryan Crawford's death, other than the story that the police have reopened the investigation. Can you give us just a little inside information?"

"Sorry, Ann Lynn. The sheriff's office is keeping a pretty tight lid on it, and I'm not covering it for the paper." I spoke truthfully, while omitting the fact that I was actually knee deep in it at the moment, though not for the *Himmel Times*.

"That's what I thought you'd say. *GO News* has had some stories, but I don't believe half of what they write. I don't want you to think I'm looking for gossip. It's not that," she said. Her cheeks had flushed a little and the heightened color went well with her silvery-gray hair.

I felt a rush of warm feeling for Ann Lynn at her dissing of *GO News*.

"No, of course I don't."

"But I knew Bryan when he was a little boy," she continued. "I was a good friend of his mother Helen's. In fact, their family lived next door to me in Omico."

"Really? You must have known Rhonda then too. She's pretty formidable."

"Rhonda was always a force, even when she was in school. There's a big age gap between her and Bryan. I remember when he was born. She'd spend hours wheeling him up and down the street in his stroller, for all the world like she was his mother. She and her mother Helen both adored him. They spoiled him more than a little, I'm afraid."

"What was he like? When Rhonda talks about him, she makes him sound perfect—handsome, smart, popular, everybody loved him."

"Well, I'd say somebody didn't, if he was murdered. Bryan was a good-looking boy, always polite. He had some charm when he wanted to use it. But he was self-centered. If he did something for someone else, it was always because it benefited him. He'd help Rhonda shovel the driveway if she was giving him a ride to school. But not if he didn't have school, but she had to get to work. But Rhonda never seemed to mind, and it wasn't any of my business."

"Did you know Bryan's first wife?"

"Tiffany? Yes, I did, but not well. In fact, I don't think I saw her more than a few times. Rhonda wasn't happy at all when Bryan married her. But I think Tiffany's parents put a lot of pressure on Bryan because she was pregnant."

"How long were they married?"

"I think about two years, give or take. She lost the baby the first year. Not long after that, her parents died in a car crash. A drunk driver hit them, such a tragedy. I remember because it was the same day my first grandchild was born. August 16, 1991. Tiffany was so young to lose both parents. Did you know them, Carol? Alice and Leo Tubbs? They owned a diner here in Himmel, on Oakland Avenue. I think it was called Leo's?"

My mother shook her head.

"Donna, you and Sam have lived here forever, did you know Bryan's first wife Tiffany, or her parents?" I asked.

"I didn't," she said. "But I do know Bryan's third wife. Does that count?"

"You know Rachelle? How?"

Donna is an outgoing person with a fairly wide circle of friends, but I couldn't see Rachelle being one of them.

"I take the yoga class she teaches at the community center."

"Do you like it? I was thinking about going," my mother said.

"Yes, I do. It's on Monday nights. In fact, I met Liz there when she first came to the area. That's how I learned about Ariana's. She stopped going after the first month or two, but I'm happy I stuck with it. I feel like it's helped my arthritis quite a lot," Donna said.

"I need to do something," Ann Lynn said. "My knees are starting to bother me, and I don't want to go the surgery route if I don't have to. Do you have to be able to bend like a pretzel?"

"No, it's very gentle," Donna said. "You just do as much as you can do and gradually you can do more and more. Rachelle, of course, is able to get into all kinds of poses, but maybe I could too if I were 30 years younger."

The conversation was quickly moving into areas that were of limited interest to me. The cookies were both gone, too.

"Okay, well, I do have to get going, and you have a dinner to plan. It was good to see you both, and thanks for the bit of Crawford family history, Ann Lynn. I'll catch up with you later, Mom."

27

As I left the conference room, a voice shouted from the newsroom, "Leah, do you have a minute?"

Maggie McConnell, a veteran journalist, left a retirement that bored her to tears to take on the editor's job at the *Times*. She's a no-nonsense woman with a low tolerance for me reporting without a license, as it were. I could tell from her tone that word must have reached her that I was poking around in Bryan Crawford's death.

As I passed through the newsroom, I waved at Troy and Allie, but I didn't stop to chat. Maggie in a mood is not to be trifled with.

"Something you want to tell me?" she asked.

The way she shoved her glasses up on top of her thick gray bob told me she wasn't pleased. Maggie can communicate a lot with the placement of her glasses.

"Like what?" I asked, assuming a mask of innocence as I sat down in the chair opposite her.

"Like that you're the newest reporter on the Bryan Crawford story? At least that's what Cliff Timmins seems to think. He called me today. Imagine my surprise when he accused you of harassing witnesses in an ongoing investigation. He wasn't very impressed with my management skills when I told him I had no idea what he was talking about. What's going on, Leah?

I've got Troy on the story with Miguel backing him up. Don't you think they're up to the job? Or is it that you think I'm not up to making assignments?"

"Maggie, I'm just doing a favor for Bryan Crawford's stepson, Adam Harrison. I told him I'd look into things, a little. He's pretty worried that his mother is going to be arrested."

"Is she?"

"It's not looking good."

"Leah, when I took this job, we agreed that if you decided you needed to flex your reporting muscles, we'd talk about it first."

"You're right, you're right, Maggie. But I'm not reporting on this. I've been very clear on that with everyone I've talked to. But I know who ran to Cliffie to complain, because she called Coop, too. Rhonda Crawford, right?"

She nodded.

"Me stammering around like an idiot because I don't know what you're up to isn't my idea of fun. I need to know what's going on in my own newsroom!"

"I apologize. I was going to tell you, but I jumped right into it first thing this morning, and I've been going at it all day."

"Did you pick up on anything yet?"

"Not anything we can use. Everything I have is off the record. Rachelle Crawford has the strongest motive, but her alibi is strong. Still, Ross keeps coming back to her, and yesterday he had her in for questioning at the office."

"That means the cops have something, but they can't prove it yet," she said. I could see that her interest in the story was outweighing her irritation at my lack of communication. "Do you know what Charlie's theory is?"

"No. I haven't talked to him yet. I'm pretty sure he won't tell me anything anyway. To hear Rhonda, the answer is crystal clear. She's all in on Rachelle. She's even doubled down and tossed in a poison theory. She threw me out when I didn't buy into it."

"Wait, there's a poison angle?"

I told her Rhonda's idea.

"Huh. Sounds pretty far-fetched."

"Yeah, the medical examiner agrees, but Cliff insisted on having additional tests run. How's Troy doing on the story? Will anyone talk? Connie said Coop and Cliff are the only ones authorized to comment."

"He's trying, but they're not giving out much. Rhonda won't take his calls. How did you get her to talk?"

"She wasn't very willing, but then I asked her to talk about Bryan and she couldn't resist. She probably won't talk to Troy because she's saving herself for Spencer Karr and his shady publication. He advised her not to talk to the *Times,* because we're too biased. I guess I confirmed it for her when I didn't jump on the poison train."

"Bottom line, are the cops ready to make an arrest?"

"I don't know. Honest."

A half hour later I was sitting on my window seat, my knees pulled up in front of me, tapping my pencil against the yellow legal pad resting on them. I'd made a list of what I'd learned, now I needed to decide on next steps.

Mitch, Bryan's former partner, was high on the list. It didn't seem likely that he'd wait 10 years to get even with him, but there was that whole "Revenge is a dish best served cold" idea. A face-to-face interview with him would be best, although first I'd have to find him.

Then there was Stephanie, Bryan's daughter. In a rare show of unity, both Rachelle and Rhonda had pegged her as entitled and selfish. Stephanie warranted some scrutiny. And maybe her mother, Bryan's second wife, did too. I added Jackie Crawford to my list, and Tiffany the first wife, too.

My phone rang.

"Hi, Marty. You must be telepathic. I was going to call you. But you go first. What's up?" I asked.

"Leah, hey there. You got a minute?"

Marty owns the A-1 Insurance Agency, which he'd purchased years ago from my grandfather. I always enjoy hearing the northern Wisconsin accent he had acquired growing up in Ashland and never surrendered.

"Well, I was just goin' over your file, and I see here that you don't have any life insurance through us. Do you have it through your paper there?"

"No. I don't have any life insurance at all. I don't feel like I need it. I'm not married, I don't have kids. Besides, I don't have any plans to die soon. Maybe never, I haven't decided on that yet."

"You could name your mom as a beneficiary. If you died, God forbid, even term insurance would be a nice payout for her. You could rest easy knowin' she'd have a little financial security even with you not there to take care of her."

"See, Marty, now you just gave me another reason not to buy a policy. I'm pretty sure I don't want to be worth more dead than alive to my mother. That could put me in real jeopardy."

"You're always kiddin' around, Leah. But insurance isn't just something for when you die."

"How's that? Isn't it just a big bet with the insurance company? I bet I'm going to die, and they bet I'm not. I pay them premiums for 30 years. If I'm still alive, they win because the policy's done, they got all my money, and they didn't have to give me anything."

"Hey, now, if you're still alive, I'd say you're the winner, right? But okay, I'm not talkin' about term insurance. You should think about a whole life policy. That's a different ball game. You pay into that—at your age the premium's gonna be pretty low—then twenty, thirty years from now, you got a real nice nest egg you can cash in on."

"Don't I have to die first?"

"Nah. Once you get some equity in it, you can borrow against it. Or you could cash it in. You could even hang onto it and turn it into an annuity, so you got a regular income from it."

"I don't know, Marty. I don't have a lot of extra cash for premiums lying around right now. Maybe later—"

Sensing he was losing the battle, he made a last pitch.

"The beauty, Leah, is you get two for one. It's an investment *plus* it's a death benefit. I always tell my lady clients, if they have a divorce situation, 'You make sure your attorney gets you ownership of your husband's whole life policy.' "

"Why's that, Marty?"

"Because it's gonna pay out for them either in cash value, or the death benefit if their ex dies. It's a solid win. A whole life policy will give you some real security, Leah."

I had let Marty ramble on about insurance not because I was interested, but to ease into why I wanted to talk to him. But I didn't want to give him false hope of a sale.

"Tell you what, Marty, if I ever get married again, I'll take out a gigantic policy on my husband. Then when we get divorced, which experience says is likely, I'll be sure and keep the policy."

"There you go, kiddin' again. I'm not tryin' to hard sell you here. I'm just planting a seed. Now, what were you gonna call me about? Are you thinkin' about upping the deductible on your car insurance? I had a couple clients do that, and ... "

"No, it's not an insurance question, it's something else entirely. You're still head of the Sports Boosters fundraising committee, right?"

"Sure am."

"I heard that the big prize at your raffle was a weekend at a bed and breakfast up north, is that right?"

"Yah, it was. We did real good with the raffle. We had a lotta nice prizes besides the bed and breakfast. Tri-Town Trailers give us a trailer that can haul two snow machines, that was a big draw. Then we had a nice little electric snowblower, had an automatic start, real nice for a single lady. Davina Markham won it, if I remember right."

"Those do sound like good prizes. But I think Mom would be interested in centering a fundraiser for the Community Players around a bed and breakfast weekend, you know, maybe tie it in with a play they do in the fall. Do you think they'd be willing to donate a weekend again?"

"Arlene's sister fixed it up with a cousin of theirs up Abbotsford way. She and her husband bought an old house a few years ago, turned it into a B&B. They gave us the weekend prize to kind of spread the word about it. And they can write it off as advertising. It couldn't hurt to ask them. I got their card here somewhere. Hold on a sec."

I waited, hearing the sound of drawers opening and closing and papers shuffling.

"Okay, here it is. It's called the Beale House Inn. Owners' names are Kelly and Robert Winston. Want the number?"

"Do they have a website? I'd like to see some photos."

"Sure do, it's www.BHinn.com."

"Got it. Hey, who won the weekend? I'd like to check and see if they enjoyed it."

"That was John Pilarski. But I don't know if they used it yet. I saw Jennifer a couple weeks ago, and I kinda put my foot in it. I asked if she liked the B&B weekend, but she didn't seem to know anything about it. I think John was planning to surprise her and I spoiled it. But I haven't seen either of them since, so I don't know."

"Okay, well, I'll dance around it delicately. Thanks, Marty."

"You're welcome. And you think about that insurance seed I planted, Leah."

"Will do."

28

I was on my laptop when Gabe called. I looked at my watch. 5:45. Hell's bells, I'd forgotten I promised to be there for dinner at 6.

"Hi, Gabe. I—"

"You haven't left yet, have you?"

"Uh, no, actually I—"

"Good, I'm glad I caught you. Dom can't find Barnacle's favorite ball. He thinks it might be under your sofa. Would you take a look and if it is, bring it with you?"

"Sure. See you soon."

That conversation had turned in my favor for a change. I'd been about to apologize for forgetting, but thanks to Barnacle, I didn't have to. I knelt down for a look under the sofa and there at home among the dust bunnies was Barnacle's well-chewed red ball. I scooped it up, grabbed my phone and my purse, and headed out.

I was calling Miguel as I went through the back door when his yellow Mini Cooper pulled into the parking lot.

"Where are you going? I thought we were going to catch up."

"I can't. I'm sorry. I forgot I told Gabe I'd have Chinese with him and Dominic tonight. But Dom will be in bed by 8. Can you come over then? I have news on the Jennifer front."

"I'll be there."

———————————

"But, Dad, I don't see why Barnacle can't come to school with me, just for one time."

Dominic, Gabe, and I were sitting on the living room sofa, comfortably full from a shared meal of egg rolls, sweet and sour chicken, and fortune cookies. Dominic was making his third try at pitching a take-your-dog-to-school-day idea to Gabe.

"Dom, no. You can ask me a hundred times and I'll still say no. It's not fair to Mrs. McCarthy to expect her to teach a class of kindergartners and Barnacle, too."

"Oliver Jordan's dog Jedi comes with him every day. It's not fair if Barnacle can't come."

"Jedi is a service dog and he's specially trained to help Oliver."

"I know, Dad, but I'm specially training Barnacle. Watch. Barnacle, go on, boy, get my backpack! You can do it!"

In response Barnacle opened one eye, raised his head, then laid it back down.

"He's just learning, Dad," Dominic said, before Gabe could comment.

"It looks like he's got a pretty long way to go. Now, come on, Dominic, I think we've discussed this enough. The school rule is no pets unless they're service dogs, and Barnacle isn't."

Dominic's eyebrows came down in a frown of disappointment, and his dark brown eyes looked reproachfully at his father. But he is a boy after my own heart. He thought for a moment, then tried a new tack.

"Okay, but Dad, you're a lawyer, right?"

"Yes," Gabe said.

"Well, Claudia DeLuca told me that her dad said lawyers fix things for people who break the rules. So, I could break the school rule and bring Barnacle—just once, I promise—and then you could fix it!" He finished on such a note of optimism that I almost laughed.

I glanced over at Gabe and saw he was having trouble keeping a straight face, too.

"That's not how it works, Dom. I help people who make mistakes that get them into trouble. But if someone deliberately breaks the rules, I don't fix it for them. They have to face the consequences. Now go get ready for bed or there won't be time for the next chapter of *Charlie and the Chocolate Factory*."

Dominic sighed as he left the room, and I heard him mutter under his breath what sounded like "I still don't think it's fair."

That's what I would have been muttering, anyway.

"Feel like a Jameson after Dominic's in bed?"

"I do, but I can't. Miguel's stopping by at 8, plus I have some work I need to get done."

"For your new series? I thought you were still in the thinking stages."

"No, that's on the back burner for now. I'm working on a couple of other things."

I filled him in first on Jennifer's situation.

"Poor Jen. I hope she's wrong," he said. "I like John. I can't see how he could do something like that to her, and to their kids."

"Me neither, but it's looking like she's probably right. I think Miguel and I are taking a road trip on Thursday. I want to find out for sure if John used the weekend at the B&B with a lady friend. It's game over if he did. But that's only part of what I've got going on."

I could hear Dominic in his room playing with his Legos instead of getting ready for bed, and I knew Gabe would have to take action soon, so I kept the recap of my inquiries into Bryan Crawford's death succinct. The part Gabe focused on surprised me.

"So, Rhonda's idea is that Rachelle put some kind of poison into Bryan's insulin, then threw the bottle away and replaced it with another one to keep anyone from finding out. Is that right?"

"Yes."

"Okay. What if the killer didn't add something to the insulin, what if he took something away?"

"I'm not following."

"I worked with a good detective once, old-school guy, kind of like Charlie Ross. He went by instinct as much as evidence. But you can't prosecute on instinct. The case he was trying to build was against a husband with a very wealthy wife, and a mistress. The wife was a Type 1 diabetic, completely insulin dependent like Bryan. One day when he was away on business, his stepdaughter came home unexpectedly and found her mother unconscious. She was near death from DKA, but the doctors brought her around. She swore that she hadn't missed an injection, but she'd started feeling unwell. She checked her blood sugar, saw it was elevated, took a dose to correct it, but it was still high. She took more insulin. She couldn't remember what happened after that until she woke up in the hospital."

"What did happen?"

"The daughter told the cops that her stepfather was having an affair, her mother knew it, and planned to divorce him. The daughter insisted that he had tampered with her mother's insulin and tried to kill her. But by the time the cops investigated, the insulin bottle she'd been using was gone. The husband said he accidentally broke it and threw it away."

"Whoa. That sounds just like the Bryan Crawford situation. Did your old-school detective get the goods on the husband?"

"Yes and no. We got a conviction on attempted murder, but not because of the evidence they found. There wasn't anything to find, because the husband hadn't put anything into the insulin. Instead, he took the insulin out and replaced it with water."

"So, when the woman thought she was injecting herself with insulin, she was just shooting water into herself?"

"Yep. Jerry—that was the name of the cop—he wouldn't let go. He pressured the mistress and she finally flipped on her boyfriend. Got him on tape admitting it too. But it was slick. No one would have known, if the daughter hadn't come home unexpectedly."

I was quiet as I ran through the possibilities in my mind. It could've worked basically the same with Bryan. The killer replaces Bryan's insulin with water, which is colorless and the same consistency as insulin. Bryan takes his injection. Doesn't feel well later. Tests his glucose levels. Takes a corrective dose of insulin. It's futile, because he's injecting himself with water. By the time he gets in the sauna, he's already on his way to DKA. All the killer had to do for clean-up was throw away the bottle and replace it with one containing insulin. It was perfect.

"Except for the video of the locked door."

"What?"

"Did I say that out loud? Gabe, you just made the missing bottle make a whole lot of sense. No wonder you're my favorite mister."

"Favorite among many?" he asked with a smile.

"Nope, favorite beyond compare," I said as I leaned over to kiss him.

"Eww. Mushy stuff. Don't look, Barnacle."

Dominic stood in the doorway in his Spiderman pajamas grinning at us, a small white speck of toothpaste in the corner of his mouth—evidence that he'd obeyed the teeth brushing order.

"Mushy, eh? I'll give you mushy," Gabe said. He jumped off the couch and swept Dom up in his arms and planted a loud kiss on his cheek.

I stood while they were both laughing and said, "I've got to go, guys. Gabe, thanks for cracking the case of the missing vial. Dominic, I'll see you later."

29

"I am exhausted. I'm getting too old for a marathon like this, Miguel. Running around all day, and then hunching over a computer for an hour. Yes, right over my left shoulder blade, that's the spot."

I leaned over the kitchen bar to give Miguel better access as his fingers massaged a knot out of my shoulder. I felt the blessed relief of a tense muscle releasing.

"You know, you're wasting your time in journalism. You could charge a hundred dollars an hour as Magic Miguel the Marvelous Massage Therapist. Where did you learn to do that?" I asked as I turned to face him and moved my now pain-free shoulders up and down.

"My friend Amanda is a masseur. She taught me. But *chica,* why are you so uptight? Tell your Uncle Miguel what's happening."

"You'd better sit down. It's a long story."

I handed him a Supper Club beer—a nice middle-of-the-road Wisconsin beverage that lives up to the Wisconsin-style praise on its label: *Supper Club. It's not bad.* I opened one for myself as well.

"I'm trying to do two different things to help two different people, and it's beginning to look like neither one of them is going to be happy with the results."

"Who else besides Jennifer?"

"Adam Harrison, Bryan Crawford's stepson."

"What? Talk to me."

I gave him the rundown on my conversation with Adam.

"I feel like I'm a lot closer to confirming Rachelle's guilt than I am to finding someone else who makes a good suspect. Now I'm down to talking to Stephanie the stepdaughter, Mitch the ex-partner, and the two ex-wives. I can get contact information on Jackie, the second wife, from her daughter, but I don't have a line on the first one, Tiffany. She doesn't seem to have an online presence at all, and I couldn't find anything on any of the people search sites either."

"Maybe she died."

"Well, that could be, I guess. She's not that old, late 40s, but you're right, people do die. I was thinking more name change, though. I'm going to check the divorce records at the Register of Deeds Office tomorrow. It's pretty common for a name change order to be in the file with everything else. Still, even if I find it, I'm not holding out too much hope that the first, or even the second, wife can give me much except some historical perspective on Bryan. The daughter, Stephanie, still holds some promise. And possibly the ex-partner Mitch."

"Does Charlie know that you're talking to people in his investigation?"

"He probably does now. I think Coop would've told him."

"He won't be happy."

"Well, then, I guess he can join the crowd. Jennifer won't be happy if we report back that John is having an affair. Coop isn't happy that I'm helping Adam. Adam won't be happy if I come up with something that makes his mother look more, not less, guilty. Rhonda Crawford is already mad. Maggie read me out for not letting her know what I was doing. Ross will just bring the we're-mad-at-Leah club to a nice even number. I probably should have told Adam and Jennifer no, but I didn't. And now, here we are."

"How can I help?"

"With the Adam thing, not at all. I told Maggie what I know, most of which is off the record and can't be used. You'll have to take your cues from her if she wants you to contact the people I talked to and dig into anything. But I could use your continued help on the Jennifer thing."

"You have it, *chica.* Every time."

"I count on that," I said, and ruffled up his perfect hair. It's an annoying habit I have that, fortunately, Miguel doesn't seem to mind.

"Now, let's see what we can find out about the Beale House Inn."

I opened my laptop and typed in the URL Marty had given me. The page opened to a slick website with a half-page photo of a three-story, yellow, Victorian-style house with white trim, stained glass windows, a tower on the left side, a large front porch, and an abundance of flower beds.

Miguel leaned over my shoulder as we looked through the description of the rooms, clicked on the photos, and checked out the guest reviews.

"Romantic weekend packages, private receptions in the ballroom, family gatherings, wine and cheese evenings, massage service, all the rooms come with a fireplace. Sounds very nice," I said.

"Did you see this part?" Miguel asked, pointing to the screen.

"Each room is supplied with a full cookie jar, replenished each afternoon," I read. "That does it. This place is perfect."

"What's our plan?"

"Let's do this. You call the Beale House Inn tomorrow. Say that our parents' thirty-fifth wedding anniversary is this fall, and we're checking out B&B accommodations for a family celebration. Ask if we can come and look the place over on Thursday."

"But how will that tell us if John was there?"

"Miguel, seriously? You're the king of small talk. We'll just chat about our friend John who told us about the place, see where that leads. We'll play it by ear."

"What time do you want to go?"

"I'd like to get started fairly early in the day. Let's say 8:30. I want to do a quick stop at the Grace and Blessings Retreat Center—Rachelle's alibi—too. It's up that way near Stratford. We can check it out and still get to the B&B by late morning. After we do our PI work, we'll find a nice place to get lunch before we drive home, and we'll be back by late afternoon. How does that sound?"

"Fun," he said with a wide smile. "We haven't had a road trip in a long time. But remember, my turn to pick the music."

"I know. But just on the way there. My choice on the way home. And for the love of all things holy, please do not make all your choices Taylor Swift. Or I'll make all of mine Backstreet Boys."

The next morning, I looked over the notes I'd been working on when Marty called, and made a to-do list for the day. Talk to Ross, get contact information for and hopefully connect with Bryan's first wife Tiffany and his second wife Jackie, follow up on Bryan's one-time partner Mitch.

To get the worst over with first, I called Ross.

When he didn't answer his cell phone, I didn't bother with a message. Instead, I tried the sheriff's office.

"Jen, hi. Hey, is Ross in?"

"No, he had an eye doctor appointment this morning. He's afraid he needs glasses. Be gentle with him."

"Aren't I always?"

"Do you want me to give him a message when he gets in?"

"No, I'll just try him again in a while. Thanks, Jen. Talk to you later."

"Wait, Leah?"

Damn. I'd hoped to get off without her bringing up John. But it was the main thing on her mind. Of course she was going to ask.

"Have you found anything out about . . . you know."

"I haven't, but I'm working on it. Promise."

"I don't mean to push you."

Before going on, she lowered her voice to just above a whisper to avoid being overheard in the office.

"It's the not knowing, that's all. He's still out of town. I'm actually glad. If I don't see him, I can pretend things are fine, like they used to be. And maybe they are, right? Maybe you'll find out that I've been worrying for nothing, and there's a simple explanation for everything, right?"

I resisted the impulse to give her empty reassurances. While it still *could* be true that John wasn't having an affair, that there was some legitimate reason for his midnight ride with an unknown woman, or his lie about giving away the B&B weekend, the odds weren't good.

Instead, I just said, "Jen, I'm so sorry you're going through this. I love you. I'll help you any way that I can."

"You can help me by finding the truth. That's what you can do."

"I will, Jen. I will."

30

I tried Ross again on his cell. This time he answered.

"Nash! I wanna talk to you. You home?"

"I thought you might, Ross. Yes."

"I'm just leavin' the eye doctor. I'll be there in 15 minutes."

As soon as he hung up, I ran down my front stairs and across the street to Wide Awake and Woke Cafe, a coffee shop that had opened a few months ago opposite my place. Ross is partial to their caramel macchiatos.

As I dashed up to the counter the bearded barista looked up from scrolling on his phone.

"Hey, Will," I said, still panting slightly from my dash across the street. "I need a medium caramel macchiato and a medium chai, STAT!"

"On it, Leah," he said, moving with practiced speed as he assembled ingredients. "What's the hurry, though? Kidnappers gonna shoot the hostage if you don't get their drinks back in five?"

"No, I have a special guest arriving shortly. I want to sweeten him up," I said.

While Will did his work, I tried out and rejected various ways to bring Ross up to speed without invoking a tirade. By the time he handed me the drinks, I had admitted to myself that nothing I said was going to make Ross happy.

"Good luck," Will said. "You know, the owner's wife is starting a yoga studio upstairs. You might want to check it out. Looks like you could use a little chill in your life."

"Thanks, but no time for chill right now. See you."

"Whadda ya doin' tryin' to help Adam Harrison? Allie tried to run interference for him with me. I told her no."

Ross delivered the words at a level just below a shout. His face was red, and his small mustard-brown eyes got even smaller as he glared at me.

"Well, I told her yes. Is Adam right to be worried? Are you going to arrest Rachelle Crawford?"

The caramel macchiato I had bought to sweeten his mood sat next to Ross, its temperature growing colder while his grew hotter.

"That is nothing I'm gonna talk about to you. Damn it, Nash. I don't need you pushin' yourself into this case, makin' things harder. Coop said you're not reporting on it, so you don't even have that for cover. All you got is your usual buttinsky ways!"

I was momentarily distracted by his use of an insult that I was familiar with from old movies. However, I hadn't ever heard the word "buttinsky" used in real life. I disputed the sentiment, but I liked the way the word sounded. I filed it away for my own future use.

"Ross, what exactly have I done that's made your job harder?"

"You pissed off Rhonda Crawford, for one thing, and she got on the phone to Cliff Timmins and now he's takin' a 'personal interest' in the case to make her feel better. So, now I gotta answer to him, too. And you stirred up things with Rachelle Crawford, and now she's lawyered up."

"Wait a minute, that's not fair. She got a lawyer because you kept coming back to her, and then you brought her in for questioning. That was before I even talked to her. Why are you so focused on Rachelle? Is it just the money motive? She's not the only one who inherits. There's Rhonda, and Stephanie, too. Rachelle's alibi is pretty tight. Did you find a hole in it?"

"I told ya, I'm not answerin' anything about this case. And I don't like you goin' behind my back with my own daughter. I also don't like you makin' her think that I'm too dumb to find the right answers, but you can!"

"Ross, come on. Allie doesn't think that and neither do I. I'm just looking for something that you—"

"What? That I missed? That I'm too stupid to know is important unless you tell me?"

"No! And you might as well quit yelling at me, because I'm not going to stop asking questions. I'm looking for something that maybe a witness was too intimidated to tell you, or forgot, or that you didn't think to ask about. You're good at your job, but you're not perfect. Neither am I. That's why maybe we could help each other. I'm not competing against you, you know. And I do have a couple of things you might like to know."

He frowned and his lips were set in a thin line. He was either considering how to kill me and get away with it, or how useful information from me might be. Or possibly both.

He reached for his macchiato and took a sip, which I took as a good sign.

"Whadda ya got?"

I told him about Mitch, Bryan's unhappy former business partner, and I gave him the information that Stephanie and her father had had a major fight about money.

"Before you say anything, I know those aren't super strong leads, but aren't they worth looking at? Or did you already know about Mitch and about Stephanie's fight with her father?"

"Yes and no, but I'm not tellin' you which is which, so don't ask."

He took another drink. He didn't sound quite as ready to take my head off. I wondered which was news to him. Mitch seemed the most likely.

"All right, that's fine. Now, your turn. What's up with the key to the sauna? I know it was found and Rachelle gave it to you. Why do you keep asking about it? Come on, help your old partner out?" I tried for a slight joke to lighten him up, but it fell flat.

"Nope. You can do what you want. You're right. I can't stop you, unless you cross a line. But I don't have to like it, and I don't have to help you."

"Fine. But because I'm the bigger person in this conversation, I'm going to give you one more thing. It comes from Gabe, so maybe you'll be more impressed. It's about the missing insulin bottle. Do you want to know what it is? Or am I crossing another invisible line?"

"Go ahead, you're gonna anyway."

He listened intently as I told him about Gabe's prior experience with insulin as a murder weapon.

"It could be, right? Injecting water instead of insulin would mess with Bryan's glucose levels pretty bad. Depending on when the switch happened, he could've already been in serious trouble when he got in the sauna, but too confused to realize it."

"Could be," Ross said. "But if you think that takes the spotlight off Rachelle, you're wrong. She's the one with the easiest access to Crawford's insulin."

"But Ross, she's not the *only* one who had access. There's Rhonda, Stephanie, maybe, I don't know her movements, but you probably do. Heck, even the house cleaner could have switched things out. Or maybe Mitch had some way of doing it that we don't know about yet. Anyway, I've given you something to think about, haven't I?"

"If anybody did, I'd say it was Gabe. He's the one who came up with the insulin idea."

"Fine. Don't give me any credit. But can you give me Stephanie's contact information? I know you have it."

"Sorry. I'm not your personal 411. Get it from your friend Adam."

"Come on. You're right here, you're just being petty."

"And you're just bein' pushy. We're not on the same page here, and I don't think we're gonna be. I can't stop you from doing anything. But I don't have to be your informant either. And I'm tellin' you, Nash, if I get hauled into Coop's office again, 'cause he got raked over by Timmins, 'cause you barged in where you shouldn't be, and I—"

"All right. All right. I've got it. But I just want to say one more thing."

"You always do."

"Just this. I'm not fighting against you, Ross. I don't think you're wrong. I'd like you to be, because I feel bad for Adam—he's the only one in that family that seems like a decent person. But so far, Rachelle looks like the murderer most likely to me, too."

31

When I texted Adam for Stephanie's cell number, he gave me some even better information along with it. I'd been trying to work a round trip to Robley College into my day, but now I didn't have to. Stephanie was at the Crawfords' packing up some of her things. I could catch her there.

I wasn't sure how Rachelle would respond to a return visit from me, but as it turned out, I didn't need to worry about it. When I rang the bell, the house cleaner answered.

"Hi, Sheila, isn't it? We weren't formally introduced. I'm Leah Nash."

"I know. I'm sorry, Rachelle isn't here right now. I don't expect her back until late afternoon."

"I'm actually looking for Stephanie Crawford. I understand she's here packing today?"

"She's here, but she's not in the house right now. She's down at the creek, looking for a rock."

"A rock?"

"She needs it for a prop, she said, for a play or something."

"How do I get to the creek?"

"Follow the pavers to the sauna. Then just go straight to the woods and you'll see a gravel path. Stay on that and you'll wind up at the creek."

"All right, thank you."

Despite the overcast sky, the temperature was what passed for warm on a March Wisconsin day, fifty degrees. And at least it wasn't raining—for the moment.

As I walked the path to the creek, the smell of wet wood and decaying leaves was more reminiscent of fall than spring. But I heard a robin singing, and I spotted a couple of crocuses poking their heads up. I felt the lift in mood that signs of winter's end always bring. As I picked up on the sound of rushing water, the trail veered to the left. I stepped into a clearing that looked like the place where woodland fairies take their lunch breaks.

A fallen tree offered a natural sitting spot. A small footbridge linked one side of the creek to the other and would be a nice place to sit and dangle your feet above the creek.

Sitting near the edge of the bank was the gazebo Adam had mentioned as a place where he liked to sit and write. I walked over to look at it more closely.

"What are you doing?" The voice behind me made me jump. I turned and saw Stephanie Crawford.

"Hi. Did you materialize from thin air? This seems like the kind of place where magic might happen, doesn't it? I'm Leah Nash, by the way."

"I drove," she said flatly. Obviously, I hadn't charmed her with my whimsical comment. "You can't see it from here," she continued, "but the road is just past those trees." She pointed upstream in the direction from which she'd come. "I know who you are, but you didn't answer my question. What are you doing here?"

"Looking for you. Sheila said you were at the creek."

Tendrils of Stephanie's long shiny brown hair lifted gently in the slight breeze. Her light blue eyes looked at me with suspicion.

"Why are you looking for me?"

"Adam asked me for help."

"Adam? Help with what?"

"He's very worried that his mother is about to be arrested. He asked me to look around a little and see if I could find anything to keep that from happening."

"It's too bad for Adam, but it's pretty obvious that Rachelle killed my father."

"Why are you so certain?"

"Because she has the best reason. She didn't like being married to my dad, but she loved his money. She killed him to keep the money and get rid of him."

The "duh" at the end of her statement was unspoken but clear.

"What makes you think she didn't like being married to Bryan?"

"Anyone could see that Rachelle was miserable and bored out of her mind. Except maybe my father. He wasn't a noticing kind of person."

"Did Rachelle tell you she was unhappy?"

"As if. She didn't *tell* me anything, but I'm not blind. Rachelle was all happy, happy when they first got married. Just having access to all that money was a thrill, I guess. She shopped all she wanted, redecorated the house, took yoga classes, met her friends for wine and tapas. But six years into the marriage she'd done the house over twice, started teaching yoga, landscaped the grounds, and she didn't know what else to do."

"So, she didn't talk to your father about that, she decided it was easier to kill him?"

"No, she tried to get him to do more 'cultural' things with her," Stephanie said, making air quotes around the word and injecting a note of sarcasm. "Rachelle is just another bougie who wants to be upscale. My dad had the money but not the class. She wanted him to take ballroom dance classes, to eat in nice restaurants, to travel to Europe. My dad wanted to spend time at his hunting cabin, eat fish boil at the Lone Pine Restaurant, and go to the Harley-Davidson Museum in Milwaukee. Rachelle was tired of my dad, but not the money. She'd signed the prenup, though, and there was no getting around that. The same thing happened with my mother."

"But your mother didn't kill your dad."

"No. She had an affair, and Rhonda found out, and couldn't wait to tell my dad. He's the one who divorced her, and she got next to nothing. Rachelle didn't want that to happen to her. So, she killed him. It's just her bad luck there's video to prove it."

"The video proves someone killed your dad, not that the someone was Rachelle."

"Come on. No one else benefits like she does. Follow the money, isn't that the saying?"

"Money isn't the only motive. Some might say your mother Jackie had a good one. She spent sixteen years married to Bryan, then she got next to nothing out of the marriage. Revenge is a strong motivator."

"Maybe when it happened, but not now."

"How's that?"

"Two years ago, my mother married the perfect man. He has money, and there's no prenup involved. He's pretty old, like in his 70s or something. To him, my mom's like a hot young chick. And she knows how to work it. Rollie does whatever makes her happy. It's the reverse of being married to my dad. Now she's the one who calls the shots. They're on a river cruise in Portugal right now. They left the day before Bryan died. Even if she wanted to kill my father, she wasn't around to do it."

"Okay, that's a pretty good alibi. But what about you, Stephanie?"

"What about me?"

"Your life was upended when your parents got divorced. That had to be hard to take."

"It was. When I went to Omico High, my squad and I ruled that school. Then we moved to Appleton. I had to start over, and we had no money, and we lived in a dumpy duplex. I was pretty mad at my dad. He could've fought to keep me here with him, but he didn't. He even let nerdy Adam have my room. I had to stay in the guestroom that didn't even have its own bathroom when I came. It was pretty tough for a while."

"What made it un-tough?"

"My mother made me see things differently."

"Differently how?"

"She told me that 'acting like a pissy little bitch,' no matter how good my reason was, wouldn't get me anywhere with my dad. He held all the cards. She said that if I wanted more from him, I'd better start being nicer to him. I was partway there because I'm pretty—no brag, it's just a fact— and my dad liked pretty women. I just learned to turn on the sweet and stop the drama. Then, I got whatever I wanted."

"Until you told him you wanted $70,000 for drama school, right? I heard you were pretty mad at your father when he told you no. Of course, now that he's dead, you'll have lots of money to do whatever you like."

I was trying to goad her into losing her cool nonchalance, but it didn't work.

"You think I killed my dad? I suppose Rachelle—or my bitchy Aunt Rhonda—gave you that idea. Or did Adam? Yeah, my dad and I had a fight. And yeah, I was mad and we were barely speaking when he died. But the night my father was being locked in the sauna I was on stage in front of 200 people. I had nothing to do with it. You can read my reviews online to prove it. They were great, by the way."

She closed her eyes to savor the memory before she quoted one of them to me.

" 'Stephanie Crawford brings the sexiness of Marilyn Monroe and the acting chops of a young Meryl Streep to the role of Alicia in the Robley College Theater Department production of *A Hole in the World*.' "

"Nice."

"Isn't it? I got a standing ovation. I have a photo of it, want to see?" She had pulled her phone out as she spoke and now was holding it out to me.

"That must have been a thrill," I said as I glanced at it.

"Yes. Good alibi, too, isn't it? I've already been questioned by the cops, and they seem pretty satisfied with it."

It wasn't just a good alibi. It was a great one. I moved on.

"Why did you ask if Adam was the one who told me about your fight with your father?"

"He was there that Sunday at dinner. And Adam is, well, so extra, isn't he? Super intense. I think he was madder at my dad than I was. He has a crush on me, did you know that?"

"I had the impression he didn't like you."

"That's because I hurt his feelings. He came after me when I left the table crying. I ran down here, actually, to the gazebo. We sat on the bench inside, and he comforted me. I comforted him back. I don't think he had ever even kissed a girl before. He got all kinds of ideas. He kept texting me, and calling me at school, and he even sent me flowers. My roommate and I nearly died laughing. I had to check him, and he took it hard."

Poor Adam. The self-absorbed Stephanie was a bad choice for him. He should have gone for someone like Allie, but people so often don't pair off the way they should—or the way I think they should, anyway.

"Maybe Adam is the one who killed my dad. If Rachelle gets the money, he gets the money. But if she gets arrested for murder, she doesn't get anything and neither does he. Maybe that's why he wants you to find someone else to put the blame on."

"Do you really see Adam that way?"

"Everybody's got a dark side, right? Let me help you out here. It's not me. It's not my mother. And okay, it probably isn't Adam. But if it isn't the most likely person, Rachelle, how about the least likely?"

"Who would that be?"

"Rhonda, of course. 'Heaven has no rage like love to hatred turned,' right? That's from a play we did last year, *The Mourning Bride*. I didn't like it, but my part was good. Zara."

"Why would Rhonda's love for her brother turn to hate?"

"Why wouldn't it? He kept choosing other women instead of her. Like Norman Bates's mother in *Psycho*."

"Sounds like you've done some thinking about it."

She shrugged. "Listen, fun as this has been, I've got to go. I'm sure you do, too."

32

As I drove back to Himmel, I thought how odd it was that everyone with a motive to kill Bryan seemed to have not just a good alibi, but an airtight alibi.

Rachelle was hours away at a retreat. Stephanie was not only hours away, she was on stage in front of hundreds of people. Stephanie's mother, Bryan's second wife, was thousands of miles away on a cruise. Rhonda wasn't hours away, but she'd been sitting by the bedside of a friend's terminally ill husband.

"Wait a minute," I said out loud, talking to myself as is my way when I'm thinking things through alone. "If her friend's husband is terminally ill, he's probably on heavy pain medication. In which case, he wouldn't necessarily know if Rhonda had slipped away for a while."

I almost called Ross to ask him if that was the case because surely he would have checked out her alibi. Then, remembering how our conversation had ended, I decided it was best to give him a little longer to chill. I checked the time. 12:30. I wasn't going to make it back to town to pick up the divorce records from Bryan's first marriage. The Register of Deeds Office closes from 1 p.m. to 2 p.m. for lunch. I called Troy.

"Have you done the courthouse run yet?"

"I'm just walking in the door. Why?"

The *Times* runs police and court briefs weekly. They're just short paragraphs, with no-frills information on who took out a marriage license, or got divorced, or was cited for speeding, or any of dozens of other relatively minor infractions. We also list building permits, doing-business-as filings, and similar news of small-town interest. Though not very detailed, the news briefs provide the building blocks of speculation for many local coffee groups, and as a result are quite popular.

"I want you to stop by the Register of Deeds Office and get a copy of a divorce file for me. Make sure you get the full case file. You might have to sweet talk Mavis, because it's an old one and she'll have to go through the paper files to find it."

I gave him the date range for Bryan Crawford's first divorce, based on Ann Lynn Bailey's memory, and the names.

"I'll check in with you when I get back to the paper. Thanks, Troy."

Troy and I walked in from the parking lot at almost the same time.

"Did you get it?" I asked.

"Here you go," he said, handing me the manila file.

"Thanks. I need some reading material for my lunch break. Did Mavis give you a hard time?"

"No. I remind her of her grandson Micah, and she likes to talk about him. Now, I always ask her how Micah's Science Olympiad team is doing. We had to pay for the copies, but she gave me the file folder for free. Plus, a mini Kit Kat from her candy jar," he added.

Troy, with his freckles, glasses, and easy blushes, looks more like a high school journalism student than a full-time reporter—a fact that he's learning to work to his advantage.

"Ah. The fine art of cultivating sources. I love to see it, Troy. Pretty soon you'll have more confidential informants than Miguel."

"I'm trying. But I'm not having any luck at the sheriff's office on the Bryan Crawford murder."

"I probably haven't helped matters there. I've had a couple of, let's say, 'tense' conversations with Coop and Ross lately. Who's giving you grief?"

"No one, it's not that. The problem is that supposedly the only ones who can give out information are Sheriff Cooper and District Attorney Timmins. And they aren't giving out much. But somehow Andrea always seems to get a jump on me."

Andrea Novak had worked at the *Times* for a hot minute, but her shaky ethics and reckless reporting got her fired. Lucky for her, those are exactly the qualities *GO News* looks for in a reporter. Spencer Karr had scooped her up. Ever since, she's made it her mission to beat the *Times* by any means necessary.

"I hoped that the forced departure of her 'special friend' Art Lamey would dry up her inside source at the sheriff's office. She must have found a new one. Can you find out who? Maybe you can flip him and make him your source instead."

"I'm pretty sure I know who it is, but I think Andrea has more to offer him than I do. I saw Deputy Lawlor coming out of her apartment early this morning on my way in to work," Troy said, pushing his wire-rimmed glasses up on his nose.

"Drew Lawlor is her source? That makes sense. I saw him lurking outside Coop's office the day Rhonda Crawford burst in with the video news. Regardless of her charms, I think he's going to be pretty sad that Andrea lured him in with her siren song. His career is going to crash on the rocks when Coop and Ross find out."

"Are you going to tell them?"

"Heck yes. Though at the moment, neither one is in a mood to welcome me into the middle of their office politics. Not that they ever are, come to think of it. Which is sad, because I have so much to offer."

"Leah, are you working on this story, too? Is that why you need the Crawford divorce file from 30 years ago?"

"I could tell you, Troy, but then I'd have to kill you. I'm working on something for a friend, and most of it, maybe all of it, could turn into nothing. Don't despair. I have faith in you. You'll find a way to beat *GO News* before this story runs its course. Thanks again for the file."

I made a PB&J sandwich and sat at the bar in my kitchen eating it as I skimmed through the paperwork in the divorce file for Bryan and Tiffany Crawford. There wasn't that much. It was an uncontested divorce for a very short marriage with very few assets— a small checking account, an even smaller savings account, an insurance policy, two cars, a mortgaged house, and the real prize, Crawford Plumbing, Bryan's fledgling operation at the time.

Rhonda had gloated because Tiffany hadn't been savvy enough to insist on a stake in the business. But regardless of the money it would be worth now, it would have tied her forever to Rhonda and Bryan. Escaping that fate might have been the better choice for her. I flipped on through the legal forms, the original filing for divorce, the initial hearing, pre-trial conference, etc. Finally, there it was, the name change order.

I was so surprised by what I saw that I had to read it twice. Tiffany Tubbs Crawford had changed her name all right. Both her names, first and last. She was now, and had been for almost 30 years, Liz Moretti. Tiffany was Liz Moretti, the executive chef at Ariana's Restaurant.

I did a quick online search to make sure our local Liz Moretti was the Liz Moretti who had started life as Tiffany Tubbs. I found a photo of Tiffany in an online high school yearbook. She was petite and pretty in the style of both Rachelle and Stephanie—small features, large eyes, light brown hair bordering on blonde. In her current incarnation as Liz Moretti, Tiffany was more curvy than petite. She wore glasses. Her hair was darker, too. Thirty years can do that to a person, but the smile on her heart-shaped face was the same, wide and dimpled.

I put in a call to Ross.

33

"I got about two minutes, Nash. What's the big surprise you got?"

Ross sat across from me in the paper's conference room, his arms folded and a scowl on his face. When I had reached him, he had just left the district attorney's office, having been summoned there by Cliff Timmins. Obviously, it had not put him in a good mood.

"I didn't say it was a big surprise, I said it was an interesting piece of information."

"Okay, whatever. What is it?"

"I found Bryan's first wife. Tiffany Tubbs. Only she isn't Tiffany Tubbs anymore. When they got divorced, she changed her name—both names, first and last. Tiffany is Liz Moretti, the woman who's the chef at Ariana's. You know, you met her at Mom's birthday party."

"Yeah, so?"

"Ross, what's the matter with you? Tiffany/Liz is one of Bryan's wives, just like Rachelle and Jackie. FYI, I connected with Stephanie today, and I found out what I'm sure you already knew. That her mother was on a cruise the night Bryan got locked in the sauna, so she's out of the picture. But Liz turning out to be Tiffany could open another possibility at least, don't you think?"

"How do you figure? She left town almost thirty years ago. She never talked to Bryan Crawford again. She didn't reach out when she moved back. I can't see any possibilities there, Nash."

"Wait a minute. You already knew Liz was Tiffany, didn't you? You've already interviewed her, haven't you?"

"I told ya, I know how to do my job."

"Well?"

"Well, what?"

"What did she say? Why *did* she come back? And why didn't she come forward when her ex-husband was murdered?"

"I already said it. She didn't come forward because she didn't have anything useful to say."

"Still, just the fact that she comes back to the area, and then her ex-husband gets murdered . . . Come on, you have to admit that's at least a little intriguing."

"She's got no motive. Why would she kill an ex she hasn't even thought about for years?"

"But maybe she has. Maybe she lied to you. Why would she come back at all?"

Even as I said it, I couldn't quite reconcile the sunny, extroverted Liz I knew with someone who would nurture a dark dream of vengeance for decades.

"You're not convincin' me of anything except that maybe you got what it takes to write fiction, the way you make somethin' outta nothin'. The amateur in you is comin' out, Nash. I know you wanna help Adam out, and you probably wouldn't mind me bein' wrong about Rachelle, but I'm not."

He pushed away from the table then, signaling the conversation was over, and he stood to go.

I stood, too, buoyed up by a rising tide of irritation at him dismissing me as though I were an idiot for even suggesting Liz warranted investigation.

"You may be willing to give this a once-over-lightly because you're so sure you're the world's best, most professional detective, but I'm not. What's her alibi? Forget it. I know you won't tell me, if you even asked her. Did you? Or did you think you didn't need to, because you already locked on Rachelle as the killer? I'm going to see Liz and ask her myself. And if I do turn anything up, I may just take it to Cliff Timmins instead of you. I'm sure he'd like to know about any gaps in your investigation."

That was a low blow, but I'd had enough of Ross and his constant digs. He'd pushed me right to the edge. Apparently, I'd pushed him, too. His face was red, and he raised a finger and jabbed it at me as he shouted.

"I don't have to interview Liz, and I don't have to question her alibi. I know exactly where she was Friday night, and the whole damn weekend. She was with me! There! Are you satisfied now?"

I stared at Ross open-mouthed for what felt like a full minute before I summoned a response.

"Satisfied, Ross? Try shocked, stunned, stupefied, staggered—any of those will do. What do you mean you were with Liz Moretti all weekend?"

"Whadda ya think it means?" he asked, slightly less truculently, no doubt regretting what his outburst had revealed.

"You're dating Liz? What about Rita?"

"Rita? Who's Rita?"

"You know, Rita. The EMT who was flirting her heart out with you practically over Bryan Crawford's dead body. Allie asked me if you were seeing someone—because of the new clothes, the weight loss, your new fondness for music. You even started wearing aftershave. I thought it was Rita. But it was Liz? For how long? And why didn't you say anything?"

"I met her last Christmas. I ate at the restaurant one night and she stopped by the table. We got talkin' and I happened to stop in the next night and we just hit it off. So, we started—"

"Wait a minute. At Mom's surprise party, when Liz was teasing you, and you got all flustered, you were already smitten, weren't you? Seriously smitten. Why the big act like that was the first time you met?"

"Because I didn't wanna have this conversation. This is my business, Nash, and it's not funny to me. I don't need you or anybody else sayin' stupid stuff to me about my life or chit-chattin' about what I do on my own time. And I didn't say anything to Allie because I didn't know if it was gonna work out or not."

"I'm sorry, Ross. You're right. I don't think it's funny. It just surprised me, is all. I like Liz. I'm happy if you found someone you enjoy being with. But you might want to pick up the pace on breaking it to Allie. She already suspects, and now it's all going to come out with a bang."

"Whadda ya mean, come out?"

"Ross, you have to tell Coop you're dating someone connected with the murder. You should've told him from the beginning."

"I didn't know from the beginning. I knew Liz was divorced and that she came from around here a long time ago, but we didn't talk about the past that much. She only told me her story after we opened up the murder investigation. She didn't want to put me in a bad position."

"Ross, you *are* in a bad position. You do realize that, right?"

"I don't see why." The crossed-arms position had reappeared.

"Then take off your love blinders so you can see the whole picture. You're dating someone who's a witness at best, and a potential suspect at worst. That could compromise the whole investigation. How do you think *GO News* will play this, if Coop doesn't get out in front of it? I can see the headlines now: *Corruption in the Sheriff's Office; Lead in Murder Investigation Sleeping with Suspect,* and don't even get me started on what Cliff Timmins is going to say after Rhonda Crawford gets hold of this."

"Liz isn't a suspect," he said stubbornly. "She isn't even a witness. She doesn't know anything. She hasn't seen the guy in almost 30 years."

"But Ross, she was married to him, and she's back in the area. Practically in the Crawfords' backyard. Ariana's Restaurant is only about five miles from their place. She has to be formally interviewed, and not by you. Come on, you know that. It has to be part of the case record."

I was shocked that love had clouded his judgment so much that he was violating basic police procedure.

"I hear what you're sayin'."

He had uncrossed his arms and he leaned a little forward, holding his hands palms up in a conciliatory gesture as he spoke.

"But listen. I don't wanna get pulled from the case just because I know someone who used to know the victim a hundred years ago. The other thing is that Liz is tryin' to get financing to buy the restaurant. She's afraid her investors might get spooked if she gets dragged into a murder investigation. This is a dream for her. I don't wanna be the reason she loses it. Especially because she's got the perfect alibi. Me. I was right there at Ariana's on that Friday from six o'clock on, same as her, until closing. She was workin', I was eatin', and then I hung out at the bar until things settled down and we went upstairs to her place. Then we were together all night. Do you seriously think if there was one iota of a chance that Liz had anything to do with Crawford's murder that I'd hold back? You know me better than that."

I was shaking my head before he finished talking, something I hate when it's done to me. But I couldn't stop myself. Ross was pitching such a bad idea. Worse, he'd already committed to it and was living it.

"Ross, no. I can't even believe you're suggesting it. Liz being part of a murder investigation might hurt her plans, but Liz not being part of the investigation could end your career. You have to tell Coop, right away. You can't put him in this position just so you can be your girlfriend's knight in shining armor. I get that it sucks for Liz that this has to come out, but it has to. It just does."

He tried one last pitch.

"It's not just Liz. If I tell Coop now, then he's gonna take me off the case. I'm workin' somethin' and it's just startin' to gel in my mind. I want to close this out. I—"

"Ross. You know that's not realistic. You can't be on this anymore. Because you were with Liz that night, you're a witness too. You're Liz's alibi confirmation. Coop has to give it to Owen Fike."

"After all the times I gave you leeway, all the times I let you in where you shouldn't be, all the things I gave you because I trust you? I don't believe this. You won't even hear what I'm sayin. I suppose this is gonna be the next big story in your damn paper."

The force of his anger surprised me, but like the song says, when a man loves a woman . . .

"I'm sorry, Charlie. But if you don't go to Coop, I will."

"Then this is it, Nash. We're done!"

He said it like he meant it, and I felt awful that it might be true. Ross was very stubborn, and he was very mad. But he was also very wrong.

When Ross left, he was as angry at me as I'd seen him in a long, long time. In his mind, I had crossed a line. In my mind, he had.

"What's the matter, Leah? You look like you just lost your best friend."

My mother had come into the conference room carrying water bottles to put in the small fridge we keep there.

"Maybe not my best friend, but I think I just lost a good one. Ross."

She put the water on the table and sat down next to me.

"Charlie? What happened?"

I realized then that I'd been running hither and yon so much the past few days that we hadn't had a sustained, substantive conversation for days. I hadn't even followed up with her like I'd said I would the day before when I'd seen her briefly with Donna and Ann Lynn.

"I'm trying to help Adam Harrison, Rachelle Crawford's son. But things aren't working out so well."

I gave her a short synopsis about my commitment to help Adam and where it had led, and ended with my discovery about Liz.

"I don't know which surprises me more. That Charlie is dating Liz, or that Liz was married to Bryan Crawford," she said.

"Mom, he got so mad when I said he had to tell Coop. He went all kill-the-messenger on me and left. I don't know if he's going to tell Coop or not. And if he doesn't, I have to."

"This is not going to be easy on anyone—Charlie, Coop, Liz, you. I hope Charlie doesn't do anything rash, like resign."

"Congrats, Mom. You just came up with the one bad outcome I hadn't thought of."

"Sorry. What are you going to do now?"

"I guess go talk to Liz. I need to get confirmation from her, though I have no doubt she's Tiffany Tubbs. Also, I'm sure she doesn't realize what a bad decision it was for Ross to stay quiet about this. Maybe once she does, she can convince him to talk to Coop before I have to."

34

I pulled into the parking lot at Ariana's at 5:30, a half hour before the restaurant's 6 p.m. opening time. I knew it wouldn't start to get busy until 7, especially on a Tuesday. I hoped Liz would have time to talk. I didn't want to wait on this conversation.

I went through the kitchen entrance and into a scene of controlled chaos. People were washing dishes, tending pots on the stove, prepping vegetables, working on the cold line making salads. Everyone seemed to be shouting to be heard above the din of banging pots, running water, and quick-chopping knives. I spotted Liz in conversation at the far end of the kitchen. She looked at me in surprise as I approached, but she smiled. That had to mean that she hadn't talked to Ross yet. I crossed my fingers that it was because Ross was with Coop, telling him the whole story.

"Leah, hi. Can you hang on just a minute?"

"Sure."

She turned back to finish her conversation.

"Trust me, Tara, you've got this. I wouldn't put you on as prep cook if you weren't ready. Take those first-time nerves and turn them into energy. You're going to be great."

"I will, Liz. Thank you. I appreciate the chance," she said, before hurrying off to her workstation.

Liz turned her attention to me, her expression puzzled but friendly.

"What can I do for you, Leah? I'm kind of surprised to see you in the middle of my kitchen."

"I'm sorry for barging in. I thought I could catch you before things got too busy. I guess I underestimated the behind-the-scenes level of busyness in a restaurant."

"Most people do. But don't worry. You caught me at a good time. I always claim 45 minutes before the 7 p.m. rush starts for myself. It's my 'me time,' as they say. I need it so I don't go crazy when everyone else does. Come on up and have a glass of wine with me."

"That sounds good, thanks."

She walked over to a door I hadn't noticed, opened it to reveal a set of stairs leading to the second floor, and beckoned me to follow her.

"This is a nice space," I said as we walked into her living room. "I'm surprised how quiet it is, considering all the noise right below us."

"The apartment came with the job. The owner of the restaurant gave me a free hand with the renovations. I made sure there was plenty of soundproofing. Not hearing any commotion from downstairs helps me get rid of that I'm-still-at-work feeling when I'm here. And my staff have strict orders not to bother me here, unless the building is on fire. Have a seat and I'll get you that glass of wine."

I sank down into an overstuffed navy chair and looked around the room. A twin of the chair I sat in was positioned across from me. A painting on the wall behind it caught my eye. It was done in that sort of gauzy Impressionist style, and featured people eating on a sunny restaurant patio. I got up to look more closely at it, and I saw that the lettering on the restaurant sign read Moretti's.

By then Liz had returned from the kitchen and handed me my wine. As we sat down, I pointed to the painting.

"The restaurant sign says Moretti's. Did you do that painting?"

"No, that's way outside my skill set," she said, and laughed. "I owned the restaurant at one time. A customer did it for me. The painting's the only thing I got out of that adventure."

"What do you mean?"

"I'll tell you my long, sad story another time. You're the one who came to talk, right? Have at it."

I plunged in.

"Liz, I know a little about your story already. I came here tonight hoping you'd tell me more."

"I'm not sure that I understand."

"I'm looking into Bryan Crawford's death for a friend. I found out that you were married to him once, and that your maiden name was Tiffany Tubbs."

She looked astonished but didn't deny it.

"Did Charlie Ross tell you?"

"No. But I know about you and him, too."

"Well."

She took a long drink of her wine. "I guess there isn't much you don't know, then."

"There's quite a bit, actually."

Although Ross had given me his version of why Liz had kept quiet, I wanted to hear it from her.

"Why didn't you come forward when the murder investigation started?"

She nodded her head, as though I had asked her a yes or no question, before she answered me.

"I know I should have. But you have to understand my marriage to Bryan was such a short, small part of my life that now it almost seems like it never happened. When I read that he'd died, it didn't have any impact on me. I'd barely thought of him for decades."

"But you loved Bryan once. You married him."

"I did. But I doubt we'd have gotten married if I wasn't pregnant. My parents insisted. I was only 18. Bryan was 23, but he was even less mature than I was. When I lost the baby, that was the start of the end. Things came to a head after my parents both died in a car crash a year later. I fell apart. Bryan couldn't cope. He had an affair—probably more than one, but I only knew about the one. I filed for divorce. It was for the best. I got to pursue my dream to become a chef, to travel, to own a restaurant. He got to pursue his to stay here and build a plumbing business. Though that was probably more Rhonda's dream than his. Bryan wasn't very ambitious."

I listened carefully for any sign of bitterness. If it was there, I didn't hear it.

"Why did you come back after almost 30 years away?"

"That's part of my sad story. After I left, I did become a chef. A good one. I worked in some great restaurants, and then I took a gig as a private chef for a hedge-fund manager and his wife. Along with a very good salary, he gave me some very good investment advice. When they moved permanently to their home in Mexico, I didn't want to go. They gave me a generous parting gift that put my savings over the top. I finally had enough money to open my own restaurant. That's it in the painting. Moretti's. It was in western Massachusetts. I was so happy then."

"Why did you give it up?"

"I didn't. More like I lost it—or it was taken from me. After four years or so, the restaurant was doing so well that I could afford to hire a manager to take care of the business side of things. Christopher handled the suppliers, and the ordering, and the accounting, and the taxes—all of that. I was free to do the things I love. I had plenty of time to develop new menus, work with local farmers on specialty items, get more active on PR for the restaurant. I even had a five-minute spot on Thursdays on a local television show. And then something I never expected happened. Christopher told me that he was in love with me . . ."

She paused to take another drink of her wine. "I can tell from the expression on your face that you know where this is going."

"No, go on, please."

"Those were sweet, sweet words to hear, coming from a handsome, charming guy 15 years younger than me. Christopher moved in with me, and I was never happier. When he offered to take care of my personal as well as my business finances, I didn't hesitate. Everything I wanted and worked for my whole life was falling into place—the restaurant, my love life, I was even in talks to write a cookbook. It was the best time of my life."

"What happened?"

"One day I discovered that Christopher hadn't just freed me up from the business drudgery I didn't like, he'd also freed up my money."

"He stole from the business?"

"He didn't pay vendors. He didn't pay state or federal taxes. He siphoned off money from the accounts. He even stiffed the staff. And then he ran away with the sous chef. I was wiped out financially, humiliated professionally, and embarrassed personally by my own stupidity. Worst of all, I lost my dream. My restaurant. I gave up so much—a chance to have kids, a family, a normal social life—to pursue that dream. And then it was gone—30 years of my life wiped away."

"I'm so sorry, Liz. What about Christopher, did he go to jail?"

"He might have, if the police had been able to find him. I'm not sure how hard they looked, to be honest. It was a white-collar crime, and I was just one more pathetic, middle-aged woman who'd been taken in by a pretty face."

"I'm sorry," I said again. "But how did you wind up back here?"

"An old friend from culinary school heard about my 'situation' through the grapevine. He owns some high-end restaurants in Milwaukee and Madison. He'd just bought Ariana's—only it wasn't Ariana's then. He thought with the location on the river it could become something special. He offered me the chance to make it happen. I was grateful and I've done my best to make Ariana's a success. Working so hard here brought me back from a pretty dark place."

"And you didn't get in touch with Bryan Crawford when you came back?"

"No. What would I say? There was nothing between us. Besides, I was still feeling pretty mortified by what happened to my restaurant. I didn't want to rekindle acquaintance with anyone, let alone an ex-husband."

"Weren't you afraid someone would recognize you and tell Bryan you were here?"

"Not really. I was a lot thinner back in the day, and my hair's darker now. I wear glasses, now, too. Besides, it's not like I was hiding. I wasn't *afraid* that he'd know. I just didn't see the point. If anyone recognized me, I wouldn't have denied it. Unless maybe it was his sister Rhonda. She was a piece of work. But nobody has. I guess that's about to end, right?"

I ignored that for the moment.

"Liz, I know lots of women change their name after a divorce, but usually they go back to their maiden name. They don't take a brand-new one, first and last. Why did you?"

"Does Tiffany Tubbs sound like the name of a world-famous chef? That's what I planned to be. I never liked my first name. As far as my last one goes, I'm sure you can imagine what fun that was in school. I'd always liked the name Liz, and my grandma's maiden name was Moretti. So, I took a whole new name to start a whole new life. And now you know my life story."

"But what I don't know is why, once you learned that Bryan had been murdered, you didn't go to the cops and tell them what you just told me."

"But I did. I went to Charlie right away. I told him everything I told you. I was kind of freaking out, though. I don't know if he told you, but I've got a real chance for a do-over, a chance to buy the restaurant. The owner and his wife are getting divorced and he's selling up. I couldn't get financing from the bank because my credit is terrible thanks to Christopher. But I've been working with some potential investors. I can't even tell you what that means to me. Maybe I don't need to. You probably feel the same way about your paper.

"I got scared that my financing would fall through if I got connected to a murder investigation. I've seen what *GO News* can do. But I told Charlie everything. And he knew I couldn't have done it, because I was with him all night. In fact, we were together all weekend. He said it would be okay, that he could keep me out of it. Leah, you have to believe me, I would never have kept quiet if I thought it would hurt Charlie. He's pretty special to me."

"But it has hurt him, Liz. Charlie was wrong. He should've talked to Coop. I'm not going to sugarcoat it. He'll be pulled off the case, and maybe worse."

"I feel sick," Liz said. And she did look pretty bad. The corners of her mouth drooped and there was the shimmer of tears in her eyes. "What should I do? Call Coop? Go into the sheriff's office?"

"I'm pretty sure someone from the sheriff's office will be coming to you, and soon."

"You know, I haven't even met Charlie's daughter yet. He talks about her all the time. He wanted to wait a while. Now she'll probably hate me for getting her dad in trouble. Charlie will probably hate me, too. This is going to be in your paper, isn't it? Me, and Charlie, and my real name, and all of that?"

"Liz, this conversation was a talk between friends, but—"

"Thank you, Leah, I—"

"No, let me finish. Troy Patterson is covering the story for the paper. He picked up your divorce file for me from the courthouse. I didn't tell him why, but he's no dummy. Ross being removed from the case will be enough to start Troy digging and he'll get here, the same as I did. And he's the least of your problems. When *GO News* gets hold of this, and they will, it could be ugly."

She looked stricken. So much for her centering bit of "me time" before she had to go down and work the restaurant crowd.

"I'm sorry, Liz. I really am."

35

I didn't call Ross when I got up Wednesday morning, although I'd tossed and turned most of the night before wondering whether or not he'd spoken to Coop, and what had happened. I thought about calling Coop as I lay in bed listening to the rain. I even reached for my phone but then stopped myself. If Ross hadn't talked to him, I'd have to be the one. And I'd rather do that face-to-face with a clear head, not a sleep-fogged one.

A few minutes later I was freshly showered, dressed in my standard work-at-home garb—a faded purple sweatshirt, matching sweatpants, and a pair of the wool socks my Aunt Nancy knits for me every Christmas. I was just tucking into a big bowl of Honey Nut Cheerios when a text came in from Coop.

Lunch today? I'll bring it.

Sure. See you whenever. I'm here all day.

I had decided to step away from the Crawford murder and the Jennifer situation, and spend some serious time developing the lead character for my new series. I had settled on a name for her, though not Rory West, the one Clinton favored. That sounded a little too Hollywood to me. I decided she was Jo Burke—for my earliest female hero, Jo March. That would give some room for mix-ups and ambiguity, as people assumed that Detective Jo Burke was a man. Having birthed and named her, I spent the morning free writing to see what her backstory was, what she loved, what she wanted, what she feared, what she regretted.

I was so absorbed in getting to know her that I jumped at the knock outside my office door. Almost everyone, including me, uses the entrance that opens on the parking lot. Coop's knock meant that he must have picked up lunch from Wide Awake and Woke across the street. Their Wednesday chili special is a favorite of his.

"Come on in, that smells great," I said. He held two drinks, two containers of chili, and a small bag that I hoped contained the coffee shop's signature frosted sugar cookies. "Here, let me grab something."

"No, I've got it balanced. Just lead the way."

While Coop put the food and drinks on the bar, I got bowls and spoons out and set them on the kitchen island. I checked the bag and found as I'd hoped, two mug-shaped frosted cookies. I put them on a plate for dessert.

"It's good to have a friend who knows me so well."

"At least well enough to know to bring cookies," he said. We ate for a few minutes without speaking and then, when I couldn't wait any longer for him to be ready to talk, I asked, "Did Ross talk to you last night?"

"Yeah, he did."

"How did it go?"

He shook his head.

"I couldn't believe it. I don't think I've ever been this angry. Charlie knows better. He's put the whole investigation in jeopardy. A good defense attorney has the perfect weapon to decimate any case we bring. And I'm not even half as mad as Cliff Timmins is."

"Coop, Ross won't lose his job over this, will he? I mean, I know he made the wrong call, and kept on making it, but Liz isn't a serious suspect. It's not like he was hiding an actual murderer."

"No, Liz isn't on the person of interest list. And yeah, I know that Charlie wouldn't lie about her alibi, and he'd never protect a killer. But that doesn't matter. A good defense attorney—hell, even a half-assed one—won't have much trouble establishing reasonable doubt for whoever we determine is the killer. All he—or she—has to do is paint Charlie as a biased investigator who was trying to protect his girlfriend, who happens to be the victim's first wife. Ask Gabe, he can tell you what a lawyer can do with that."

"I don't need to ask Gabe. I can see it myself. All the defense needs to do is give the jury reasonable doubt. Charlie and Liz's connection makes that easy. The fallout from that makes a mess of both their lives."

"Yep. By trying to 'protect' Liz, Charlie made it worse for both of them. If he had just come to me right away, I would have pulled him from the case. Owen Fike would have interviewed Liz and in all likelihood, if things checked out, her connection to Bryan Crawford would never be public."

"Are you going to fire Ross?"

He sighed and his anger left him like air from a punctured balloon.

"I don't know. I honestly don't know. I put him on paid administrative leave, and I assigned the case to Owen. But Cliff is pressuring me hard."

"But you're the sheriff. You have the final decision on personnel issues. If Ross loses his job, it will just about kill him. He's in love, Coop. He's always been a good cop. People do things they normally wouldn't when they're in love."

I didn't add, *Look at you and Rebecca*, and mentally gave myself some good karma points for the day.

"This is a screw-up on a major level. I need some time to figure things out. What are you going to do with it as far as the paper goes?"

"I'm not doing anything, but Troy probably is. He picked up Bryan Crawford's first divorce file for me yesterday. When you issue an update about Owen taking over the case—"

"Cliff and I talked. We're not going to release that at this stage."

"Boy, I'm not sure that's a great decision. In case you don't know it, you've got a leak in your department."

"I know that. I'm just not sure who it is yet."

"I can help you there."

I explained about Troy spotting Drew Lawlor at Andrea's apartment.

"It might not be him, but I also caught him hanging around outside your office right after Rhonda Crawford left in high dudgeon that day. He said he had just stopped to read a text. Maybe he was actually texting Andrea telling her that you, Ross, and I had video of the locked sauna door. *GO News* was all over that."

His phone rang then, and he looked at the caller ID.

"Just a sec. I should take this."

"Sure."

As I got more ice for my tea, I heard Coop say, "Hey, you. No, no problem."

He listened for a few beats, then said, "I'm just finishing up lunch with Leah. I'll stop by your office on my way back."

Another beat and then he laughed and said, "No, it's great. You're not interrupting. I'm looking forward to your surprise. I could use one—the nice kind—today. See you soon."

When he hung up, I asked, "Kristin?"

"Yeah. She said she picked up a surprise for me."

"I gathered that. Any idea what it is?"

He shrugged.

"Not a clue. It could be a new ball cap, or some bagels from the Elite, or once she got me flowers. I never know with Kristin. It's kind of fun."

"I'm sure it is. Is Kristin involved in the Crawford thing at all?"

"Not yet, but if we're ever able to make a case after what Charlie did, she'd be second chair. For now, Cliff just has her writing up the press releases. He doesn't want to share too much of the glory. Though if this goes south, he might set her up to take any blame that could come his way. You know Cliff."

"Indeed I do."

"Kris could easily do Cliff's job. He knows it, too. That's why he keeps her in the background. It'll be a good thing for her career if he does get elected judge."

"Yes, I think she's good. Certainly better than Cliff. She seems good at making you happy, too. You know, Mrs. Schimelman asked me the other day when I thought you guys were going to get engaged."

I expected him to laugh it off, but he didn't.

"You never know," he said. "Seeing you and Gabe with Dominic sometimes, it makes me wonder if it's time for me to be thinking about a family, too."

"I'm not thinking about a family. I'm not ready to take on a commitment that big right now. Are you sure you are? You just got elected sheriff, you're in the middle of your first big crisis, and Kristin's on the brink of getting a chance to move up in her career."

"Am I sure? No. But sometimes you go with sure enough, if you don't want to miss out on a good thing. Anyway, this is probably a conversation I should have with Kristin, if I have it at all, right?"

I experienced a slight hollow feeling in my chest, like something was slipping away.

"Right," I said.

He looked at his watch. "I should get going."

"Wait, you didn't have your cookie," I said. "And we didn't finish talking about the Crawford case. I don't know if Charlie told you, but I gave him some information I picked up about the daughter, Stephanie. And do you know about the wild card in the deck, Mitch Toomey?"

"Leah, this situation with Charlie doesn't change anything. I'm still not going to tell you what I know, or don't know."

"You told me about Liz."

"No, you told Charlie, and Charlie told *me* about Liz."

"Well, there, see, you owe me. I found out about Liz and I learned about Stephanie and about Mitch Toomey on my own. What I don't know is if Ross already checked them both out and discarded them as persons of interest. If he hasn't, I'm just saying they're worth a look. I know Rachelle makes an attractive suspect, but it wouldn't hurt to look elsewhere, too, right? Unless, of course, Ross already broke her alibi. Did he?"

"I hope if I'm ever suspected of a crime, I've got you in my corner, because you never stop swinging. All I'll tell you is that I've got all of Charlie's case notes, and so does Owen. Rachelle is not the only person we're looking at. Enough said. Okay?"

"Fine. I'll eat my cookie and shut up. And if you don't want yours, I'll save it for later."

After Coop left, I called Gabe. I'd already texted him, but he hadn't answered. His phone went to voicemail. I called his office and got Patty, the administrative assistant for Miller Caldwell and Associates, where Gabe works.

"He's in court all day, and he had a lunch meeting with a new client, Leah. He should be back in the office by five or so, do you want me to give him a message?"

"No, that's okay, Patty. He probably told me that, but I've been running kind of crazy the last few days."

"And how is that different from most of your days, Leah?"

Patty reminds me a little of Mrs. Santa Claus in looks, but her personality has more of a Mrs. Landingham—the president's secretary on *The West Wing*—energy.

"I feel very seen, Patty. You can tell him I called, but I'm sure we'll connect later."

After I hung up, I felt a little bad that I probably hadn't been listening when Gabe told me about his work week coming up. He always listens very patiently to mine. And I never bought him red Henley T-shirts, or new ball caps, or flowers, like Kristin did Coop. I should work on being a more thoughtful girlfriend. I added it to my to-do list.

36

Despite my assurances to Patty, Gabe and I didn't manage to connect beyond a short, late-night texting session. Dominic had brought some kind of bug home from school and had spent the evening and part of the night throwing up.

I called to check on him—and Gabe—as soon as I woke up.

"How's Dominic feeling?"

"Much better physically, but he didn't get much sleep and he needs a day at home. He's pretty upset. He's missing Dinosaur Day at school. I'm going to stay with him and work from home today."

"Aw, I wouldn't want to miss Dinosaur Day either. I'd volunteer to stay with him, but I've got that road trip with Miguel planned."

"What road trip?"

"Didn't I tell you Monday? We're going to check out the B&B for Jennifer?"

"Oh, wait. Yes, you did, sorry. I remember. It doesn't seem exactly right to wish you good luck, though, because if you find what you think you're going to, it's going to be pretty hard on Jennifer."

"I know, but she's got to know one way or the other. This limbo is killing her."

"Dad? Daaaad?" I could hear Dominic's voice in the background.

"Hey, I'll catch up with you later. Tell Dominic I hope he feels better."

After I ate a quick breakfast of toast and orange juice, I went downstairs for a quick conversation with Maggie before Miguel and I left for points north. I was worried that *GO News* might stumble on some of the things I'd discovered and scoop us, especially because of Andrea's connection to Drew Lawlor, and Rhonda Crawford's trust in Spencer Karr. I couldn't lay everything out to Maggie, because most of it was off the record. But I could point her in a couple of directions. I poked my head in her office as she was settling in for the day.

"Got a minute?"

"I thought you and Miguel were going on a joyride today."

"We are," I said. "But I've picked up a few things on the Crawford investigation. Expect a news release on—"

"A shake-up in the investigation leadership? Ross is out?"

"How—"

"You're not the only one with connections, Leah. It's all over cop world already. Troy's on it."

"Did he tell you he thinks—"

"That Drew Lawlor at the sheriff's office is in bed—literally—with Andrea Novak? Yes. We're on that, too."

"Okay, great! Just one other thing. Troy might want to—"

"Get a copy of the file you had him pick up at the courthouse Tuesday? Done and dusted."

"I feel like we're playing reverse Watergate here. I'm Deep Throat and you're Bob Woodward, but you're the one with all the answers."

"I've been on the team a long time, Leah. I know how the game is played. Enjoy your day with Miguel, he deserves some time off. You do too, I'd say. You're looking a little peaky."

I knew that I should be glad that Maggie and Troy had everything well in hand, but I couldn't help a twinge of disappointment that they so obviously didn't need my help.

Miguel picked me up in the parking lot, his smile wide as he sat behind the wheel of his bright yellow Mini Cooper convertible. It's not my favorite car to ride in during the winter, but in Miguel's mind, spring begins March 1 regardless of the weather. He had insisted we take his car for its first big trip of the season.

We weren't even out of the parking lot before he asked me the real story behind Ross being taken off the Crawford case.

"That hasn't been released yet. How did you know?"

"Andrea Novak isn't the only one who has sources," he said. "But why?"

"It's a pretty big mess."

I told Miguel the backstory with strict parameters about the off-the-record parts, which was basically all of it until Troy got hold of Liz's real identity. Which, I was sure, was imminent.

"Oh, I'm so happy Charlie has a girlfriend! That's why the V-neck sweaters, and the aftershave, right? That is very sweet, Charlie dressing up for Liz, his bae. "

"Miguel, seriously, did you hear what I just said, all of it? Yes, it's nice Ross has a love life headed in the right direction, but his career isn't. I asked Coop if he was going to fire him, and he wouldn't answer yes or no. Ross is on very shaky ground right now."

"I don't believe Coop would fire Charlie. He made a bad decision, but Charlie, he's a good man."

"I agree, but Rhonda is going to put the pressure on Timmins, and Timmins is going to put the pressure on Coop, and Coop is going to put the most pressure of all on himself. You know how high his standards are. And he's trying to clean up the office after the ethical wasteland Art Lamey left behind. I'm worried for Ross. I'm also feeling conflicted."

"About what?"

"I want to help Adam. Finding a better suspect than Rachelle is the only way to do that. But the best thing for Charlie would be to find something that bolsters his case against Rachelle. It would show his instincts were right."

"And even if he did a wrong thing hiding Liz, it didn't change the investigation."

"Exactly."

He didn't say anything for a few seconds, then he turned to me, smiling again.

"You just have to follow the leads. You can't change who the killer is, even if one way it's bad for Adam, another way it's bad for Charlie. And when you can't change things, you know what you do?"

"What?"

"You dance! With my girl, Taylor Swift."

He turned on the music loud, and he began singing to "Shake it Off." My heart wasn't in it, but he was trying hard to cheer me up, so I joined in half-heartedly. As it turned out, the more we sang and car danced our way up north, the happier I began to feel. Miguel has that effect on me.

We'd been on the road for just over an hour and a half when a roadside billboard caught my eye. *Grace and Blessings Retreat Center. Find Your Bliss.*

"Miguel."

He was singing too loud to hear me.

"Miguel!" I shouted. He took his eyes off the road and looked at me, startled.

"Our exit is coming up. The Grace and Blessings Retreat is just five miles east of here. According to the billboard, you'll be able to bliss out there, too."

We traveled a few miles down a dirt road, passing a sign and a turn-off that read "Parking for GBR Center." A quarter mile later, we came to the drive for the center itself. Built of wood and stone, the two-story structure had a wing on each side that seemed to disappear into the woods behind. It looked like the building was being pulled back into the forest from which it had come.

We parked out front and walked through the main door to a lobby furnished with several futon-sofas, a couple of similarly styled chairs, and a scattering of patterned area rugs on the polished wood floor. The walls were hung with paintings depicting the center in each of the four seasons. No one was at the reception desk, but there was a small bell and a sign asking visitors to ring it, which we did.

Within a few minutes, a woman with a long gray braid over one shoulder came into the lobby from the hall to the left. She smiled in greeting as she approached us, her face creasing in pleasant laugh lines around her eyes and bracketing her mouth.

"Hello, I'm Maura. I'm the manager here. How can I help you?"

"Hi, Maura, I'm Leah Nash and this is my friend Miguel Santos. We're on our way somewhere else, but we noticed your billboard and took a detour to see what Grace and Blessings is all about. Do you have time to answer some questions for us?"

"Of course. Please, sit down." She pointed to one of the sofas, and as we settled on it, she brought a chair over so that she could face us as we talked. As she sat and folded her hands in her lap, she radiated a sense of calm.

"Now, what would you like to know?"

"Well, what exactly is it that you do here?"

"We help people find their true center by giving them space and time to spend in silence, in meditation, and in thought. We offer both group and individual retreats, some silent, some not. Are you interested in a retreat?"

"Maybe. Tell me more about the silent retreats."

"Usually, we have between 15 and 20 guests. They arrive together on a Friday afternoon, check in, and turn in all electronic devices. Dinner is at 5:30 each evening. Breakfast is at 7:30 and lunch is at noon. On the first evening guests are able to talk and get acquainted, but the silence begins after Kirtan, our chanting session at 8 p.m. The silence continues until breakfast Monday morning."

"Does everyone attend Kirtan?" I asked.

"Well, we don't take attendance, but most guests do. It's a beautiful experience. The room has excellent acoustics, and it's already darkened, illuminated only by candlelight when guests come in. Without being able to see anyone clearly, when the chanting starts, it feels like we're all joined together as one soul."

She gave a little shake of her head and smiled.

"I'm sorry. I've been told I can wax a little too poetic at times, but it's my favorite part of the weekend."

"What do people do the rest of the time?" Miguel asked.

"We offer lectures featuring some excellent teachers, as well as group guided and unguided meditation. There are yoga sessions each morning and evening. We have a lovely pond on the grounds, surrounded by trees, with benches for sitting and thinking, or meditating. There are lots of paths for walking meditation through the woods as well. Some people take part in every session we offer, some pick and choose, and a few don't attend any at all. Each person who attends creates their own experience."

"Where does everyone stay?"

"The east wing of the building has individual bedroom suites. We also have three very small, single-person cabins available. They're furnished with a bed, a small desk and chair, a refrigerator, and a microwave. Some people prefer to bring their own food, though meals are included in the price of the retreat. If you're looking for complete solitude, you can find it there. Sometimes guests check in to a cabin on Friday and that's the last we see them until Monday morning checkout."

"You mean they don't even see anyone else? For all weekend? They could get sick. Or have a heart attack. There's no phone, no internet? No one checks on them?" Miguel appeared horrified at the thought of no human contact for nearly three days.

Maura laughed gently, and she put a hand on Miguel's arm.

"We haven't lost anyone yet. There's a phone in each cabin that rings in up here. If a guest needs us, we're just a call away. But if privacy is their preference, we try not to intrude."

"I want to be sure I understand, Maura," I said. "If I signed up for a silent retreat weekend, I could request a private cabin, arrive on Friday, park my car in the lot down the road, check in here, and then not see anyone again until Monday morning. Or I could choose to pop in and out of lectures, or yoga, or meals, or whatever if I wanted to during the weekend. Is that right?"

"Exactly right. You can structure the retreat any way that is right for you, within the parameters we have. And we offer retreats that aren't centered around silence, too. Are you interested in joining our email list, Leah?"

"Thank you, but I hate to add any more emails to my inbox. I can just check the website and find news and updates there, can't I?"

"Yes, certainly. We always post what's happening at the center on our website. We have some brochures at the desk if you'd like one."

"Thank you so much, Maura. It was very nice meeting you."

"You as well. I hope we see you again one day."

37

When we were in the car and pulling away from the retreat center, I turned toward Miguel.

"Do you have the same idea that I do?"

"I think so. You go first."

"Rachelle's alibi seems solid, but up close it's as full of holes as my vintage Backstreet Boys T-shirt. She could come and go at that retreat any time she wanted, and no one would even miss her."

"She could have driven up here on Friday afternoon, checked in at two o'clock, and then driven back home to lock her husband in the sauna," Miguel said.

"It's certainly possible. It's a tight timeline to lock her husband in at 6:15 and make it back here for 8 p.m. Kirtan. But the beauty of her story is that no one can prove that she wasn't there, given the dimly lit setup Maura described."

"Do you think Charlie knows this?"

"I'd bet on it. It's probably why he keeps hammering at her alibi. But so far, Rachelle hasn't cracked. If she holds firm, she might get away with it."

"So now you think she did it?"

"I don't want to think that for Adam's sake, but it's sure looking that way. And so far, I haven't found a good alternate suspect. Listen, I didn't want to risk shutting Maura down by asking specifically about Rachelle. But now I've changed my mind. I think we should stop in on the way back and get right down to it. Did Rachelle opt for a private cabin, did Maura see her during the weekend? If so, when? She probably won't give us names of anyone else at the retreat, but she might let us talk to some of the staff. Maybe someone saw Rachelle driving away or coming back on Friday, or on Sunday when she went back to unlock the door."

"You think she went back on Sunday? Why? Couldn't she just unlock the door of the sauna when she got home on Monday morning, then cry, and scream, and call 911?"

"Yes, but it would be a risk. Everyone knew that Bryan was planning to go to his cabin on the weekend, so she could be sure no one would go out to the house and rescue him from the sauna before he died. But if he didn't show up at work on Monday morning someone might go to the house to check on him. If the sauna door was still locked that would ruin Rachelle's plan to make it look like a natural death from diabetes complications."

I was quiet for a minute as I ran through things in my mind.

"The insulin thing fits, too. She wanted to be sure that Bryan would be weakened enough by the time he got into the sauna to actually die over the next three days while she was gone. Replacing his insulin ensured that."

"That is cold, *chica*. In fact, that is frigid. If it's true, I feel very sad for Adam with such a *mamá* as her."

"Me, too, but there it is."

"Are you going to talk to Charlie about this?"

"I'll try, but he's pretty upset with me about Liz. Besides, I think he probably has a pretty good idea already, and that's why he's been so focused on Rachelle. I'd still like to know what the sauna key has to do with it, though."

"What about Coop and Detective Fike?"

"They've got the case file Ross was working on, so whatever he knew they know already. But yeah, I'll tell Coop what we found out today, just in case. Adam's the one I wish I didn't have to talk to."

"What will you say to him?"

"I can't give Adam any of the supporting details without messing up the investigation. I'll just have to say I couldn't find anything to help. I wish I'd told him no when he asked."

"Why didn't you?"

"Oh, it's a long story. I'll tell you someday. But for now, we need to change focus. We're almost at the B&B. And I don't have a great feeling about how Jennifer's situation is going to work out, either."

The Beale House Inn looked just like the photo on its website. This early in the spring, the flowers were the only thing missing.

"I love it!" Miguel said as we walked up the porch steps.

A sign on the door invited us to come in, and we stepped into a small entry that smelled of beeswax and lemon. A carved wooden staircase curved up to the next floor, and to the right was an open room with a row of windows that let in plenty of light. The large room was furnished with well-padded leather club chairs, a long sofa, and a freestanding bar.

A woman in jeans and a bright yellow sweater came running lightly down the stairs, her strawberry-blonde ponytail swinging with each step.

"Hi, you must be Miguel. I'm Kelly Winston. I saw your car drive up, I was doing a little vacuuming up in the tower suite."

She had reached the bottom of the stairs and offered a handshake to Miguel before she turned to me.

"Are you Miguel's sister?"

She looked slightly puzzled, as though trying to work out the genetic code that had produced two such different-looking people from the same DNA.

"I take after the Irish side of the family," I said, by way of explanation to her unasked question. "I'm Leah."

"Good to meet you. Come on into the lounge."

Once we were seated, Kelly said, "You mentioned that a friend of yours had been here and that's how you found out about us, Miguel. I forgot to ask who it was."

"John Pilarski. I think he was here in February. Do you remember him?"

"I do. I remember because when he called to book, he said he was looking for a quiet getaway. I told him it's always pretty quiet this time of year. It didn't work out that way, though. He said he didn't mind, and I guess if he recommended us to you, he must have meant it."

"Why would he mind? How did things turn out?" I asked.

"Oh, it's nothing bad," she said. "It's just that the Historical Society got into a bind and had to find a new venue for their wine and cheese fundraiser. I told them they could hold it here. But when John and his wife Jennifer checked in around 8:00, instead of a low-key, romantic evening, they walked right into a crowd of laughing, talking, drinking people who came for the fundraiser."

Miguel's eyes had widened with astonishment at the mention of Jennifer. I gave a discreet shake of my head signaling him to get his chill back on.

38

"It sounds like just the kind of evening they'd enjoy, Kelly. Both of them love to mingle, especially Jennifer," I said.

"Not so much that weekend," Kelly said with a smile. "They didn't stay long at the reception, and we hardly saw them the rest of the time they were here. No surprise there, though. It's what usually happens when guests come for the Romance Package. They get breakfast in bed Saturday and Sunday, and a catered dinner in their suite on Saturday night. Typically, we don't see much of those couples. After all, they're here to spend time with each other, not with us."

I died a little inside on behalf of Jennifer, who would have loved to come to the Beale House Inn with her husband. But John had not only used a romantic bed and breakfast weekend on his girlfriend, he'd even signed her in as Jennifer. That was the lowest of low blows.

Kelly jumped up then and talked over her shoulder as she hurried across the room.

"I was going to show you the room we use for receptions, but we had a malfunction with the overhead sprinklers in there a couple of days ago. It's an addition we had built in the back to accommodate larger groups. We've had more trouble with the new wiring and plumbing there than we've had in the whole rest of this 130-year-old house."

When she reached the bar, she darted behind it, bent down, and resurfaced with a laptop in her hand. She opened it and beckoned for us to join her.

"I've got some photos of the room here. I took them at the wine and cheese thingy to use for a brochure, but I haven't done anything with it yet. They'll give you an idea of the dimensions of the room and what we could do with it for you."

Kelly seemed so happy at the prospect of a large family party booking and she was so accommodating that I felt increasingly guilty about our ruse. But there was no going back now. Maybe after all this was behind us, Gabe and I could come for a weekend. I might be able to persuade Coop to bring Kristin, too, and my mother would be here in a hot second with Paul.

"See that gorgeous stained glass window? It's pretty in the candlelight but it's stunning on a summer or fall day. Have you got a date set yet?" Kelly asked, pulling me back from my thoughts of future reparation to present day deception.

"Ah, no. Their anniversary is October 27, but that's on a Tuesday. We're thinking the weekend before, or the weekend after. We just want to hit the general vicinity. It's more important that everyone can be there than that it's on the exact date."

"Sure, I understand."

As she spoke, she'd been scrolling through photos. "Oh, here we are, this gives you an idea of how the room accommodates a crowd."

She turned the laptop slightly so both Miguel and I could look.

"We had maybe 60 people or so here that night. You can see they aren't too crowded. There's enough room for everyone to stand and move around without bumping into the walls, or each other. Oh, look! There's your friend John and his wife in the corner by the fireplace," she said, zooming in on the man who was clearly John, leaning in toward a woman who was clearly not Jennifer.

But I recognized her. Rachelle Crawford was the woman with her hand on his arm, smiling up at John.

We played it as cool as we could with Kelly, but it was hard. I made an abrupt excuse about lunch plans we had to get to, and asked her to AirDrop the photo to me, so we could show the reception room to the rest of the family. Miguel couldn't contain himself once we got in the car.

"*Chica*! John, he's having his affair with Rachelle Crawford! I cannot believe it! This changes everything, yes?"

Though we were both stunned by the revelation, Miguel was more animated about it, flinging his hands so wide that I leaned over and grabbed the steering wheel.

"Hey! Easy there. Yes, this changes everything. Holy hell. Rachelle and John. Rachelle wasn't covering up the killing, she was covering up her affair. The weekend retreat was an excuse for her B&B weekend with John," I said.

"Poor Jennifer!"

"Yes. What an asshat he is!"

"Rachelle and John, they must have come separately. Rachelle, she checks in at Grace and Blessings, and John comes later and picks her up, right?"

"I think so. Then Sunday after checkout they went their separate ways, John back home and Rachelle back to the retreat center. Then she drives home on Monday morning, thinking everything went off just fine. Only when Rachelle gets home, Bryan is dead, and before she knows it, she's the prime suspect in a murder investigation."

"But then, when the police keep questioning her, and her son is so worried about her, why doesn't Rachelle just tell the truth? John is her witness and Kelly at the bed and breakfast is, too, and all the people at the wine and cheese party that saw her. She can prove she didn't lock Bryan in the sauna."

"Maybe John convinced her to stick to her retreat story, so he wouldn't have to get involved. It's a hard one to disprove. Unless the police turn up someone who saw Rachelle coming or going when she shouldn't be, which they obviously haven't, or she'd be arrested by now, her alibi holds. There's also the Rhonda factor."

"What do you mean?"

"Well, if I were Rachelle, I'd avoid invoking the wrath of Rhonda for as long as possible. Rhonda's in charge of distributing Bryan's estate.

According to Rachelle, she's already slow-walking it. If she found out Rachelle had cheated on her brother, she might try to cut her out of inheriting altogether. I don't know if that's even possible, but I'm sure Rhonda would tie things up in court as long as she could. I'm no Rachelle fan, but it's John who disgusts me."

"But both of them had the affair, and both of them deceived their partners."

"Yes, but John betrayed his wife *and* his girlfriend. Jennifer by having the affair, and Rachelle by letting her twist in the wind alone. If he really cared about her, he'd have stepped up and come clean. It looks to me like he wanted the thrill of an affair, but the comfort of his marriage. And he was willing to lie to both the women in his life in order not to face any consequences."

"I don't approve of cheating. Also, now I don't approve of John. Jennifer must divorce him," Miguel said, sounding very fierce. Despite how bad I felt for Jennifer, the incongruity of Miguel passing judgment so firmly made me laugh.

"No, don't laugh at me. I am serious. There should be no cheating in marriage."

"Hey, I don't disagree. But I will say that no one knows what goes on inside a marriage except the two people in it. I love Jennifer, and I like—or anyway I used to like—John. However things move forward, it's their call. I'm going to refrain from giving advice. I'd suggest you do the same, Dr. Love."

"What are you going to do now?"

"I'm going to talk to Rachelle first, and give her a chance to come clean to Adam. He should hear this first from her, not me. I doubt he'll care that she betrayed Bryan, but he might feel that she betrayed him as well. He was in obvious distress, and she let him suffer by not telling him the truth. "

"Rachelle was trying to protect Adam, don't you think?"

"I'm sure that's what she's telling herself. And maybe it's true. Anyway, that's for them to work out. After I talk to Rachelle, I'll go to Jennifer. That's going to be a hard conversation to have. Then I'll talk to Coop and Ross. I'm pretty sure this is information they don't have. I haven't told either one of them about Jennifer because she wanted to keep it out of work."

"What about the *Times*? What are you going to tell Maggie?"

"That we know Rachelle has a much better alibi than the retreat weekend. She was with John. But that she needs to independently confirm what we found out, because we were just in help-a-friend mode, not reporting mode. It's probably better if Troy takes the lead on this, so things don't get muddied between what you and I did and what the actual reporting is. Sorry for dragging you in, and now keeping you out."

"It's okay. I wouldn't want to interview John anyway. Too hard to stay objective. This day didn't turn out to be so much fun, did it?"

"No, Miguel, it sure didn't."

"I guess we don't need to go back to the retreat center now, either."

"No, I guess we don't."

We both fell silent then. Neither of us felt like the festive lunch we'd planned, so we didn't stop. Miguel turned the music on, but there was no singing on the return trip.

39

I didn't call ahead, because I didn't want to give Rachelle an opportunity to say no or ask me to just tell her on the phone. I started with no preamble when she opened the door.

"Is anyone else here, Rachelle? I need to talk to you in private."

"What are you doing here? I told you before, I don't want you talking to Adam, and I don't have anything to say to you."

"I know about you and John."

Her eyes widened and she took an involuntary step back, which gave me an opportunity to slip inside.

"I have proof of your affair. And I have proof where you were the night Bryan was killed."

She rallied for a minute. "I don't know what you're talking about. I was at Grace and Blessings Retreat Center. I have the receipts."

"Yeah? Well, I have the truth. I know that you signed in at the retreat, but I know you didn't stay there. I also know—"

She cut me off.

"Please. Sheila is here. Come into Bryan's office with me. We can close the door."

I followed her through the living room to her deceased husband's mostly empty office—just two chairs and a desk. The shelves were bare and there was nothing on the desktop. Rhonda was right. Rachelle had done a thorough clean-out of all things Bryan. I moved swiftly past her and sat in the executive chair behind the desk. No way was I going to cede the power position to her. She had rallied enough to challenge me as soon as she took her seat in the guest chair.

"Whatever you think you know, you're wrong. I wasn't having an affair. This is ridiculous. I hope you haven't given Adam your wild theory. I don't want him upset. I—"

"Stop. Just stop. When I said I know, I mean, I *know*. I've talked to Maura at Grace and Blessings. I know the setup, and I know how easy it was for you to slip away. And I've also talked to the owner of the Beale House Inn. I know you were with John Pilarski—"

Her eyes widened with shock and she started to speak again, but I rolled right over her.

"Don't bother to lie, Rachelle. She said you two took full advantage of the Romance Package weekend John won in the raffle. In fact, I have a picture of you and John here on my phone, looking very cozy at the wine and cheese reception."

I showed it to her, including the metadata showing the date and time the picture was taken.

She drooped like a wilted flower after looking at the photo. Her shoulders were hunched, her head was bowed, and she was twisting the wedding ring that was still on her finger. I couldn't help it. I felt a slight, very slight twinge of sympathy for her. Enough to let some of the anger drain from my voice.

"Rachelle, I haven't talked to Adam yet. I think you should be the one to tell him where you were, and why you lied. And I hope you do it before the police come back for more questioning. It's a crime, you know, to obstruct a police investigation. And your lies made them waste a lot of time on you."

"I couldn't help it."

"Of course not."

"You don't need to be sarcastic. Maybe you just don't understand what it's like to be in love with someone. To feel like you can't breathe when you're not with him. What it's like when you're finally together. John and I didn't mean to fall in love. We couldn't help it. We were in an impossible situation."

I found it hard to see quiet, John Denver-ish looking John Pilarski as half of the passionate romance Rachelle described. Although Jennifer had fallen in love with John, too.

"Why was it impossible, Rachelle? You love him, he loves you. You just tell your respective spouses and get on with it. You don't lie, and hide, and sneak around. If your love is such a grand passion, then own it and deal with the fallout. It seems pretty simple to me. Hard, maybe, but simple."

I had a fleeting thought that the harsh words I said to Rachelle had more to do with my own latent anger at the woman my ex-husband had an affair with than they did with the present situation.

"It isn't simple. John's wife has cancer. It was in remission, but it's come back and it's terminal. The doctors don't know how long she'll last. It could be a year, maybe a little longer, but there's no cure. He can't ask her for a divorce now. It would crush her spirit. It might even kill her. That's why John didn't want me to tell the truth to Detective Ross. It's because of his wife Jennifer. We're just trying to be good people."

I was dumbstruck. I literally couldn't get a single word out. Actually, I could barely even formulate a word in my head. My response was entirely visceral and nonverbal. That anger that I'd let go of at least in part a minute ago rushed back in. I'd been right in what I'd said to Miguel. John wanted the thrill of an affair and the comfort of a marriage. He'd lied to both the women in his life. I almost said as much to the weeping Rachelle, then decided Jennifer had the right to know, first.

"Rachelle, I'll wait until tomorrow. But if you don't talk to Adam, I will."

———————————————

"Hi, Jen. Are you super busy at work? Got time for a coffee break?"

"Leah, hi. I'm not at work. I'm at home. I took a sick day because I was up all night with the twins. They both came down with a stomach virus that's going around the school. The worst seems to be over. They're sleeping now. Can you come here?"

"Sure, yeah, I can do that. I'll be over in fifteen. Unless you need me to pick something up for the kids? Slush Puppies from JT's, ginger ale, or whatever to soothe their troubled tummies? Gabe went through the same thing with Dominic last night."

"Thanks, but I think they're going to sleep for at least a couple of hours. Leah, do you—that is, have you—is there anything—"

I cut off her fumbling attempt to ask the question I knew was foremost on her mind, so that I wouldn't have to give her the answer over the phone.

"Okay, then, I'm on my way. See you in a few."

The Pilarski home is a gray, two-story house built in 1920 from a kit ordered from the Sears catalog. All the precut pieces were shipped by rail to Himmel along with instructions for how to build the house. Apparently that was a thing back then and catalog homes are found all over the United States. I only know that much about it because Jennifer had researched the history before she and John bought it. They'd fallen in love with it even though it was in pretty bad shape. Jennifer had done a lot of work on it, and to be fair—which I didn't feel much like being at the moment—John had, too.

When I knocked lightly on the front door and stepped into the hall, I didn't get the warm and welcoming feeling I usually did when I visited. The house was quiet, probably because the kids were sleeping, not rough-housing upstairs. There was no enticing smell of cookies baking or a hot dish in the oven. I didn't hear the crackle of a fire in the fireplace that would normally accompany a damp March afternoon. Jennifer was sitting on the sofa, lost in thought. She looked up, startled, when I said hello. She hadn't even heard me come in.

"Leah, hi. Sit down. Do you want something to drink?"

She began to get up as she asked. I motioned her back down and joined her on the sofa.

"No, Jen. I'm fine. It's awfully quiet here today," I said, not wanting to start the conversation we had to have.

"Yes. Ethan and Nate had a pretty tough night and morning. They both more or less collapsed at the same time. I don't expect them to wake up for hours. Probably at their normal bedtime."

"You look pretty tired yourself. Are you feeling okay?"

Instead of answering, she put her hand on mine and said, "Leah. I know why you're here. You found out something. Just tell me, please."

And so, after taking a deep breath, I did. When I finished, she didn't cry. She didn't ask any questions. She just sat there, staring at me.

"Jen? Let me get you a glass of water."

She still didn't say anything.

"Are you okay?"

I knew it was a stupid thing to ask. Of course she wasn't okay. I hurried into the kitchen and got her a drink, and I grabbed a box of Kleenex from the cupboard, too. I handed both to her as I sat back down and waited.

She was crying now, not sobbing, just tears welling up and spilling down her cheeks.

"I'm so sorry, Jen. I'm so, so sorry," I said.

"How long?"

"How long have they been seeing each other? I don't know. A while I'd guess, but I didn't ask Rachelle."

"I can't believe this. This can't be happening. He can't not love me anymore. What am I going to do? I don't want him to leave me. And Nate and Ethan, they'll never understand. I can't, I can't, I—"

She couldn't get the words out because she'd started hyperventilating, her breath coming in short gasps.

"Jen! Slow down, just breathe. Come on, deep breath in and out." I held her hand to give her an anchor, something to pull her to the present and away from awful-izing about her future.

After a minute she began to breathe normally again.

"Here, take a drink."

She gulped down the water.

"I wasn't paying enough attention to him. Maybe he felt like I didn't appreciate him. It's just with the kids, and my job, and school—"

"Stop that. Stop it right now. You've always been there for John. This isn't about you, it's about him."

"It takes two people to make a marriage, Leah. It isn't just John's fault. I don't know what I did or what I didn't do, but the blame is half mine, too."

"Okay, no. Sure, there are two sides, Jen, but that doesn't mean they're

50/50. You're the one who put aside your own goals to support John. You're the one who juggles work, school, home, pretty much alone because John is gone so much. All John has to think about is his job and himself. And thinking about himself is pretty much a full-time occupation, I'd say."

"I could quit school, go back later. Maybe we could go to counseling. What's this Rachelle like? I suppose she's blonde and beautiful? With little tiny feet, and a little tiny waist, and a little tiny voice, just like Tisha Baumgarden. Remember her? She dated John before I did in high school. I couldn't believe he chose me over her. I've been meaning to go on a diet, I know I should lose some weight. I—"

"Jen! There is nothing wrong with you. You want to go to counseling, then go. You want to lose weight, fine, do it. But do it for yourself, not because you think you're not good enough. You're better than good enough."

"How could he take her for a weekend and sign her into that bed and breakfast with my name? What kind of sick asshat does that?"

Her voice had suddenly strengthened. She began rubbing at her cheeks as though if she scrubbed hard enough, the Kleenex in her hand could wipe away her pain along with her tears.

"I hate her. I hate him and I hate her. I'd like to kill them both! And don't tell me I shouldn't feel like that."

Okay then, we'd run through denial and bargaining already. I knew she'd cycle back and forth through a whole range of emotions for a long time to come. But I was glad we were at the anger stage at the moment. I do better with anger than guilt.

"Hey, I'm totally down with that feeling. You're talking to the queen of revenge fantasies here. What they did was stupid, and selfish, and thoughtless, and cruel. But we can come up with some kind of revenge that won't involve you going to jail afterwards. I'll give it some thought."

"Do you think John wants a divorce? Do you think he wants to marry Rachelle?"

"I don't know. Maybe he doesn't want either. Otherwise, why all the lies to her and to you? Jen, you need to think about what you want, not what John wants."

"I can't think until I talk to him. He's supposed to be home today. I—"

Jennifer stopped and looked up at the sound of the back door opening, and then closing with a bang.

"Jen? Jennifer!"

As we looked up, John came running into the living room.

40

"Jennifer, I need to talk to you. I—"

"Hello, John."

He stopped short when he saw me. John is tall and lanky, a quiet man who always seemed content to let the extroverted Jennifer take center stage. I noticed that he had ditched his wire-rimmed glasses. His eyes were a deeper shade of blue than I recalled, and that spoke to me of tinted contacts. His clothes were different, too. Instead of a sport coat with an open-neck shirt, he wore a well-cut suit with a tie that Miguel would have swooned over. I wondered if his makeover had been done by Rachelle, or for her.

For a second he didn't seem to know what to say. Obviously, Rachelle had called him, and he'd come rushing home to do damage control. He found his voice and said, "Leah, I need to talk to Jennifer. Alone. Could you please go?"

I started to stand, but Jennifer grabbed my wrist.

"I want her to stay," she said, then turned to me. "Leah, don't go."

I didn't want to stay. It was too painful to watch, and I was too angry at John to be in the same room with him for long. But I sat back down to calm her, and to wait for the right moment to slip away.

"All right, Jen. I'm here."

She turned to John then and the anguish in her voice made my heart hurt.

"John, when I look at you, I can't believe that it's true. That you lied, and lied, and lied to me. Why did you do it, John, to me, to the kids, to our family? Don't we mean anything to you? Was it always a lie, from the very beginning? When did it start? When did you stop loving me?"

John moved quickly to the sofa and sat down on the other side of Jen. He tried to take her hand, but she pulled it away. He ignored me and focused directly on her as though I weren't there.

"I never stopped loving you, Jennifer. I just got so mixed up. I didn't mean for it to happen. I love you, but I made a mistake. A bad mistake. It was just . . . I don't know. I've been so miserable, and you were so busy, and you were so proud that I got that big promotion. I didn't want to tell you how hard it's been, the kind of pressure I'm under at work. I have to prove myself every day. Mark Horgan thought he was a shoo-in for the job. Ever since I got it, he's done everything he can to undermine me.

"The stress, it's been unbelievable. A few months ago, I stopped at a coffee shop in Omico, and that's when I met Rachelle. We just talked a little in line, and then we had coffee together. That was all. I didn't plan on starting anything. But she was there the next time I stopped in. We talked some more. She was a good listener. We were just good friends, at first. But she wasn't happy either, and, well, after a while, it just happened. That's all. I didn't mean for it to."

I just about had to physically clap my hand over my mouth to keep from offering my opinion about John, his stress relief program, and his refusal to take responsibility for his own actions. But Jennifer didn't need my help.

"It didn't just happen, John. You chose to have an affair with this, this, Rachelle. You lied to me over and over again, for months. And you signed into the bed and breakfast with her, and she used my name! How could you do that? Don't bother to lie, Leah talked to the owner. She saw a picture of the two of you there, too."

John looked at me as though he would have happily throttled me, were it not for Jennifer sitting in between us.

"I'm not lying now, Jennifer. I promise. I know that I hurt you and if I could take it all back, I would. But I swear to God, I love you and I want to find a way to fix this," John said. "I was going to end it with Rachelle anyway, I swear. You and the boys are everything to me."

Okay, I had to get out of there. This was giving me PTSD. It was the same kind of manipulative excusing that my ex-husband had used on me. But John wasn't Nick, and Jennifer wasn't me, and I needed to take myself and my emotions out of the picture and leave them to it.

I stood up and said, decisively this time, "Jennifer, I'm going to go. You and Nick—I mean John—need to have this conversation alone. Call me, anytime."

"But Leah—"

"No, Jen. Let her go," John said, and then he turned to me.

"If you hadn't interfered, if you hadn't gone to Rachelle, none of this would even be happening. Jennifer didn't have to know. She wouldn't be feeling like this if you hadn't interfered. I was planning to end it with Rachelle."

"John, that's not fair. I was worried. I asked Leah to—"

"It's all right Jen, I've got this."

I was willing, even eager, to bow out of their private discussion. I was not, however, willing to let John shift the blame for Jennifer's pain to me.

"Just when were you planning to end it, John? When I talked to Rachelle, she seemed to think that if it wasn't for your poor wife's cancer treatment, you'd be with her right now. But you're such a noble soul you couldn't leave Jennifer until her terminal illness ended, according to Rachelle. And how long were you going to let Rachelle twist in the wind as a murder suspect? You could have gone to the police right away and told them that she was with you all weekend. Her son has been worried sick about her. I always thought you were a good guy, John. Now it looks like you were just a good actor."

I noticed then that Jennifer was staring open-mouthed at her husband, as though she were looking at something disgusting on the bottom of her shoe. I realized then where my anger had led me. I'd left out the part about John giving Jen a fatal disease as a way of keeping his wife and his mistress, too. I had decided that was just too much for her to hear. But now I'd let my fury lead me to do it anyway.

"You told your girlfriend that I had cancer? That you had to wait until I *died*? Oh, my God, did I ever even know you? Who are you?"

As John attempted to get out of the very deep hole to which I had unintentionally added several more feet, I got my jacket off the chair where I had tossed it and slipped away. Neither of them seemed to notice.

41

My wipers could barely keep up with the rain as I headed from Jennifer's house on the outskirts of town over to Coop's. It had rained off and on all day, but up north it had been a light splatter hitting the windows. It was a downright downpour in Himmel. As I drove over the bridge, I looked down at the water and realized with a start that it had risen considerably since the last time I'd paid any attention, which was more than a week ago.

When I got to Coop's, I knocked on the door, then walked into the kitchen. The tantalizing aroma of cooked onions, chicken, carrots, thyme, and whatever else goes into chicken and dumplings almost knocked me off my feet.

"That smells so good, Coop! You don't have to ask me twice, yes, I'll have some," I said.

"Actually, I didn't ask you once, but sure, help yourself. It's in the crockpot."

I took a plate from the cupboard and dished myself out a generous helping, got a glass of water, sat down, took a bite, and savored it before I said, "Thank you. You saved my life. I haven't eaten anything substantial since breakfast, and it's been a very draining day."

"Why's that? I stopped by the paper today. Courtnee said you and Miguel were out having fun while she had to be at work because receptionists don't get time off anytime they want. She wasn't very happy she got left behind."

"Miguel and I were on a mission, we weren't just joyriding."

I told him about Jennifer and John, and why Miguel and I had gone to the Beale House Inn.

"She hasn't been herself at work. She gets real quiet and just kind of stares into space sometimes. I asked her once if anything was wrong, but she didn't want to talk about it. I guess I know why, now."

"And that's not all. When Miguel and I got to the B&B, guess who we found out John is having an affair with? No, never mind, don't guess, you never will. Rachelle Crawford. Now guess which weekend he was with her at the Beale House Inn, which is less than half an hour away from Grace and Blessings Retreat Center. No, never mind, I'll tell you. She was with John all weekend while Bryan Crawford died in his sauna."

The surprise on his face was very satisfying. Then I gave him the full rundown of what had happened both up north and then with Rachelle, Jennifer, and John.

"Well, what do you think?"

"I think it's something to add to the mix that could be important. You don't mind that we're going to check your homework, do you?"

"Of course not. But you think finding out Rachelle was with John all weekend is just something 'to add to the mix?' Doesn't it upend your case against her?"

"We don't have a case against Rachelle. We don't have a case against anyone yet. We're investigating everyone involved. I'm glad you shared what you found. I don't know if we would have uncovered it."

"But it's not a game changer?"

"No, but mostly because this isn't a game. It's a murder investigation."

"Come on, you know I'm not making light of it. It just seems to me that this information means someone else should come into focus as Bryan's killer."

"Like I said, we're investigating everyone."

"But you'll be shifting attention from Rachelle now, won't you? Who's in the crosshairs next? Stephanie, the daughter? How about Mitch Toomey, the guy who blames Crawford for everything bad that's happened in his life? And of course, there's Rhonda. She makes a nice dark horse suspect, don't you think?"

"It wouldn't break my heart if it was her, but I just don't see it. Her story that she was providing respite care holds up. She had to give the man medication at specific times. He was restless and alert because of his pain. He would have known if she'd left him alone. Their security camera would have shown her leaving the house, too. It didn't."

"What about Stephanie? I don't like her."

"You should have told me that right away. I would've had Charlie move her to the top of the suspect list. Why don't you like Stephanie?"

"She's like a smart Courtnee. She has Courtnee's ruthless self-absorption, but she also has a brain. That's a dangerous combination. I know she's got one of the better alibis. Standing on stage in front of an audience is pretty good. But her father was crushing her dream of going to New York. And she was furious at being thwarted. Maybe she decided to un-thwart herself. With her father dead, she's free to do whatever she wants—at least as soon as Rhonda loosens the estate purse strings."

"Like you said, her alibi is strong."

"Okay, fine. You're not telling me anything about the case. I get it. At least tell me what's going on with Ross. I've called him a couple of times, but he won't pick up. When I text, he won't reply. How long before you let him come back?"

"I'm still not sure that I'm going to. I respect Charlie. I like him, too. He's a good cop. But he put himself, me, and the whole sheriff's office in a really bad position. I can't have him back on the Crawford case, that's for sure. I don't know that I can even have him back in the office at all."

"No, don't say that, Coop. It would gut him."

"I have to be able to trust the people I work with to be honest with me. Charlie wasn't."

"That's pretty hardline of you. Technically, he didn't lie. He just didn't tell you about Liz. He loves her, I think. He wanted to take care of her. That's understandable, isn't it?"

"Yes. But it still wasn't the right decision. This is tough, Leah. It just is."

He sounded so discouraged that I felt bad for pushing him.

"When you clear the Crawford murder, that'll improve things, right? People can move on, and it'll be your first big win for the office."

"You'd think so. But I was in a meeting with Rhonda and Cliff Timmins yesterday. I don't think that lady is ever moving on. Not unless Rachelle Crawford is arrested, tried, convicted, and sentenced to a hundred years in solitary. No matter how many witnesses there are who can prove she wasn't anywhere near that sauna."

"You need to keep an eye out for *GO News,* too. If Lawlor is the leak, and he gives them something about Charlie and Liz ..."

"I'm aware. If Lawlor is feeding information to Andrea, he's out. And he'll have a hard time getting a job at another law enforcement agency, too."

"How are you going to find out for sure if he is?"

"Timing is everything, Leah. I'm going to give him a chance to hang himself, and we'll see what he does."

"That sounds like fun. Can you do Andrea at the same time? And can I watch?"

"What about freedom of the press? I thought you had that tattooed over your heart."

"*GO News* isn't real press, and she isn't a real reporter. Both of them are a blight on journalism. And don't get me started on how frustrating it is that readers can't seem to tell the difference between reporting and opining."

"I feel a rant coming on."

"Not that I couldn't, but I'll spare you. And even though you've been so very tight-lipped about what's happening with your investigation, if I find out anything useful on mine, I'll let you know."

"Wait, you're still going to be pursuing this? You found out about John for Jennifer, and you can truthfully tell Adam that you gave the cops something new to think about that takes the focus off Rachelle, at least for now. Why aren't you done?"

"Because it's not over. I don't know who killed Bryan Crawford yet."

While I was helping Coop clean up the kitchen, I nicked my finger on the paring knife I was washing and went to the bathroom for a Band-Aid. I was a little taken aback by what I saw there. A woman's robe hung on a hook, and on the shelf was a small makeup bag and a hair dryer. Obviously, they belonged to Kristin. I keep some things at Gabe's, too. It shouldn't have surprised me. But it did.

I heard the kitchen door open as I walked down the hall, and when I came in, Kristin and Coop were laughing together as he helped her towel dry her long auburn hair. I waited a second in the doorway, suddenly feeling like I didn't belong there. Kristin glanced up and smiled.

"Hi, Leah. It's turned into a monsoon out there. I got soaked just coming in from the car," she said. Then she stepped away from Coop and said, "That's good, babe. Thanks."

"You're welcome," he said. "Here, hand me your towel. I'll throw it in with a load right now."

As he left the room, she turned to me.

"Coop didn't tell me you were coming over. How are you? I haven't seen you in forever."

"He didn't know. I just barged in and demanded dinner, and he fed me. I'm heading out now."

"Oh, don't go, please. I'd love to catch up a little. You never did call and set up a day to shadow me at work. I'm going to put on some coffee. You can stay, can't you?"

While she spoke, she'd been opening cupboards and drawers, getting out coffee, and cups, and spoons. She moved about the small kitchen with the ease that familiarity brings.

I felt weird again. The same way I had when I saw Kristin's things in the bathroom. As though she belonged here now, and I didn't. It wasn't like with Rebecca. Kristin wasn't flaunting her "ownership" of Coop, and she wasn't deliberately trying to make me feel out of place. It was the opposite. She was welcoming me into their space. But it was clear that it *was* their space, hers and Coop's.

"Sorry, no coffee for me. I have to run. I'd still like to job shadow you for a day, though. Things are just a little crazy for me right now. I'll call you later if that's still okay."

"Of course it is. You're sure you can't stay? I'd love to hear how your writing's going. Have you got a plot figured out yet?"

She's a nice person, and I knew she was sincere in asking me to stay. But I suddenly couldn't wait to get away.

"No, thanks, but I can't. I promised to be somewhere, and I'm late already. Have a good night. Say goodbye to Coop for me. I'll call you for lunch soon—or you call me. Either way."

I grabbed my jacket but didn't even finish zipping it up before I opened the kitchen door and ran through the pouring rain to my car.

42

"Oh, I'm so sorry for Jennifer. It's a terrible feeling to realize that your marriage isn't what you believed—or wanted to believe—it was," my mother said.

On the way home I had realized I didn't feel like driving back to a dark apartment and sitting alone thinking about how easy Kristin and Coop seemed together, and more to the point, what that meant for my relationship with him. When I drove down my mother's street and saw the light on in the kitchen, it drew me like a beacon through the fog.

"I guess we both know that feeling. But I never in a million years would have predicted this for Jennifer and John. They seemed so, I don't know, solid, I guess," I said.

"Do you think they'll try to put things back together? Divorce is always so hard, but with kids as young as hers it's complicated, too."

"It's too early to tell. You know Jen. She usually just rolls with whatever comes along, but this is pretty big. Besides the whole infidelity thing, personally, I'd find it pretty hard to forgive a husband who gave me a fake terminal illness so he could string his mistress along."

"Yes, that would be a definite deal-breaker for me, but we've all got different break points and blind spots. You put up with things from Nick that I never would have, and I put up with things from your father that you wouldn't have."

"Why is that? Are we all masochists under the surface?"

"No, but I think that we're all unconsciously drawn to people who can help us grow—even if that growth comes through pain. There's always a lesson at the core of the hurt. If we can figure it out, we don't need to repeat the experience in another bad relationship. I hope that's true for Jennifer."

"You've been bingeing Oprah's *Super Soul* podcast again, haven't you?"

"Yes. Would you like me to recommend some episodes? I'd be happy to curate a list of things you need to think about."

"Is there one about how to handle it when your best friend gets a new best friend?"

I hadn't intended to say that. It just popped out.

"Ah, Coop and Kristin."

My mother's intuitive awareness of things that I don't even realize are on my mind can be irritating, but it does save time.

"Yes. I was just over there. I had dinner with Coop, and Kristin came over, so I left."

"I thought you liked Kristin."

"I do. And I'm happy that Coop's happy. It's just, I don't know ... I went to get a Band-Aid after I cut my finger while I was helping Coop do the dishes. I noticed some of Kristin's things in the bathroom, and it just hit me. They're like, 'together' together. Everybody's right. They probably *will* get married."

"And that's a bad thing because?"

"It's not bad. I mean, yay for them. But it's going to be different for me and Coop. When they're married, things are going to change."

"Of course they are. Things are always changing. What do you want, for you and Coop to stay 12 years old, and have a secret tree house just for the two of you, and ride your bikes, and have fun adventures together all day?"

"You say it like that's a bad thing," I said, only half-joking.

"Leah, I know you know this, but maybe you need a reminder. Life isn't Never Never Land, and you aren't Peter—or Petra—Pan. Coop's going to get married sooner or later. I hope that you and Gabe do, too. I'd love to be a grandmother before I'm too old to enjoy it. Things will change. Fighting that fact will only make you miserable. You're not going to like this . . ." She paused.

"Then how about you don't say it?"

But she continued undeterred.

"You sound a little like what my grandmother used to call a dog in the manger."

"Okay, I'll bite—pun totally intended. What's a dog in the manger?"

"It's from a fable about a dog lying on a manger full of straw. When a hungry cow tries to take some of the straw to eat, the dog snarls and bites at him. The dog is keeping something that he doesn't want, just so someone else can't have it."

"So, I'm a dog, Kristin's a cow, and Coop is a pile of hay?"

"Stop it. You know what I'm saying. You don't want a romantic relationship with Coop, but you don't want Kristin to have one either."

"That's not true."

"Isn't it?"

"No. And if you can't see that, well, let's just not talk about it anymore."

My mother hadn't exactly eased my troubled mind. In fact, she'd said several things that had made me more agitated. I postponed going home yet again in favor of the company of Father Lindstrom. Although he sometimes says things I don't like, they have the advantage of not carrying any of the weight of mother-daughter baggage. Which makes them less irritating to hear. And, more often than not, he makes me feel like, flawed though I am, I'm a fairly decent person overall. Sometimes I need to get external confirmation of that.

When I knocked on his apartment door, he opened it the way he always does—with a smile and an expression on his face that said there was no one he'd rather see standing there but me.

"Leah! Come in, come in. I'm having a small glass of Benedictine B&B. Can I tempt you?"

Father Lindstrom's fondness for the herb liqueur blended with brandy, and my extreme aversion to the taste, is a not-that-funny joke between us. But it's our joke and we repeat it often.

"No, thanks. I'm not mad at my tastebuds tonight. A glass of white wine would be nice if you have it, though. It will pair nicely with the whining I came over to do."

When we were seated in his living room, Father Lindstrom in a recliner so large his feet barely touched the floor, and me on a loveseat that had seen better days, I dithered a bit before bringing up the topic on my mind.

"So, if the budget committee at St. Stephen's decided it's not feasible to rebuild the rectory, and the priest's house is now basically this apartment, when are they going to spring for some decent furniture? No offense, Father, but the decor isn't exactly homey."

When the rectory had been destroyed by fire, the parish had gotten together and donated a very eclectic collection of cast-off furniture to furnish his new apartment. Some was okay, like the king-size recliner Father was sitting in, but not suited for the room—or the small stature of the tenant. Some, like the frayed pink loveseat I sat on, were ready to be put out by the side of the road. And none of it looked like it belonged together.

"There's some talk of that, but I'm quite comfortable here and the money can be better used elsewhere in the parish."

"Maybe so but I think this loveseat has reached the end of its days," I said.

"You may be right," he said, noticing that I had scooted forward so that I was basically perching on the frame to avoid being sucked into its lumpy depths.

"Why don't you move to the rocking chair?"

"No, that's all right. I'm not going to stay long anyway. Just dropped by to chat."

He smiled then and took a sip of his drink and waited. Father Lindstrom is very at ease with waiting.

It didn't take long for me to break.

"So, one of my friends—well, it's Coop, I guess I might as well say it. I think he and Kristin Norcross—he brought her to Mom's birthday party—I think he might want to marry her. I don't want him to. Does that make me a bad person?"

"I never think of you as a bad person, Leah. But some context would help me. Why don't you think he should marry? Do you have an objection to Kristin, or do you feel that Coop shouldn't marry anyone?"

"Wow, Father. Way to cut to the heart of the matter. If I wanted to hear hard truths, I could have stayed in my mom's kitchen. I'm kidding. Sort of. But basically, that's what she said, and I don't like how that sounds."

"How does it sound?"

"Like I'm a selfish, immature, bad friend."

"And are you?"

"How can you look so kind and gentle and ask me such tough questions?"

"Sometimes asking tough questions is the kindest thing we can do for each other, Leah."

This time, I was the one who held the silence. Not long enough to beat the master, Gregory Lindstrom, but long enough for me to allow my real feelings to surface.

"All right. Here's the thing. I already know what it's like when Coop gets married. I went through it once before when he was with Rebecca. I know we'll stay friends. He won't just toss me overboard, and I know that Kristin, unlike Rebecca, wouldn't ask him to, either.

"But Kristin will come first. She should, that's what marriage is about. I get it. But I'm not used to coming second in his life. I like the way things are now. I like him with Kristin and me with Gabe, but Coop and I still tight, still right there to catch each other if we fall. It's Kristin he'll be playing catcher for if they get married. And I'm going to miss having him backing me up."

Even as I spoke, I cringed inwardly at how the words sounded out loud. My mother was right. I *was* Petra Pan. Not only did I not want to leave Never Never Land, I didn't want anyone else to, either.

"What if you marry Gabe, do you have the same fears that you and Coop will no longer be close?"

"I'm not marrying Gabe."

The words came out so quickly and decisively, they surprised us both.

"Does that mean that you're not ready to marry Gabe now, or that you've decided that you never will be?"

"Gabe and I have an agreement. We like things the way they are."

I realized that wasn't answering his question, but I also realized I didn't know the answer to it. Or did I?

"You know what, Father? Thanks for the wine, but I think I'll reflect on my unconscious motivations in solitude. At another time. A long time from now. It's getting late and I should go."

His pale blue eyes looked directly into mine. I looked away first.

When I got home from Father Lindstrom's, I remembered I hadn't let Gabe know about my road trip with Miguel. But it had been such a long, emotionally draining day that I just didn't have it in me to go over everything with him. I texted with a promise to call the next day.

I had a hard time falling asleep when I crawled into bed. I kept thinking and replaying from different angles my conversations with my mother and Father Lindstrom. I didn't like the conclusion I came to. I wasn't a good friend to Coop. I was a self-centered one who only wanted him to be happy if it was convenient for me.

Well, admitting the problem is the first step, they say. But I wasn't sure I had the strength of character to take the next one—that is, to accept my lesser role in Coop's life with grace. I turned to the guiding principle that is always there for Nash family members: a problem ignored is a problem solved. When my mind drifted to Father Lindstrom's question about Gabe, I doubled down on the motto, and finally fell asleep.

I woke early but not refreshed. I checked my phone and found a text from Adam Harrison that had come in around midnight.

My mom told me the truth. Thanks.

That was all, but it was enough. Rachelle had come through for Adam, finally. Though I wondered what spin she'd put on her story.

I pulled on my robe and flip-flops and slap-slapped my way to the kitchen for toast and a cup of coffee to clear the brain fog. I needed to focus, because I had a busy day lined up. Review the notes from my interview with Stephanie, see how Jennifer was doing, find Bryan's ex-partner Mitch, wait for Ross to respond to the texts and emails I'd been sending. I didn't have time for personal drama. I pushed thoughts of Coop and Gabe firmly to the bottom of my list.

I was heading for the shower when my intercom buzzed. I looked at my watch and saw it was just seven—pretty early for a visit. I pressed the buzzer.

"Yes?"

"Leah, it's Allie. I know it's early, but I need to see you."

43

"Coffee?" I asked as Allie sat down at the kitchen bar.

"No, thanks. I don't have very long, I have to get to school."

"Okay, what's up?"

"I talked to Adam last night."

"So, you know about his mom and her affair?"

"Yeah. Adam feels good because now she's got a witness who can prove where she was when his stepdad was killed. She told Adam she didn't admit it before, because she didn't want him to think bad about her. But she changed her mind because she didn't want to lie to him anymore. Is that true?"

We were moving into the dangerous waters of half-truths here. I didn't think much of Rachelle, but Adam obviously did. It had probably meant a lot to him that she seemed to finally be putting his feelings above her own. Maybe it was a starting point for a better connection between them. Who was I to cast doubt on her motives? I settled on a true but noncommittal answer.

"I don't know how Rachelle feels or what her motives are. Only she does."

"Well, I think you gave her a chance to tell Adam first, didn't you? Otherwise, she would still be lying. I didn't say that to Adam, and I won't.

But I just like to know what's really true. I'm kind of like you that way, I guess."

"Don't say that in front of your dad. He'll cancel me for sure," I said, but I was touched. "Listen, Allie, this is for your ears only. I did talk to Rachelle and I suggested it was best if she came clean with her son before she talked to the police. But she's the one who decided to do it. We can't know for sure why. Does that satisfy your need-to-know?"

"Yeah, it does. I get why Adam is so happy. I used to want my mom to do something, anything, to show me that she cared more about me than she did her boyfriends. I don't trust Mrs. Crawford, but she's Adam's mom, not mine. I won't say anything to him."

Allie and I might share some characteristics, but she was already a lot smarter than me. At her age I would have been telling my friend that his mother was an asshat—with predictably bad consequences.

"I think that's wise."

"I hope things turn out better for him and his mother than they did for me and mine."

"Allie," I said, reaching out to touch her hand. "Your mother—"

"No, it's all right. I'm over it. It's not like she was ever that much into being a mother. She's probably a lot happier with the guy she took off with than she ever was with me. I like living with my dad, and he needs me. He needs you, too, Leah."

"How's he doing?"

"He's just sitting around in his sweatpants watching the Weather Channel. At least he finally told me he has a girlfriend. He had to, to explain why he's not on the murder investigation, and why he's on leave."

"How do you feel about Liz and your dad?"

"Okay. I mean I don't know her, but I told you before I thought my dad was seeing somebody. I'm glad he is. Only now he isn't. He's not seeing or talking to anybody. That's my other thing I wanted to ask you, Leah. Would you please talk to him?"

"Allie, I've tried. I've called him, I've texted, I've emailed him. He's just not answering. He was so mad at me because I told him he had to tell Coop about his connection to Liz. I'm not sure he'll ever talk to me again."

"He will, I know he will. Sometimes with my dad, you just have to be as stubborn as he is. Please, Leah, try again. Just go over and pound on the door. He'll let you in. I know deep down he'd like to see you."

"All right. I'll give it one more try. But it won't be until later. I've got a list of people to see, things to do first."

She jumped up then and hugged me.

"Thanks, Leah. You never let me down."

"You know how to put on the pressure, Allie. I'll do my best with your dad, but that's all I can promise."

"Your best is always great. I have to go, or I'll be late for class. See you later."

That was definitely not true, but sometimes a little hero worship is a very soothing balm for the soul.

After Allie left, I took a shower and was drying my hair when the phone rang.

"Hi, Maggie. What's going on?"

"I take it you haven't seen the latest *GO News* story."

"No, but I'm guessing it isn't good. Let me call it up."

The headline jumped out at me as soon as I opened the *GO News* site.

Crawford Murder Case in Chaos—Former Lead Detective in Bed with Suspect

"Oh, hell."

"It gets better, and by better, I mean worse. Read it. I'll wait."

I scanned the story under Andrea Novak's byline quickly. In essence it said that Charlie Ross had been suspended for compromising the murder investigation because he was having an affair with the victim's ex-wife, Liz Moretti, who was living under a false name. It framed the "no comment" they got from Liz as something sinister, instead of an attempt to maintain some shred of her privacy.

"This is bad. But for once a *GO News* story is basically true, though the slant is, as always, sensational. Their readers are going to love it. Andrea got one thing wrong, though. Ross is on paid admin leave, he's not suspended. I wonder if Coop made sure Lawlor got hold of the wrong info and passed it on to Andrea. He said he had something in mind to catch him. What have we got on the story?"

"Troy's working on it. He already got the Liz-used-to-be-Tiffany information from the file. He called Rhonda for comment and got a quote from her that's not very flattering to Liz. He's waiting on a call back from Coop to confirm Charlie's situation. We'll have it up later this morning. Unlike *GO News,* we like to confirm our information, even if it means we miss out on a scoop."

"Did he get any comment from Liz?"

"Nope. She's not talking to anybody. I don't blame her, I guess. I don't suppose you have anything to add?"

"No. But between Troy and Miguel, I'm sure they'll deliver. Listen, Maggie, I do have something else on the Crawford case that you'll want to follow up on."

I gave her the condensed version of how my favors for Jennifer and Adam had converged to give Rachelle an alibi and Jennifer a heartache.

"I told Coop what I found out. He didn't have the John and Rachelle affair information, but I couldn't get anything from him about where their investigation is."

"This is good, Leah. We'll start digging. I don't see how *GO News* could know anything yet about the Rachelle angle. We can beat them on that."

"You know, Maggie, sometimes it's not so fun to be in the reporting business."

"Like when the facts that come out hurt people you care about?"

"Yes. I know we have to report it out, the good, the bad, and the ugly. If we don't, if we start picking and choosing, then we've got no credibility. But I wish I could keep Jennifer's private pain out of this. I don't see a way to do it, though, because Rachelle's affair with John is part of the case."

"Do you know what Jennifer is going to do?"

"No. She's hurt right now and angry, too. But she and John have a history together. Plus, there are the kids to think about. And she's been in love with John since high school. She might stick with him."

"I play pickleball with her mother. Bea thinks John is a wrong'un."

"She does? I don't think Jennifer knows that."

"Bea doesn't want her to. John was Jennifer's choice and Bea never wanted to let the fact that she can't stand John cause a rift between her and Jennifer."

"Jennifer thought that if she told her mother that she was afraid John was having an affair, her mom would just tell her to live with it."

"Sometimes mothers and daughters don't communicate very well, I guess. I know I didn't with my mother. You're lucky, Leah. You have a good relationship with Carol."

"Yeah, I guess I am, Maggie. But it takes a lot of work sometimes."

"Anything worth having is worth working for."

She changed the subject abruptly.

"Anyhow, mission accomplished for you, right? You found the answer to Jennifer's question. And you got Adam Harrison something that will help his mother. I guess you're done now."

"Not quite yet. I mean, if Rachelle is out of the picture, who's in? You know me, Maggie. I can't stop now."

"How's Coop feel about that?"

"I think you know the answer to that."

44

When I hung up with Maggie I got started on my day. I reread my notes on Stephanie, looking for anything that might be a flaw in her alibi. Then I went online to the Robley College Theater Department site. I found a detailed page about the production of *A Hole in the World* that included cast photos and biographies, as well as information on the producer, director, stage manager, and all of the crew, and reviews of the production. I read everything, including the review that Stephanie had quoted so proudly to me.

"Stephanie Crawford brings the sexiness of Marilyn Monroe and the acting chops of a young Meryl Streep to the role of Alicia in the Robley College Theater Department production of *A Hole in the World*."

She hadn't been lying about that. But she hadn't given me the whole quote, either. The next line read, "Even though she doesn't appear until the beginning of the second act, her impact on the play is palpable." I thought for a few minutes. Then I phoned my mother.

"Leah, why are you calling? I'm right here in the office. Come down, I brought apple bread."

"Thanks, but I can't right now, I'm working on something. I have a quick question—or two. When you guys do a play for the community theater, when is the call time?"

"A half-hour before the curtain goes up. So, 7:30."

"Does everyone in the play have to be there at the same time? I mean the whole cast, even the ones who aren't in the first act?"

"They should be. It's bad for morale if everyone doesn't convene together with the director before the play starts."

"You said *should*, so that means it doesn't always happen, right?"

"Not always. Once in a while someone has a legitimate reason to be late —a family crisis or something like that and the director would accept that."

"What happens if I have an important part in the play, but I don't have a legitimate reason, I'm just late? Would my understudy step in?"

"Leah, this is the Himmel Community Players, not Broadway. Sometimes we have a hard time getting a cast together at all. We don't have understudies. If you were late, the stage manager would be hunting you down, and if necessary, sending someone to drag you in by your hair. And you probably wouldn't be cast again. Why are you asking me about the theater?"

I ignored her question in favor of another one of my own.

"What if when I got there, I said my car ran out of gas and my phone wasn't charged, but I made it in time to go on and turned in a great performance, would all be forgiven?"

"Not if I were the director, but maybe."

"Okay, one more question. Are you familiar with the play *A Hole in the World*?"

"Yes. It's a favorite of mine, as a matter of fact. I pitched it to the theater board, but we didn't have enough young people to fill out the cast, so we decided against it."

"How long is the first act?"

"About 45 minutes. Why are you asking me all these questions? You've never had an interest in theater before."

"I'm just trying to work out an idea. I'll talk to you later. Thanks, Mom."

It had dawned on me when I read the second line of Stephanie's review, the one she hadn't quoted to me, that I'd found a hairline crack in her alibi. I might be able to split it wide open. The play started at 8:00 Friday night. Robley College was two hours away from the Crawford house. As Stephanie had told me—and showed me with her curtain call photo—she had the perfect alibi. There was no way she could have locked her father in the sauna shortly after 6 and walked on stage at 8:00 p.m.

Except she didn't have to be on stage at 8:00. She came on at the top of the second act, which wouldn't have started until around 8:45. She could have locked the sauna door at 6:15 and driven back to the theater with time to spare before she had to be on stage.

I felt a sudden surge of excitement. I began looking for contact information for the director or the stage manager. Then I was hit with a wave of doubt. Ross would have checked her alibi. Wouldn't he have seen the same thing I had? But it would be easy to miss the part about Stephanie not coming on until the second act, especially if he was already leaning toward Rachelle as his prime suspect. I shook my head to clear away the second-guessing. It didn't matter if Ross had checked it out, I needed to do it for myself.

Mackenzie Daley was the stage manager for *A Hole in the World*. But the online student directory only listed email addresses, no phone numbers. I went back and read her bio. She worked as a student assistant in the Theater Department. I called the general number.

"Theater Department, student assistant Trina, how can I help you?"

"Hi, Trina, I'm trying to reach Mackenzie Dailey. Is she in?"

"Sorry, Mackenzie doesn't come in until Monday. Do you want to leave a message?"

Hell's bells. I didn't want to wait that long.

"Well, maybe you can help me. My name is Andrea Novak."

I had to stifle a sneeze then, no doubt the result of the sudden spurt of growth at the end of my nose from the whopper I had just told. I play it straight most of the time—always if I'm going to quote a source—but this situation called for a little subterfuge. Okay, a big subterfuge.

"What can I do for you?"

"I work for *GO News*, it's an online news service. Maybe you follow us on Twitter?"

"I'm not that much into news," she said, a trace of polite apology in her voice, but no interest.

"Okay, well just to give you some background, the father of Stephanie Crawford, a student at Robley, was murdered last month, and—"

"Wait! Stephanie's dad was murdered? I knew he died but I didn't know somebody *killed* him!"

"Yes, it's a tragedy, and *GO News* is doing a story on the aftermath—how everyone is coping, what they're feeling, how they're finding the strength to go on. I've talked to all the family to build out what their life was like before the murder. But we're obsessive about getting the facts right. I just need to confirm that Stephanie was on stage at Robley the night her father died."

"Yeah, she was. I should know, I was doing props."

"It's hard to think that at 8 o'clock when Stephanie walked out on that stage, full of life and confidence, at that very moment, her father lay dying. I heard she gave a stellar performance. It's so sad that her father never knew."

"She was good that night, but in my opinion she's no Meryl Streep. And she wasn't on stage at eight. She didn't come on until the second act. And she was almost late for that. Nothing new there."

"I thought it was a cardinal sin in the theater to be late for a performance."

"It is, but it helps if you're the stage manager's BFF. Stephanie was late for rehearsals all the time, and nothing happened to her. I could've played Gillian, my tryout was really good. And I'd never be late. It's so unprofessional. But the director said Stephanie looked more like the part."

"That's ridiculous. Good acting transcends appearance. Take Barbara Stanwyck. She wasn't conventionally pretty. But she played femme fatales convincingly by the sheer force of her performances. Look at her in *Double Indemnity*."

"Who?"

Trina was obviously not a classic film fan. I moved back to my main point.

"It must have thrown things into a tizzy if Stephanie was late opening night."

"You'd think. When she didn't show for call time at 7:30, I told

Mackenzie that I could play the part. I knew all the lines from being prompter when the actors first went off book. She told me to chill, that Stephanie called and said she had car trouble, but she was on her way. And she did get there before the end of the first act. But still, I could've done it just as well."

"I see. Okay, well, then thanks, Trina, I—"

"Hey—sorry, I forgot your name—but I'm not going to be in your story or anything, am I? You won't quote me on anything I said about Mackenzie or Stephanie, will you? I wouldn't want—"

Though I was a touch sad she didn't remember my fake name Andrea Novak, and thus Andrea would feel no future repercussions from this interview, on the whole it was probably for the best.

"No, no worries. It was just us talking. Nothing you said was for attribution. Thanks for your time, bye."

45

Stephanie's solid alibi was a thing of the past, and I had just widened the likely suspect pool. Car trouble was the flimsiest of excuses. Being late didn't mean that Stephanie had killed her father, but she'd have to come clean about her whereabouts to take her off my list.

Mitch Toomey was up next and the first thing I had to do was find him. Leah Madsen at Crawford Plumbing and Electrical had said she thought he lived outside Hailwell. I tried a search online, but the only Toomey in the area was an 87-year-old woman named Della. She lived in Delving, not far from the county line in the eastern part of Grantland County. It wasn't anywhere near Hailwell, but she might be a relative of Mitch's. She had a landline, so I gave it a try. It rang quite a while and I was just about to hang up when someone answered.

"Hello?" The speaker sounded slightly out of breath, as though she'd been in a different part of the house when the phone rang.

"Hi. My name is Leah Nash. I'm looking for Mitchell Toomey. Does he live there by any chance?"

"Could you speak up a little, dear? I'm out of batteries for my hearing aid. I meant to drive into town to get some yesterday, but it was raining cats and dogs. Not that I'd melt, mind you, I'm not sweet enough for that. But I hate getting wet."

I was encouraged by her cheerful and detailed response. Thank goodness for the extreme extroverts of the world, who are always happy to engage with strangers, and rarely question their motives.

"Yes, sure, sorry," I said, amping up my voice and repeating what I'd said.

"Mitch did stay with me for a while, but he moved in with a lady friend, oh, it must be four or five years ago. Over in the trailer park in Hailwell. I haven't seen him, though, for a year or more. He used to stay with us a lot when he was a boy. He was kind of a son to my husband Bob. We never had any kids of our own. He and Bob loved to go fly fishing together." She gave a small sigh, then said, "But you didn't call to hear me walk down memory lane. What do you want Mitch for?"

"Somebody told me he did electrical work."

"Oh, I wouldn't hire him for that, dear."

"Why? Isn't he good at his job?"

"He used to be a real good electrician back 15 or 20 years ago, but he's drunk more than he's sober these days. I hate to say it about my own nephew, but it's true. Mitch's dad Earl, that was my husband's brother, he was the same way. It hit Bob pretty hard when Mitch started going down the same path as Earl. It's a sad, sad thing, but you can't fix it for him, I used to tell Bob. Now, me, I like a little gin and tonic now and then, but for people like Mitch the stuff is just poison to them. Now, where did you say you're from?"

I hadn't, but it was clear she was a little lonely, and it didn't hurt me to spend a few extra minutes with her. As the conversation went on, Della found the holy grail that friendly people look for in every encounter with a stranger—a shared connection.

"You're from Himmel, you said?"

"That's right."

"You wouldn't know Miguel Santos, would you?"

I shouldn't have been surprised, given Miguel's reach, but I was.

"I do, very well. Is he a friend of yours?"

"Yes, he is. He came by with a crew of volunteers from the Commission on Aging last fall and raked up my lawn. Such a handsome boy, and so nice. I wanted him to meet my neighbor's daughter Autumn. When I told him that he laughed. Then he told me he was gay. I told him I was an equal opportunity matchmaker, just give me his specifications. I listen to his podcast every week. I just love him. How do you know Miguel?"

"We work together. I'm part owner of the *Himmel Times*."

"Ohhh. You're Leah *Nash*. The crime writer. I've got to get those batteries for my hearing aid. I thought you said Lee Cash. Are you working on a true crime book about Bryan Crawford? I read all about his murder in the paper. Is that the real reason that you're looking for Mitch? Because he used to be a partner with Bryan?"

She was quick as well as curious.

"I'm not working on a book, but I do want to talk to Mitch. Do you know what happened between him and Bryan, why the partnership ended?"

"To hear him tell it, he was the backbone of that business and Bryan cheated him every which way to Sunday. I just tune him out when he gets talking like that. I don't know what happened, but I expect that Mitch's drinking had a lot to do with it."

"You said he lives in Hailwell, do you have his address?"

"I'll have to get my address book and look it up, hang on a minute."

She was back in less than that and gave me both the address and a phone number for her nephew.

"Thanks, Della. It was nice talking to you."

"I'm glad you called. Stop by next time you're out this way. And you tell Miguel hello for me, and I'm still looking for the perfect match for him."

"I'll do that."

The Whispering Pines Manufactured Home Park was a pretty depressing place. The lots were small and close together, and although they might sprout a few blades of grass in the summer, at the moment they were muddy and pocked with puddles. The brown needles on the bedraggled pines that enclosed the park seemed to give the lie to the term "evergreen." Several leaned alarmingly, looking as though the next big wind would topple them over.

As I drove down the rutted gravel road that wound through the park, I realized I had done Della a disservice. When she had referred to it as a trailer park, I'd imagined that she was just using the term a lot of people her age did to refer to modular and manufactured homes. However, her description was closer to reality than my imagining had been.

A few of the places fell into the category of manufactured homes. They were double-wide, several with small front porches, carports, and window boxes waiting for spring flowers. But most were old-fashioned trailers, true mobile homes without the wheels, sporting dinged and dirty aluminum siding and metal skirting on the bottom. Many had concrete blocks serving as front steps.

Mitch's place, or more accurately that of his "lady friend," was at the end of Jack Pine Lane, number 34. It was a single-wide mobile home with blue and white siding. I could see white curtains at the windows, and there was a gravel path leading to the front steps, which were wooden, with a handrail, and sheltered by a striped metal awning. A bright yellow bird feeder stood a few feet from the door.

Either Mitch had it more together than his aunt believed, or his lady friend was good with home repair. The short driveway next to the house was just long enough for two cars, and one was already there, a dented dark blue Volkswagen sporting a weathered, half-gone Packers bumper sticker. I pulled in behind it and walked up to the front door.

I knocked and waited, heard stumbling around inside, waited some more, then knocked again. Finally, the door was flung open.

"Hi, are you Mitch Toomey?"

"Who wants to know?"

The man who had answered the door spoke in a raspy voice as he swayed slightly and leaned on the door for balance. He gave off a sour, boozy smell and his nose was reddened with the broken capillaries of the habitual drinker. He had to be Mitch. I knew that he was Bryan's age, early fifties, but his lined face and pouchy eyes made him look much older. I didn't bother with any subterfuge.

"I'm Leah Nash. I'm here to ask you about Bryan Crawford."

"What about him?"

"You do know that he's dead, right?"

"Bastard ruined my life, that's what I know."

"I'd like to hear about that. Do you have a few minutes?"

46

I didn't wait for an answer, instead I acted as though he had invited me in, and began to step through the door, forcing him to step back. The fact that he'd already begun his drinking for the day could work in my favor if it loosened his tongue.

The living room was sparsely furnished but immaculately clean with a small sofa in a floral pattern, a patched brown vinyl recliner, and a flatscreen television on a stand. A shelf held a few framed family photographs. There were no books, no plants, and none of the ornamental knickknacks that most people have on display.

Judging by the half empty glass of amber liquid sitting on a small table next to the recliner, that was Mitch's preferred seat. I took a spot on the sofa and waited for him to settle down on the chair.

"Whadda ya say your name was?" he asked, after taking a long drink. The slur in his voice was more pronounced than I'd noticed at the door, and my heart sank a little. He might be too far gone to carry on a conversation.

"Leah Nash. I heard that you used to be in business with Bryan Crawford. I wondered if you could tell me something about him?"

"I can tell you he's a lying two-faced son-of-a-bitch who stole my company. Is that what ya wanna hear?" He flung out the hand that held his glass of liquor, and some of it sloshed out with the movement.

"Why did he steal your company?"

"Because . . . because he's a cheater. He didn't wanna gimme my share. I was the best damn electrician in three counties. People begged me to work for 'em."

He stopped again for a long drink, closing his eyes as he did. When he opened them again, he returned to his rant.

"Now I got no money, no family, no friends. Him and his sister, they stole me blind. Said I wasn't pullin' my weight. That's bull!"

He drained his glass, and then, in one of the wild swings of emotion that can come with being drunk at 10:30 in the morning, he began to cry. Clearly, this was not going to work. I stood to leave.

"Mitch, I can see you're not feeling very well. Maybe we can talk tomorrow. I'll call later and—"

We both turned at the sound of a door opening at the opposite end of the mobile home.

A woman's voice called out as footsteps came down the hall, "Mitch, Carl said you didn't give him the lot rent for this month yet. I—"

She stopped as she arrived at the living room and we both stared at each other. I was the first to recover.

"Hello, Sheila."

Rachelle Crawford's house cleaner was Mitch's "lady friend."

She looked rapidly back and forth between me and Mitch, obviously confused by the presence of a virtual stranger in her living room. Mitch ignored both of us and closed his eyes as he leaned back in his recliner.

"Sheila, I—" Before I could explain my visit, Mitch made a snuffling sound and jerked upright again. He looked at us with bleary eyes and said, "I gotta take a nap."

Standing unsteadily, he waved off Sheila's move to assist him and tottered unsteadily down the hall, to what I assumed was a bedroom. Then a door shut, and a soft thud followed. No doubt Mitch, flopping onto the bed.

"I don't understand why you're here. Did you say anything to Mitch about me working for Rachelle?" Sheila's voice was tense.

"Why? Is it a secret?"

"How did you find me?"

"Find you? I wasn't looking for you, Sheila. I'm not exactly sure what's happening here. Can we sit down for a minute and talk this through? I think we're both a little confused."

I sat back down on the sofa, and Sheila perched uneasily on the edge of Mitch's chair.

"I got Mitch's address from his Aunt Della. I came to see him because I know he was Bryan Crawford's partner at one time. I agreed to look into the murder for a friend. So—"

"You think Mitch is involved?"

"I don't think anything just yet."

That wasn't strictly accurate. I had come hoping to discover some present-day link between Mitch and Bryan that might be connected to the murder. I hadn't expected to find that link to be Sheila.

"You know, Sheila, I don't even know your last name."

"Why would you? I'm just the cleaning lady. That's what you think, isn't it?"

"No, it's not. Look, I just came to see Mitch because I thought he might be able to give me some background information on Bryan."

"Well, he can't." Her tone was flat and decided.

"I can see that he can't today, but—"

"You didn't answer my question before. Did you say anything to Mitch about me working for the Crawfords?"

"No, I barely talked to him at all. I only got here a couple of minutes before you did. I had no idea that you lived with Mitch. I also have no idea why you're so worried that I might have mentioned you work for the Crawfords, and I also still don't know your last name."

"Keller. My name is Sheila Keller. Mitch doesn't know that I work for them. I don't know what he'd do if he found out. He hates them all so much. And he should. Bryan and his sister used him. They wanted his customers, and they wanted his crew, and they wanted his reputation. When they had all that, they cheated him out of his partnership."

"That doesn't quite match the story I've heard."

"From who? Rhonda? What did she tell you? That they had to get rid of Mitch because he was drinking? That's not true. Oh, I know what he looks like now. But he's a good man, and he used to be a successful man. If it wasn't for Bryan Crawford, he still would be."

"Were you with Mitch when he and Bryan Crawford split up their partnership?"

"No. That was before I met him. But he told me all about it. People like the Crawfords, they think they can walk all over people, stab their friends in the back. Bryan and Mitch were best friends in high school. Mitch's business was way more successful than Bryan's. He was the one doing Bryan a favor by going into partnership with him. And then look what it got him."

"Sheila, you sound like you hate the Crawfords as much as Mitch does. Why on earth did you go to work for them?"

"Because we need the money. The pay is good. People like us, we don't have a lot of choices."

"Did Bryan know about your connection to Mitch?"

"No, none of them do. I'm invisible to them. I clean at Vivienne's Nail Salon in Omico every Saturday. One day last year, Rachelle was Viv's last client. I heard her complaining that she couldn't find a reliable house cleaner. I was looking for more work, so I told her I could do the job. Viv vouched for me, and Rachelle hired me right there."

"But if you're so worried about Mitch knowing you work for her, why did you take the job?"

"I didn't know who she was until she gave me her full name and her address. She offered me $10 an hour more than any of my other jobs, and I get a lot of hours there. Always two days a week, sometimes three. Maybe that doesn't mean much to you, but it sure does to us. I couldn't turn it down. Mitch hasn't had much work lately."

I wondered how long "lately" had been. If Mitch started drinking so early that he was half gone by late morning, "lately" was probably a very long time.

"How long have you and Mitch been together?"

"Four years. I met him when I waitressed in a bar. Don't look at me like that."

"Like what? I'm just listening."

"No, you're not. You're thinking Mitch is a loser and I'm a loser for being with him. You feel sorry for me. You don't need to. Mitch works whenever he can, but it's hard for him to get places since he lost his driver's license. He's not always like this. He's going through some things right now," she said.

"What's he going through?"

"His son won't talk to him anymore. Said he didn't want Mitch around his kids, told him he was a terrible father, and he wasn't going to give him a chance to be a terrible grandfather, too. How could a son say that to his own father? It was so cruel. That's what set Mitch off a couple of days ago. He was doing real good until then."

"Mitch was on the wagon?"

"Well, no, not that exactly, but he was trying to cut down, tapering off, you know."

Yes, indeed I did know. I'd had a brief relationship once with a man who drank too much. I was familiar with the excuses, the promises, and the concept of enabling. He, too, had been a "good man." But alcoholism is a nasty disease, and it doesn't determine its victims based on their character, or lack thereof. When I had stopped enabling Connor, he had found someone who would. Someone probably very like Sheila.

"Sheila, if you think I'm judging you, or pitying you, or whatever, I'm not." I was, a little, but you know. "Your life with Mitch is your business. But are you sure that the way he told the story about his partnership with Bryan is exactly the way it happened? I've been around alcoholics before and I—"

"Mitch isn't an alcoholic. He just drinks too much sometimes. He wouldn't if it wasn't for all the bad things that happened to him because of Bryan Crawford. That's why I feel fine about taking his money—well his wife's money, now, I guess. It's not much payback for what he did to Mitch."

"Is Mitch looking for payback? Are you?"

"Why wouldn't we be? But I guess you could say we got it. Bryan's dead, and Mitch is still here. I don't have anything else to say. I'd appreciate it if you didn't tell Rachelle about Mitch. I still need that job."

"I won't say anything to Rachelle. But the police might."

"The police?" The look on her face was both surprised and worried. "They already talked to me when Bryan died. I don't know anything. I told them that."

"Well, I found out about you and Mitch. I imagine they will, too."

47

My unexpected encounter with Sheila had given me something new to think about. Mitch was still very bitter about the way he felt he'd been treated. And he blamed Bryan for his current circumstances. Resentment is a very ugly thing. But Mitch was way too deep into his drinking to carry off a revenge plan. However, Sheila wasn't. And Sheila had access—to Bryan's insulin, to his supper and sauna routine on Fridays, to the weekend schedule of the family.

Maybe her taking the job at the Crawfords' wasn't by chance. Maybe she'd planned it, with Mitch's urging. She was certainly devoted to him. Was she devoted enough to kill for him? That seemed like a stretch.

I had a lot of thoughts swirling around in my head. I needed to bounce them off someone.

"Sorry about the limited menu," I said, handing Gabe his cheese sandwich. "I was going to treat you to a real lunch, with waiters and everything, but—"

"No need to apologize. I'm the one on a short lunch break. A quick sandwich is all I have time for. Besides, the company is excellent, and the view is beautiful," he said, and smiled.

We were sitting on the window seat in my apartment, looking at the car and pedestrian traffic three floors down.

"It's fun to watch people scurrying down the street, knowing they have no idea I'm watching them. It's like my mini Mt. Olympus here, right? I love the view, but it's not exactly beautiful."

"Maybe I wasn't talking about the view out of the window."

I shook my head and smiled.

"Okay, not that I don't enjoy flattery, but that isn't why I brought you here. I want to run something by you before you have to rush back to court to fight for truth, justice, and the American Way."

"I think that's Superman. I feel like I have more of a Batman vibe. But go on, you've got my undivided attention."

I brought him up to speed on John and Rachelle.

"You can see the implications, right? Rachelle was with John, so she wasn't locking her husband in the sauna, but somebody did. I have two new ideas."

I told him about Stephanie's flawed alibi.

"Let me be the defense attorney that I am, here. Just because Stephanie was late to the theater, it doesn't necessarily follow that it's because she was killing her father. She could have been somewhere else entirely."

"Yes, I know. But she has such a good motive. All that money."

"Lots of spoiled children will inherit money when their parents die, but very few of them kill for it."

"You're just trying to ruin all my fun, aren't you? But I have another rabbit to pull out of the hat."

I explained the surprising situation with Sheila Keller.

"Okay, this time you've got easy access, but is the motive that strong? Revenge after all this time seems a little shaky. And it's second-hand revenge at that. Bryan didn't do anything to Sheila, it was Mitch he wronged —if he even did."

"Ah, but it doesn't matter if he did or not, as long as Mitch believes he did. He has a motive, but he doesn't have the wherewithal to do anything about it. But Sheila is a classic co-dependent. She's taken on all of his grievances, real or imagined, and embraced them as her own."

"Sounds like it's time to pull out your legal pad and do some paper and pencil thinking. And speaking of thinking ... "

"Yes?"

"What do you think of a week in New York in June? The weather should be good. I can show you more of my favorite haunts. We barely scratched the surface on our long weekend."

"What made you think of taking a trip to the city?"

"Lucy called last night. Her grandmother died yesterday afternoon. She's going to be there another week or so taking care of things, and then she's coming here to spend a week with Dominic. We talked about him going back with her, but it's so close to the end of the school year, we decided he should stay with me and finish out. I thought you and I could both take him back when school's over. The three of us will have a great time. What do you say?"

I suddenly felt boxed in. I fought the impulse to blurt out a quick no. Why did I feel so pressured about a fun vacation? My intermittent but usually troublesome inner voice—conscience, instinct, beaten-down guardian angel, I'm not sure which—popped in uninvited. *Because you know you have to stop playing with Gabe's feelings.* I shook my head to silence it.

"Leah, you're shaking your head no. Why don't you want to go?"

"No, I do, I do. It's not that. I was just thinking how to fit that in with my new life's work as a fiction writer. I haven't even started the book yet."

"It's not for almost three months. You'll be well on your way then and ready for a mid-book break. Come on, say yes."

What on earth was the matter with me? I couldn't bring myself to commit.

"It sounds great, Gabe. Let's talk more later, you've got to get going and I have to get busy."

"You're right," he said, looking at his watch. "I'm due in court in 15 minutes. We'll make plans later. Bye!" He leaned in to kiss me quickly and I heard his footsteps pounding as he raced down my front stairs.

48

I hesitated before I knocked on the front door. Despite Allie's pleading and her assurances that a visit from me was just what Ross needed, I steeled myself for a hostile reception. I got it.

"Whadda ya doin' here?"

Ross looked bad. He hadn't bothered to shave. The result wasn't a sexy, stubble beard. It was more of an I'm-at-deer-camp beard. His hair was sticking out in the back, and he wore baggy gray sweatpants and a frayed gray sweatshirt to match.

"Hi, Ross. I'm just checking on you. You haven't answered any of my texts or my voicemails."

"Ya think there might be a reason for that?" He favored me with a fierce scowl.

A gust of wind sent a burst of rain onto my neck. I shivered.

"Charlie, it's cold out here. Could I please come in for just a minute? I think we should talk, don't you? Allie's worried about you. I brought you a caramel macchiato."

I hoped the combination of his concern for Allie and his sweet tooth would give me an edge. It seemed to work. He stepped aside, leaving the door open, and walked toward his den. I followed. We sat in the same places we had on my last visit—he on his plaid rocker-recliner, me on the brown sofa. I handed him his drink.

"Thanks."

"You're welcome."

I waited, thinking that he might want to open the conversation with a bit of venting and verbal bashing of me. But he just sipped on his hot drink and stared at the Weather Channel, which was predicting more rain for our area of Wisconsin. I tried a weather gambit to break the ice.

"So, looks like we're in for it, doesn't it? It feels like it's been raining for six months straight. Might be time for Coop to stop building furniture in that wood shop of his and start on an ark instead."

He didn't answer.

"Ross, come on, did you invite me in just to watch you drink coffee and monitor the weather? I know you're mad at me. Can't we at least talk it out?"

He still didn't answer, and I began to feel a little irritated myself. I had a ton of things to do, none of which included coaxing him out of his bad mood as though he were a cranky toddler.

"Okay, fine. I was going to update you on some pretty interesting developments in Bryan Crawford's murder. I'm sure you're not getting anything from the sheriff's office right now. But I'm not staying just to beg you to talk to me."

I stood to leave.

"Wait." He picked up the remote and turned off the TV.

"Sit down." He put his chair in the upright position and turned to look at me. I accepted the conciliatory gesture for what it was and returned to my spot.

"You want some water or something? You didn't bring anything for yourself."

"No, I'm good."

He waited a second, then looked down at his hands and began talking in a rush.

"I'm sorry, Nash. I'm not mad at you. I'm mad at myself. I'm embarrassed, if you wanna know. That's why I didn't answer your texts or calls. I haven't even talked to Liz. Just texted and told her I was sorry. I'm just so pissed off at myself and ashamed at the same time."

"Ross—"

"No. Now I got started, let me finish. You were right. I screwed up. Bad. I was tryin' to protect Liz, but I made it worse. I knew better. But Liz is ... she's ... it's because I ..."

His voice trailed off and he wouldn't look at me.

"Because what? Because you care about her, Ross? Maybe even love her? It's okay to say that, you know. You made a bad call, but when you care about somebody, sometimes you do the wrong thing for the right reason."

He finally looked up then.

"Don't let me off the hook like that. But yeah, I guess I like Liz a lot. Maybe I might love her. Are you happy?" He scowled at me to cover his discomfort at revealing his feelings.

It would have been comical, if he wasn't in so much trouble and misery.

"Of course I'm happy, Ross. That's great. And when this is over—"

"No, I gotta say this. I wasn't just thinkin' about Liz. That was just part of it. I didn't wanna give up the case for myself. I didn't want Owen Fike to take over my murder investigation."

"I thought you liked Owen."

"It's not him, Nash. He's all right. It's me compared to him. He's got the fancy college degree. He's a lot younger than me. Coop's gotta look to the future. I'm old school, I know that. I'm not up on every new thing like Owen is. I'm not as brainy as him. But I'm still a good cop. I wanted to prove that by solvin' the Crawford case. I got maybe a dozen years to retirement. I don't wanna spend those years running security at the county fair. Now I balled up the investigation and I might not even have a job."

It was exceedingly painful to witness the usually self-confident Ross brought so low.

"Ross, Coop respects you. I know he values you. Sure, Owen's got a degree and he's smart. But you've got more experience and you're smart, too. You did a dumb thing, you're paying the price for it now. When this is over, you'll be back on the job. Coop doesn't play favorites and he doesn't hold grudges. You know that."

I firmly pushed down the memory of Coop's unwillingness to reassure me that Ross didn't need to worry about his job.

He looked up then and gave me a half smile.

"Nice try. I appreciate it. But I don't see it that way. I don't mean Coop's a bad guy. But I kinda boxed him in by not tellin' him about me and Liz. You saw *GO News*, right? They're makin' it look like I'm some corrupt cop. And that Coop's in on the corruption if he doesn't fire me. It's BS, but a lotta people read it. I'd like to take that smug little bastard Spencer Karr and knock him six ways to Sunday."

I was glad to hear a little bit of fire in his voice with that last sentence.

"Ross, as satisfying as that image is, there's only one thing that's going to quiet *GO News* down. Lucky for you, I know what it is."

49

"Whadda ya mean?"

"I mean that I stand ready to stand by my partner. The detective team of Nash and Ross is not going down in flames. With my brains and your experience, we've got this."

"Got what?"

"Got the murder of Bryan Crawford well in hand. Keep up, Ross."

"Wait a minute. Does Coop know whatever you think you know?"

"Yes. Well, most of it. We're going to get this investigation wrapped up and *GO News* punched down. I've got solid new information on Stephanie Crawford, a surprising fact about Sheila Keller, *and* something on Rachelle that's going to make you rethink everything you think you know. Do you want to hear it, or not?"

He stared at me for a second as though weighing whether he was in or out. Then he said, "Fine. Tell me what you got. Start with Stephanie Crawford."

I had planned to lead off with Rachelle and John, but maybe it was better to present him with two plausible alternatives before I demolished his Rachelle theory.

I explained how I'd found the flaw in Stephanie's alibi through a full reading of the review Stephanie was so proud of, and a conversation with the disgruntled props manager, student assistant Trina.

"Now that we know she didn't arrive at the theater until after eight, that opens a lot of possibilities, don't you think?"

"I don't believe it!" He shook his head, a disgusted look on his face.

"Ross, just because you don't like what I found out doesn't mean it's not true."

"Nah, that's not it. That was good work, Nash. Real good. I made a mistake. Looks like I'm gettin' to be an expert at that. I had Drew Lawlor check Stephanie's alibi. He said the stage manager confirmed it. He didn't go the extra mile, like you did, and he shoulda."

"About Lawlor, Ross. I think he's the source for the leaks coming out of the sheriff's office the last few weeks. I'm almost positive he's the one who leaked the story about Liz and you to *GO News*."

"Yeah? I knew he was a suck-up. I didn't think he'd take the risk of leakin' information to the press. I need to have a little talk with that pissant."

"Don't. Coop knows and he's handling it. Eyes on the prize, Ross. You want your job back, right?"

He nodded.

"Okay then. I've got an idea for breaking Stephanie's half-assed alibi."

"What is it?"

"I'll tell you when it works out. If it doesn't, then this conversation never happened. Now, have you heard the name Mitch Toomey before?"

"Yeah. He was Bryan Crawford's partner. The partnership split up because of Toomey's drinking."

I must have looked crestfallen, because Ross said in a teasing voice, "Hey, come on, what did ya think I was doin' all this time? I found Mitch Toomey, too. But if you're goin' to pitch him as the killer, you can stop right there. If Crawford was killed on impulse—shot to death, say, then maybe. But Toomey is too deep in the bottle to plan somethin' like this murder. Besides that, he's had 10 years to pay the guy back, why now?"

"How did you get on to Mitch?"

"I'm a detective, Nash. I detected. Besides, I remember when Crawford Plumbing and Electrical was C&T Plumbing and Electrical. I asked Rhonda and she told me about Mitch Toomey. I don't know if it went down like she said, but she was on the money as far as Mitch havin' a real serious drinking problem."

"You talked to him, then?"

"I caught up with him at his favorite bar, and he wasn't that far from fallin' off his stool at three in the afternoon. He had plenty to say about how Crawford done him wrong. But there's no way the guy could mastermind a murder. You got a knack for findin' things out, Nash. I'll give you that. But you're not a detective."

Normally, the smugness with which he said that would irritate me. At the moment, however, I was glad to see that he was coming out of his funk enough to goad me.

"No, but I'm a journalist, and like I keep telling you, my job isn't that different from yours. I just can't arrest people. Which is something I'd really like to add to my job description, by the way. But let's table Mitch for a minute. What do you know about Sheila Keller?"

"The house cleaner? Enough. She's not in the picture. No motive."

Now it was my turn to be smug.

"Oh? She lives with Mitch. Has for the past four years. And she's very devoted to him."

It probably doesn't speak very well of me, but I felt a pleasant rush of satisfaction at the surprise on his face. I could see Ross recalibrating things as I waited for him to weigh in.

"Okay. Ya got me. I didn't know that. I think I see where you're goin' with it. Sheila coulda done the killing with Mitch eggin' her on. But murder's a big risk to take for a grudge that old, especially when it's not even your grudge. How'd you get on to her?"

"I'd like to say it was my superior detective skills, but actually, I stumbled across her by accident. I went to see Mitch at the trailer park where he lives. I didn't get anywhere because he'd already been drinking pretty heavily. I was leaving when Sheila walked in. I don't know which of us was more surprised."

"My grandma always said it's better to be born lucky than smart."

He started rocking his chair back and forth then, frowning as he did.

Then he said, "There's somethin' else. It's not much. So, don't go gettin' all carried away, but it's there."

"What?"

"A coupla days after we opened the investigation, this guy, George Wynn, calls. Strikes me as the nosy neighbor type, which is just what you want in a case like this. He lives a ways down the road from the Crawfords. Late Sunday afternoon of the weekend Crawford died, old George heard a real loud car comin' from the Crawfords' end of the road. He looked and saw a VW bug headin' north. He didn't get a license plate, and he wasn't sure of the color either. Just that it was a dark one. We checked. No one in the family drives a VW, so it went in the file."

"Ross, Sheila Keller owns a VW bug. It's dark blue. And I heard her tell Rachelle that she was afraid she might get a ticket, because the muffler was going."

"All right, hold on there, Brenda Starr. There's lots of VW bugs on the road."

"But how many people with a VW had a reason to be in the Crawfords' neighborhood on that particular Sunday night?"

"The car coulda come from another house on that road. And George said it *could've* come from the Crawfords' driveway, not that it did. Are you throwin' your Stephanie theory overboard already?"

"It's not a theory, it's just a possibility. And I'm not throwing it overboard. But you already said no one in the family owns a VW. That includes Stephanie."

"What about a boyfriend?"

"I don't know that she has one."

"Might be worth checkin' on. Your trouble is, you're looking to complicate things. Sheila may be in love with the guy, but deep down she's gotta know Mitch is kiddin' himself when he blames Crawford. She's not gonna risk prison for some half-ass payback plan. This murder isn't about some *Count of Monte Cristo* revenge plot from 10 years ago."

It always throws me off track a little when Ross makes an unexpected literary allusion, as he did with his *Count of Monte Cristo* reference. But I resisted the urge to pursue its source.

"I suppose you're still stuck on Rachelle. Well, I can see why. I almost came over to your side while I was trying to help Adam. But what I found out yesterday changes everything!"

I tried one of Miguel's dramatic pauses, but it didn't work as well for me as it does for him.

"Just tell your story, Nash."

I went through what Miguel and I had discovered the day before.

"After we visited Grace and Blessings, and I found out how easy it was to come and go there, I was all in on Rachelle, like you. But finding out about Rachelle and John, well, that put an end to that."

He was rocking his recliner back and forth again, rubbing his chin between his thumb and index finger as he did.

"Now that's real interesting, Nash."

I had expected him to be a little more upset at having his primary suspect ruled out.

"It's a little more than interesting, don't you think? Rachelle was with John Pilarski. I didn't get that wrong, Ross. There's a witness plus photos. What else do you need?"

"I'm not doubtin' what you found, Nash. I'm thinking about what it means."

"It means Rachelle didn't kill her husband. She couldn't have. She was lying, but not about that."

"Take it easy. Her whole alibi bothered me from the get-go, even before I knew her weekend retreat story had as many holes as a cheese grater. See, Rachelle was so helpful it made me suspicious. Showed me her credit card receipt, photos she took on the grounds, the brochure with the weekend agenda, the whole deal. When I called the retreat center, I saw how she could've worked the killing.

"My idea was that she checked in, then turned around and drove back to Omico in time to lock her husband in the sauna, then drove back to the retreat. Then she did it all over again on Sunday, only this time to unlock the door, in case anyone from work drove over to check on Bryan when he didn't show up. It would put the kibosh on her plan if the door was locked."

"Ross, I can't believe I'm saying this, but we had a mind meld. I thought the same thing after Miguel and I talked to the manager at the center. But then we went to the bed and breakfast and found out that's where she was all weekend. That's when I knew it wasn't her."

"See, that's where we're different, Nash. What you just told me about the B&B, that's what's makin' me think it *was* her."

50

"Wait. What? Why?"

"Isn't that supposed to be Who, What, Why?"

"Don't try to be funny, Ross. How can it possibly be Rachelle? She was with John."

"Yeah. That was the part I needed."

"You're going to have to walk me through this, slowly."

"Listen and learn, Nash. Listen and learn. First, I put the focus on Rachelle because she had it all: motive, means, and opportunity. And I knew her alibi wasn't that solid. But my idea for how she killed Crawford was too complicated. All that drivin'. She woulda had to be on the road five times over the weekend. There was a good chance someone would see her comin' or goin' one of those times. I couldn't find anybody that did, though. But I still liked her for it because of the way the retreat place is set up. No one could prove she wasn't there, but she couldn't prove she was, either. That's when I started thinkin' harder about the missin' sauna key."

"I know you kept asking about it. Why?"

"I guess you could say the key was the key."

"You could, but I wouldn't. What about the key?"

"It made me see how she coulda done it."

"Ross, I know you're enjoying this, but I'm not. Just come out with it, please."

"Rachelle had a partner. She works her end of things, makes sure everybody's gone for the weekend, messes with Bryan's insulin so he's in trouble before he gets to the sauna, then she goes to the retreat. Only now we know she went to the B&B. Same difference, she was away from the scene of the crime.

"Meanwhile her partner waits in the woods for Bryan to show up, and locks him in. Then, he comes back Sunday, unlocks the door, and everything's copacetic. Rachelle rolls in Monday morning, does her boo-hoo act, and they're home free. Until the trail cam messes them up. And the key."

"I'm still not getting the key."

Ross answered with, for him, surprising patience.

"When you and me were at the Crawfords' the day Bryan's body was found, you know I asked Rachelle about the key. The guy had to unlock the sauna to get in, so what happened to it? I didn't get a good answer, but after the M.E. said Bryan died from natural causes, I didn't spend any more time thinkin' about it. What really brought it back to mind is that as soon as we reopen the case, like magic, the key turns up. It was under the mat all along, and I just missed it, Rachelle says. I didn't miss it. It wasn't there.

"I didn't need Rhonda to point me in Rachelle's direction. Spouse is always my first look. But like I said, I couldn't come up with a clean way for her to do it. Then when all of a sudden the missing key turns up, it got me thinkin'. I start wonderin' if she maybe had a partner help her kill her husband."

"Why did the key make you think that? Why didn't you just assume that she'd dropped it or slipped it in her pocket and forgot because she was in a hurry? Then she found it later and put it under the mat?"

"I do think that it got put in a pocket and then dropped or maybe lost. But if Rachelle had done that, she wouldna looked so shocked that first time when I asked her where was the key. She wasn't fakin' it. She had no idea what I was talkin' about. Why? Because her partner is the one who had the key."

"Then why didn't her partner tell her that he forgot to put it back, so she could think of an answer if you asked about it when the body was found?"

"Rachelle was at her silent retreat. No communication, so if the partner drops it in his pocket because he's in a hurry, or loses it somewhere, he can't let her know. And it doesn't seem to matter. Bryan's death is natural causes, so no more questions. But when the case gets reopened as a murder investigation, they get spooked and they want the key question to go away. So either he finds it and they put it back, or there was a spare and they put that one under the mat. She sticks to her story about the dumb cop who couldn't even see what was in front of him, and there's no way to prove it isn't true."

"Ross, there were two keys. Rachelle told me one got lost months ago. But she could've planted the spare under the mat for Adam to 'find.'"

"It works for me."

"So, who's the partner?"

"I thought maybe her kid."

"Adam? That's crazy."

"It wouldn't be the first mother-son murder tag team in history. I saw right away the kid had no use for his stepdad, but he loves his mother. If she told him Crawford was beatin' her up or threatin' her or somethin', who knows? Then there's the money. The two of them would be fixed pretty good if they got away with it. But Adam had a fireproof alibi. He left with his friend Cameron's family for Chicago after school on Friday, and he came back with them Sunday night at midnight. So, then I thought maybe Stephanie partnered with Rachelle."

"But she and Rachelle hate each other."

"But they both get big money with Crawford dead. Maybe they put their feelings aside for a couple mil. I sure could. But you just gave me the answer. Rachelle's partner was John."

"John? No. No, you're wrong."

"Sorry, Nash. I think yes. What time did you say they checked in at the B&B?"

"Around 8:00."

"There you go. Plenty of time for John-boy to lock Bryan in the sauna and drive up to get Rachelle for their romance weekend. What time is checkout at the B&B?"

"Three o'clock. Don't say it. John would have plenty of time to drop Rachelle off and stop by to unlock the door of the sauna. Oh, Ross. You have no idea how much I don't want that to be true."

"I hear you. This is gonna be real bad for Jennifer. But you gotta admit, it works. I told ya before, Nash. Murder always comes down to four motives: love, lust, loathing, and loot. Here you got two of the four, love—or lust, take your pick—and loot. It's a real deadly combo."

"But it's just so hard to think that John, this guy I've known since high school, that he and Rachelle were frolicking at the Beale House Inn *knowing* that Bryan was dying in that sauna."

"It ain't pretty, but no murder is."

"Okay, well, how about this? The partner theory works, but it might not be what actually happened. There's still Stephanie. We don't know why she was late to her play. And don't forget Sheila's VW. What was she doing over there on Sunday afternoon?"

Ross smiled, then shook his head.

"You never wanna give up, do ya? That's your trouble—but that's your edge, too, Leah. It's why you're good."

The unexpected compliment shocked me into silence. I looked closely to see if his expression showed some level of sarcasm, but I didn't detect any. And he'd called me "Leah," not Nash. First names are the marker of real emotion between us.

"Thank you, Charlie."

"Yeah, well, don't let it go to your head. I didn't say I agree with ya. My gut's tellin' me it's Rachelle and John. And they could get away with it, as long as they don't turn on each other. There isn't a whole lotta evidence and my screw-up just makes it that much harder."

"Do you think they might turn on each other? If it is John and Rachelle, I mean?"

"Depends. Last time I talked to her, Rachelle was wound pretty tight. She could be ready to snap. John, I don't know about."

"I doubt he will. He's such a stone-cold liar that he told Rachelle that Jennifer had cancer, and that's why he couldn't leave her. I don't have any sympathy for him. But Ross, adultery's one thing. Murder's a whole other level of evil."

"Well, it's Owen Fike's case to solve now. And he sure won't want any advice from me—or you either, for that matter. He's not as easy-goin' as I am about you pokin' your nose in."

"I already told Coop about John and Rachelle. He didn't know, but he didn't seem that excited about it. I was hoping he'd tell me where they are in the investigation, but he wouldn't give me anything."

"Nash, I keep tellin' ya, the sheriff's office doesn't work for you. And it doesn't have to work with you, either. You're not part of the equation. You got no business expectin' Coop to tell ya anything. He can't do it."

"Well, you're telling me things."

"That's different. For one thing, I'm not the sheriff; for another, I'm not even on the force right now. For third, well, this is a special circumstance."

"Admit it. You miss me and we have a special partner bond."

"I'm not admittin' anything."

"That's okay. I can see it in your eyes. What are you going to do while I'm hitting the streets, taking down names, and kicking butt?"

"I'll be wishin' I was back on the case. But since that's not gonna happen, I'm gonna lay low and try not to do anything to push myself deeper in the hole I dug."

"Can I make a suggestion?"

"Can I stop you?"

"Take a shower. Shave. Put on something besides sweatpants. Call Liz. She's going through a lot, too. Her whole life—the bad marriage, the name change, losing her restaurant—it's all out there for people to read about with their morning coffee and donuts. You guys should help each other get through this. Invite Liz over Sunday for dinner. The restaurant's closed. Besides, Allie needs to finally meet her, don't you think?"

"Maybe, yeah, I guess."

I could tell from the way his face brightened that he liked the idea.

"Well, you do what you need to. I've got to get going. I'll keep you in the loop."

When I got home, I poked my head in the newsroom before going upstairs. Maggie's door was closed. I could hear my mother and Courtnee talking out front. I didn't bother to ask where Miguel was. When I got upstairs, I tried his phone.

"*Chica,* where are you?"

"I'm home. Listen, I have a mission for you tomorrow, do you have time?"

"Yes. It's Troy's weekend. What is it?"

"I love that you always say yes to me before you ask what it is. I need more of that in my life."

I hit the highlights of my day, including Stephanie's alibi fail, and Sheila Keller's surprising connection to Mitch Toomey. I didn't tell him about the Rachelle and John theory yet.

"What do you need me to do?"

"Find out why Stephanie was late to the play. I think she'll respond a lot better to you than to me. Especially if you tell her you want to interview her for your podcast. You can say you're going to be in her area tomorrow and you'd like to chat in person with her about the idea. She'll say yes. Her ego won't let her say no."

"But if being in the play is her alibi, why would she tell me she was late?"

"Don't underestimate your charm—or her narcissism. Plus, you're not from the police, you're not interviewing her for the paper, it's for your fun podcast. She'll have her guard down. As far as she knows, Rachelle is still the lead suspect."

"What about *GO News*? Are they following the Stephanie and Sheila leads?"

"I don't think so. That would take some actual reporting, not just relying on an inside source. I feel your pain, Miguel, at the way they have of beating us to the punch. But Spencer Karr and his minion Andrea will get theirs someday."

"Do you think so?"

"No. But it makes me feel better to say it. Anyway, we need to focus on what's in front of us now. Namely why was Stephanie so late to the play. Are you in?"

"Always. What are you doing this weekend, working on your book?"

"Yes. I owe Clinton a murder, a victim, and a killer. Plus, an assortment of suitable supporting characters. That's my plan for the weekend, except for a short trip to Vivienne's Nail Salon in Omico tomorrow."

"You're getting a mani-pedi? I thought you didn't like strangers touching your feet."

"No, I'm not going for a manicure. Sheila Keller cleans there on Saturdays after the salon closes. I'm going to press her and see if she still belongs on the list or not."

"What if both she and Stephanie don't belong?"

"I don't want to think about that right now."

51

I parked my car in the lot behind Vivienne's Nail Salon at 3:15 on Saturday afternoon. Sheila Keller's dark blue Volkswagen was already there. So was a silver van, and I waited for a few minutes in case it belonged to Vivienne herself. I wanted to see Sheila alone.

I had just decided the owner must be someone from one of the other stores in the little strip mall when a woman with bright red hair and equally vivid lipstick hurried out of the building, just in time for a dollop of water to roll off the awning over the back door and drop down her neck. Her shoulders shot up involuntarily as the cold water hit its mark, but she didn't break stride on her way to the van. Nor did she glance my way.

No one answered when I knocked on the back door, but when I tried the handle it opened. Once inside I followed the sound of running water to a small storage room filled with shelves of nail polish, manicure brushes, brightly colored disposable flip-flops, towels, and other supplies. Sheila stood at the sink with her back to me, much as she had the first time I met her at the Crawfords'.

"Sheila?"

She jumped at the sound of my voice and turned.

"You. How did you get in?"

"The back door was unlocked. I—"

"I don't have to talk to you. Besides, I'm working. I can't have people here."

"I won't take long. And you don't have to talk to me, you're right. But I'd like to hear your story. You might want to test it out on me, before the police come. And they will be coming."

Her face was impassive, but I saw the fear in her eyes at the mention of the police.

"I don't know what you're talking about. I already talked to the police. I told you that."

"Sheila, they know your car was in the Crawfords' driveway on Sunday afternoon, the day before Bryan Crawford's body was found." That wasn't strictly true, but from Sheila's reaction, I could tell that it hit home.

She blinked nervously. Her eyes darted around the room. I wasn't sure if she was looking for an escape, or for something to use to whack me with. But unless she could make a weapon out of a foam toe separator, I felt like I was pretty safe.

I also felt like a bully as I saw her eyes fill with tears that began to spill down her cheeks. She wiped them away roughly with a chapped, red hand, and her lips trembled.

"I didn't do it. I didn't. And I don't know anything. Why would I kill Bryan? Because he cheated Mitch? That's how life is. There's the ones who take, and the ones who get taken from. There's no sense fighting it. You'll never win. Even if Mitch and me wanted Bryan dead, we didn't do anything about it."

"Then why were you at the Crawfords' place on Sunday?"

"I went there to look for my earring."

"Your earring?"

She pulled back the bandanna that covered her head and revealed a small solitaire in her ear.

"Mitch gave them to me last year for my birthday. They're real diamonds."

"Very pretty."

They were sparkly, that's all I could attest to. My uneducated eyes couldn't tell the difference between diamonds and Diamonique. Although it seemed unlikely that the rambling wreck of a man that was Mitch could have pulled the money together to buy diamonds—even very small ones.

As though reading my mind, Sheila said, "He sold his fly fishing rod to buy them for me. One his uncle gave him. It was real special to him. But he sold it to buy me the nicest present I ever got. I wear them every day."

"And you lost one at the Crawfords'?"

"I didn't notice until Saturday. I didn't want to say anything to Mitch. I tore up our bed, looked all over the house. I even emptied the vacuum and went through all the dirt in the bag. I looked in my car, pulled the seats out, everything. I couldn't find it. I went to the Crawfords' on Sunday to look for it, in case it fell out when I took my bandanna off after I finished cleaning. I have a key, and the code for the alarm. I knew they were all gone. I found it in the master suite and then I left. I never went near the sauna. Why would I?"

"If you noticed you lost it on Saturday, why did you wait until Sunday afternoon to go look for it?"

"Mitch, he had a bad weekend. I can't leave him alone when he gets like that. But he was pretty much settled down by Sunday."

By settled down, I took it she meant passed out.

"Why didn't you tell the police you were there on Sunday?"

"They didn't ask me. You don't give the cops what they don't ask for. It's always trouble."

"Where were you the Friday night Bryan got locked in?"

"I was waiting tables at the Bluegrass. I fill in there sometimes to earn a little extra. I was supposed to be there at 6, but I had to find Mitch. He was at Ernie's Tavern. Amber the bartender's a friend of mine. She said she'd keep an eye on him until I got off from the Bluegrass at 11. When the cops started talking to everybody, I asked Petey, he's the owner, to say I got to work there at 6, if anybody asked."

"It's not a good idea to lie to the police."

"Yeah? Well, I'm kind of an expert in bad ideas. So, do you believe me, or what?"

"Yes, I believe you. But the police may not. Do yourself a favor when they come back to you, and they will. Don't lie to them this time."

I had known from the first that Sheila's motive for killing Bryan wasn't very strong. But when Ross told me about her car on the Crawfords' road that Sunday night, I let myself hope that maybe Jen could catch a break. Now it looked like the only thing standing between John and a murder charge was Stephanie Crawford.

52

After I got back from seeing Sheila, I texted Miguel to see if he'd had better luck than me. When I didn't get a reply from him right away, I turned my attention to writing to pass the time.

As Clinton had predicted, I found that I enjoyed being the decider of all things in my imaginary world. I gave Jo Burke several siblings, both genders, to allow for intertwining conflicts and future complications and callbacks. Her father was alive, but not living in the area. Her mother had to be dead. Otherwise, I ran the risk of my own mother assuming that Jo's mother was really her in disguise. That had the potential for discussions I wanted no part of. I was toying with the idea of having my first murder victim be the unscrupulous publisher of an online news publication, but then decided to save that for another book. Finally, around 7 o'clock, my phone rang.

"Miguel, hi! Did you talk to Stephanie? Did you find out anything useful?"

"Yes, but I don't think it will make you happy."

"No signed confession from her then?"

"No. But I know what made her late to the play. What about Sheila Keller?"

"No good. I'm pretty sure she didn't do it, and neither did Mitch. I'm ready, give me the bad news. What's Stephanie's story? No, wait. Come over and you can commiserate with me."

"I can't tonight. I'm on my way to McClain's to meet my friend Trevor. We're playing on his team in the dart tournament tonight."

"All right, then just give me the highlights—or maybe I should say lowlights. I can rub the salt of disappointment in my wounds by myself later."

"It was very easy to get Stephanie to see me. She said she listens to my podcast."

The note of surprise in his voice was genuine. Even though the link on our website to his pod, *Miguel Says,* is clicked multiple times a day, and the download numbers are steadily climbing, he still doesn't quite get how popular he is.

"Miguel, who doesn't listen?"

He ignored me and continued.

"I went to meet with her at her apartment. We just started to talk, and she got a phone call. She asked me to get her some ice and a glass of water from the kitchen. I think because she didn't want me to listen. It took me a minute because I spilled some. Just when I got it wiped up, the front door banged open. Boom! A man came in shouting. Stephanie, she started shouting back. I waited in the kitchen. I could only hear the loudest parts."

"Which were?"

"He cried and begged for her to take him back. She said no, he was pathetic, and it was over weeks ago. Then more yelling, and he shouted, 'I'll tell my wife.' And she said, 'I don't care.' Then the door banged again, and he left."

"Did you get the details from her?"

"Of course I did. But it's not good news if you want Stephanie to be the killer."

"All right, just tell me."

"His name is Morgan. He's married to the chair of the Theater Department. Stephanie didn't want his wife to find out, because she needs a recommendation from her to get into the acting school in New York. That's why he said he was going to tell. But Stephanie said he never will, because he's a loser and if his wife throws him out, he won't know what to do."

"She's a sweet girl, isn't she? I'm guessing Morgan is her alibi?"

"Yes. She was with him in the afternoon before the play. But when she had to go, Morgan, he wanted her to stay a little longer. She said no, she had to leave for the performance. They were walking to the car and arguing. Morgan took the car keys and threw them way far away toward the woods behind his house. He was sorry then and they both looked for them, but it took so long that she was almost late. She broke up with him after that."

"Not that I'm on Team Stephanie, but Morgan trying to ruin her big night is a pretty good reason to dump him."

"I know, I know. But still, he was crying very hard today and she was like Brrr! to him. I couldn't help it. I felt a little bit sorry for him."

"It sounds like the way she treated Adam after she was done toying with him."

"Her brother?" His voice was suitably horrified.

"Stepbrother. Still cringey, though, I agree. Stephanie's one of those women who likes to manipulate emotions, especially male emotions. Sometimes to get what she wants, like with her father. Sometimes just for fun, like with Adam and maybe Morgan. She's got more than a touch of her Aunt Rhonda in her, I'd say."

"Stephanie wouldn't like to hear that she's like her aunt. She spilled a lot of family tea to me."

"Like what?"

"That Rhonda is mean and nasty, and pushed Stephanie's mother out and tried to push Stephanie out. That she didn't want anyone to get next to Bryan except herself. That Adam is so extra she can't stand to be around him for very long. That she's happy it was Rachelle who killed Bryan, because now she won't have to share the money with her. Also, that she will try to make her Aunt Rhonda sell the company because she wants the money not the business. And it will be payback for all the mean things she did. Stephanie is very pretty, but she has a cold, cold heart. So, *chica*, we know it's not Sheila, it's not Stephanie, and it's not Rachelle. Who is left to be the killer?"

"Ross has a theory that kind of turns Rachelle's alibi upside down. It's looking like he might be right."

I gave him the John and Rachelle murder team rundown.

"Oh, no! Poor Jennifer."

"I know."

"What are you going to do?"

"Wait and see, I guess. I'm out of ideas and even though I don't want to believe it, what else is there? I can't tell Jennifer, that could screw up the investigation. But I can't leave her alone in her misery either. I just hope Owen and Coop wrap things up quick. It's going to be awkward tap-dancing around the truth with her. Remind me to never try to help anyone again. I feel like I made things worse."

"No. You don't want Jennifer married to a killer, do you? You're feeling bad because you like to fix things and this time you can't. Come down to McClain's and have a drink with me and Trevor. You can cheer for our team in the dart tournament."

"Thanks, but you don't need Debbie Downer with you tonight. Is Trevor the one who's a dental hygienist?"

"No, that's Darren. Trevor works at the Commission on Aging."

"Oh, wow, that reminds me. I forgot to tell you hello from one of your fans, Della Toomey. She's Mitch's aunt. Also, she'd like you to stop in and see her when you're out her way."

"Oh, she's a very nice lady. I will."

"And you're a very nice boy, Miguel. Go, enjoy your night. I'll talk to you soon."

53

The next morning, I knew what I had to do, but I put it off as long as I could. I dreaded talking to Jennifer so much that I did the floors, washed, dried, and folded two loads of laundry, made a grocery list, and even cleaned the bathroom to avoid calling her. What was I going to say?

"Hey, Jen, remember how crushed you were to find out that John was having an affair? Well, allow me to totally flatten you. Your husband might not just be a philanderer. He might be a killer, too."

Finally, around one o'clock, I made the call.

"Hey, Jen. How are you doing?"

"I thought I was getting to the numb stage, but the latest *GO News* story made my blood boil, so I guess not."

"From today? What is it? I haven't looked yet."

"Oh, nothing much, but Charlie's not their lead story anymore. I am."

"You? Why?"

It couldn't be because *GO News* knew about John and Rachelle already. It was too soon. Besides, if they had that information, Jennifer wouldn't be the story, John would.

"It's all about me getting fired. But I *wasn't* fired. Coop put me on paid leave. He said once he knew about John and Rachelle, he didn't have a choice. I suppose he found out from you?"

"I had to tell him, Jen, because it's part of a murder. I'm sorry, but I did go to you first."

"No, I understand. Because Rachelle's part of the case, her affair with my husband is part of the case. And because he's connected to the case, I can't be anywhere around it. I get it. I'm not mad at you, or Coop. I'm mad at John and I'm mad at *GO News* for getting the story wrong."

"What does the story say besides you were fired?"

"That I was part of 'rampant corruption' in the office. Andrea made it sound like my 'firing' was linked in with Charlie. She threw in a few anonymous quotes about my long-standing relationship with the sheriff—she probably got them from Spencer, or just made them up. We went to high school together, for heaven's sake! I should be glad, I guess, that they didn't sniff out anything about John and Rachelle yet."

"Andrea crossed a big line there, Jen. You're not a public figure or an elected official. You could sue them for libel."

"You sound like Coop. He called Miller Caldwell and got him to threaten Spencer with legal action. That must have scared Spencer a little bit. He said it was an 'honest mistake' caused by a misunderstanding on the reporter's part. As if. He said he'd put up a correction. Of course, I'm sure there'll be a follow-up story that will make it even worse. I hate Spencer and that little witch Andrea!"

"I'm sorry," I repeated, "but I'm glad you're in a fighting mood. How are the boys doing? Have you and John talked to them about things yet?"

"No, not yet. We're trying to keep it together around them. They're young enough not to understand, but old enough to have a lot of questions. Their school is on spring break next week, so my parents came this morning to take them for a few days. John and I are going to see a counselor tomorrow."

"So, you're thinking about staying with him?" I tried to keep my voice neutral.

"You don't think I should, do you?"

"No one can make that choice for you, Jen."

"But you don't think I should. I can tell by your voice."

"What I think is that you and John have to work this out. I hope the counselor you see helps. No matter what you decide, I'm there for you, however you need me to be."

Shortly after I hung up with Jennifer, I got a call from Adam.

"Leah, I thought everything was okay with my mom and the police. She talked to them on Friday and told them about her real alibi—this guy she's been seeing. But then today, a different cop came to the house. He was leaving when I got here, and Mom was really upset. She said she wasn't, but I could tell she'd been crying. Is this starting all over again? Do you know what's going on?"

My first thought was that Owen Fike was following up on the John and Rachelle theory Ross had come up with. But I didn't know, and there wasn't anything I could say about it to Adam even if I did. I avoided a direct answer.

"I'm not working with the police, Adam. But your mom did lie to them before. They have to check and cross-check everything. There might be a few details they want her to clarify."

"She just keeps pacing around the house. I have a bad feeling. I heard her talking on the phone and she hung up as soon as I came into the room. I think she was talking to her lawyer. Do you think she's getting arrested?"

"Adam, stop. If your mom was talking to her lawyer, that's a good thing. He'll know the right thing for her to do."

He went on as though I hadn't spoken.

"I called my dad, but I shouldn't have. They don't get along. He said I should go stay with him. But then she'd be here alone. I can't leave her without anybody. She's worse now than she was when I talked to you the first time. It's like it's taking everything she has to hold it together. I don't know why I'm telling you this. I just don't know anybody else to tell. I shouldn't have called you."

His voice broke toward the end, like he was struggling to hold back tears.

He was nearly an adult, but at the moment he sounded, and probably felt, like a lost little boy. How was he going to feel if his mother was arrested? He'd blame me, probably, for providing the link between John and Rachelle. I just hoped he wouldn't blame himself for getting me involved.

"It's okay that you called. But Adam, there isn't anything you can do. Your mother has to work through whatever's on her mind herself. She's been under a lot of strain. Keeping secrets takes a toll. Maybe giving her a little space is the best thing."

"She told me to go over to Cameron's and hang with him for a while."

"Well, then you probably should do that. She might be ready to talk to you when you get back."

"Yeah, I guess. I'm sorry. I don't know why I called. It's not like you can do anything. I just ... I don't know. Thanks."

He hung up before I could reply. I was relieved. I had nothing to comfort him with, and though I wasn't lying to him, I had been walking a line I didn't like. Much as I had with Jennifer. At that thought I realized that Jennifer hadn't said anything about John being questioned by the police. But if Owen or someone else had re-interviewed Rachelle, surely they'd talked to John, too. That was probably something else he was hiding from Jennifer.

As I sat down to work, the sun that had been making its first effort in several weeks to give us some respite from the rain gave up and disappeared. This was getting ridiculous. It was as if some giant hand was wringing out a dirty sponge over the whole county, then pausing just long enough to sop up more before squeezing it out again.

Still, I actually prefer gloomy weather to sunny when I'm writing. I'm less distracted then. I was pretty glad to return to the imaginary corner of Michigan's Upper Peninsula that I was creating. At least there I could help the people I cared about. In real-life Himmel, I couldn't do anything to stop the freight train of pain bearing down on Jennifer, on her little boys, and on Adam.

After I'd put in a good stretch of work, my stomach began rumbling and I realized it was dinner time. I got up and rummaged around in the freezer, looking for a frozen dinner that I was sure was buried under bags of frozen vegetables, frost-bitten ground beef, and a box of freezer pops. Then my phone rang.

"Hi, Gabe, what's up?"

"It's not Gabe. It's me, Dominic. Dad and I made dinner. Can you come over? It's roast beast. With mashed potatoes! And we have cake for dessert!"

"Dominic, you are my favorite friend. How did you know I was starving? And I love roast beast. What kind of cake?"

"Chocolate with white frosting. But we didn't make that. We bought it at the bakery."

"Hey, if the cake is chocolate and the frosting is thick, I'm there. What time do you want me?"

"Now time. I'm hungry."

"Perfect. I am, too. See you in a minute."

When I tapped on Gabe's front door and walked in toward the kitchen, Gabe poked his head around the corner. His expression when he saw me was pleased, but surprised.

"Leah! You picked the perfect time to come by. I'm just taking a pot roast out of the oven. You can join us for dinner, can't you?"

I looked at Dominic, who was peeking out from behind Gabe, a huge grin on his face.

"Dominic Hoffman, did you invite me over without asking your father?" I asked with mock sternness.

"Yes," he said, then began to giggle.

Gabe reached down and lifted him up in a hug, which made him laugh so much he got the hiccups, which in turn made Gabe and I join in.

"It was Barnacle's idea, Dad. It's a good surprise, right?" he asked between gasps of laughter as he caught his breath. Of late, Dominic had begun making the claim that he was taking orders from Barnacle whenever his own behavior was in question.

"Yes, it's a good surprise," Gabe said as he set Dom back down. "I hope Leah doesn't mind being tricked."

"Absolutely not. The roast beast smells delicious, and I am so, so hungry."

My stomach gave a very loud growl at that moment, which set Dominic off again, and the laughing continued on and off all the way through dinner.

54

After dinner, Dominic changed into his Spiderman pajamas and we watched his current favorite movie, *Spiderman: Into the Spider-Verse*. He has seen it approximately 10,000 times and still finds it perfection. I'm less enamored, but I enjoy his enjoyment.

When the film was over, Gabe scooped him up and said, "Okay. School tomorrow, time for bed. Say goodnight to Leah."

"Goodnight, Leah. I hope we see Spiderman when you and Dad take me to Mom's when school is over. We might, because Spiderman lives in New York. Like me and Mom."

I smiled at Dom, and said, "You never know. Sleep well."

When Gabe came back into the living room after tucking Dominic in, I said, "Why did you tell Dominic that I was going to New York with you guys?"

He looked puzzled.

"Well, you are, right? We talked about it Friday."

"Yes, I know, but I told you I wasn't sure I could make it, with the new book and all. We said we'd talk more about it."

"I don't remember it that way. But let's talk about it now, then. It's more than two months away. You'll be ready to take a break. It's only for a week.

In June the weather will be great, and there are so many things to see and do. You'll love it. Trust me, the Hoffman men know how to show a girl a good time."

Although his tone was light and teasing, I felt like I was getting backed into a corner again. That's when my inner voice chose to pop in. *Oh? This is a surprise to you? You've been feeling like this for weeks.*

"It's not that, Gabe. I always have fun with you and Dominic. I just think ... that is, it feels like I ... I'm just not sure where my head is right now. The Crawford case is coming to a close, I think, and it's going to be bad for a lot of people I care about. And you can tease me about writing fiction, but I *am* kind of scared to do something that different. A trip to New York is too much right now. It's just not a good idea. Gabe, it's not . . ." I stopped because I wasn't sure how I wanted to end that sentence.

"It's not what, Leah? What are you trying to say?" The teasing tone was gone.

"Nothing! I told you. I'm just too busy to think about things now. Don't make a big thing about it."

"I think maybe it is a big thing," he said, his eyes dark and serious. "Something isn't right between us. You're pulling away from me."

"What? No, of course I'm not. Where is that coming from? Just because I can't go to New York when I'm in the middle of writing a book?"

"Leah, we've always been honest with each other. Something is wrong between us. What is it?"

"No, there's nothing wrong. I just . . . it's just . . . oh, I don't know what's the matter with me."

"Leah, I'm in love with you. I know I've made that clear. But I've tried not to push you, to give you space. I know commitment scares you. But I thought if I was patient enough, if I loved you enough, you'd get past that. But you're never going to, are you? At least not with me."

I was stunned. My first instinct was to reassure him, to say that he was wrong. But I couldn't. Because I realized that what he had said was true. I struggled to find the words to express feelings I hadn't let myself acknowledge were there until that moment.

"Gabe, you're smart, kind, sexy, funny, any woman would be lucky to have you. And Dominic is a great kid. I love you both. But you're right, I'm not in love with you. It's not because you aren't a wonderful person. You are. It's me. I told you once I'm not very good girlfriend material. You deserve someone who is."

"What did I do wrong?"

"Nothing! Except fall for the wrong person, I guess. Gabe, I'm so very sorry that I'm hurting you. I didn't mean to just blurt it out like that. I didn't even know it's what I was thinking. You did everything right. I'm the one who didn't. I should have been more honest with myself and with you. But I liked you so much, it was so fun being with you, that I convinced myself if we took it slow, I could fall in love with you. But it didn't happen. And you deserve to have someone who's crazy in love with you. I know you're probably angry with me, and you have every right to be. I'm so sorry."

"I'd like to be angry at you, Leah. This would be easier if I was. But I'm not. You can't help it if you're not in love with me, any more than I can help it that I am with you. I suppose this is the part where I'm supposed to say, yes, you're right. It's for the best. But I can't, Leah. It might be the best for you, but it's the worst for me. I don't know what I'm going to do without you in my life."

"Gabe—"

"No. Please don't say that you'll always be in my life, we'll always be friends. Right now, I don't want you as my friend. I want you the way we were. Or the way I thought we were. I'm not ready to pretend that's not how I feel. I need a little space. It's going to take a while to pick myself up off the floor. Okay?"

"Yes, sure. I understand."

He gave me a sad smile and said, "I don't think you do. But I have a favor to ask."

"Anything I can do, I will."

"I'll tell Dominic tomorrow. He's going to need to know why his dad is feeling so sad. But do you think you could talk to him, too? Let him know that you're still his friend? He got drop-kicked pretty hard when Lucy and her husband divorced. He stepped out of Dom's life like he'd never been in it. He needs to know that our break-up doesn't change your feelings for him."

"Sure, yes, of course. Whenever you want, just let me know."

"Thank you. I will."

He stood then, and I did, too. I wasn't sure whether to hug him or not. But he reached out and wrapped his arms around me. As he hugged me, he whispered in my ear, "I will never meet another woman like you, Leah."

Then he dropped his arms and I left.

55

I started crying as soon as I got in the car. I sat there for a minute, then called Coop. I needed someone to process this with.

"Leah, hi. No, I can't tell you what's going on with the Crawford investigation."

"No, no, I know."

I struggled to keep my voice steady. "I wanted to talk to you about something else. Can I come over?" Normally, I would have gone without asking, but with Kristin so much in the picture it seemed like I should get permission in case he was busy.

"Ah, sure, yeah." I caught the hesitancy and backed off.

"It sounds like you're busy. I can catch up with you tomorrow."

"No, I'm not busy. Kristin's bringing a pizza over in about half an hour. Come now, and then you can stay and join us."

"No, no, that's all right. I already ate. No worries, it's not a big thing. I'll just catch you later," I lied. Then I hung up before he could say anything else.

When I got home, I saw my mother's car in the parking lot. She comes in to work some evenings because, she says, she can get more done in two hours alone in the office than she can in four hours during regular business hours. I wasn't in the mood to say hello, or anything else.

I went straight to my place, poured a Jameson, sat on my window seat, and wondered if I'd made a terrible mistake. Two hours ago, I had a stable relationship with a good man who thought he was lucky to have me. Now, I was alone in the dark, drinking myself into maudlin self-pity, with no one to blame but myself.

I got up for another Jameson and brought the bottle with me this time. I pulled the afghan off the back of my sofa as I walked by. I set the bottle on the floor, my glass on the seat, wrapped myself in the blanket, and scrunched into the corner. As I drank, I thought about how things rarely go the way I want them to.

It wasn't just my relationship with Gabe that I'd handled badly. It was the whole Crawford thing from the moment Adam asked me for help. I should have said no from the beginning, no matter how forlorn he'd looked, and how much Allie had wanted me to help. I should have told Jennifer no, too, and stuck with it. All that I'd managed to do was the opposite of what Adam and Jennifer wanted me to do. Thanks in part to my poking around, it looked like Rachelle was a killer, and John probably wasn't just an asshat, he was a murderer, too. Yay, me.

I lifted my glass and was surprised to see it was empty. As I leaned over to get the bottle for my third drink, there was a tap on my door. My mother. She has the key code to the security door at the bottom of the stairs.

"Come on in, Mom. It's open."

"Why are you sitting in the dark with just that little lamp on?"

She flipped on the kitchen light. Her glance took in the glass in my hand, the bottle on the floor, and my woebegone appearance.

"What's wrong?"

"Nothing's wrong. I'm just drinking alone in the dark, thinking about what a swell life I have, and how everything I touch turns to gold."

"I'm not sure what you're talking about, but I think I'll get a drink for myself, and a big glass of water for you. It looks like a box of Kleenex wouldn't hurt, either."

She grabbed the bottle of Jameson and took it to the kitchen. I didn't protest. When she returned, she carried a glass of water for me, a shot of Jameson over ice for herself, and a box of tissues tucked under her arm. She distributed the items, then took a spot next to me.

"All right. What's going on?"

There are times in life when you need to be on your own. And there are times when you realize, no matter how old you are, you need your mom. Without preamble I spilled out what had happened with Gabe, and how bad I felt about it.

"I didn't mean to hurt him. I didn't even know I was going to say those things to him. We were just having a nice, regular, fun evening. But when Dominic said that about going to New York, and then Gabe was trying to convince me I should, it just, all of a sudden, I felt like I couldn't breathe. Like I was almost going to have a panic attack. I just blurted it out. Mom, he was so stunned, so hurt. I feel awful. And I know you like him a lot, and you want grandkids, and you think I should get married to him and ... but I can't, I just can't."

She pulled me into a hug. I leaned into her as she patted my hair and said, "There, there. It's all right. It's okay," as though I were six years old. When I finally finished, my nose was stuffy, and her shoulder was soggy with my tears. I reached for the box of tissues and blew my nose.

"Leah, of course I like Gabe. He's a very likable man. And yes, I would love to have grandchildren, but I don't think you should marry him, or anyone else, if you're not in love with him. You can't help how you feel. I'm sure it was very hard to tell him it's not going to work. I think you did the right thing. I've been expecting it for a while."

That took me by surprise.

"You have? Then why did you keep talking about grandchildren and how great Gabe was and all that?"

"Part of it was teasing and part was wishful thinking. Deep down I knew you'd never stay with Gabe."

"How did *you* know that? I didn't know that."

"Because you've never stayed with any man for very long. You always find a reason to leave."

"That's not fair. I married Nick. And look how that turned out."

"Okay, I'll give you that one. Nick is a narcissist. You had to leave. But Gabe isn't, and neither were most of the other men you've been involved with. But there's always something wrong with them in the end, isn't there? What do you think that is?"

"Mom, they ended for different reasons. It's not like I have one go-to deal-breaker for a relationship."

"Don't you?"

"I hate it when you're cryptic. What are you saying?"

She hesitated for a second, then plunged in.

"Remember when I said you were a dog in the manger about Coop? That you didn't want him, but you don't want Kristin to have him either?"

"Yes, I recall that tender mother-daughter moment when you told me I was selfish and immature. I thought you were here to comfort me, not to make me feel worse."

"That's not exactly what I said. And I'm not trying to make you feel worse. This is as hard for me to say as it will be for you to hear. Contrary to what you seem to think sometimes, I try to avoid being the caricature of an interfering mother. But you need to hear this."

"I'm all ears," I said in a sarcastic voice that conveyed I was anything but.

"Leah, please, listen to what I'm saying without throwing up your defenses. I think the real reason you walk away from relationships with men who are smart, and funny, and kind, and sometimes crazy about you like Gabe, is that they're not Coop."

"Oh, come on, Mom. Coop is my best friend."

"Let me finish. I've watched you two together for more than twenty years. You are each other's go-to person in every situation, good or bad. You're the first one there if he needs you, and he's been there for you more times than I can count. You were devastated when he married Rebecca, and not because you hated her. You feel the same way about his relationship with Kristin, and you *like* her. Sweetheart, you are so brave in so many ways, but you are a coward when it comes to love. You've had plenty of chances, but you turn everyone away who isn't Coop. He's the one you're in love with, but you're too afraid to admit it."

I stared at her, speechless. I don't know if it was the Jameson or the crying jag that had beaten down my defenses. But I saw with sudden, blinding clarity the truth of her words. A truth I'd been hiding from for a long time.

"Leah? Don't you have anything to say?"

"Mom, it's too late. I waited too long."

I told her about the accidental kiss Coop and I had shared on election night, and the text he'd sent me afterward.

"But then he didn't say anything. And I didn't want to ask him about it. I mean, he would have followed up if he really meant it. He didn't. So I didn't. Now he's with Kristin. I already told you, they're 'together' together. She has her stuff at his house. She knows where all the dishes go. She just goes in and out of his house, like, like …"

"Like you do?"

"No, like the person he wants to be with. I called him tonight, you know, after I left Gabe's. I wanted to tell him what happened, but he was too busy to talk."

"Is that what he said? It doesn't sound like Coop."

"No. He said Kristin was coming over and we could all have a jolly chat together. I may be slow, but I'm not stupid. He's with Kristin, he's happy. That's it, end of story. I am not going to blow up our friendship by exploding some big, awkward, unwanted truth bomb in the middle of it. This isn't a movie, so I'm also not going to run over to Coop's house with a stack of signs and a boombox to reveal my true feelings like I'm that guy in *Love Actually*."

"Leah—"

The look on her face was so sad, it almost undid me all over again.

"Mom, thank you, for being here, and for listening to me fall apart, but I have to put myself back together. Now, I hope you'll join me in reaffirming the code of the Nash family, *A problem ignored is a problem solved*."

I tried my best to keep my voice light, but it cracked a little at the end.

"Leah," she started again.

"No, Mom, I don't want to talk about it anymore now, or ever. This conversation never happened. And don't say anything to Coop or anyone else about this, either. Please. And don't you dare look at me with sad eyes and ask me if I'm okay tomorrow. I'll be fine. I'm always fine."

56

Unexpectedly, given all the turmoil of the day, I slept like the dead that night and didn't wake up until my intercom buzzed at 8:30. I stumbled into the living room and pressed the button to answer.

"Yeah?"

"Hi Leah, it's Allie. I've got some cinnamon rolls your mom made. She wants me to run them up to you."

"Oh, okay. I'll unlock the door. Just come on in."

I caught a glimpse of myself in the mirror as I spoke, and it wasn't pretty. I went in the bathroom, splashed cold water on my face, pulled my hair back in a ponytail, brushed my teeth, and threw on a robe. There wasn't anything I could do about my puffy eyes or my red nose. I heard the door open, and I caught the scent of warm cinnamon rolls.

Allie looked up as I came in.

"Leah, don't you feel good? You look—"

"Like death warmed over? Yeah, I know. I think I'm catching a cold."

I reached for a tissue and blew my nose to lend credence to my lie. "What are you doing here, Allie? Shouldn't you be in school?"

"It's spring break this week. Courtnee's on vacation, so I'm filling in for her. Here," she said, shoving the plate toward me. "Aren't you supposed to feed a cold?"

"I'll have some later. I'm just waking up. I think coffee's the answer for me. How was your weekend?" I asked, suddenly remembering that I'd advised Ross to invite Liz over on Sunday. I hoped that hadn't turned to ashes, like everything I touched.

"It was nice. I got to meet Liz, she came over for dinner yesterday."

"Did you like her?"

"Yeah, I did. It sure put Dad in a better mood. She brought the meal, which was delicious, and I bought the dessert at the Elite. We ate, we talked, we watched a movie. It was all good, right up until she left."

"What happened?"

"Dad was helping Liz on with her coat and knocked over her wine glass. There was still some in it. It left kind of a big stain on the sleeve."

"Yikes."

"Yeah. She was chill, said not to worry. But Dad was all upset. He said he'd buy her a new one, and she said no, and that went on for a while. Then they started getting a little flirty about it and that was too much for me. I'm happy Dad's happy. But I don't need to see middle-age love in bloom. Finally, I had to step in. I said I'd drop it off at the cleaners this morning before work. If Mr. Hayward can get the stain out, great. If he can't, then Dad can take Liz coat shopping."

"Way to handle things, Allie."

She grinned.

"Somebody's got to take charge. And Mr. Hayward said he thinks he can do it."

"How's your dad doing today?"

"Better. At least he's out of his sweatpants, and he's fixing the dishwasher, not watching the Weather Channel today. That's progress, right?"

"Sure sounds like it."

Although I'd feigned interest in Allie's story of her dad's romance, I'd only listened with part of my mind. The other part had returned again and again to the admission I'd made to my mother—to myself, as well—poking and probing at it like a tongue exploring a sore tooth. And just like the tongue returns the message that the sore tooth is still sore, my mind confirmed that it was still true. I was in love with Coop, and it was way too late to do anything about it.

Scores of times when I might have said something flashed through my mind, but I'd been too dense or too unwilling to admit how I really felt about him. And all right, too afraid. I liked the safety and comfort of solid friendship. Girlfriends and boyfriends, husbands and wives, can come and go, but real friends, best friends, stayed. I knew for sure that I always wanted Coop in my life. If I told him how I was in love with him, and he didn't feel the same way, it would be the worst thing that could happen. I'd expose my secret self, I'd embarrass him, make things weird between us, ruin everything. I hadn't picked up the slightest sign that he felt anything toward me but the strong, steady affection of deep friendship. If he had, he would've said something before now. I knew that for sure.

I shook my head to clear the useless ruminating. I hadn't said anything up to this point, and it wasn't worth the risk to say anything now. Time to get on with things.

First, I called Ross to give him the sweet satisfaction of hearing me admit that I'd come to the end of the line in my search for an alternate suspect. His theory had to be the right one.

"I don't see how either Stephanie or Sheila could have done it. I tried pretty hard to figure out a way to make it be Rhonda, but I don't see that either. Looks like our first case as partners is about to get wrapped up."

"I told ya, we're not—"

"Partners. I know, Ross. But kind of we are. Be nice to me, or I'll change my mind and put you in my book after all."

"Don't even kid about that. Hey, did you hear from Coop that he gave Lawlor the boot, or am I breakin' news?"

"No, I haven't heard from Coop. Good. That should set *GO News* back a little."

"I can't believe that little pissant with his 'yes sir,' 'no sir,' all the time was spyin' on the whole office for *GO News*. He just drove his career into the ground."

"Yeah, well, what we do for love, I guess. But here's hoping Coop's good decision-making continues, and you're back on the job soon. I think Owen's closing in on Rachelle. I heard from Adam. They interviewed her again yesterday and she was pretty shaken, according to him."

"I feel for the kid. Not much worse than having your mother in jail for murder."

"Except maybe your husband," I said, thinking of Jennifer. "Actually, there's no contest. They're both equally awful."

"Yep. I—oh, hey, I got a call comin' in. Talk to ya later."

I sat down to do some writing. I didn't feel much like being around people at the moment. But now that I wasn't fixated on who murdered Bryan Crawford, I couldn't seem to stop obsessing over my newfound feelings about Coop. I alternated between being absolutely sure that the best thing to do was nothing, followed by that pesky little voice saying *But you don't know that, do you? What's the worst that can happen?*"

"Utter humiliation, permanent damage to our friendship, and a lifetime of not being able to look him in the eye ever again," I answered out loud.

I forced myself to return to writing strings of words purporting to be sentences that I would no doubt delete when I re-read them. But at least it kept my mind away from places it wasn't healthy to go.

When someone knocked on my door around four o'clock, I knew it had to be my mother. She was doubtless checking up on me after last night's meltdown. I had to admire her restraint in lasting this long. I opted to pretend the night before had never happened, and hoped she'd fall in line. Foolish dream.

"Hi Mom," I said brightly. "Thanks for the cinnamon rolls."

"I don't know why. I see you didn't eat any. Allie told me you're coming down with a cold. Are you?"

"Nope. False alarm."

I continued tapping my keyboard and looking at my screen, the way you do when you want to let someone know you're so busy you don't even have time to tell them you're so busy, so please, go.

"Leah, about last night—"

Clearly, signaling I didn't want to talk wasn't working. I'd have to confront it head-on.

"Mom, stop. I was tired, I was down about hurting Gabe. I had one Jameson too many and I got a little weepy and incoherent. That's all it was. We don't need to go over it again."

"*In vino veritas*, Leah. Or in your case, *in Jameson veritas*. You always let your guard down when you've had a few drinks. That's when your real feelings come out."

"Okay, thank you. I'll file that away for future review. But I've got a ton of work to do. I—"

She walked over to my desk then and pushed down the lid of my laptop. I felt a surge of genuine anger.

"Mom, you don't have any right to interfere. It's my life. I don't want to talk about it."

"I'm not going to talk about your life. I'm going to talk about mine. I don't want you to make the same mistake I did."

All right, that piqued my interest. My mother does know how to create a good hook.

"What mistake is that?"

She pulled up the extra chair and sat next to my desk.

"I was very much in love once. His name was Alex. If there is such a thing as a 'soulmate,' he was mine. But to be with him, I had to take a risk. In the end, I couldn't do it. I was too afraid. But Leah, sometimes when I think about him, and I still do, I feel such a fierce wave of longing and regret that it takes my breath away. Hon, you don't want to get to be my age and still wonder what your life might have been, who you might have been. What I know is that while you *may* suffer from the fallout of taking a risk, you most certainly *will* suffer from the regret if you don't."

She stood up then, leaned over, and dropped a kiss on the top of my head and left without another word, as I stared after her.

57

My hands were clammy as I gripped them tightly on the steering wheel, sitting in the dark, in my car, across the street from Coop's. I felt like a stalker staring at his house. I'd been parked there for 15 minutes, after driving around the block three times. Pretty soon the neighbors were going to call and report me as a suspicious vehicle.

Still, I couldn't seem to pull into his driveway, as I would normally have done. Because there wasn't anything normal about this. I was on the verge of changing, quite possibly ruining, my friendship with Coop. I'd spent hours pacing my apartment after my mother left, playing both prosecutor and defense in the case of Leah's Head versus Leah's Heart. First one side presented compelling arguments, then the other knocked them down. The problem was, there was no jury and no judge in this courtroom, just me, trying to figure out what the right thing to do was.

I imagined myself laying it all out there in front of Coop, only to have him look embarrassed, his eyes sad and full of sympathy as he tried to let me down gently. It would be so awful. I'd flush with humiliation, make some kind of stupid joke. Say let's forget it ever happened. He'd agree and smile uncomfortably. But he wouldn't forget, and neither would I. Everything that was so easy between us would become so hard. He'd pity me but feel constrained around me. I'd be mortified and awkward around him.

The very thought of the conversation and the possible outcome made me shudder.

But it wasn't that much better when I imagined a different outcome. Sure, I let my mind's eye show me a picture of Coop smiling down at me, taking me in his arms, telling me that he felt the same way, he just hadn't believed that I did. I thought about his mouth on mine and the warmth and strength of him holding me in the kind of hug we'd never shared before. I shuddered then, too, but for entirely different reasons. But even that outcome was fraught with danger. Love doesn't always last—maybe rarely does. Look at me and Nick, my mother and father, Jennifer and John. What if Coop and I fell out of love with each other? What if we went through a soul-crushing break-up and when we weren't lovers anymore, we weren't friends, either?

And yet. What if I didn't tell him, and I never knew how he felt, and we just went on forever like that butler and the housekeeper in that really slow movie with Anthony Hopkins and Emma Thompson?

"Oh, stop it. Take the leap or don't, but quit sitting here angst-ing out about it. This isn't a Hallmark Channel movie," I said out loud, disgusted with myself.

A light went on in Coop's living room. I watched him walk across it to put a book down on the table next to his easy chair. He was done with dinner, kitchen tidied up, and he was ready to sit down and read. It was now or never. There wouldn't be a better time. I rubbed my sweaty hands on my jeans, put the car in drive, looked up again at the window, and realized it was going to be never.

Coop was still standing as Kristin came into the room. She said something to him, then reached up and put her hand on his cheek. I watched as he wrapped his arms around her, and she lifted up her face for a kiss. The exact scene from my Hallmark daydream. Only I wasn't in it, was never meant to be. I took my foot off the brake, pulled away from the curb, and drove home.

I didn't drink Jameson. I didn't call my mother, or listen to sad music, or go to see Father Lindstrom. I went home and sat in the rocking chair in front of the fire with a scrapbook on my lap. My mother had given it to me when I graduated from college. I hadn't taken it down from the shelf in a long time.

Each page was filled with memories of family and friends, and I looked at all of them on my way to the one section at the back that was dedicated wholly to me and Coop. The two of us on our bikes, racing around Riverview Park. Coop showing off the stitches he'd needed in his finger after literally saving me from an oncoming train. Both of us delivering copies of the neighborhood newspaper I'd established at age 11.

Then there was Coop hugging me after I won the Forensics Tournament for broadcasting in high school. Me dumping a bucket of water on his head after he hit the winning home run for the baseball team. Both of us leaving for college freshman year. Me working at the *Himmel Times* on summer break, Coop coaching Little League. Both of us drinking our first legal beers at McClain's after we had each turned 21. The last picture was of us smiling, wearing our graduation caps and gowns, his arm across my shoulders, mine around his waist.

When I closed the book a thousand more memories of our intertwined lives eddied through my mind, alive with the exuberance of childhood, the awkwardness of adolescence, the growing surety of young adulthood. Always throughout the ebb and flow of our separate lives, the current of friendship had pulled us back to each other no matter how far apart we'd drifted. It wasn't dependent on romance or passion. It ran on trust, and acceptance, and, yes, love, but not the romantic kind. The kind that's born of deep-rooted friendship.

I was glad then, that Kristin had been there. That I hadn't said anything, hadn't done anything that could alter that friendship.

I'm not so good at fantasy romance, but I'm great at reality. If there had ever been a chance for us, it was gone. Coop had moved on, he'd found Kristin, and they were a good match. He'd never have to tell her to stay out of his business, to calm down, to think things through, to stop being stubborn. She was like him. Steady, honest, true. They were much better romantic partners than he and I would ever be.

I had moved from friend, to would-be lover, and back to friend in less than 24 hours on one of the shortest, most unexpected, and most painful journeys of my life. And I had taken the trip without Coop even knowing. Thank goodness. Things had worked out the way they should. I knew that was true.

So, why did tears keep dropping with soft plops on the cover of my scrapbook, in steady counterpoint to the rain hitting against the windows?

58

The next morning I spent a considerable amount of time standing under the hot water in the shower, repeating my new mantra: *Get over yourself and get on with things.*

At 8:30 I sat down with a bowl of Cheerios and clicked on the *Himmel Times* site to see what we had as the lead story for the morning. As soon as I read the headline, I called Maggie.

"Rachelle Crawford is dead?!?"

"Good morning to you, too, Leah."

"Maggie, what happened? When?"

"I take it you didn't get past the headline," she said dryly.

"Maggie, just tell me."

"The kid, Adam, found her body last night."

"Oh, no! Did she ... was it suicide? I talked to Adam Sunday. He was worried about her state of mind."

I felt a stab of guilt as I recalled the pain in his voice, and how I'd had nothing to offer him but empty advice about giving his mother space. Space enough to spiral deeper into depression and kill herself?

I realized Maggie was still talking.

"Don't know yet. Could be. She was found face down in a creek on the Crawfords' property. Body would've washed downstream, but it got caught on some rocks. She could've walked in the water to drown herself, or she could've slipped and fallen. Or somebody could've killed her."

"I know the spot. What was she doing there?"

"That's the question, isn't it? Her son said she walked down there sometimes. She liked to sit in the gazebo by the creek and watch the water run by. Pretty rotten weather for sitting by the water, if you ask me."

"Is there an estimate for time of death?"

"Not yet, at least not one that we've got. The kid got home from a friend's last night around 9. House was dark, but Rachelle's car was in the garage. He thought maybe she'd gone to bed early, but when he checked, she wasn't in her room. She wasn't in the house at all. He texted her, called her, but got no answer. She's got an iPad with one of those apps that tells you where you left your phone. He checked and it showed up down by the creek."

"Was she already dead?"

"That's what he says. He spotted her in the water, ran down, managed to drag her out and up higher on the bank. She wasn't breathing and there wasn't any pulse. He called 911."

"How do we know so much about this already? I can't believe Coop released a statement that detailed this fast."

"He didn't. It's our boy, Troy. A neighbor of the Crawfords' he interviewed last week took a shine to him, gave him a call around 10 last night."

"Is his name George Wynn?" I asked, thinking of the guy down the road who had spotted Sheila's VW near the Crawford house.

"How did you know?"

"Something Ross told me. So, what did he have to say?"

"He told Troy all hell was breaking loose, cop cars, ambulance, the whole circus at the Crawfords' property. Like I always say, nosy neighbors are a reporter's best friend. When Troy got there, yellow tape was up, and the medical examiner was with the body. Owen Fike spotted Troy, he gave him a 'no comment,' and told him to beat it."

"I take it Troy didn't?"

"He moved on, but he didn't leave. He saw Adam wrapped in one of those silver blankets, leaning against the back of the ambulance. He went over and asked him how he was doing. Then, maybe because they're close to the same age, Adam started talking and everything spilled out. And it's all on the *Times* website right now, and even better, *GO News* doesn't have it yet."

"Do you know where Adam is?"

"Allie texted him. He's home. His dad's coming in from Ohio later today."

"Okay. You know, Maggie, it makes a big difference if Rachelle's death was suicide, or accident, or murder. Did you—"

"Leah, you're in danger of crossing the line from interested but hands-off owner to micromanager again. Yes, I know it makes a big difference. Yes, I tried to play the friendship card and called the medical examiner myself. Connie wasn't playing. All I could get was a wait-and-see until the autopsy is done. That's supposed to be later today."

"Sorry. But when you know the results, let me know, will you?"

"Sure, if I can remember. Things are getting a little crazy here. We've got some flooding in the northwest corner of the county. Another stationary front has moved in. With all the rain we've already had, the emergency manager tells me that could mean big trouble. Troy's working on that story and the Rachelle Crawford thing, because Miguel has to report for jury duty today. They don't usually pick reporters for a jury, so I hope he'll be in by this afternoon, but who knows?"

"If I can help with anything, Maggie, let me know."

"Aren't you supposed to be writing a book? We'll manage as long as the stringers don't let me down."

I couldn't stop thinking about Rachelle's death. In medical examiner terms, the cause of death is the specific injury or disease that leads to death. The manner of death is how the person died—natural, accident, suicide, homicide, undetermined. It was pointless for me to speculate until the autopsy came in. But I've always found pointless speculation hard to resist.

Rachelle's death could have been accidental. The creek was running fast, and the rain made the rocks slippery. If she had walked down to look at the water, she could have slipped, fallen, and drowned. Nothing to do with Bryan's death, except maybe a kind of justice if she and John had killed him.

But she could have killed herself, too. According to Adam, after Owen had talked to her on Sunday, she'd been agitated, nervous, upset—the way you'd be if the walls were closing in on your crime. Owen was working hard to get her to confess. Maybe John was working even harder for her to hold firm to their story. That was a lot of pressure, perhaps mixed with guilt and remorse. Was it enough to make her kill herself, though? Wouldn't she be more likely to just cave and confess to Owen?

But if she had told John that she wanted to tell the truth, or if he'd seen the same mounting anxiety and fragility in her that Adam had, maybe the manner of death was homicide. John had killed her to make sure she didn't flip on him. If he succeeded in making it look like an accident or suicide, he could get away with putting all the blame for Bryan's death on Rachelle.

Which one was the real answer?

59

I alternated between writing, sort of, and refreshing both the *Himmel Times* site and the *GO News* page, just in case Maggie got too busy to call me with the autopsy results.

Finally, around two o'clock, my phone rang. Of course, I'd left it on the kitchen counter when I had gone foraging in the cupboard for something to eat. I dashed from my office to get it and answered without bothering to look at the caller ID.

"Maggie, what did you find out?"

"Leah, it's Gabe."

He sounded different—hesitant, as if unsure of his reception.

I overcompensated with a cheerful, hearty response.

"Gabe! Hi, sorry, I was expecting a call from Maggie. How are you?"

I cringed as soon as I said it. How did I expect him to be?

"I'm fine. I was wondering, that is, I talked to Dominic. About us. He seems okay, but the thing he most wanted to know is if you still like him, and if you're still his friend. I told him yes, but I think he'd like to hear it from you. Would it be all right if I stopped over with him today, after I pick him up from daycare around 3:30?"

"Oh, Gabe, sure, yes. I'm here all afternoon."

"Okay, thanks. I guess I'll see you then."

We both hung on for a few seconds of dead air, then each of us said a hasty goodbye.

I hate the aftermath of a "friendly" breakup. If you're the breaker, you feel guilty and sad. If you're the break-ee, you feel hurt and sad. In both cases, you walk on eggshells trying not to make the other one feel worse. If you're lucky, after a while you might get comfortable with each other, but sometimes you never do. I would hate to lose Gabe from my life.

Around 3:30 my intercom buzzed, and when I answered, a small voice said, "Hi, Leah. It's me, Dominic. And my dad. Is it okay to come up and see you?"

"Absolutely. I've been hoping you'd stop by."

When I opened the door, Dominic rushed in and gave me a hug that nearly knocked me over.

"Hey, it's good to see you. What do you have there?" I asked as he waved a paper in my direction.

"It's a picture. I made it for you. See, it's me and Barnacle and you and Dad. We're swinging at the park."

"I can see that. It's great. I especially like Barnacle on his own swing."

"Yes. Dogs can't really be on their own swing in real life, but he told me he wants to. So, I thought of it in my imagination and then I drew it."

"You did a wonderful job. Let's put it on my fridge."

Dominic took the picture from me and ran to get the magnets to put it on the refrigerator. Gabe was still hanging back in the doorway.

"Come on in, please. I've got coffee on and I've got cookies."

"Actually, I uh, I need to run a quick errand. I'll do that while you two talk."

He barely met my eyes as he spoke, and my heart sank at the awkwardness between us.

"Oh, sure, okay. See you in a few."

I closed the door and saw that the picture was already in place, and Dominic was clambering up on a seat at the kitchen bar where he'd already spotted the plate of cookies.

"These are for us, right?"

"Right. Would you like some water, too?"

"Yes, please."

When I was sitting down across from him, he said, "Leah, my dad said you aren't his girlfriend anymore, but you're still his friend."

"That's true."

"Don't you like him anymore?"

"Yes, I still like him very much. But I think we should be friends, not boyfriend and girlfriend."

He nodded solemnly as he chewed on his cookie. After he swallowed and took a drink of water, he said, "My mom and my other dad, they got divorced."

"I know."

"But they didn't stay friends. Now, I don't see my other dad anymore. Do you still want to be my friend?"

"Dom, of course I do. You and I will always be friends."

"Can I still stay overnight at your house sometimes?"

"Of course you can."

"Will you still stay overnight at my house?"

"I don't think so. For grown-ups, that's more of a boyfriend/girlfriend thing to do."

He nodded as though processing my answer.

"My dad said that he's sad. Are you sad, too?"

"Yes, I am."

"Then why don't you just stay the same way?"

"Well, the thing is, your dad is so great that he should have a great girlfriend. But I think that I'm better at being just a regular friend. So, we're going to be regular good friends, and then one day he'll find the right girlfriend for him. It's okay to feel sad when things change, but we won't be sad for always."

He chewed on both the cookie and my explanation for a minute. When he finished, I prepared for another emotionally fraught question.

"Okay. Are you going to eat your cookie? Because I would like it if you aren't."

And that was it.

A few minutes later Gabe returned from what I was sure was an imaginary errand. We did casual chatting for a minute, uneasily. After we said goodbye, I watched them as they walked down the stairs together. Dominic was talking a mile a minute, and Gabe was holding his hand and nodding. I felt a lump in my throat at the thought that I wouldn't be a part of that anymore. At least not in the way I had been. But at the same time, I knew that what I'd said to Dominic was right. Gabe deserved a great girlfriend, and that wasn't me.

In the end it was Ross, not Maggie, who gave me the autopsy results on Rachelle.

"Nash, did ya hear? Rachelle Crawford was murdered. Things aren't lookin' good for John Pilarski, I'd say."

"Are you sure she was murdered? I've been waiting all day for Maggie to call me with the autopsy results, but she hasn't yet."

"They're not out officially. Steve Northam just gave me a heads up on the QT."

"How was she killed?"

"She had a wound on the side of her head, like she coulda slipped and fell on the rocks, then drowned. Or somebody coulda hit her with a rock. The killer mighta got away with it only Connie's good at her job. She found marks on Rachelle's neck and shoulders where somebody held her down."

"And you think it was John."

"You don't?"

"No, I do. In fact, I already worked out that scenario. But I've been hoping the autopsy would show accident or suicide as the cause—for Jennifer's sake."

"I get that. I don't like to think how this is gonna hit Jennifer, either. But the suspect pool for Crawford's murder is pretty much dried up, and Pilarski is the fish left gaspin' for air. He made his play to get rid of Rachelle, trying to make it look like an accident or suicide. It didn't work and he's left holdin' the bag for her murder and Crawford's too, I'd say."

"It won't be that easy to prove, though. John's only tie to Bryan Crawford's death is his relationship with Rachelle. He can say she did it all and he knew nothing about it."

"He can say that, yeah, but is a jury gonna believe him? His motive for killing Rachelle was to keep her quiet. Why would he have to keep her quiet, if he didn't help her kill Crawford? I think he's goin' down for both. We'll see. But I thought you should know what's up. Jennifer's going to need a friend."

"Thanks, I appreciate it. Partner."

I hung up before he could contradict me.

I tried Coop then. He couldn't feel any better about the way things were heading than I did. He didn't pick up. I didn't bother with a voicemail. He'd know what I wanted when he saw my number.

If he didn't call me back, it would be because he couldn't give me anything and didn't want to have a discussion about it. I debated calling Jennifer but decided to wait for her to call me if she wanted to talk. I didn't want to lie to her, but I didn't want to tell her I thought John was in imminent danger of being arrested either.

60

When my phone rang early the next morning, I thought it might be Coop with news about John. It wasn't.

"Leah, they arrested John! They think that he killed Rachelle Crawford, and Bryan Crawford both!" Jen's voice was high and panicky, and she was talking so fast I could barely understand what she was saying.

"Jen, Jennifer! Slow down."

"I can't. I have to get him a lawyer. Will Gabe do it? I have to call Gabe. I have to call John's parents. The boys! What am I going to tell the boys? I can't believe this is happening. How could Coop do this? He knows John. He—I can't, I can't!"

Finally, she was overtaken with sobs, and I was able to break through.

"Jen, I'm coming over."

"No, you have to help me."

"I will, that's why I'm coming over."

"No, you have to go see Coop. You have to tell him it's a mistake. John didn't kill anybody. He couldn't. He had an affair. That doesn't make him a killer! You can fix it, Leah. You can talk to Coop. You can make him see they've got it wrong."

"Jen, they wouldn't have arrested John without some evidence. What did they say when they took him into custody?"

"I don't know. I wasn't here. I ran out to the store because I needed milk. John was asleep. When I got home, the police car was in the driveway. When I got inside, Owen was handcuffing him!" She ended the sentence on a wail.

"Jennifer, what did Owen say? He must have said something to you."

"Yes. He said he was sorry! What does that even mean when he's taking John to jail! He told me I couldn't see John until after he had his first appearance in court. He's going to be in jail for at least a day without me even being able to talk to him. You could, Leah. You could get in. Miller could help you. You need to talk to John. I'm sure he can explain. Then you could talk to Coop. This is so wrong. You could—"

Her fear and her desperation were making her thoughts careen all over the place. If I'd been with her, I might have been tempted to slap her across the face to shock her out of it, the way they always do in the movies. Instead, I tried the verbal equivalent—short, sharp, final.

"Jennifer, no."

It worked. Jen stopped her chaotic stream-of-consciousness freak-out. She stopped talking at all. The only thing I could hear was the harsh rasp of her breath. Into the silence I said, "Jen, I can't try to intervene for John with Coop."

"Why? Why can't you?"

"Because I don't think John is innocent. I know you don't want to hear this. Owen didn't arrest John on a whim. He's going on something more than John's affair with Rachelle."

"Well, he wouldn't even know about the affair if it wasn't for you, would he? You're the one who told Coop about John and Rachelle. If you hadn't, no one would even know. He slept with Rachelle, yes. But he didn't kill her and he didn't kill Bryan! He's the father of my boys, and he didn't do it. I know he didn't. He wouldn't be in jail now, if it wasn't for you. I asked you to help me, not to ruin my life. And now that you have, you won't even try to make it right!"

"Jen, we can't talk this through on the phone. I'm coming over."

"No! I don't want you here. I don't want to see you, Leah. I don't know if I ever want to see you again!"

"Please, Jennifer—"

She hung up.

I stared stupidly at my phone for a minute. I knew it wasn't my fault. But right then, with Jen's accusing, fearful, desperate voice still ringing in my ear, it sure felt like it was.

I ran downstairs to see Maggie. The newsroom was empty, but she was in her office.

"I just talked to Jennifer. John's been arrested. Do you know? Why didn't you call me?"

Maggie pulled her glasses down from the top of her head and settled them on her nose before she looked up from her computer.

"It's been just a touch busy around here, Leah. Miguel got picked for jury duty yesterday, and the trial went into a second day, so he's out today, too. Troy just called in with the autopsy results, and to say that John Pilarski's been arrested, so you're as up on the news as I am. The stringer I had lined up to cover for Miguel just bailed on me, it's deadline day, and, oh yeah, we've got a flood watch that could turn into a warning any minute going on. Any questions?"

"No. Sorry. I didn't mean to sound so demanding. I'm pretty shaken about John, that's all. Did Troy have anything on why they arrested him?"

"Not from the cops or the DA. But he got a hint from the one-man neighborhood watch, George Wynn. He called Troy after he called the cops. Seems that George was past the Crawfords', goin' home from work around 5:15 Monday afternoon. John was backing out of the Crawfords' driveway and nearly hit him."

"When was Rachelle killed?"

"Between three and eight p.m. is the time of death window, but Connie loaded it with lots of caveats—the body being partially in the water, the rain, the cool weather, for all I know the phase of the moon. Just once I'd like to meet a medical examiner who wasn't wishy-washy about time of death."

"What does *GO News* have?"

"So far, just the autopsy results. They must not have the John and

Rachelle connection yet or they'd be all over it. With Lawlor out now at the sheriff's office, it looks like Andrea lost her inside source."

"He's definitely fired, then?"

"That's what we heard, but all we've got from the sheriff's office is that he's no longer employed. They haven't confirmed he was fired, and we don't have time to chase that down right now. You said you talked to Jennifer, what does she know about John's arrest?"

"Nothing. Owen didn't give her any reason, but there's got to be more than just the fact that John and Rachelle had an affair. The neighbor guy seeing his car at the Crawfords' would be one factor. Maybe there were texts on Rachelle's phone. You said that locating her phone is how Adam found the body, so the cops must have that."

"Right." She shook her head. "We've got enough news for two editions this week. Too bad I only have half a staff. Like they say, when it rains, it pours."

As she spoke, a low roll of thunder rattled the windows.

"Forget I said that. What we don't need is any more rain."

"You said there's a flood watch. What part of the county? Just the northwest?"

"Mostly, the Apple River is pretty high and so are a lot of creeks that feed into it."

"What about Ponder Dam?"

"I talked to the emergency manager early this morning. It's not good. The spillway degradation is serious. It's possible the water will overtop the dam, and if that happens, the strain could make the whole thing go."

"Holy cow, I didn't realize things were so bad. Listen, if you need help, call me. I mean it. I can jump in, write a story, take some photos, whatever."

"For now, just keep your fingers crossed. I've got calls in to a couple stringers, and the weatherman says the front is supposed to move on today, so we'll see."

"Okay, well, you know where I am."

61

Back upstairs, I couldn't get Jen's words out of my head. She couldn't mean that she never wanted to see me again. We'd been friends since kindergarten. She was just hyper-emotional, like anyone would be, I assured myself.

John had probably convinced her that Rachelle was some kind of femme fatale who had cast a spell he couldn't resist. But that he had realized it was Jennifer he loved, and she had believed him. When everything came out, Jennifer would face the facts. She was super loyal, and she had a very forgiving heart, but she wasn't stupid. I was counting on her forgiving heart to restore our friendship. The only thing that might keep that from happening was if John really hadn't killed Rachelle and Jen couldn't forget that I'd said I thought he had.

But that was pretty much impossible. I'd already laid out the only three scenarios that fit the facts. The first two, accident and suicide, had been ruled out by the autopsy. That left murder. Rachelle and John killed Bryan, and when the police began closing in, Rachelle panicked, and John killed her to shut her up. That was the only answer that made sense. Unless . . .

What if Rachelle killed Bryan with an accomplice, but it wasn't John?

No. I was grasping at straws, trying to find a way to make John not guilty so Jennifer wouldn't be devastated. The facts were the facts, and the sheriff's office had tracked enough of them down to arrest John. It wasn't my job to second-guess the police investigation.

It was my job, however, to get my new series going. I sat down in my office and opened my laptop. I researched winter storms in the Upper Peninsula, outlined the structure of the sheriff's office in mythical Makwa County, and even tried to write a story arc for the first three books in the series. But nothing worked. No matter how hard I tried to push the idea back down to the murky depths of my mind, it kept popping back up like the bobber on a fishing line.

Finally, I gave up resisting. I let my thoughts roam free to see if anything came together. Okay. Rachelle was Bryan's wife. When a husband dies, his wife is often the killer. But Bryan had *three* wives.

Rachelle, who had the means, motive, and opportunity to kill him. Jackie, Stephanie's mother, who had a possible motive, revenge, but no opportunity. Liz, who had no means, no opportunity, and no motive except maybe regret that all she got out of the marriage was a half share in two paltry bank accounts, a small house with a big mortgage, and . . .

Unexpectedly, I heard the Northern Wisconsin sound of insurance man par excellence, Marty Angstrom, in my head.

" . . . *you should go for a whole life policy . . . I always tell my lady clients, if they have a divorce situation, you make sure your attorney gets you ownership of your husband's whole life policy . . . it's gonna pay out either in cash value, or the death benefit if your ex dies. And that death benefit appreciates, too. It's a real good deal, there.*"

I began digging around on my desk for the divorce file from Bryan's first marriage, my mind racing. I flipped impatiently through the papers to find the division of property. Bryan and Liz split the checking and savings accounts, each took one of the cars, Bryan kept sole ownership of Crawford Plumbing, and Liz got the mortgaged house and an insurance policy. A whole life policy in the amount of $100,000. Marty had given me the clue weeks ago, but it hadn't registered.

I grabbed my phone and called him.

"Hey, Leah, how's by you?"

"Hi, Marty. I'm good. I just have a quick question for you. If I had a $100,000 whole life insurance policy, what would it be worth after thirty years?"

"So, you been thinkin' about what I said, eh? Well, now that depends on a coupla things, your interest rate, if you borrowed against it, what company you took it out with, if—"

"I just need a general idea. Say I never borrowed against it or took cash out or whatever. I just paid the premium for thirty years. Give me an idea what it's worth today."

"Well, I'd say maybe around $75,000 if you cashed it in—you'd maybe have to pay taxes on it; it depends, though. Now, your death benefit, that would have a real nice appreciation, might be up right around $150,000 give or take. And there's no income tax on that. Let me set up an appointment, we can talk—"

"Sorry, Marty, I have to go. Thanks, I'll talk to you later."

My next call was to Miller Caldwell.

"Hi, Miller. Quick question. Do you know how much Ariana's Restaurant is listed for?"

Fortunately, Miller is used to random, abrupt queries from me, and he didn't waste time questioning me about why I was asking.

"It's not officially listed yet, Leah. It's my understanding the owner's given a prospective buyer some time to come up with the financing. If that falls through, though, it will go on the market."

"Okay, but do you know how much he's asking?"

"I believe it's in the neighborhood of $500,000. It's a prime piece of real estate, and the restaurant is thriving, so it's a bargain at that price. I understand there's a divorce situation involved."

"If I wanted to buy it, and I had investors who agreed to finance the purchase, they wouldn't cover the whole amount, would they? I mean, I'd still have to come up with a down payment, right?"

"Most certainly."

"How big?"

"Twenty percent would be typical, so about $100,000."

"Okay. Thanks, Miller. Bye."

62

I pulled a legal pad from my drawer and took it and a pencil into the other room to sit on the window seat and organize my thoughts.

Liz wanted to buy Ariana's, but needed $100,000 in addition to her investors' backing. Rachelle wanted to leave Bryan, but not without money. They both had a financial motive to kill Bryan. Rachelle had the means and the opportunity to do it, but as the spouse, she'd be the prime suspect if Bryan was killed. Liz, on the other hand, was an unlikely suspect. She was an ex-wife who hadn't seen him in 30 years, with no obvious financial motive. Who even knew about the insurance policy after all this time?

Killing Bryan would be high risk for Rachelle because any investigation would focus on her immediately. But for Liz, murdering Bryan would be low risk—ostensibly she had no motive.

Liz needed money. Rachelle wanted money. A dead Bryan was the way they could each get it. Separately, it would be difficult to pull it off. But together they could make it work. But how had they gotten together? When did the paths of wife number one and wife number three intersect, and how had it led to murder?

I tapped my pencil on the edge of my pad as I chased a memory that I couldn't quite grab hold of. It had something to do with Ann Lynn, my mother's friend. But what was it?

I jumped up and began pacing around the apartment, trying to will the memory to come forth. It would not. I flopped back down on the window seat in frustration, drew my knees up, and rested my chin on them. I stared mindlessly out the window at Wide Awake and Woke across the street. I gradually registered that a number of women were wandering through the door carrying yoga mats. Will, the barista, had mentioned that the owner's wife was opening a yoga studio on the second floor—not my cup of tea, or coffee either.

Then it hit me. The conversation I'd had in the conference room of the *Times* with Ann Lynn, Donna, and my mother. Only it wasn't what Ann Lynn had said that was niggling at the back of my mind. It was Donna's casual remark. She'd mentioned that she knew Rachelle because she went to her yoga class. The yoga class where she'd also met Liz.

That was it, that was the connection, Rachelle's yoga class. That's where she and Liz had first met. From there it was fairly easy to hypothesize how they'd come to collaborate.

They hit it off at yoga class, then go out for a glass of wine or whatever afterward one night. During the usual get-to-know-you chat, they realize they have a husband in common. After the initial astonishment, they laugh, maybe commiserate about Rhonda, the sister-in-law from hell. Liz says she'd rather Rhonda didn't know she was in the area. Rachelle understands. She won't mention it to Bryan, because he would surely mention it to Rhonda. And anyway, she and Bryan don't talk much. They live almost separate lives, Rachelle admits.

The friendship grows and Liz confides one night that she wants to buy Ariana's, but she doesn't have the down payment. She has an insurance policy on Bryan that she got in the divorce, but the cash-in value isn't enough. Rachelle says she's got a different money problem. She wants to divorce Bryan, but with the prenup, the only way she gets anything is if he dies. Liz says face it, Bryan's worth more dead than alive. They both laugh. Until they don't. And a murder plot is born.

They work things out pretty much the way Ross and I had imagined it, only with Liz as the co-killer instead of John. Rachelle handles the setup, making sure no one is home that weekend, switches out the insulin for water, then leaves to establish her alibi. Liz takes care of locking Bryan in the sauna during her regularly scheduled "me time" at the restaurant. Having trained her staff well, she knows there's no danger anyone will venture up to see her and discover she's not there. Ross is down in the restaurant eating or at the bar, knowing Liz is busy but they've got the whole weekend together and he's happy enough to wait until she's off work. He knows about her "me time" between 6 and 7, but he has no idea she's left the building. No one does, because she slips down the outdoor back stairs to her apartment. The restaurant is less than five miles from the Crawford house.

On Sunday she goes back and unlocks the door. That's when their first bit of bad luck occurs. Sheila's car comes down the road on her way to check for her lost earrings, its loud muffler rattling as she pulls in the driveway. Liz gets spooked and takes off, forgetting to put the key back under the mat. She doesn't get a chance to tell Rachelle before Ross asks about it, but it doesn't seem that important.

Rachelle arrives home on Monday, goes to the sauna, opens the door, Bryan is dead, she calls 911. It's all going just as they planned. The death is declared natural, caused by diabetic complications. She and Liz are home free. Until Rhonda finds the trail cam footage, and starts harping about the missing insulin bottle, and Ross begins thinking about the key.

I made another quick call, this time to Connie Crowley.

"Leah, I told you before, I'm not the go-to for autopsy results. Only Cliff Timmins or Coop are authorized to talk to the press."

"I'm not the press, Connie. This is just me, and it's not even about an autopsy, exactly. It's about the toxicology report on the samples you sent in after Rhonda pitched a hissy fit about poison. Is it back yet?"

"Came in yesterday. This is off the record, right?"

"Yes, same as I told you last time."

"Just checking. There was nothing there. No mystery poison that changed the original cause of death. It was DKA, like I said."

"Connie, my boyfr—that is, my friend—Gabe told me that he prosecuted a case once where a husband substituted water for his wife's insulin, and she went into a diabetic coma. Is it possible that water was substituted for Bryan's insulin?"

"Sure, it's possible. Blood sugar's a funny thing, it doesn't react the same in everyone, or even the same way every time in the same person. A lot of factors can affect it. Messing with Bryan's insulin could've been a little insurance to make sure he died. But substituting water for insulin could be chancy, too. If his glucose levels shot too high, too fast, he might have gone into DKA too soon. Like at work, when people were around and could help him, instead of when he was alone and locked in the sauna. Still, killing someone at all is full of risk, isn't it? You think that's what the missing insulin bottle was all about?"

"I do, but there's no way to prove that."

"True. Rachelle's not going to be doing any talking."

When I hung up the phone, I felt a sense of triumph similar to the one you get when you've finished putting an Ikea table together and there are no extra bolts or screws left over.

I had a theory that accounted for the missing insulin vial, how and why Bryan died at the hands of two of his wives. It also accounted for Rachelle's death. Liz had done it when she saw that her partner in murder was about to crack under the strain. The only thing it didn't account for was John's car being at the Crawfords' the afternoon Rachelle was killed. But it could be that the helpful neighbor George Wynn had been wrong about the time, or even about seeing John. Eyewitnesses often make mistakes.

And, I had to admit, so do I. This time, though, I was pretty sure I had it right.

I had to talk to Ross. He was going to be really torn up about Liz. But he had to know the truth. I called to make sure he was home and alone. Awkward isn't the word to describe what it would be like if I showed up on his doorstep unannounced and found Liz there.

His phone rang several times, then his voicemail came on.

"Ross, call me as soon as you can. It's important."

I called Coop while I waited for Ross to return my call, but I had no luck there either. I left a longer message for him. I gave him the key points of my theory so that he'd call me back as soon as he could. Then, I waited. When my phone rang 15 minutes later, it wasn't either of them.

"Hi, Maggie."

"Leah, I have to eat my words. I do need some help. I don't have anyone to shoot photos and we need some high water pix from the west side of the county. Have you got time to handle it?"

"Yes, sure. I can do that. Anything particular?" I'd rather be active than sitting around waiting for a return call from Ross or Coop.

"The covered bridge would be good, showing how high the water is. A barricade at a closed road would work, too. But be careful. Keep your phone nearby so you hear any flash flood warnings. I don't want you getting swept away."

"I will. I'll be there and back before you know it."

63

The countryside around me looked pretty normal as I drove out of Himmel. But once I got past Omico, I saw field after field with standing water and ditches that were over halfway filled.

It was still a shock when I got to the covered bridge and saw how high the water was. I pulled over and took a couple of pictures, then I walked to the other side and moved upstream along the bank to get a better angle for a few more. I wanted a good shot of the black, rain-soaked tree limbs bending like skeletal arms toward the rushing water. Maggie would probably favor the shots I'd taken of the bridge. But I might keep the one of trees for myself. It would make a nice print for my office wall.

It didn't seem like it had taken me that long, but by the time I walked back, the water had risen level with the planks of the bridge. I hurried to my car, Maggie's warning to be careful in my head. As I buckled in, an emergency warning sounded on my phone.

"The National Weather Service has issued a flood warning for portions of Grantland County . . ."

The artificial, disembodied voice proceeded to identify the areas under warning. One of them was exactly where I was.

I threw the car in drive and surged forward across the bridge, intent on getting to higher ground. No need to panic. Just a mile and a half down I could cut over on Linwood Road, and take it to the top of Caroll Hill. I'd be high enough there to be out of reach of any flood waters. From that vantage point I should be able to shoot some great video of the waters rising.

I'd only gone a few hundred yards when rain began pounding down on my car like a thousand tiny jackhammers. The sound was deafening. My windshield wipers couldn't keep up. I leaned forward squinting to see more than a few feet ahead of me. Water had begun overtopping the ditches on either side.

Scenes from every flood disaster documentary I'd ever seen danced through my head. I drove as fast as I dared. Water sprayed out from my tires like I was piloting a hydroplane instead of driving a car. I clenched my hands tightly on the steering wheel. The car hit a huge pothole. The impact bounced me up toward the ceiling and wrenched the wheel from my slippery grip.

I grabbed it back and tried to straighten the car as it fishtailed and swerved scarily close to the water-filled ditch on the left. By an undeserved miracle, I managed to get the car under control. I forced myself to move forward at a slower speed.

I claimed the center as my lane because it took so much effort to keep the car steady on the gravel road. I longed for the reassuring taillights of a car ahead of me, but I was the only driver careless enough to get caught in the middle of a flash flood warning. Maggie had told me there was a watch, she had told me to be careful. But no, I had to jump around playing Ansel Adams taking artsy photos while the water kept rising. If I'd just taken the bridge photo and moved on, I'd be at the top of Carroll Hill by now, instead of trying to drive in visibility that was just slightly better than looking through gray gauze.

I stoked the anger at myself to keep the fear at bay. It wasn't working that well. I began repeating out loud, "I can do this, I can do this, I can do this." It was hard to loosen my fingers enough to hit the answer button on the steering wheel when my phone rang, but I was desperate for human contact.

"Ross, I'm glad to hear your voice."

"Nash, we were wrong. It's not John Pilarski. It's *Liz*! Liz and Rachelle together."

I was so shocked that Ross had reached the same answer as me that I forgot my peril for the moment.

"Ross, how do you know?"

"I found the sauna key. The guy at the cleaners handed it to me when I picked up her jacket this morning. He said there was a hole in the pocket and it slipped down between the lining. It's orange on top with a yellow S, just like the key Rachelle gave me after Adam "found" it under the mat. Liz played me like a fiddle, all this time. I thought I was protecting my girl-friend. I was covering up for a murderer! How could I be such a dumbass!"

"Ross, I'm so sorry. You're not a dumbass. Or if you are, we both are. Liz had a motive. She had an insurance policy she got in the divorce from Bryan. It's worth $150,000 to her. She needs it for the down payment on Ariana's."

"She killed two people so she could buy a damn restaurant?"

"It's not just a restaurant to her. It's her dream. People will do a lot to keep their dreams alive."

A loud clap of thunder startled me, and I jerked the wheel. "Shit!"

Ross didn't seem to notice.

"You and me need to go see Coop, lay this out for him. Can you meet me at the sheriff's office?"

"I would like to, Ross, but I'm a little busy trying to outrun a flood just now."

"What? Where the hell are you, Nash?"

"I'm on Wheaton Road—"

"You gotta get off that road! There's a flood warning out. What are you doin' there?"

"I'm trying. I was out taking pictures. It was a watch, not a warning, when I started. I'll be fine as soon as I get to Linwood, then I—"

"No, you won't! Christ, half of Linwood is washed out. You can't get down Storey either, the bridge is gone."

"Damn, Ross, that doesn't give me many choices." I tried to keep my voice even, but it wobbled a little.

"Where are you right now?"

"I think I'm almost to Linwood, but it's hard to see in this rain."

"Okay, okay, you're gonna be fine. When you get to Marion, take a right."

"But that's going to take me to the Apple River. I want to get away from the water, not drive into it."

"It's the only high ground you can get to from where you are. Listen, I don't wanna scare you, but the spillway's failin' at Ponder Dam. If the dam goes, I'm not sure even that's gonna be high enough."

"That's your way of not scaring me? Also, did you forget Ariana's is there, and Liz? I don't want to run from a flood into a murderer's arms."

"You don't have a choice. She's probably evacuated already. And if she hasn't, just play it cool. She doesn't know what we know. Now, listen, the only way you're gettin' outta there is by plane or by boat. I ain't got a plane. I'm goin' to get a boat."

"Ross, this is too risky for you."

"Nah. I used to be on the Marine Rescue team for the county. It's a piece of cake. When you get to Ariana's, get inside. Keep your phone on. As soon as ya see me comin' or hear the motor, run down to the dock. If Liz is there, don't do anything stupid. I'll take you both back, and we'll handle it from there. I gotta go. For once, do like I tell you!"

The rain was still hitting so heavy that I missed the turn for Marion Road and had to back up, cursing myself all the while. Driving was a little easier once I got on it, though, because the road was asphalt not gravel and there were no ditches along the side to worry about. When the road began to rise, some of the tension left my shoulders, and I stopped looking in the rearview mirror for a wall of water bearing down on me. I would've felt a whole lot better, though, if Ross hadn't told me the dam was ready to go.

I'd covered a dam break once, when I worked in Michigan. It was pretty horrifying. I didn't know how many good karma points I had banked. Realistically, probably not that many. Nevertheless, I cashed them all in with a prayer for the dam to hold, Ross to be safe, and both of us to live to tell our tale to Coop. I was going to throw in a wish that Liz not be at the restaurant, but I didn't want to overload my prayer. Ross was right, I could deal with her. When necessary, I can pretend with the best of them.

64

I breathed an audible sigh of relief when I finally made it to the empty parking lot at Ariana's. Temporary safety was better than no safety at all. I pulled around to the back, wishing very hard that Liz's van wouldn't be there. It was.

Maybe I could just climb the fire escape leading to the back door of her apartment. I could huddle under the awning and from that vantage point I'd be able to see Ross coming from a long way off. Or the river bearing down on us from the dam break. It would beat making nerve-racking casual conversation with Liz knowing that she had killed two people, while I worried if I might be next.

Then, I saw the only thing short of Captain America arriving on the scene that could have given me a fiercer jolt of happiness and relief. Coop's SUV. Why and how he came to be there didn't matter. I knew with certainty that everything would be all right.

Until I walked through the door and saw Liz holding a gun, and Coop on the floor, his back propped against a counter, holding his arm as blood seeped out between his fingers in a bloom of red.

"Coop!" I ran over and knelt beside him. His face was pale and drawn from the pain.

"I'm okay, Leah."

He struggled to get the words out.

"No, you're not!"

I looked up at Liz and shouted, "Why did you shoot him?"

"Shut up," she said, her gun now pointing at both of us. "I have to think."

"You have to think? You have to think? You just shot Coop!"

I jumped up, my eyes darting around the restaurant kitchen looking for what I could use to make a tourniquet to staunch the flow of blood.

"Stand still!" Liz shouted in a voice so loud and harsh that it temporarily stopped me in my tracks. That and the gun she was pointing at me. If I was going to save Coop, I had to find a way to get the gun from her. I had to lull her into a moment of carelessness. I forced myself to speak in calm, measured tones. I didn't let myself think of Coop slowly bleeding on the floor behind me.

"Liz, please. Just let me try to stop the bleeding. Then we can talk. Whatever happened, we can work it out. But if he dies ..."

"I said shut up! I have to figure a way out. That stupid, selfish bitch! She ruined everything!"

I froze. Liz gave her head a shake. She was losing it. The gun was still pointed at me. I glanced back at Coop. His hand was still on his arm, but blood was still seeping out from under his fingers, and his breathing sounded shallower. I tried to keep Liz talking to buy more time.

"Rachelle, right? If she'd stayed at the retreat like you planned, if she hadn't gone to that bed and breakfast with John—"

"I should've found another way, just done it on my own. First, she doesn't know about the trail cams. But we could still make it work. Her story was true. She was at the retreat. She was safe. Then I find out she had to sneak away to go screw her boyfriend! It was a perfect plan, but she didn't follow it. I was calm. I told her, 'They can't prove anything. You didn't do anything. I took all the risk. Just keep saying you were at the retreat. But the stupid bitch couldn't do it."

"You must have been furious. You did all the hard stuff. You locked

Bryan in the sauna, you went back and unlocked it Sunday. Rachelle had it easy, and still she wrecked everything."

That was obviously the wrong thing to say, because it brought her focus back to me.

"No, you! You wrecked everything, digging around in my old divorce file! We had it all set. No one even knew who I was. Then you came along, and it all went to hell. I didn't want to kill her. I didn't even want to kill Bryan. It wasn't personal for me, like it was for her. I had to get rid of him so I could get the money for my restaurant. All that planning, all that work, all gone because of her."

"You arranged to meet Rachelle at the gazebo so you could kill her, didn't you?"

"I couldn't trust her. I had to stop her. She was going to take me down with her. They were supposed to think she killed herself. Now everything is ruined!"

"Liz, there's no point in killing us. It's over. You can't get away. Charlie knows everything. He's got the proof. He found the key to the sauna. It was in your jacket."

"You're lying."

"I'm not. There was a hole in your pocket. It slipped behind the lining. The cleaner gave it to him today when he picked it up. Put down the gun, Liz. Don't make it worse for yourself."

She shocked me by laughing loud and long.

"Worse for myself? Worse? Worse than losing the one thing I gave up everything for? I was so close to having my own restaurant again. I talked to Charlie this morning. He told me John Pilarski had been arrested. I thought, 'Okay, it'll be all right now. Pilarski can take the blame for Bryan and Rachelle. He should. I can still pull this off.' And then he showed up," she said, pointing the gun in Coop's direction.

"Why did you have to shoot him?"

"He was asking too many questions. Like you. I hate you! This is your fault. You cost me everything that matters to me. My restaurant, my second chance, it's all gone now. At least I can make you pay!"

"Wait! Liz, you—"

At that second the emergency warning signal blared from my phone.

Liz jumped. I rushed forward, turning so that my left shoulder slammed into her soft belly, keeping my weight on the ball of my foot to maintain momentum. I knocked the wind out of her, and the gun flew from her hand. It landed by Coop's foot. I scrambled for it as she tried to catch her breath. He kicked it over to me. As I grabbed it, he slumped over. His hand fell from his arm and I knew he'd lost consciousness. As I moved toward him, I heard a sound behind me.

Liz held a butcher knife. She moved toward me, her eyes wild with rage. But her fury was no match for the violent anger that coursed through me at what she had done to Coop. I didn't hesitate. I shot her. She stumbled. I shot her two more times. She fell. It took a few seconds before I processed the words the emergency warning kept repeating. Ponder Dam had failed. Three-point-four billion cubic feet of water was rushing toward us. I threw down the gun and turned to Coop.

65

His eyelids fluttered, but he didn't come fully awake. Without his hand pressed against the wound in his arm, blood was flowing at an alarming rate. I jumped up and ransacked drawers for something to use as a tourniquet. I grabbed a large tea towel and found a flat table knife to serve as a windlass to tighten the tourniquet. Then I tugged Coop from his slumped-over position so that he was flat on the floor. I kept up a running stream of chatter to steady my nerves. I was about to put into practice in real life something I'd only ever done before on a silicone dummy in a first-aid class. If I did it wrong, he could lose his arm. But if I didn't do it at all, he could bleed to death.

"Okay, here we go. I've got the towel folded to make the tourniquet. Now, I'm wrapping it around your arm, there we go. I'm tying a nice half-knot, and here comes the table knife to use for the windlass. Okay, I tied that in place, and we're ready to go. This is going to be a little rough, but I know you can take it."

I began twisting the knife to tighten the tourniquet. I knew I had to get it super tight in order to stop all the bleeding. Coop's eyes had opened. He gritted his teeth, but he didn't complain. The blood slowed as I twisted, but it hadn't stopped. I had to get the tourniquet even tighter to increase the pressure.

I steeled myself and gave one more good, hard twist. Coop let out a groan, but the bleeding stopped.

"Almost done. I just have to take the tails of the towel, twist them around the windlass to keep it nice and tight, then around your arm, with a good, strong knot to make sure the knife doesn't slip and the pressure doesn't let up. There!"

Sweat was running down my face and I wiped the back of my hand across my forehead.

"Thanks, Leah," Coop managed to say.

"Hey, we did good. You're all set for the ride home. Ross is on his way."

"So is all the water from Ponder Dam. Hope Ross makes it first." His voice was so hoarse and low I had to bend close to hear it.

"Sure he will. We're a long way from the dam. It might not even get here. No worries. I might just give him a call, though, ask him to speed it up a little," I said in a fake cheery voice that fooled neither of us.

As I picked up my phone, the kitchen door flew open.

"Nash! You were supposed to be at the dock. Can't you do what I tell you just once? We gotta get—What the hell happened?"

Ross took in Liz lying motionless, me, my hands covered with Coop's blood, and Coop, lying on the floor beside me.

"Liz is dead, I think. I shot her. She tried to kill Coop. He's lost a lot of blood. But I think I got it stopped."

Without a word he went to Liz, checked to make sure. Then he turned back to me.

"We gotta go," he said. "We gotta outrun the water from the dam break."

"Ross, we're on high ground here. I don't know if we'll be able to get Coop down to the boat. Maybe we should stay?"

"No, we can't take the chance. For one thing, that tourniquet can't stay on for more than two hours. For another, that's a gunshot wound, and they're dirty. He needs to see a doc pronto. Also, we don't know how far that water's gonna travel, or how high up it'll reach if it gets here. We got no choice. We gotta go."

"Get me standing. I can make it," Coop rasped out.

We helped him struggle unsteadily to his feet. As Coop leaned heavily on the counter, Ross and I exchanged uncertain glances.

"I can do it," Coop said.

That was the last time he spoke. With Ross on one side and me on the other functioning as human crutches, we haltingly made our way to the boat and half dragged him in. Ross had rescued us using one of the two marine patrol boats the sheriff's office has for summertime search and rescues. I didn't ask him how he'd been able to get it. I didn't care if he'd stolen it. I just wanted to get Coop to a hospital.

"There's some blankets in that chest over there," Ross said as he started the engine. "Cover him up and stay close to try to keep him warm. We're gonna be fine. At least the damn rain slowed down."

As we left the dock, he used the radio on the boat to call ahead for an ambulance to meet us at the city dock in Omico. I cradled Coop's head and shoulders in my lap, and I prayed.

Ross pushed the boat to its maximum speed. We bounced and swayed with each wind-whipped whitecap we hit. Coop had begun shivering beside me, despite the two blankets. He was only semi-conscious, and he didn't talk. Neither did I. There weren't any words for the fear I was feeling. It had seemed like so much blood on the floor where he had lain. And there was still the flood coming after us. A rampaging flood is like a monster, roaring through the land, ravaging everything in its path. And it had to be closing in on us.

"Ross, how much farther?"

"About five minutes. I been pushin' as fast as I can. He doin' okay?"

"Yes, fine. He'll be fine," I said. I didn't want Coop, if he could hear me, to think I had any doubts. Although my mind was filled with them.

I saw the flashing lights of the ambulance long before we reached the dock. I almost wept.

"Coop, we're nearly there."

I squeezed his hand, but he didn't respond. As soon as we docked, Ross and I jumped out and away to give the EMTs the room they needed to work. As they loaded him in the ambulance, I moved to go with them.

Ross grabbed my arm. "Leah, there's no room for you. Get back in the boat. My car's at the dock in Himmel. I'll get you to the hospital, don't worry."

Coop was in surgery when we got there. I tried to call my mother to tell her what happened, but I started crying so hard Ross had to take over.

"I'm sorry, Charlie," I said when he finished talking to her, and I had more or less pulled myself together. "It's just—"

"Leah, you're havin' a helluva day. No need to be sorry."

His words and the kind look in his eyes set me off again. He got up and brought an entire box of tissues over, wrapped me in a hug, and held me until I finally stopped. I pulled away and sat up straight. I blew my nose and wiped my eyes.

"Okay. I'm done. Thank you, Charlie. Thank you for rescuing us, thank you for being here, thank you for everything you've done today."

"It's all right," he said, obviously embarrassed. "You saved my girl once, Leah. I told ya then I wouldn't forget. Let's just quit all this thankin' and cryin' now, okay?"

"Okay, but Charlie, there's something else. Liz, I killed her."

"I know. You told me."

"No, but I shot her, and I shot her again. And then again. Charlie, I wanted to kill her. I don't know if—"

He cut me off. I'd been about to say that I wasn't sure I'd had to shoot her three times. I didn't know if I'd truly killed her in self-defense or for revenge. I didn't feel any remorse when I did it. I didn't feel any right then either, just the awareness that I had killed another human being.

"We don't need to go over that now. You did what you had to do. Don't second-guess yourself, and don't get all wishy washy when you talk to whoever investigates. Hear me? You had no choice. You shot Liz in self-defense."

I realized that he was warning me. If I expressed any doubt about self-defense to the police, I could find myself in a bad situation.

"Yeah, I hear you," I said. "Are you all right, Charlie? I mean with Liz and everything?"

He shook his head.

"No, I'm not. Let's not talk about that now either, okay?"

"Okay."

———————

Things are pretty much a blur after that. I know that Ross stayed with me, my mother came, Miguel, guys from the sheriff's office, Coop's father, Dan. Kristin might have been there, but if she was, I didn't see her. I didn't see much of anything except the door that I knew a doctor would walk through to tell me how Coop was.

People tried to coax me to the cafeteria for some food, but I refused. Someone handed me a sandwich, but I couldn't eat it. My whole self was focused on radiating all the energy and strength I had to Coop. He had to be all right. Time didn't go slowly, it didn't go fast, it didn't go at all. I sat suspended in a state of not knowing, just waiting.

But as soon as the door swung open, Coop's dad and I both jumped up. As we walked toward her, I tried to read the doctor's expression. She wasn't smiling. I grabbed Dan's hand, hard. The doctor was talking, but to my fatigued and anxious brain, her words were disjointed fragments I couldn't link together. Coop had lost a lot of blood, that was bad. The bullet had exited the wound, that was good. He'd needed a transfusion, that was bad. The scans showed no serious damage, that was good.

It wasn't until Dan began thanking the doctor profusely that it finally penetrated my fear fog. Coop was all right. He wasn't fully awake from surgery, he'd have to stay in at least a day, he'd be in pretty severe pain from his arm, and he'd need a sling for a while, but he was okay. As the doctor left, Dan turned around with a huge smile and two thumbs up, and everyone began hugging and laughing and hitting each other on the back with relief.

I felt the adrenalin surge that had kept me upright and functioning since I first walked into Ariana's kitchen desert me. I was completely exhausted.

Dan turned to me and said, "I don't know if you caught the doc say it. He's still in recovery. When he comes out, only one of us can see him at first."

"Dan, you're his dad, I'm just his best friend. You should go first. I'll come back later."

"Leah, I don't want to hear you use the word 'just' in front of 'his best friend' ever again. After what you and Charlie did?" I saw the sheen of tears in his eyes that he quickly blinked away.

"Forget it, Dan. Consider it payback for Coop saving me that time from the train. I'll remind him that we're even when he wakes up."

66

My mother drove me home and I endured—maybe even enjoyed—her fussing over me. She made me dinner while I showered, didn't ask me anything while I ate, and even after, kept her questions to a minimum.

Maggie, Troy, and Miguel were tied up covering the dam break, so I didn't have to contend with their professional or personal need to know either.

The story of who killed Bryan Crawford and Rachelle could wait a day. *GO News* would get nothing from me, Ross, or Coop, and we were the only ones who knew what had happened. I had questions myself.

Thankfully, I knew now that there would be plenty of time to get the answers from Coop. I drove my mother home after I ate. With my car quite probably under water or even floating down the Apple River, I had to use hers to go back to the hospital to see Coop. But I made one stop along the way.

"I've been going over and over what happened. When Liz came at me with that knife, I felt so much anger. I know how to use a gun, Father. I'm a good shot. I could have tried for her knee, or her arm, or . . . but I didn't.

And I shot her three times, even after I knew she had to be dead. I felt glad."

I was sitting with Father Lindstrom at his kitchen table, an untouched cup of tea in front of me. With almost no preamble, just the briefest framing so he'd understand why I was there, I'd spilled out everything that had happened at Ariana's hours before.

"Self-survival is an instinct we all have. The human race wouldn't be here if we didn't. It's very natural that your first reaction was to feel happy that you're alive, not sad that Liz was dead. How do you feel now?"

"Guilty. I guess that's why I'm here. I want you to tell me that I'm not."

"I can tell you that. I believe that. But you're the one who has to accept that in your own heart. And as hard as you are on yourself, it may take a while."

"You can't give me a shortcut? You know, a quick 'go forth and sin no more?'"

"I can pray that you learn to treat yourself with the loving kindness that you deserve."

My eyes filled with tears then, for about the millionth time that day. I was going to be the one who needed an IV pretty soon, not Coop, if I didn't stop crying every time something good, bad, or sad happened to me.

"Thanks, Father. You're just about the nicest person I know. I'll try. But you know me, I'll probably be back again."

"I'm always here, Leah."

It was after nine when I got back to the hospital. The lights had been dimmed in the rooms and hallways for the night. Dan was still sitting by Coop's bed. Coop had an IV in his arm, and he was hooked up to monitoring equipment, but his breathing was good.

"How's he doing?" I asked in the hushed voice that a quiet hospital room evokes.

"The nurse says fine. They gave him something for the pain when he woke up a little while ago. He fell back asleep," Dan said in a similarly muted tone.

"He looks a little pale still. Did he wake up enough to say anything?"

"He said he wanted to go home. I take that as a good sign. I was going to call and tell you that you might as well wait until morning. But I figured you'd want to see him for yourself."

"You were right. I'm glad he's sleeping, though."

He nodded. "He probably won't wake up again for a while. I think I'll go get some sleep myself."

"Good idea. I'm going to just sit here for a few more minutes."

"All right. I'll see you tomorrow," he said, patting my shoulder as he left.

I took the chair he had vacated, and I pulled it closer to the bed. I put my hand on Coop's.

"Coop," I whispered, "are you awake?"

He didn't answer, and he didn't move. Satisfied, I took a deep breath, and then began to say what I'd decided I had to, during that seemingly endless boat trip down the river.

"I went to your house to tell you something important last week. Only when I got there, I saw you and Kristin through the window. I saw her touch your face, and kiss you, and I watched you hug each other like two people in love. I knew then—I know now—that I was too late to say what I should have said a long time ago. So, I left. But today on the boat when I held your head in my lap, and I was so scared you wouldn't make it, I wished that I had been brave enough to tell you that night. I promised myself that if you didn't die, I'd do it."

I stopped there and took a drink from the water on his side table. This was tougher than I had thought it would be. I swallowed hard, and then rushed the words out.

"So, okay, this might not count as brave, because you're unconscious and you can't hear me. But maybe it's better this way: absolute honesty with no messy aftereffects. Here goes. You know I love you, I've told you that lots of times. But what you don't know, and how could you, because I didn't even know, I'm also *in love* with you, Coop. I don't know when it happened. Maybe I always have been. And I've always been too afraid of losing what we have to risk telling you, or myself.

"But I want to say this now. Whenever I've looked across the room at the best times and the worst times of my life, you've been there. You've made the awful times, like when Lacey died, bearable. You've made the happy times, like when I signed my first book contract, even better. It's you I always look for, and it's you I always want to share the good and the bad parts of life with. No one knows me better than you. There's no one I have more fun with, or count on more, or get madder at, or laugh louder with, or cry harder with than you. My mother thinks the reason I never stay with any man is because none of them are you. I think she's right. I wish I had said this all before, instead of waiting until you fell in love with Kristin. But I didn't know. And maybe telling you that would have made everything weird between us. And, well, that's all. I'll work myself out of being *in* love with you, I guess. I don't have a choice. But I know I'll never not love you. You're the best man I know."

I stood then and leaned in to kiss him on the forehead. As I did, he opened his eyes.

"Could you say that again? I'm kind of groggy. Start with the part about being in love with me."

I jerked back up to standing.

"You were awake? You were awake the whole time? Oh, God," I said, and put my face in my hands. "I asked you if you were awake and you didn't answer me! This is so humiliating. Forget everything I said. Please, don't tell Kristin."

"I don't need to. She already told me. Last week, when you saw us in the window? That was goodbye. Kristin broke up with me. She said she couldn't compete with you, and it was time we both realized it. She was right, Leah. You had me the first time you said, 'You're not the boss of me' when we first met. I'm crazy in love with you."

I dropped my hands and stared at him in genuine surprise.

"You never told me that. How was I supposed to know that?"

"My timing was always off. Plus, I saw how you treated the guys who came in and out of your life. I didn't want to be that disposable. And then, when I was just about ready to take a chance, you married Nick. And after that blew up, I didn't want to catch you on the rebound. Then you moved south and got involved with Connor. After you came back to Himmel, you got with Nick again. And then there was Gabe. You didn't give me much of a chance."

"Oh, stop it! You were head over heels with Rebecca and you would have laughed in my face if I'd said I was in love with you."

"Okay, I can't explain Rebecca. But I would never have laughed at you. What about Gabe? I like the guy, but I hated it when you started seeing him."

"I broke up with him because I couldn't love him the way he wanted me to. Only I didn't know you were the reason."

"I tried to steal you away from him, but you just blew me off. Remember election night, when you kissed me by accident and said you were sorry? And then I texted you and said I wasn't? I thought that was pretty clear. But you never said anything after."

"*I* never said anything after? You never said a word. And I've got a news flash for you. A two-word text that says, 'I'm not,' isn't exactly a declaration of love. When you didn't follow up, I thought it was just a mistake, like you started a text and didn't finish it."

"How about I finish it now?"

He reached up with his good arm and put his hand on my face to draw me closer. I leaned in toward him, and when we kissed this time, there was no mistake about what he meant.

67

Coop didn't get released from the hospital until Saturday, and his dad insisted on spending the night to make sure he could function on his own with only one good arm. It was just as well, because I was crazy busy at the paper. I didn't do any of the reporting, but I helped out as copy editor. Between the flood coverage and the Liz-Rachelle-Bryan Crawford story, we had a lot of words going out. It turned out Owen Fike had his hands full, too, so he didn't talk to me until Sunday morning.

The flood waters had reached Ariana's parking lot, but not the restaurant itself, so the crime scene was intact when he was finally able to get to it. When he questioned me, my story matched the evidence, the autopsy on Liz, and Coop's hazy recollection. I was in the clear on the shooting—at least in the eyes of the law.

Owen met then with Ross and me together. Most of what we told him didn't come as a big surprise. When he took over the case, he began working with the two-person theory Ross had been playing with for Bryan Crawford's murder. He also started digging into Liz's background. But when John and Rachelle's affair came to light, his interest in Liz had faded. John's arrest for Rachelle's murder was the result of a text message found on Rachelle's phone, setting up a meeting with John at her house at 5 o'clock the day she died. When the neighbor identified John as the driver of the car backing out of the Crawfords' drive a little after 5, that seemed to clinch it.

John admitted being there but swore that Rachelle wasn't home when he arrived. He said he had waited a few minutes, but then left. He hadn't wanted to come in the first place. He'd already told her it was over between them. She hadn't taken it well and he was afraid she might do something "crazy." Not afraid enough, apparently, to call her or look for her, though.

At the crime scene at Ariana's, they'd discovered a burner phone in Liz's purse. She'd made a call to Rachelle in the morning on the day Rachelle was killed. Owen's theory was that Liz had arranged to meet Rachelle at the gazebo that afternoon and had killed her then. She was probably already dead while John waited for her up at the house.

I already knew from Coop that he'd been at Ariana's because of my voicemail. He was out checking on the flooding when he got it and had planned to stop there anyway to make sure Liz knew about the flood danger. After he got my message, he tried to shake her up a little. He opened with the flooding situation, and then moved on to Rachelle's death. He said he'd heard that she and Liz were friends.

She denied it, said she'd never met Rachelle. Which he knew was a lie. He told Liz they both needed to leave and he'd drive her to safety. She went to get her purse. When she came back, she had the gun out. He tried to talk her down, but she shot him. That's when I came in.

On Sunday, Adam Harrison left with his dad for Ohio. He called Allie to say goodbye before he left, but told her he didn't want to see or talk to me or anyone else.

John Pilarski had been released on Saturday. Miguel said he was staying at his parents' house. I'd called Jennifer and texted, but she hadn't answered yet. I decided to let it lie and hope for the best.

Rhonda Crawford was satisfied with the outcome, not just because Bryan's killer was found, but because it turned out to be Rachelle, as she'd insisted from the beginning. Stephanie was probably the only one truly happy. She would get Rachelle's share of the money. I wondered if she'd follow through on her plan to force her aunt to sell Crawford Plumbing and Electrical. Given what I knew of her and her toxic family, I thought she probably would.

Dan Cooper went home on Sunday afternoon, persuaded that Coop could manage on his own. My mother sent a dinner over to Coop via me. I was a little worried about whether things would feel odd the first time we were alone together after everything. But they didn't. Not at all. We laughed, and we argued, and we cleaned up the kitchen, just like we'd done hundreds of nights before. Except it was better, because when we watched a movie afterwards, Coop slipped his good arm around me and I found that nestled on his shoulder was a very comfortable place to be.

When the film was over, I kissed him and then said, "Do you need help with anything before I go? This is your first solo night with your bad arm."

"Well, now that you ask, I could use a little help."

"Sure, what can I do?"

"Can you tuck me into bed?"

"Sheriff Cooper, are you trying to seduce me?"

"I am. Is it working?"

"What about your arm?"

"I think we'll manage."

And, reader, we did.

DANGEROUS DECEPTION: Leah Nash #9

Leah Nash uncovers a tangled web of deception, delusion and obsession —with a dead police captain caught right in the center.

The murder of police captain Rob Porter sends shockwaves through the small town of Himmel. And when a member of Rob's own department is arrested for the crime, everyone is stunned.

But journalist Leah Nash isn't buying it.

To her, the motive isn't plausible, the evidence is thin, and the investigation smacks of an overconfident detective eager to solve a high-profile murder. So when Leah's asked to do some digging for the defense, she jumps at the chance.

Leah starts tugging at a few loose threads in the case and discovers that Rob Porter was keeping some very ugly secrets—and not just his own.

As she nears the truth in a twisting tale of ulterior motives and long-buried guilt, a killer with everything to lose will do anything to stay hidden.

ACKNOWLEDGMENTS

Although writing is a solitary profession, I'm helped along the way by many people. The friends and family who give me encouragement, listening ears, and cookies all had a hand in this book. As did the beta readers who responded with constructive criticism, and whose gimlet-eyed readings picked up on typos, missed words, and random punctuation. Of course, I never take for granted the unwavering belief and unflagging enthusiasm of my first and favorite reader, my husband Gary, who is always ready with chai lattes, shoulder rubs, and something to say that makes me laugh. And last, but never least, I can't leave out the readers whose interest in and enjoyment of Leah's story inspires me to keep on writing. Thank you one and all, for getting *Dangerous Waters* across the finish line.

ABOUT THE AUTHOR

Susan Hunter is a charter member of Introverts International (which meets the 12th of Never at an undisclosed location). She has worked as a reporter and managing editor, during which time she received a first place UPI award for investigative reporting and a Michigan Press Association first place award for enterprise/feature reporting.

Susan has also taught composition at the college level, written advertising copy, newsletters, press releases, speeches, web copy, academic papers and memos. Lots and lots of memos. She lives in rural Michigan with her husband Gary, who is a man of action, not words.

During certain times of the day, she can also be found wandering the mean streets of small-town Himmel, Wisconsin, looking for clues, stopping for a meal at the Elite Cafe, dropping off a story lead at the *Himmel Times Weekly*, or meeting friends for a drink at McClain's Bar and Grill.

Sign up for Susan Hunter's reader list at
severnriverbooks.com/authors/susan-hunter

Printed in the United States
by Baker & Taylor Publisher Services